After service in the Royal Air Force, John R. McKay worked for seventeen years for Greater Manchester Fire Service as a control room watch manager, before leaving to take up other challenges including writing.

He lives in Wigan with his wife, Dawn, and has two daughters, Jessica and Sophie.

He is a keen football fan and open water scuba diver and is currently adding the finishing touches to two further novels, which he hopes to release in the near future.

He can be found at www.johnrmckay.com

Follow him on twitter @JohnMcKay68

and on Facebook at www.facebook.com/JohnRMcKayAuthor

THE ABSOLUTION OF OTTO FINKEL

John R. McKay

THE ABSOLUTION
OF
OTTO FINKEL

Vanguard Press

VANGUARD PAPERBACK

© Copyright 2015
John R. McKay

ISBN: 978 178465 043 8

Vanguard Press is an imprint of
Pegasus Elliot Mackenzie Publishers Ltd.

www.pegasuspublishers.com

First Published in 2015

Vanguard Press
Sheraton House Castle Park
Cambridge England

Printed & Bound in Great Britain

For the children of Drancy

Suffer little children, and forbid them not to come unto me, for of such is the kingdom of heaven.

(Matthew 19:14)

PROLOGUE

BRITTANY 1964

The man in the black suit and grey overcoat sat in the dark near to the window. Fixing his heels into the carpet he pushed back with his legs, sliding the chair backwards along the floor until it touched the wall. Using the thin strip of light at the side of the curtain, where it hung away from the window and allowed the dim glow of a nearby streetlamp to penetrate the darkness, he re-checked the automatic handgun he held firmly in his right hand. He did not want to adjust the curtains or switch on a lamp for fear of someone outside seeing him. No one could know he was there. There was only one man he wanted contact with tonight and as yet that man had not returned to the second floor hotel room.

Although he already knew it to be in good working order, a round firmly wedged in the chamber and the silencer screwed on tightly, he checked it again nevertheless. The man in the black suit and grey overcoat had waited a long time for this, almost a quarter of a century, and there could be no problems. Not now. There could be no room for any mistakes.

He had been sitting in the chair for over an hour and he was desperate for a cigarette although he knew smoking one would do nothing to calm his nerves. Instead he fiddled with the edges of his moustache, continually twirling the whiskers together and then releasing them, before starting the process over again. He had meant to shave it off having been told recently that men with facial hair looked at least ten years older than their less hirsute contemporaries. This ratified something that someone long ago had told him, but he had found neither the time nor the inclination to do so. That same person, all those years back, had said that it gave him an air of authority and for that reason alone he had kept it adorned for so long.

He looked towards the door. He could hear the laughter of a young couple passing in the corridor and saw their shadows break the light at the foot of the door as they walked by. They were speaking French but he could not make out what they were saying although he was virtually fluent in the language having visited France many times throughout his life. He blinked and rubbed his eyes with the back of his left hand, keeping his gun hand free and the weapon continually trained on the door.

He was tired. Tired beyond belief. Tired of the whole thing. But this night, this cold and wet September night, it would all come to an end, and maybe then he could finally get some real sleep.

Another fifteen minutes passed and he was beginning to think that his prey would never return, that he had somehow found out what was awaiting him in his hotel room and had simply disappeared, like he had done all those years before. But then he heard footsteps approaching the room and instinctively knew it was him, that the time had finally arrived.

He adjusted himself in the chair once more, took a couple of deep breaths and then concentrated on holding the gun steady, supporting the wrist with his left hand to prevent it from shaking.

He heard the key turn in the lock and then the door opened slowly. The man he had not seen for so many, many years entered the room and pressed the light switch. Nothing happened. The man with the gun, sitting in the darkness had taken the bulb out on entering the room to prevent the dazzling effect it would have had after being sat in the dark for so long.

With irritation the man shut the door and walked to the side of the bed to turn on a lamp not noticing him or sensing another's presence in the room.

'Leave it,' said the man in the black suit and grey overcoat sharply. 'Sit on the bed and don't move.'

Startled, the man who had entered the room fell back onto the bed, looking in the direction of where the voice had come from.

'What… Who…' said the man in German, squinting his eyes.

'Don't speak,' interrupted the man in the black suit and grey overcoat in English. He was surprised at how calm he was feeling.

'I have a gun and it's pointed at your stomach,' he continued. 'Do not make any attempt to leave, or to shout, or come any closer otherwise I will pull the trigger. I will not hesitate, believe me.'

'Who are you?' replied the German. 'Why are you doing this?'

'You don't remember me?' asked the man in the dark suit and grey overcoat. 'Well, it has been some time I suppose, so I will forgive you for that. Nevertheless, I know who you are and, more importantly, what you are.'

'I do not understand,' said the German nervously. 'I am just a simple businessman on a business trip. I do not know what you want with me.'

'I know who you are,' replied the man with the gun and then said his name to confirm it. He could see the man twisting nervously in the half-light, sweat appearing at his forehead.

'Who?' he replied. 'I do not know him. I do not know of whom you speak. I am Heinrich Vogel, a businessman from Austria.'

'You really don't recognise me do you?' said the man calmly from the chair. He leaned to his left and switched on a bedside lamp to reveal his features to the German sitting on the bed, who was unable to move with the shock of what was happening.

The German again squinted his eyes as he scrutinised the man sitting calmly in the chair, no hint of recognition in his eyes.

'I've been looking for you for some time, my old friend, for a very long time, and let's face it, you know that don't you?'

'What are your intentions?' asked the German suddenly. 'Are you going to shoot me here? In this room?'

The man in the dark suit and grey overcoat did not reply.

'Who do you work for?' continued the German. His voice was now getting thick with despair, realising that this could be the final conversation he would ever have and was trying to get some sense from it. 'British Secret Service? Mossad? The Americans?' he added nervously.

The man laughed humourlessly. 'None of the above,' he replied. 'I suppose you could say that I work for myself, if anyone. But who I work for is of no importance right now. I suppose you could also say this is about the choices we make in life. You see, people make choices in their lives that affect others, either directly or indirectly, and more often than not they have no idea what the consequences of those decisions will be. You have made choices in your life that all of us have regretted, maybe even yourself. Your choices, and mine for that matter, have led us to this moment. Right here. Right now.'

The German leaned closer and looked into his eyes.

'Yes,' he said after a while, his confidence gaining strength. 'Maybe I do recognise you.'

PART ONE

BRITTANY 1928

CHAPTER ONE

Jack Graham loved his summer holidays. This was the third time in as many years that the family had stayed at the Hotel Britannique belonging to Madame and Monsieur Descartes, the old French couple who never smiled and looked in Jack's opinion, to be around a thousand years old. He had received, along with his younger brother, Francis, a sharp slap across the top of the head from their mother due to them both laughing loudly on seeing old Monsieur Descartes drop a pot of coffee in the dining room, spilling the contents on the floor and exclaiming, 'Merde! Merde!' in a high pitched voice that had reminded him of the toucan he had seen in London Zoo during the Easter holidays. Jack laughed again as Francis whispered, 'Clumsy old fart,' not realising his mother could hear him. She had apologised for their behaviour but was not quite sure whether the old man understood what she was apologising for. Their father, Stephen Graham, who had sat quietly saying nothing, whilst attempting not to laugh, was unable to prevent a smirk from appearing upon his face. His wife glared at him and raised her eyebrows, to which he shrugged at her with feigned innocence.

Two days earlier, Jack's mother and father, along with Francis, three suitcases, a picnic basket and two fishing rods, had collected him from the boarding school he attended in Hampshire and driven to Portsmouth to catch the overnight ferry across the English Channel to St Malo for what was becoming their routine annual trip to France and the Brittany coast. Jack's father had remained silent as the vessel slowly made its way to the walled French port, often wandering alone on the deck lost in his own thoughts, not wishing to be disturbed. Their mother had told them not to bother him during the journey. Jack was now old enough to understand that a great and terrible war had occurred in France not too long ago, in which his father had taken part, and maybe it was this that he reminisced as he stood, leaning against the gunwale, smoking the old pipe with the foul smelling tobacco that Jack hated, as they approached the land of his nightmares. Jack was old enough to understand that it was probably for this reason that Stephen Graham looked significantly older than his thirty-eight years, his hair completely grey and face haggard and worn. Jack had wondered why he would ever want to set foot in France again if this was the case, let alone visit it willingly on a family holiday.

They had arrived at the small, quiet hotel, mid-morning and dropped off the suitcases in the two rooms they had been allocated on the first floor, before heading out into the sunshine to explore the surrounding area. The hotel was half a mile outside the main town, a short walk from the beach, where fishing boats could be seen from the windows, bringing their catches back to the harbour, to sell at the markets and local restaurants. It was in good repair, had four floors with nearly thirty rooms, and a large dining room, which served continental breakfasts and coffee. It had a limited menu for evening dinner, most guests choosing to eat at one of the many restaurants and cafés in the immediate vicinity. It was not exactly the Ritz but it served their purposes well, and it was clean, which was the most important thing in Margaret Graham's opinion.

The previous year Jack's father had taken the boys to the harbour where they had been allowed to use their new fishing rods from the sea wall and marina. Although they had not caught a thing all day, Jack had become obsessed with angling and had pestered his father to take him fishing during the weekends he spent away from the boarding school. And now, in his own modest opinion, he had developed into an expert angler.

They paid for bicycles for the day from a hire shop that they knew from their previous visits and enjoyed the rest of the afternoon cycling around the town stopping only to eat lunch al-fresco in a local park. It was only here that Jack's father's normal jolly countenance had returned and he was his usual jovial and chatty self, laughing and joking with his two boys and having fun often at them and their mother's expense. He would make fun of the way Francis's dark fringe tended to stick up, defying gravity no matter how much he attempted to comb it down and then he would turn his attention to Jack and remark how much he looked like a friend he used to know in the army, who was nicknamed Scruffy Joe on account of how his unkempt appearance would always get him in trouble with the regimental sergeant major.

He would also have fun with his wife, Margaret, telling her she looked like a Hollywood movie star and she would laugh good-naturedly, indulging him, allowing him to enjoy this time with his family, even though she knew that some of what he was doing was a front to hide the true melancholy he had been feeling since his return from this very country a decade earlier. She had asked him, a year or so ago, if he would like to ever return to the battlefields of the north, to pay his respects once more to those who had fallen and to maybe purge the demons from the past that she knew still haunted him in his dreams at night. But he had refused. It was still too soon, he had said, still too raw. Maybe one day in the future, but not now, not just yet.

That evening, after eating out at a small restaurant near the waterfront, they had returned to their rooms and all fallen into a deep sleep until waking that morning and going down for breakfast. Jack had noticed a couple of other young boys, roughly his own age, eating at other tables and wondered if they too were there on holiday.

On the table next to the Grahams sat another couple with a young boy. The father was dressed formally in a suit and tie, had dark hair slicked back with oil and wore small round spectacles with thick lenses. His wife did not seem to speak a lot, only to answer her husband when he addressed her and the young boy did not speak at all, sitting up straight and eating his meal in what Jack thought could only be described as the "correct and proper manner", something according to his mother he had not yet mastered, despite his twelve years. The boy looked quite small and was probably older than he appeared, he thought, blond hair side parted and deep blue eyes that were both intense and pensive. When he noticed Jack observing him he turned his head away quickly, avoiding the eye contact Jack had tried to make.

Further along, at a table near to the door sat another family. Jack knew these to be Italian as he had seen them the previous day checking in at the reception desk in the lobby and wondered why Italians would travel all this way when they had so much coastline of their own to enjoy. He had never been to Italy but had seen books and photographs of the sights there and hoped one day to visit. The city of Rome, with its marvellous Coliseum and stories of Julius Caesar and Mark Antony, and of ancient great battles and conquests, both fascinated and intrigued him. He knew where it was on the map and thought it the oddest shape for a country, reminding him of a large heeled boot.

There were four of them. The father looked a lot older than his wife. Or was he the grandfather? Jack was not quite sure. He was bald with grey hair at the sides and gave the impression that he was an important man from wherever he came from. His wife sat facing him and would smile affectionately whenever he spoke, responding with a chirp in her voice that Jack thought quite comical. The two children, a boy of around twelve years old and girl perhaps a year younger, who looked a miniature version of her mother, sat quietly and well-mannered as their parents conversed happily.

At a table in the corner sat another boy, alone, quietly sipping at a glass of orange juice, the croissant on the plate in front of him untouched, an expression of total boredom upon his young features. His curly brown hair was unkempt and uncombed and the clothes he wore had obviously seen better days; the holes in the elbows of his pullover proof of this. As Monsieur Descartes passed him, he leaned over and pushed the plate closer toward him, saying something sternly in French. Jack could not see the man's mouth as it was covered by a huge bushy moustache, but the deep tone resonated across the room causing a few of the guests to turn and look over to see what was happening. The boy picked up the croissant and reluctantly put it in his mouth, biting off the end and chewing at it laboriously. Jack theorised the boy was probably related to Descartes in some way and wondered why he was sitting at the table without parents or any other company.

Noticing her son looking around the room at all the various hotel guests Margaret said, 'Jack, stop staring at people. It's rude.'

'I wasn't staring,' he replied. 'I was just looking.'

'Please don't contradict your mother,' said his father.

Jack did not respond and quietly turned his head to face his brother across the table. Then Stephen Graham too had a quick look around the room curiously to see as to what and whom Jack was observing.

He caught the eye of the man on the next table, the one with the blond son and silent wife. The man smiled at him and Stephen smiled back out of politeness.

'Forgive me intruding,' said the man in a heavy German accent. 'I was wondering how old your boys were.'

Stunned at hearing the accent, Stephen replied robotically, 'Jack here is twelve and Francis is not quite eleven.'

'Ah,' said the German smiling politely, 'I thought so, I thought so.' He paused for a moment to take a sip from his coffee. 'My boy here, Otto, he is twelve years also. We are visiting my wife's family for a few days. For a holiday you see. We are from Dortmund. Well, I am... my wife is actually French. I was wondering...'

Jack's father turned his head away and looked down at his plate, ignoring the German's attempt at friendly conversation. The German stopped talking but continued to look in the direction of the Grahams.

Jack's mother smiled awkwardly at the German, who responded by looking from her to her husband then back to her, all the time maintaining a smile. It was obvious to Jack that his father was making every effort to ignore the man and it intrigued him as to why his father would behave in such a rude and out of character manner toward the stranger. Jack and Francis stared at their father who smiled at them when he caught their eye.

'If I have offended you in any way…' said the German slowly.

Stephen Graham put down his knife and fork and turned around to face him.

'If you have offended me! I am British and you are, as you have just told me, German. Your very presence in the same room as me offends me…'

'Stephen!' said Jack's mother sternly. 'Stop it. This is hardly the place… The children.'

'I am sorry you feel that way,' said the German, the smile remaining fixed to his face as though a permanent feature. 'But I can understand. I take it you were involved also. I saw my friends killed at Passchendaele and Verdun. A truly terrible business for both sides, don't you agree?'

Stephen Graham looked at his wife and turned back to the table, ignoring the man once more. 'I have no interest in talking about such matters,' he said. 'Please refrain from addressing me in such a manner.'

'Of course,' said the German apologetically. 'I am sorry to have caused you such discomfort.' With that he turned back to his family and spoke to them quietly in German. They did not respond to his words.

'Stephen,' said Jack's mother after a while. 'Are you all right?'

'I'm fine, Margaret,' he replied, picking up his coffee cup and taking a sip. After a short while he sighed and turned to face the German family again. 'Excuse me. Can I apologise for my little outburst just now? It is quite unlike me to be so discourteous.'

'That is fine,' said the German, still smiling.

Stephen Graham again turned away.

'So what business are you in?' asked Margaret Graham politely, seeking to alleviate the heavy atmosphere that existed between the two men.

'I am a university lecturer,' he replied. 'I teach foreign languages. English and French mainly but also a little Italian now and again.'

'How long are you here for?' she asked. She was aware of her husband's unease with holding a conversation with him but did not wish to look rude herself.

'We are here for a week,' replied the German good-naturedly. 'We are here to visit my wife's parents. Their house is very small, so that is why we are staying in this hotel. They are very old now. It is a good opportunity for Otto here to see his French family. However, I fear he is getting bored as he has little to do.'

Without thinking she replied, 'Maybe he could tag along with my two boys, Jack and Francis here. They are going fishing today while we visit the cathedral.'

Jack shot his mother a harsh look. This was all he needed, he thought. He already had to put up with Francis's ramblings when he was fishing and now his mother was suggesting he look after a German stranger's boy who probably spoke little or no English. Francis turned his head to look at the young boy who seemed oblivious to what was being suggested, the straight serious expression not having changed once since the conversation began.

The two English brothers looked at each other and frowned. Rather than make any comment, they continued with their breakfasts in silence. Whatever was decided they would have to live with, there was not much they could do about it now.

The German turned to his son and spoke to him in his native tongue. The boy replied in what Jack thought was a slightly too high a pitched voice for a boy of his age. He sounded like a girl. Although Jack did not know him and had no reason to, he made a decision there and then that he would not like him. Maybe this was because of the way his father had taken an instant dislike to the adult, no doubt because of the past that they both shared. He did not want to betray him in any way even if that meant an unwarranted low opinion of someone he did not even know.

'That is very kind,' replied the German to Jack's mother. 'Otto would like to join them in their endeavours if it is not too much trouble. I fear we older ones bore him slightly and mixing with children his own age will be nice for him. Maybe he can improve on his English too.'

'There,' she said to everyone. 'That's settled then.'

'Thanks, Mum,' said Jack sarcastically when the German family resumed their own conversation.

Jack's father ate the remainder of his breakfast in silence.

CHAPTER TWO

The three boys left the hotel a half hour later, fishing rods, fold-up chairs and packed lunches firmly held under their arms and headed for the sea wall, which overlooked the beach on one side and the harbour on the other. The two English boys had fished there before with limited success and were hoping for a good day. They had been told by their parents to be back at the hotel by three o'clock and their mother had checked that their watches were in good working order to ensure there would be no reason for any lateness.

Otto Finkel, the young German boy, had met with them in the hotel reception and as they all walked along the Quai Saint-Louis towards the Esplanade de la Bourse he trailed a couple of paces behind them, finding it difficult to keep up with the pace that the two Graham boys were setting. They both chatted happily together ignoring their German gate-crasher. However, Francis would occasionally look back to see if he was keeping up, whereas Jack on the other hand, showed no interest in the boy whatsoever.

After a fifteen minute walk they arrived at the sea wall and set up their equipment. As they only had two chairs, Otto was forced to sit on the hard ground at the side of them. He chose to sit by Francis as he could sense the tension and unfriendly aura that Jack was giving out and he did not wish to antagonise him in any way.

They set up their rods and cast out into the sea, which was fairly calm. Jack loved the peacefulness of the process. Although gulls shrieked loudly overhead, he found the whole thing very relaxing. He could sit back now and enjoy the sunshine; the sound of the sea lapping against the wall ten feet below them sounded wonderful to him. A few people passed them as they strolled to and from the small lighthouse at the end of the sea wall, some looking over at them curiously.

After a while Francis broke the silence. 'How long do we have to do this for?'

Jack turned to him, 'As long as it takes. All afternoon maybe. Why?'

'Because it's boring,' replied his younger brother.

'No it's not. Not when you catch something. It will be worth it then, honestly.'

Francis frowned and began whistling.

'And how long will you be doing that for?' asked Jack calmly.

'As long as it takes… All afternoon maybe?'

They both broke into fits of laughter but after a few seconds Jack suddenly stopped laughing and looked over to where Otto sat, he too enjoying the moment.

'What are you laughing at?' he snapped at the German boy.

'Your brother made a joke,' replied Otto in perfect English.

Jack was stunned into silence. He had not expected the young, quiet German boy to understand anything that they had said. Indeed, this was the first time that he had actually heard the boy speak since they had set out. He tried to say something in response, but taken by the surprise of it he only let out a croak, which made both Francis and Otto laugh even louder.

'You should see your face!' said Francis. 'You weren't expecting that were you.'

'No, I bloody well wasn't,' replied Jack and then turned away from them to look out at the water, feeling embarrassed and foolish.

Francis turned to Otto. 'How come you can speak English so well?'

'My father is a foreign language teacher. I can speak French too,' he replied enthusiastically, happy that he was now being included. 'My mother is French.'

'So how come they are married if they are both from different countries?' asked Francis innocently.

'Because she was a bloody collaborator,' interrupted Jack viciously.

Francis turned to his brother. 'What does that mean?'

'It means that she probably got with him during the war. Well, that's what Dad was saying earlier anyway.' He turned to Otto. 'Is that what happened?'

'I do not know,' he replied defensively. 'It was before I was born so I do not know of such things. All I know is that we visit my mother's family once a year but they do not like my father for some reason. My parents do not include me in their conversations.'

Jack was not sure if the boy was telling the truth about how much he knew of his parents' courtship but he was suddenly filled with a sense of sorrow and compassion for the young German boy sitting on the ground before him. It was surely not his fault and it was unfair to be nasty for no other reason than his own father disliked Germans because of his experiences during the war. Otto Finkel probably had few friends and being away from home, albeit for only a week, with a domineering father and a mother who said nothing, could not be much fun either. Jack made a decision that Otto could be part of their group and could tag along with them for the remainder of his trip.

Jack smiled at him in apology for his rudeness. 'If you want to, you can cast out for me if you like,' he said after a while.

'I do not know how,' replied Otto.

'It's okay, I'll show you,' said Jack standing up and reeling the line in. 'It's quite easy when you get the hang of it.'

Four hours later, with precisely no fish caught, they decided to call it a day and to take the fishing rods back to the hotel. Once they had dropped them off the three boys decided to go for a walk around the old town and look at the ships and boats out to sea from the harbour, as they still had some time before they were to meet their parents.

As they were about to leave the building from the front door, they found their exit blocked by a huge man wearing blue overalls. He was in his early twenties, well over six feet tall and heavily built. His hair was untidy, his face grubby and pockmarked; he had obviously had a bad dose of acne at one point. An attempt at a pencil moustache adorned his upper lip but failed to have the debonair style he was looking for due to one side being clearly longer than the other. He looked down at them and spoke gruffly in French.

'I'm sorry,' replied Jack, 'we don't speak French. Je suis Anglais. Anglais.'

'Ah, Anglais,' said the man and then continued to babble away in French once more.

Jack and Francis looked at each other and laughed, which only served to frustrate the man standing before them.

'He's asking for a password,' translated Otto helpfully.

'A password?' said Francis. 'Tell him "farts".'

With that the three boys started to laugh hysterically, although Jack was unsure if Otto was laughing just to join in or if he actually understood what had been said and their sense of humour.

The man started to speak quickly, tripping over his words, and the boys stopped as he was clearly getting agitated and frustrated.

Monsieur Descartes appeared from the office behind the reception desk and called over. 'Claude, Claude.'

The man blocking the boys looked over and suddenly became sheepish and submissive. A brief exchange of words took place between Descartes and Claude, as they now knew him to be called. After a moment, Claude looked quickly at the boys, smiled and hurriedly moved away and up the stairs to the first floor, leaving them free to leave the hotel.

Once outside, Jack said, 'What was all that about do you think?'

'No idea,' said Francis. 'He looked a bit simple to me.'

'What do you mean, "simple"?' asked Otto. 'I do not know what you mean by that.'

'A bit thick,' replied Francis. 'Retarded. Stupid. An idiot.'

'Okay,' said Otto. 'Yes I believe he is a bit simple, as you say it. It looks like he must work for the hotel. Maybe he is a janitor.'

'Right,' said Francis slowly. He said no more as he did not want to admit not knowing what a janitor was, especially to someone who did not speak English as a first language.

Jack laughed, sensing his brother's ignorance of the word. 'It's like a caretaker, Frank.'

'Yeah. I know what a janitor is,' replied Francis, irritated at his brother's patronising tone.

'Yes,' Jack looked at Otto as he replied to Francis. 'Of course you do, Frank. Of course you do.'

CHAPTER THREE

For the next two days the three boys met up at breakfast and then hurriedly left their parents to take the fishing gear down to the harbour. Although they were unsuccessful in catching a single fish, they spent the time talking and laughing and enjoying each other's company. Jack learned that Otto's father had, as his own father had suspected, met his mother during the time of German occupation in the north of the country during the war. Otto's mother's family had not been very happy with the arrangement and had refused to meet him. They had not exactly disowned their daughter but could not bring themselves to accept that she had married a member of the occupying forces. This had meant that she had to leave France at the end of the war and go to Germany to be with her husband.

Jack could see the reasons why Otto's grandparents would feel this way but he wondered why they should hold a grudge so long after the war had ended. It made no sense to him. It was all so long ago.

'Sometimes people find it hard to forgive,' surmised Otto, casting out into the sea with Francis's rod. Francis was lying on his back on a towel he had laid upon the ground, his eyes closed as the two older boys fished. 'I think sometimes people find it hard to move on and accept things for what they are. I heard my mother once say that you cannot help who you fall in love with.'

'So what do you think of your grandparents?' asked Jack. 'Are they okay with you?'

'Not particularly,' replied Otto thoughtfully. 'They moved down here after the war to get away from the shame of what their daughter had done, I suppose. I don't really know.'

Jack looked over to him and smiled. He had better change the subject, he thought. He did not want Otto to get upset.

'What do you think of that French boy who sits on his own at meal times?'

Otto looked at him blankly.

'The one who sits at the table in the corner of the dining room at meal times? I think he must be some sort of relation of the old bloke with the big moustache, Mister Descartes.'

'Oh yes. I know who you mean. I think he is the grandson of the owner.'

'Where do you think his parents are?'

'I have no idea.'

'Maybe we should ask him to join us,' said Francis, raising himself up onto his elbows.

They turned to look at him.

'I thought you'd fallen asleep,' said Jack.

'I nearly was,' replied Francis yawning. 'I don't understand how you find all this fishing so interesting. It's rubbish.'

'In your opinion, not mine,' said Jack.

'Maybe we should,' said Otto. 'Maybe we should ask him to join us. We could find out his story then couldn't we? It might be interesting.'

'It's got to be more interesting than sitting here watching you two fishing,' said Francis sarcastically, lying back down and shading his eyes from the sun with his hand.

'What do you think his story is?' said Jack to the two of them.

Otto shrugged.

'Who knows?' said Francis. 'Who cares anyway?'

Jack ignored him. 'Maybe he's been sent away from his parents because he's committed a big crime. Maybe he's on the run from the police or something like that.'

'Or maybe he's just on holiday like us,' said Francis quietly.

'If you want my opinion,' said Otto, 'I think Francis is more than likely to be correct.'

'Spoilsports,' said Jack.

CHAPTER FOUR

Thirteen year old Jean-Luc Descartes sat alone on the sofa in the reception area of the Hotel Britannique. He was beyond bored and his grandfather was starting to irritate him. Ever since he had arrived from Lyon the previous week the old man had done nothing but moan and nag at him and it was clear that his grandparents did not particularly want him there. Did they really think that he was happy sitting around the hotel all day long with nothing to do other than read books and wish he was somewhere else? Even making fun of that idiot Claude was becoming tiresome.

He had not wanted to come to Brittany in the first place, but was pretty much forced to do so by his mother. His father, whom he never knew, had died during the war at some place called Verdun and his grandparents had no other family besides him. His mother could not make the trip as she needed to work "to make ends meet" as she put it, but had set him on the train last Wednesday with a ticket to Paris where he was to change for the onward journey to St Malo. He had expected someone to meet him at the train station but there had been no one and he had had to walk, with his heavy suitcase, the three miles to the hotel after getting directions from a kindly station master. Upon his arrival he found that he had not been expected until the following week, there had been some kind of mix up in communication, and there had been no room available for him. He had spent the first two nights on the floor in the idiot Claude's room and had been given the attic room at the very top of the hotel once it had become free.

His grandparents had been too busy to occupy him and expected him to create his own entertainment. They told him there was plenty to explore in the town and he should take himself off and go and do just that. However, Jean-Luc thought that he had not yet to see all that his own town had to offer so could see no reason why he had to travel across the whole of France to look at someone else's that meant absolutely nothing to him. He had no interest in the sea, St Malo or an old couple, who frankly meant nothing to him either as they were no more than strangers; he was there purely out of duty to his mother and his long dead father.

Jean-Luc was aware that people had been staring at him, particularly in the dining room at meal times when he would notice other residents looking over as he ate the food his grandfather would put before him. The women's faces wore expressions of pity whilst their husbands would watch with a sense of curiosity and sometimes what looked like revulsion. Jean-Luc was not sure if it was the oversized and threadbare clothes he wore, donations from a neighbour that he was happy to wear to prevent his mother from spending money that she frankly did not have, or the curly hair he purposefully wore too long that was altogether different from every other boy he knew of his age. Whatever it was it did not seem to sit right with them.

Frankly, he did not care what other people thought of him. His bohemian looks generated welcome attention from the local girls back home and for this reason he was happy to be different to all the other boys and not to conform to how strangers, and family for that matter, thought he should look. Some of the boys back in Lyon would pick fights with him, mocking him for how he looked and for having a Jewish mother but Jean-Luc did not let that bother him as he was more than capable of taking care of himself.

He had watched over the past couple of days, with a slight degree of envy, the two English brothers form a friendship with the odd looking blond German boy and had secretly wished he could join them on their trips out. They always seemed to be in good spirits, carrying their fishing rods and paper bags packed with sandwiches as they set off to try their luck in the St Malo waters. Claude had told him that he had seen them fishing from the sea wall and thought they would have better luck at a small cove he knew that was not too far from the hotel. Jean-Luc had feigned indifference and instead had mocked him out of boredom, asking him what exactly he knew of angling anyway. Claude had hung his head and walked away. Jean-Luc had felt guilty later at his own intolerance and lack of charity and promised himself he would not be so cruel in future. After all, Claude may be big and stupid, but he was by no means a bad person.

As Jean-Luc sat there, his mind wandered to the future and what it would mean for him. One day, he thought, he would move to Paris and write fantastic novels from an attic flat overlooking the Seine and the Eiffel Tower. He would write about the adventures he would have and the places he would visit. He would be poor at first, this he knew, but then he would become famous like Alexandre Dumas or Victor Hugo and make a fortune and buy a huge house off the Champs Elysees…

"Why don't you go out and do something constructive?'

Jean-Luc jumped, startled by the gruff voice that had interrupted his daydreams. His grandfather looked down at him, a cup of coffee in his hand.

'You sit around all day doing nothing. I do not see the point of your trip if you are not to enjoy the sunshine.'

'I do not have any friends here,' replied Jean-Luc, and then inwardly cursed himself for sounding so lame, so pathetic.

'Well, go out and make some,' replied his grandfather sharply. 'There are plenty of children your age about. I'm sure that you can find someone to play with. I do not have the time to entertain you and to occupy you with things to do. You have to try a little harder to find something to do.'

Jean-Luc realised the old man was right. He did have to make more of an effort otherwise he would go mad. Sitting around doing nothing was starting to depress him. However, he could not show that he agreed that the old man was talking sense; his pride would not allow it and despite him wanting to smile up at his grandfather and tell him that he really would try harder, something within him prevented him from doing so and this is what made Jean-Luc truly sad. He would ease himself out of this melancholy at his own pace and would not be forced out of it by his grandparents. Even he could not understand why he was being so stubborn and cursed himself for it. He knew his behaviour was not exactly virtuous.

Then Jean-Luc realised the old man had asked him a question but he had not been listening and had no idea what it was. He stared up at him blankly.

'You're not even listening to me now are you?' said a frustrated Descartes.

Jean-Luc could not find a suitable reply.

CHAPTER FIVE

Upon returning to the hotel that afternoon the three boys came across Claude sitting on the steps at the front of the building smoking a cigarette. On seeing them approach he looked over and called to them.

'What's he saying?' asked Jack to Otto.

'He is asking if we have caught anything,' he translated.

Otto shouted back to Claude something in French that Jack and Francis had no understanding of and Claude again replied, standing up. He walked over to the boys, babbling away excitedly and gesticulating with his arms.

Jack looked from Claude to Otto and then back again.

'He is saying that we are fishing in the wrong place if we want to be more successful,' said Otto when there was a break in the conversation. 'He says he knows of a little cove where there are a lot more fish to catch. Mullet and bass and others he does not know the name of. He says that he could show us where it is if we want.'

'Tell him thanks,' said Francis, 'and that we'll bear it in mind.'

There was something about Claude that scared Jack. He was not sure if it was the sheer size and look of the man or the fact that he was not as other adults. His voice was very gruff and when he spoke he seemed to have an angry way of expressing himself. Maybe this was because he was not as intelligent as others his age and this frustrated him, but it scared Jack nevertheless.

'Come on,' he said to Otto. 'Let's get inside.'

On entering the reception area they saw Monsieur Descartes in conversation with the quiet boy they had discussed earlier, the one who sat alone at breakfast. The boy was sitting in a chair at the side of the reception desk and was being more spoken at than engaging in a two way conversation. Descartes was bending forward towards him, his face only inches away from his and he seemed to be lecturing him over something. But the boy sat uninterested, looking away from his grandfather's face. When he saw the three boys walk in with their fishing gear, he looked over. Catching Jack's eye he smiled and raised his eyebrows as if to say, "get me out of here". Descartes stopped talking, looked over to the three of them and stood up straight. He said nothing and turned away, walking back to the office behind the reception desk.

'I wonder what all that was about,' said Francis.

'Beats me,' replied Jack. He was not altogether too interested.

'I think his grandfather was telling him to get out and to stop sitting around the hotel all day,' said Otto helpfully.

'Oh right,' said Francis. 'Maybe we should ask him to come with us to the beach this afternoon then, like we said.'

Jack shot his brother an annoyed look. 'Oh come on, Frank,' he said. 'He's a miserable little bugger and we don't speak French.'

'Otto does. He could be our translator,' he replied smiling.

Otto turned to them both. 'I am sorry but I have to be with my parents this afternoon. They are visiting my grandparents again and they want me with them. If he goes with you, then you won't have me with you to translate.'

'Well, we'll have to forget it then,' replied Jack and headed for the stairs.

Francis said goodbye to Otto and joined his brother. They returned to their room and after a minute their parents knocked on the door to tell them to hurry as they wanted to get a bite to eat before setting off for the beach.

'Can we ask that French boy to come with us?' asked Francis. 'I feel sorry for him spending all day sitting around the hotel with nothing to do.'

'Which French boy is that?' asked his father.

'I think he's the grandson of the man with the big moustache.'

'Oh come on, Francis,' said Jack. 'This is supposed to be a family holiday and we already have a German tagging along each day.'

'I thought you liked Otto,' said Francis turning to him.

Jack looked at his father sheepishly. 'Well, I do… a bit…'

'It's okay, Jack,' said his father smiling at him. 'You don't have to dislike him on my account.' Turning to his younger son he said, 'It's very nice that you are thinking of others, young man, and if you want to ask him along then it's fine with me.'

'That's settled then,' said Margaret on hearing this. 'We will ask the permission of his grandfather when we go downstairs.'

CHAPTER SIX

Monsieur Descartes had been extremely grateful when they had finally got him to understand what they were suggesting. From what they could make out, he had been very frustrated with his grandson for not finding something to do other than sit around the hotel and he was concerned that the boy would start to get into mischief to relieve the boredom that he was undoubtedly feeling. However, the boy did not seem too pleased when he was told that he would be accompanying the English family to the beach that afternoon.

So they all found themselves, thirty minutes later, on the beach, the Fort Nacional to their left and the English Channel facing them. The sun shone down warming their faces as they lay on their towels, enjoying the peace and tranquillity of the location; the only noises were the gulls flying and squawking overhead and the surf as it hit the beach twenty yards in front of them. The beach was not too busy, only a couple more families in their immediate vicinity, but more seemed to be arriving as they set themselves up.

Margaret lay reading a book while Stephen sat up smoking a cigarette quietly, his thoughts to himself. Francis had tried to engage in conversation with the young French boy but had only succeeded in getting his name, Jean-Luc Descartes. Everything else the young boy said none of them could understand. In the end he had given up and lay on his back with his hands over his eyes, shielding them from the sun.

Jack was not very pleased that the boy had come along at all as he did not care too much for his miserable face and his interest in him had waned earlier when Otto and Francis had mocked him regarding his thoughts on the boy's story. The boy had dark hair that Jack thought too long and dark eyes. He wore clothes that were somewhat inappropriate for the heat of the day; long trousers, boots, a pullover and a jacket, all of which had seen better days, probably hand-me-downs from someone who Jack knew not. All in all, he thought, quite an odd character.

Jean-Luc too had given up on trying to converse with the English family and lay back slightly away from them. The look of total boredom that had adorned his face had never left at any point.

After a while Francis sat up and spoke to his brother. 'Do you want to go for a paddle?'

'Not particularly,' said Jack. 'I'd sooner be fishing to be honest.'

'But we never catch anything,' said Francis. 'It's boring.'

'Maybe we should investigate it more thoughtfully,' he replied. 'What was it that big fella told us? He knows where the good fishing is.'

'Which big fella is this?' asked their father, who had been listening to the two boys while he smoked.

'I think he's called Claude,' replied Jack, looking to his father. 'Otto thinks he is the handyman or something… at the hotel.'

'Oh, him.'

Margaret looked over. Placing her book to her side she said, 'I don't want you going near him. He's a strange fellow and I'm not too sure about him.'

'Oh there's no harm in him,' said her husband, taking a drag from his cigarette. 'He's just a little simple, that's all. I don't think there's anything to fear about him.'

'Well, he told us that he knows where there is some good fishing, Dad,' said Jack. 'He knows where we can get sea bass and mullet.'

'You can get that at any restaurant you like,' interjected his brother who then proceeded to laugh at his own wit hysterically.

Ignoring him Jack went on. 'We haven't caught a thing all the time we've been here. It's ridiculous.'

'Sometimes it works out that way,' said his father sympathetically. 'But you must listen to your mother. If she's not happy with you speaking to him, then please avoid him if you can.'

Hearing Claude's name being mentioned Jean-Luc looked over.

'Claude?' he said enquiringly, straining to understand what the English were saying about him.

They all turned to him.

'Claude,' he said again and then put his finger to his temple and put out his tongue, as if to indicate what he thought of the handyman's intelligence, or lack of.

The two boys laughed loudly, their father smiled, but their mother was not impressed. 'It's not nice to make fun of people,' she said, 'particularly when they are less fortunate than yourselves.' She picked up her book and then lay back to read it once more.

Jean-Luc put his hand down and looked at her, a look of sadness on his face as he understood that she was not too pleased with him and what he had insinuated. He looked to Jack's father who smiled and shrugged. Then he pointed at his wife, put his finger to his own temple and pulled out his tongue. Jean-Luc and the two Graham boys laughed. Margaret looked at them all for a second, frowned, then went back to reading her book.

Jack looked at the laughing Jean-Luc.

'Fishing?' he said. 'Do you like fishing?'

Jean-Luc frowned at him.

'Dad,' said Jack, 'what's French for fishing?'

'*Peche* is fish, I think.'

'Peshing,' said Jack to Jean-Luc. 'Do you like peshing?'

Jean-Luc looked at him blankly as Francis and Stephen Graham burst into an uncontrollable bout of laughter.

Frustrated, Jack made another attempt to get Jean-Luc to understand. 'Peche, peche,' and pointed to the sea.

A look of understanding came across Jean-Luc's face.

'Ah. La pêche.' He then continued to speak at a fast rate pointing towards the sea to the left of the Fort Nacional. Jack heard Claude's name mentioned a couple of times and also "Le Grande Be" and "Le Petite Be" which he knew to be the two small rocky islands not too far from the coast.

'Has anyone got any idea what he's saying?' asked Jack.

'I do,' came a heavily accented voice from behind them.

They all turned around to see another family sitting on the sand a few yards away from them. They must have arrived in the last couple of minutes without the Grahams noticing. It was the Italian family from the hotel. Jack recognised them immediately as he was quite taken with their dark Mediterranean looks and often found himself staring at the girl without realising it. He instantly flushed as he realised that he had probably made a fool of himself in front of her. Her brother stared at him with interest.

The person who had spoken was the father. Or was it the grandfather? Jack was not too sure as the man was obviously many years older than the woman who accompanied him.

'He is saying that a man named Claude, who I believe works at the hotel, tells him that there is good fishing to be found near the Grand Be and the Petit Be, over there,' he pointed in the direction of the two islands, but Jack did not turn to look. 'And at a small cove he knows. He says that if you go fishing there you will be sure to catch some large ones.'

Jack did not say anything, aware that the two children were staring at him and he flushed some more. 'Thank you,' he whispered.

Jack's father looked at him and frowned before replying to the Italian gentleman. 'Thank you, Mr...'

'Roncalli,' said the man rising from the sand and walking over to Stephen Graham. Extending his hand to him the two adults shook. 'Cesare Roncalli.' Turning to his family he said, 'May I introduce my wife, Leola, my son, Marco and my daughter, Sophia.'

'Pleased to meet you all,' he replied then introduced his own family, including Jean-Luc.

'I have seen you all in the hotel,' said Mister Roncalli. 'I take it you are here on holiday.'

'We are,' replied Stephen Graham. 'This is the third year we have been here. We used to holiday in Devon but decided to take the ferry across here one year and fell in love with the place. Now it's become a regular thing. Are you on holiday too?'

'Kind of,' he replied smiling. 'I was here on business for a few days and so thought I would bring my family and make it into a little trip. We go back to Turin in a few days' time.'

'That's nice...'

The adults continued to make small talk for a few more minutes.

Francis decided to try again with his brother. 'Shall we go for a paddle then or what?'

'Oh go on then,' he replied. 'Anything to shut you up.'

Jean-Luc, with his boots off and trousers rolled up, and the two Roncalli children joined them and they all set off across the beach to the sea.

Margaret sat up and shouted after them, 'Be careful, children.'

Jack turned his head and shouted back, 'Yes, Mother.' He turned back and noticed Sophia Roncalli smiling at him. He raised his eyebrows and she let out a little giggle. Feeling himself flush again he sprinted ahead and was first into the water.

CHAPTER SEVEN

That evening Otto returned with his parents and found the Grahams in the hotel sitting room. His parents walked to the opposite side of the room to avoid any clash between the two men but Otto approached them, smiling. Seeing him Jack and Francis stood up and met him in the middle of the room where they sat down at a table together.

'How did it go with your grandparents?' asked Francis.

'As expected, I suppose,' he replied quietly. 'I cannot see us visiting them that often from now on. There were some harsh words between my parents and them. I think my father wants to go home now but my mother wants to stay a little longer.' He glanced over to where his parents were sitting. 'However, I think my father will have his way and we will be leaving very soon.'

'That's a shame,' said Francis sadly. 'You will have to give me your address so we can write.'

'Thank you. I would like that. What happened with you two today? Did you go to the beach?'

'Yes,' said Jack enthusiastically. 'We made a couple more friends too. Marco and his sister. The Italians who have been staying here.'

'Ah yes,' said Otto. 'I know who you mean.'

'Not forgetting Jean-Luc,' said Francis.

'Ah, so he went with you then?'

'Yes,' said Jack. 'He's a bit quiet to tell the truth but he seems okay. We can all go out tomorrow together if you like. It might be fun. We could take a look at the boats and see if we can find a better place to fish.'

'Oh must we?' sighed Francis sitting back in his chair.

Jack looked at his brother. 'Yes we must. I'm not leaving here without having caught anything. The lads back at school will laugh at me if I tell them that.'

'Then lie to them then.'

'I'm not doing that,' responded Jack sharply. 'I'll catch the biggest bass in the sea. That's what I'll do.'

'I wouldn't bet on it,' muttered Francis.

Jack ignored him and turned to his German friend. 'What do you think?'

'I see no reason why not. Like you say, it might be fun.'

Otto looked over to where his mother and father were sitting and saw that they were deep in conversation, their heads close together. Jack noticed a look of nervousness appear on his face.

'I think I had better re-join my parents now,' he said. 'Goodbye until morning.'

He stood up and left them, not waiting for their response.

The two brothers returned to their mother and father and sat back in the two chairs they had vacated earlier.

'We will be leaving for home the day after tomorrow,' announced Margaret once they were settled.

'I thought we were staying until Monday,' said Francis aghast. 'Why are we leaving early?'

'Your father has to return to work,' she explained. 'Something has come up that he must return for. A very important meeting.'

Stephen Graham pulled down the newspaper he was reading and looked over the top of it at his two sons.

'I'm sorry, boys,' he said. 'Can't be helped I'm afraid. Something has come up that I can't get out of. I got word earlier this evening by telegram that I must return as soon as I can. We will catch the early morning ferry on Thursday. There's nothing I can do about it.'

With that he pulled the newspaper back up and continued to read it.

Jack and Francis knew when not to argue and this was such a time. They were not quite sure what their father did for a living but knew that it was very important and that they were still deemed too young to understand.

Jack sighed and sat back. No point in getting upset about it, he thought. Like his father had said, there was nothing that could be done, so they would have to make the most of their last day in St Malo. Jack felt an immense sense of frustration at his lack of success in catching any fish and now he only had one day in which to turn that around. He looked at his brother who looked as crestfallen as he did about the holiday being cut short. They had both made a new pal in Otto Finkel and had started to develop a friendship with Jean-Luc, Marco and Sophia. It upset him to know that he would have to leave all that behind, to return home to finish off his summer break there and not with his new friends, even if that was only to be for a few days more.

Jack stood up and beckoned to Francis.

'What?' said Francis irritably, annoyed that his brother was disturbing his melancholy.

'Come with me a minute,' said Jack and walked out of the room.

Francis rose and followed him. 'What do you want, Jack?'

'Look,' said Jack. 'I don't want to go home yet either, but there's nothing we can do about it is there? At least let's make the most of our last day here.'

'What do you have in mind?' asked Francis curiously.

'I'll tell you shortly,' replied Jack. 'But first let's go and find Claude.'

CHAPTER EIGHT

Marco Roncalli sat on a bench outside the restaurant looking at the boats in the harbour. His mother and father were still inside, paying the bill for the very average meal that they had just consumed, his sister Sophia waiting patiently behind them.

It was quite a pleasant evening, a slight breeze blew in from the sea bringing with it the pleasing aroma of saltwater and he could hear the chains that secured the vessels in the harbour clanking gently against their moorings. Altogether it was an atmosphere that he found quite engaging and for a few moments he was lost in the peace of it all.

Overall he had had a good day. He enjoyed spending time with his family, especially his father whom he loved devotedly. Cesare Roncalli was a kind and considerate man and very religious. He wished for no more that his children would be happy and hoped one day that Marco may take up the priesthood. As it stood, Marco had no objection to the course his father would wish his life to take, but had discussed with him that he wanted to keep his options open. Although he was only very young, he was old enough to realise that he could not make such a huge decision just yet. For now his father would have to be content that his son was a conscientious altar boy at the Church of the Blessed Sacrament on the outskirts of Turin. They would have to see how it progressed from there, if at all.

Marco was keeping these options open because he realised that his good looks had caught the attention of girls his own age as he would often catch them staring at him in the classroom. He was at an age that made him wise enough to realise that the feelings this generated within him would probably not be conducive to the celibate lifestyle that being a priest would require. His teacher, Signor Nardavino, had once told Georgia Salvaggi to stop staring at him and concentrate on her work, much to the embarrassment of them both but to the enthusiastic, and highly vocal, teasing of the rest of the class. Marco stood tall for his age with a mass of thick black hair and very dark eyes, his skin a shade darker than the rest of his friends. He was also aware that his sister, even though she was a year younger than he, caught the attentions of the local boys due to the way she too looked. He had even caught the elder English boy, whom they had spent some time with that afternoon, staring at his sister and had he not been such a gentleman himself, he might have asked him to put his eyes back into their sockets.

However, the time he had spent that afternoon with the English boys and their rather odd French companion had been most enjoyable. Their company had been fun and it was good to play with some boys his own age and not have to spend the whole holiday looking after his younger sister, even if she was good fun to be with most of the time.

He had watched, over the past couple of days, the two English boys and their newly acquired German friend leave the hotel with fishing rods and packed lunches and had been slightly aggrieved that he had not been asked to accompany them. They seemed to be having a lot more fun than he himself was having. He was grateful that they had got along so well that afternoon and secretly hoped that he would be able to join their little clique over the coming days.

He heard the door to the restaurant open and turned to see his family exiting the building. He stood up.

'Hey, Marco,' said his father pleasantly. 'What did you think?'

'I've eaten much better at home, father,' he replied honestly.

'Me too. You can't beat good home cooking can you? Especially the way your mother does it.' He looked at his wife who smiled at him delightedly.

'Have you had a good day, my boy? You seemed to get along well with those children on the beach today.'

'Yes. They were nice enough. For Englishmen.'

'Hardly men,' Cesare laughed. 'But I know what you mean. Why don't you ask to join them tomorrow? I believe they have been going fishing with that German boy, the one with the rather odd father. You might enjoy it.'

'I might just do that,' he replied. 'As long as it's okay with everyone else.'

His mother took his arm as they walked along the pavement towards the hotel. 'It's fine with me,' she smiled. 'Whatever makes you happy.'

Marco smiled to himself. He loved his family, each and every one of them. He had always felt content and could never remember any time in his life where he had not felt so. He had no idea what sadness felt like.

CHAPTER NINE

After breakfast the following morning Jack and Francis went in search of Otto. They found him in the foyer sitting on a sofa waiting for them as he had been the previous few days.

'Same thing again today?' he asked as they approached.

'With a slight difference,' replied Jack. 'This is our last day and we aren't leaving here without having caught anything.'

Otto raised his eyebrows questioningly.

'We saw that Claude fellow last night and asked him if he could show us where the good fishing is,' explained Jack.

'How did you manage that?' asked Otto. 'I thought you knew no French.'

'I don't,' said Jack. 'I used a lot of miming and stuff but I think he got what I meant. He's going to meet us at the front of the hotel later on and take us to where we will be able to catch something.'

'I'm not sure about this,' replied Otto. 'Do you think it's okay to be going off with him?'

'We'll be fine,' said Jack.

'What do you think?' said Otto turning to Francis.

'As long as he catches his flaming fish I don't really care,' he replied. 'This is getting on my nerves.'

'Anyway,' interjected Jack. 'We'll take Jean-Luc and ask that Italian boy to come along too. There'll be plenty of us so there's no need to worry.'

It was very easy to persuade Jean-Luc and Marco to join them in their adventure and, after gaining permission from their parents, fifteen minutes later the group of five boys followed behind the beaming hotel janitor as he led them, like the Pied Piper, to where he claimed they would be able to catch fish as big as he was.

As they walked, Jack looked around at his companions. He was not sure but he felt that he was the only one of them who was even remotely excited at the prospect of what the day would bring. Francis was his usual indifferent self and Jack knew that he was tagging along only to keep his big brother happy.

Being part of the group seemed sufficient for Marco and Jean-Luc no matter what it was that they were to do with their day. Marco was glad of some male company away from his sister and Jean-Luc content not to be left on his own. Jack was aware that he had become group leader and everyone was following his wishes. He put this down to there being two Grahams and that the group had been added to one by one leaving him as the default head of them all. It had not happened by choice or democracy.

He glanced to his left where Otto walked beside him. Now here was a strange one, Jack thought. He had grown to like and appreciate the young German boy even though he had reservations about him at the start. Their fathers maintained a cordial, polite attitude towards each other whenever their paths crossed but both tried to avoid that happening if possible. However, they were happy for their sons to spend time together as they knew their friendship would be brief. The more Jack thought about Otto the more he thought of him as something of an enigma. He rarely spoke when he was in the presence of his parents, unlike himself and Francis who were generally included and even encouraged to participate in any conversations their parents had, but when he was in their company he was always vocal and expressed his opinions in a clear and thoughtful way. He was extremely intelligent, fluent in three languages and getting by in a fourth wherever it was needed. It was obvious to Jack that Otto was far more clever than any individual in the group and probably more intelligent than all of the others put together. However, he was quite content to go along with any idea that Jack, or Francis for that matter, would suggest, whether it was good, bad or just plain ridiculous.

Jack had no idea where Claude was leading them. He had put his faith in this dim-witted Frenchman to finally end his fishing drought and had established the boys' security in the fact that there were five of them and one of him. Safety in numbers and all that, he grinned to himself. He had not told his mother of what they would be doing as he knew that she would have put a stop to it. She was clearly opposed to any of them being with Claude, for a reason that Jack could not fully understand and if she found out that he had gone against her wishes then he knew that he would be in serious trouble with both parents. But then, he thought, they did not really need to know. As long as he caught the fish that had been eluding him all week then everything would be all right. Everything would be fine and he could go back home happy and with his head held high.

As they walked through the streets heading out of the town, Claude a good ten yards in front of them, periodically looked behind to check that the boys were keeping up, Jack felt a great sense of contentment. The sun was shining, he was in good company and he was about to achieve what he had been attempting unsuccessfully to accomplish all week. What could possibly go wrong?

He was aware of Otto looking at him. 'You look pleased, Jack,' Otto observed.

Jack turned to look at him. 'Do I?'

'You do. I hope that we are able to get something today. Please don't be disappointed if it does not happen.'

'Oh it'll happen all right. Don't you worry about that, my friend.'

Upon saying these words Jack noticed the German boy's face illuminate. It was as though someone had given him a fantastic gift that no one else in the world could own, something unique and priceless. His whole face seemed to beam with joy and Jack saw what he thought may be a tear in Otto's eye. Jack hoped that it was the slight breeze that was in the air that had caused it, the sudden cold causing the eyes to water but he was not so sure. He turned his head away to avoid any embarrassment and looked ahead towards Claude who was hurrying along, suddenly feeling uncomfortable with Otto's reaction to what was a perfectly innocent remark.

Claude turned to them and said something that Jack did not comprehend but was obviously an encouragement for them to keep up.

'Okay, okay,' said Francis irritably. 'We're going as fast as we can. It's not going to go anywhere is it?' Marco and Jean-Luc smiled at him. Although they did not know what Francis was saying, they could tell exactly what he meant.

After a few more minutes Claude turned off the road and they followed him down a path that led towards a cluster of four large boulders and upon reaching them they saw, on the opposite side, steps that led down to a small cove. As they walked down the steps, which wound around out of sight of the roadway where they had just been, Jack could see that this natural inlet was sheltered on three sides by rock walls and he realised that they would be unobserved by anyone only a few yards away on the main road. He also understood that there was only one way in and one way out and that was the route by which they were currently taking.

He looked at the water here and saw that it was quite calm compared to what he could see further out to sea, where the white caps of larger waves were clearly evident as they rolled and crashed against the rocks at the entrance to the cove. If any fish were in here, he thought, they would be at his mercy. This would be a good day; he had no doubt about it. Claude had come good with his promise of a better location that was for sure. He turned to the others and grinned at them, ignoring the looks of apprehension on some of their faces.

At the bottom of the steps was a natural stone platform with a drop of a couple of feet to the water. Tethered to a metal ring fixed to the ground in front of them was a small rowing boat with two oars tucked inside. The boat had obviously seen better days but Jack saw that it looked in good order, robust and sturdy and, more importantly, dry inside, an indication that there were no leaks and it was perfectly seaworthy.

Claude stopped and turned to them, his face alive and excited. He started to babble very quickly in French and Jack turned to Otto for a translation.

Without looking at Jack, his eyes firmly fixed on the large Frenchman, Otto said: 'He is rather pleased with himself. He says that you can fish from here and you will be sure to catch some large ones as long as your bait is good. He says for us to be careful near the water's edge. He is going to leave us here if we are happy for him to go and he will see us later.'

'Tell him thank you,' said Jack. 'Tell him I will bring him back a huge sea bass for his supper.'

Otto translated Jack's words and Claude broke out into a huge smile. He walked past the boys returning to the stone steps, patting Jean-Luc's head affectionately as he walked by. The boys watched him go up the steps and just before he was out of sight he turned and waved to them. They all waved back before he turned and was gone.

'Well,' said Jack enthusiastically. 'Let's get started then.'

'If we must,' sighed Francis. 'If we must.'

*

Francis sat up and looked around. He had fallen asleep for a few moments, the heat of the morning sun and the sound of the sea lapping gently against the stone jetty having a soporific effect upon him. After two hours his brother had caught only three fish and none of them could be described as huge exactly. He thought of the promise Jack had made earlier to the janitor and was amused that Claude would be having a very light supper this evening.

Jack had refused to give up his rod to allow the others to try their luck but Francis had readily handed his over and they had taken turns in using it, with no success. Jack was now sitting alone, away from Marco and Jean-Luc who were laughing together, encouraging each other to cast out further and finding amusement in their quite hopeless attempts. Francis could see that his brother was annoyed that they were not taking it very seriously and had set himself away from them as he complained they "were scaring the fish away".

He looked for Otto and saw him sitting at the bottom of the stone stairway reading the book that he had brought along with him and Francis was annoyed with himself for not having done the same thing himself.

He called over to his brother. 'How are you doing?'

Jack turned to look at him. 'Not as well as I thought we would, to be honest.'

'Oh well,' said Francis. 'At least you've caught something today. There's no need to be embarrassed in front of your school pals.'

Jack could not tell if his younger brother was being sarcastic so did not reply.

A short while later Jack stood up and reeled in.

'This is hopeless,' he said exasperatedly. 'We're getting nowhere again here. We need to be further out.'

Francis was suddenly filled with a sense of dread. He did not like his brother when he got himself worked up like this. As far as Francis was concerned, this had been a successful trip. So far this week they had not caught a single fish and now, after only two hours, Jack had three, albeit it rather small, at his feet in front of him.

'You've done all right, Jack,' he said encouragingly. 'This has been a good morning.'

'It's our last day,' replied Jack loudly. 'We've got to do better than this.'

Jean-Luc and Marco looked over, stopping what they were doing, Jack's raised voice having alerted them to a potential confrontation between the two brothers. Otto put down his book and stood up.

'There's no need to shout at me,' said Francis calmly. 'It's only fishing. It's supposed to be enjoyable isn't it?'

'It is,' said Jack.

'Well, not to me it isn't. Especially when you get frustrated like this.'

'I'm not getting frustrated,' said Jack, again too loudly for Francis's liking. 'Stop shouting at me.'

Otto placed his book on a step and walked forward.

'Come now,' he said. 'There's no need to fall out over this.' Turning to Jack he said, 'We still have hours yet, haven't we? I am sure that you will catch something big shortly. It just requires a little more patience.'

'We're running out of time,' replied Jack. 'We have to leave for England tomorrow and I really want to get a big one before I go.'

Jack looked from Otto to Francis and then the rowing boat they had spied earlier caught his eye and he paused. The other four noticed his attention was distracted and turned to look at the boat.

'I don't think that's a good idea,' said Francis slowly, reading Jack's thoughts.

'I haven't said anything,' replied Jack calmly.

'Yes, but I know what you're thinking.'

'It isn't a good idea,' said Otto. 'In fact I think it's a very bad idea.'

'I haven't said anything,' Jack repeated.

Jean-Luc and Marco, who had been watching the conversation intently, without understanding a word, were starting to realise what was happening and began talking in their native tongues. Jack looked at them both blankly.

'They are agreeing with me and Francis,' Otto translated before Jack could ask him. 'They too feel it is a bad idea.'

'Okay, okay,' Jack was irritated. 'As I have already told you all, I haven't said anything.' He paused. 'But then again, if we take the boat out to the middle of the cove I bet we can get something.'

'No, Jack,' said Francis. 'It's too dangerous.'

'No it's not,' he replied. 'Look at the water, it's really calm. We could row out not too far and see how we get on. Just for a few minutes. If we don't get anything after a few minutes then we can row back and I promise I'll give it up. We can go to the beach or something if you want. Anything you like. You can choose.'

'No, Jack. Claude said for us to be careful and this isn't being careful is it?'

'Listen to your brother, Jack,' said Otto. 'He is talking sense.'

Ignoring him, Jack marched over to where the boat was tied and stood looking down at it. 'It looks safe enough,' he said. 'It's dry inside and looks strong. If you are all too scared to take a little rowing boat out a short distance on calm waters then that's your look out as far as I'm concerned. It's not my fault that you are all a bunch of chickens.'

'I'm not a chicken,' said Francis defensively.

Jack started to make a chicken sound and looked from one boy to the other, indicating that all four of them did not have the same courage as he did.

Otto was starting to get annoyed. 'We are not chickens, as you call us, Jack. We are just not foolhardy or stupid.'

'Who are you calling stupid?' said Jack aggressively.

'I'm not calling anyone stupid,' replied Otto. 'I am just saying that I do not like your idea.'

'Jean-Luc!' shouted Francis, interrupting the developing argument.

While Otto, Jack and Francis had been engaged in conversation, Jean-Luc had made his way to the boat and had climbed down into it. He was now busy picking up one of the oars and examining it. Jack turned to the others.

'Look,' he said, pointing to the boat. 'Jean-Luc's not soft. He's up for it.' Turning to Otto he continued, 'Are you going to let a Frenchie get the better of a German again? Like we and they did in the war… Well, are you?'

Otto looked at Jack and then at Francis. He offered Francis a small smile and then without another word he stepped into the boat where Jean-Luc assisted him in sitting down at the bow. Otto looked up to Jack.

'Come on then, brave English boy. Show me what you can do.'

'For God's sake,' said Francis. 'What are you all playing at? This is ridiculous.'

'Come on, Frank,' said Jack smiling. 'We can't let a German get the better of us now can we? What would Dad say?' He passed his rod down to Jean-Luc and then stepped into the boat, seating himself opposite Otto who looked at him with a serious expression on his face. It was obvious to Francis that he was infuriated with what Jack had been saying to him.

'I don't believe this,' said Francis. He saw no option but to join his brother. He did not believe that he had much of a choice, so he too stepped into the boat, which rocked unsteadily as he put his foot into it.

'Careful,' said Jack. 'Try not to capsize us you clumsy sod.'

'We shouldn't be doing this,' said Francis, finding a place to sit behind his brother.

'Oh shut up,' responded Jack.

Marco, who had watched what had taken place with a look of total bewilderment, approached them and looked down into the boat.

Jack looked up at him. 'Come on,' he said. 'Room for one more. Or are you Italians as soft as Germans?'

Otto glared at him and Jack replied with a smile. 'A bit of fun Otto, that's all. Try not to be so serious.'

Marco looked up to the sky and then took out a gold chain from beneath his shirt. Attached to the chain was a small crucifix, which he raised to his lips.

'Come on, choirboy,' said Jack, 'Get a move on.'

Marco looked at Jack, his face expressionless and then stepped down into the small craft and positioned himself at the side of Francis.

'There are too many of us in here,' said Francis. 'The boat isn't big enough Jack. It's dangerous.'

'We're fine, stop worrying. We'll just row out a little way and see how we get on.'

'We won't be able to cast off properly, it's too tight in here.'

'Oh shut up.'

'You should listen to your brother,' said Otto calmly. 'This is not a good idea.'

Jean-Luc stood up and reached over to untie the rope that secured the boat to the metal hook and then sat back down. He placed the oar against the platform and pushed. As the boat drifted away from land, he put the oar into the water and indicated for Jack to do the same with the other and together they rowed the small wooden boat toward the centre of the cove.

No one said a word.

*

Claude had returned to the hotel and been employed by Monsieur Descartes in unloading a food and drink delivery before he was asked to fix a door that one of the residents had complained was a little stiff. Once this was done he returned to the office and asked if there was anything else he was needed for.

Monsieur Descartes did not look up from the newspaper he was reading and told him that he was free to do what he wanted for the rest of the morning and he would see him again after lunch. Claude returned to his room in the attic and changed out of his overalls. He lay on the bed for a few moments wondering what to do with himself and then sat up. With a free couple of hours, he thought, he might as well see how the boys were getting on at the cove.

Closing the door behind him, he returned to the reception area and told Monsieur Descartes he would be going out for a couple of hours. Descartes raised his hand in acknowledgement and carried on reading his paper.

Claude was getting excited. The boys, particularly the elder English boy, had been very grateful for him showing them the cove and Claude was desperate to know if he had been successful in catching anything of note. The truth was that Claude did not know if the cove would yield any better results than the sea wall or the other venues the boys had tried prior to today and he hoped that they would not be disappointed if their trip was as fruitless as the others.

As he hurried along the road on the way back to where he had left them, he noticed people looking at him with somewhat odd expressions on their faces as he passed them. He had grown used to people staring at him, whispering behind his back and sometimes, particularly when he was in a bar or cafe, openly making fun of him. But today he did not care, today was a day where people, albeit children, would appreciate him. Today was going to be a good day.

On the water the brickbats were still flying. For some reason, unbeknown even to himself, Jack would not let up on mocking the other four boys, Otto in particular. Francis had been trying to stop his brother from continuing with the insults but was getting nowhere and was becoming more and more frustrated with the whole situation. Jean-Luc and Marco sat quietly, the latter clearly looking uncomfortable and wishing he was somewhere else.

'Can you give it a rest now, Jack,' said Francis. 'Enough is enough. You have your wish, we're all here in the boat with you so please stop.'

'Okay,' replied Jack. 'I'm sorry. Now pass me the bait and let's get these fish caught.'

He looked to Otto. 'I'm sorry, Otto,' he said apologetically but Otto did not reply. 'Oh suit yourself.'

Francis passed Jack the bait and watched as he organised the line. The others had to move to allow him to complete the task causing the boat to rock from side to side. They clung on to the side of the boat nervously.

'Careful, you'll have us over!' shouted Francis. 'Be careful.'

'Stop worrying and give me a hand,' said Jack.

'This is making me nervous,' said Otto anxiously.

After a few moments, with everyone watching, Jack was able to cast out into the water. Once the float was settled he turned to the others.

'Come on, there's another rod.'

No one seemed interested in joining him and the second rod remained at their feet in the rowing boat. Jean-Luc watched indifferently and, to Francis, Marco seemed uneasy, clearly wishing he was back on land and anywhere else but with them.

After a few minutes, no one having said a word, the boat began to bob a little higher in the water. Instinctively they all gripped the sides. Francis looked behind him to where the cove exited to the open sea and could clearly see the waves getting higher.

'Jack, I think we ought to get back to land. It's getting too rough.'

'Just a few more minutes,' he replied, but Francis could see that he too was clearly worried about the sudden change in the current.

Marco said something in Italian and took out his crucifix and kissed it again. Otto looked at him.

'Yes, Jack,' he said. 'I think it's time we headed back.'

Without saying a word, Jean-Luc placed his oar back into the water and indicated for Jack to do the same. As he did so, a wave hit the boat causing it to rise and fall sharply, water spraying over the side and hitting them.

'Come on, Jack,' shouted Francis. 'Let's get back.'

Realising that he did not really have a choice, Jack reeled in the line as fast as he could. 'Come on, Jack,' repeated Francis as another big wave hit the boat, 'Hurry!'

'Okay, okay.'

With the line reeled in Jack placed the rod at his feet and then took hold of the oar and placed it in the water. Smiling apologetically at Jean-Luc he indicated for him to row.

After a few minutes they realised that despite all their efforts they had not travelled any closer to land and, if anything, had drifted further out toward the entrance of the cove and the open sea. There was a current underneath the boat that was proving difficult to fight against.

'We aren't getting any closer,' said Francis fretfully. 'I told you this was a bad idea.'

'Oh shut up, for God's sake. We are trying our best!' shouted Jack at his brother.

With Marco gripping his crucifix in the hope of a divine being taking care of them, Francis gripping the side of the boat as though his very life depended on it and Otto sitting as deep into his seat as he possibly could, the two boys struggled and strained against the sea to drag the small craft to the safety of the jetty. With each stroke they took, more water would crash over the side, spraying them all as the wind began to gain strength. Francis was able to look again at where the cove met the open sea and could see the waves getting higher and crashing against the rocks with frightening force. He started to weep.

Jack and Jean-Luc strained at the oars in a desperate effort to get them all to safety. With each stroke they breathed out hard, the exertions starting to take their toll. However, Francis could see that finally they were beginning to make some progress and offered them encouragement.

'Come on, lads. Keep going!'

Francis judged that they were around forty-five yards from safety when he spied a figure on the platform waving out to them.

'Someone's there,' he pointed.

Jean-Luc, sensing the different tone in his voice looked up. 'C'est Claude.'

'Yes, it's Claude,' he agreed and waved back at him. 'Come on, Jack, try harder!'

'I can't,' he replied and stopped rowing, Jean-Luc doing the same. 'We're beat. Someone else needs to take over for a while.' Francis noticed that both boys were sweating profusely and realised that they did not have the energy to continue. They needed to swap over rowers.

'Come on, Otto,' he said. 'We need to help out. Let's swap seats with them.'

Otto looked at him fearfully. 'I don't feel safe. Can't Marco do it?'

Francis looked at Marco who had his eyes closed and appeared to be praying.

'No,' he said. 'I think you are stronger and, anyway, we need his prayers to give us the strength. Come on, let's swap seats with them.'

Francis raised himself from his seat and slid his body over the top of his brother, as Jack moved backwards under him. The boat rocked violently as another wave hit it causing them to grip tightly, fear paralysing them for a moment as they tried to regain their balance.

As they settled into their new positions, they could hear Claude shouting at them.

'I don't think he's too pleased,' remarked Francis. 'We are going to be in so much trouble.'

Jack leaned back in his new seat, panting and wiping the sweat from his forehead with his sleeve. 'Maybe this wasn't such a good idea after all.'

'You're not kidding!' said Francis as another wave hit the boat causing it to rise and fall in the water. 'Come on Otto, you need to relieve Jean-Luc, he's done in.'

Jean-Luc was clearly exhausted. He leaned over the oar and did not look up when his name was mentioned. His long curly hair was plastered to his forehead by a mixture of sweat and saltwater and he was panting heavily. It was clearly obvious that he could not carry on.

Otto looked at him nervously then spoke to him in French. Jean-Luc raised his head and shook it before looking back down again.

'We need to give him a minute,' said Otto, 'I do not think he can move yet.'

'He'll have to,' replied Francis. 'We are in danger of losing the ground that they've made. We could drift out further if we don't carry on rowing.'

Otto spoke again to Jean-Luc who nodded. He placed the oar in the boat alongside them then stood up. The boat rocked violently forcing him to sit back down quickly.

'Jesus!' exclaimed Jack, suddenly alert again, 'Be careful or you'll have us all over.'

'How are we to do this?' asked Otto.

'The same way me and Jack did,' replied Francis. 'But it needs to be done quickly.'

Claude's shouts now carried clearly to them. It was obvious that the man was not only annoyed that they had taken the boat out, but was getting agitated that they had put themselves in danger and he could do nothing about it.

'Come on, you two,' Francis insisted. 'Hurry up.'

Sensing the urgency in his voice Jean-Luc and Otto looked at each other. Jean-Luc spoke to Otto who nodded quickly, a look of total fear upon his face. A second later both boys stood up in the boat and twisted around to exchange seats. As they did so, another wave hit the boat causing it to rock to the left. Jean-Luc fell back into his seat but Otto fell forward.

What happened next seemed to occur in slow motion. That is how Francis would describe it later. As he looked on, totally helpless and unable to do anything about it, Otto fell forward. He heard the dull thud as his head hit the side of the boat, his head and face crashing against the metal housing where the oar fitted. At first Francis thought that the liquid that hit his face at the same time was more spray from the sea but on examination later, he realised it was Otto's blood. Otto's limp unconscious body fell to the side and before he could reach out a hand to grab him, he had slithered overboard and disappeared beneath the waves.

For a second all four boys were frozen. The shock of what had just taken place before their eyes left them unable to speak or react. As the waves continued to crash against the side of the boat, they sat there, unable to speak, unable to move.

Eventually the silence was broken by Jack. 'Come on! Quickly,' he said moving to the side of the boat and looking down. 'We've got to get him back in.'

It was like a rallying call and all at once the other three boys started to move.

Francis looked over the side but could see no sign of Otto. Jean-Luc grabbed an oar and placed it vertically in the water as though fishing for him, prodding and rotating the wooden pole in a frantic search for the young German boy. Jack had started to take off his jacket and shoes.

'What are you doing?' asked Francis desperately.

'I'm going in for him,' shouted Jack. 'This is all my fault. He's going to drown.'

'You can't,' said Francis, his eyes filling with tears. 'You'll drown too.'

'I have to do something,' he replied and before his younger brother could stop him, Jack was over the side and into the water. For a second he floated there, treading water, getting his bearings and accustomed to the coldness of the water, then taking a deep breath he dived under the surface and kicked down.

And then he too was gone.

CHAPTER TEN

'In your own words. Tell me what happened next.'

Francis looked at the gendarme, Henri Le Bot, and wiped the tears from his eyes. His father handed him a handkerchief and he blew his nose loudly before handing it back to him.

'Come on, son,' he said. 'Just tell the gentleman exactly what happened after that.'

Francis had returned to the hotel to find the police already waiting for them. Each boy had given their account of what had taken place in the cove and now it was his turn. He looked again at the young gendarme who was sitting across the table from him, a black notebook in front of him to which he was transcribing the conversation, waiting patiently for Francis to continue. Like Monsieur Descartes, who stood in the corner of the dining room watching quietly, Le Bot had a large bushy moustache, which was an attempt to make himself look older than he really was. He had taken off his hat to reveal a completely shaved head and for some reason this slightly intimidated Francis. However, his father was beside him and held his hand under the table, squeezing it gently occasionally in encouragement.

'Well, when Jack went under I thought that was it,' he sniffled. 'I thought that there was no way he would find Otto and he would drown too. I began to scream and shout and nearly went in myself but Marco was holding me back. Jean-Luc kept splashing the water with the oar, I don't know why, and then I noticed someone else in the water. While we had been watching what was going on around us, Claude must have jumped in and swam over to us.'

He paused again. This was getting harder and harder the more he related his story. He looked at his father who smiled at him and nodded for him to carry on. He was there for him, he didn't need to say anything.

'And what happened after that?' asked Le Bot, looking up from the notebook.

'Jack came up with Otto... on the other side of the boat. Jean-Luc shouted something, I don't know what 'cause I don't speak French and we turned round and saw him there. Otto looked asleep and there was blood pouring from his head, I think it was 'cause he banged it on the metal thing before he fell into the water.

'Jean-Luc held out the oar and Jack tried to get hold of it but his head went back under the water. He was struggling to keep himself and Otto up and I think that he was really tired. Then Claude swam to them and got hold of Otto and pushed him to the boat. We grabbed his clothes and tried to drag him on board but the boat was wobbling and the sea was really choppy still and we were in danger of capsizing, so then Marco jumped to the other side of the boat to give it some balance and me and Jean-Luc pulled Otto out of the sea and into the boat with us. Jack and Claude were pushing as we were pulling, which made it easier.'

'You need to slow down a little, son,' said his father quietly. 'The policeman has to write this down.' Francis looked across the table at Le Bot who was writing very quickly in an attempt to get down everything he said correctly.

Le Bot looked up at Stephen Graham and smiled. 'Merci.' Looking at Francis he said, 'And then what happened?'

'Well, we needed to get Jack into the boat too. He was really tired and he looked in danger of slipping back under the water but Claude was there to hold him up. Marco looked after Otto while me and Jean-Luc tried to pull Jack in. With Claude's help we were able to get him in and he was coughing and spluttering and puking all over the place, it was horrible.'

'Puking?' asked Le Bot raising his eyebrows.

'Being sick,' said Stephen, 'vomiting.'

'D'accord,' he replied and continued writing.

'Shall I carry on?' asked Francis and when the gendarme nodded at him he continued. 'Claude was the only one left in the water but we realised that there was no room for him. There wasn't really room for the five of us as it was and Claude is really big. At first he tried to get in but when he did the boat nearly toppled over.'

Francis began to weep. 'There was no room for him, Dad, there really wasn't. We didn't know what to do. If he got in the boat, then we could have all ended up in the sea and I can't swim that well can I?'

'So what did you do?' asked Stephen Graham quietly, squeezing his son's hand gently under the table. 'Come on. Just tell the truth. You've nothing to worry about.'

The tears were now pouring down Francis's face and he sniffed again loudly. Le Bot, sitting opposite, watched him quietly, his pen poised ready to continue.

'We stopped him from getting on board. We had to. He could have ended up killing us all. I just sat there with Jack who was now sitting up and Jean-Luc was holding the oar against him to stop him coming in, but it wasn't just him. No one tried to stop Jean-Luc and we all were saying for him to not let Claude in. When he realised that we weren't going to let him in the boat, he shouted something and then turned to swim back to land. The sea was still quite choppy but it had calmed down a little bit by now, but we had drifted a little further out. We watched as Claude started to swim back but he looked exhausted. We just sat watching as he swam for a while and then he just disappeared. He just vanished. We couldn't see him anywhere. It was awful.'

Francis was now sobbing.

'Can we take a short break?' his father asked the gendarme.

'No,' Le Bot replied. 'He might as well finish, there cannot be much more to tell.'

'Come now, Francis,' said his father, 'Stop your crying and tell the policeman what you know.'

Francis took a deep breath. 'Well, we had to get back to land, so myself and Marco started rowing as fast as we could. Jack was in a bad way and Otto was still unconscious. We rowed and rowed and it was really hard but the sea was getting calmer and we managed to get back. When we got to the jetty, Jean-Luc jumped out and ran off to get some help. He came back a few minutes later with some people and Jack and Otto were taken away. That's it. That's what happened.'

He covered his face with his hands and sobbed into them. Stephen lifted his hand from under the table and placed it around his shoulders. He did not speak.

After a while, when the gendarme had finished writing in his notebook he asked him, 'So what happens now?'

'Well, from what I know,' he replied with a sigh, 'Claude Lavoie is missing believed drowned. There is a search team out now still looking for him. As you know, your son and'—he flipped a few pages in his notebook searching for a name—'Otto Finkel... are both in the local hospital. From what I have gathered it looks like your son has a little bit of shock and mild hypothermia but I do not know about the Finkel boy.'

'He'll be fine though, right?' said Stephen.

'Monsieur, I really do not know,' he replied. 'We will need to take a statement from your other son, Jack, as soon as he is able to do so and then we will take it from there. If Lavoie is found alive and the Finkel boy is all right then this will go down as little more than a bad day. If, however, they are not then things may take a more official course. Let us pray they are both okay.'

'Yes,' agreed Stephen, looking at his son who was still holding his face in his hands. 'Let's… Is it okay for us to go now? My wife is at the hospital and I need to see my son.'

Le Bot placed the notebook and pen in his jacket pocket and stood up. Retrieving his hat from the table and placing it on his head he said, 'Yes that is fine. When are you to return to England?'

'It was supposed to be tomorrow, but my plans may need to be altered now.'

'Okay. Depending on how things turn out it may not be possible to leave just yet.'

The gendarme left the room. Stephen did not respond. He looked at Francis, who had now taken his hands away from his face, and sighed.

'What am I going to do with you two?'

Francis looked at him. A whimpering "sorry" was all he could muster in response.

CHAPTER ELEVEN

Jack and his mother returned to the hotel a few hours later, accompanied by Stephen and Francis who had met them after the interview with Le Bot. Jack had taken in a few mouthfuls of sea water, which he had mostly vomited back out inside the boat, or once on land, and the doctors had told them that with a few hours' warmth and rest he should be fine. When Stephen attempted to broach the subject of what had taken place, Jack could not bring himself to speak. The only thing he was concerned about was if they had found Claude and if Otto would be all right.

'Hopefully,' replied his father. 'From what your brother tells me it was you who dragged him out of the water. If you hadn't done that then he would surely be dead by now.'

'Yes,' said his mother, more sternly. 'But had you not got into that boat in the first place or gone against my wishes then none of this would have happened now would it?'

Jack looked at his mother but did not respond.

Turning to Francis she said, 'And why didn't you stop him? You would have known that it was a silly idea and now there is a child in the hospital with a big hole in his head and a man somewhere out there who is probably dead.'

Francis turned away from her and began to sob.

'Margaret,' said Stephen loudly. 'Enough. What's happened has happened and there's not a lot we can do about it now. The boys know what they did was wrong but shouting at them like this will only make matters worse.'

'What am I to say to that boy's mother? What am I to say to the mother of that poor man? You tell me that, eh? Just tell me because I have absolutely no idea.'

'I don't know, dear, but all this shouting will get us nowhere.'

'You are sometimes too soft with them, Stephen. You really are. This whole thing is just terrible.'

Stephen Graham sighed and looked at his wife. 'Margaret. Maybe you're right. Maybe I am a little easy on them from time to time. But if you had seen the things I've seen in my time then you too would cut them a little slack. What happened out there was ridiculously bad but in the end it was just boys being boys gone too far. No one intended for this to happen, least of all these two. They are not bad lads, they are just normal kids, sometimes mischievous granted. They will be punished that is for certain. But not here. Not now. We will wait until we get home and then we will think of a suitable tariff.'

They were disturbed from their conversation by the front door opening behind them and Heinrich and Catherine Finkel strode in. On seeing the Grahams standing talking in the lobby Heinrich marched purposefully over to them, before his wife could prevent him.

'You,' he said pointing menacingly at Jack. 'You, boy. What were you thinking? Do you realise what it is you have done?'

Placing himself between his son and Finkel, Stephen said, 'Now hold on, Finkel. If you want to speak to someone about this then you address me and not my son. Do you understand me?'

'Of course I understand you, Englishman,' he said venomously. 'Your boy is an idiot. Otto could have died.'

'But he hasn't, has he, German?' replied Stephen. 'And if it wasn't for Jack here, your boy would be lying at the bottom of the sea at this moment and not in a hospital bed. Jack pulled him out and saved his life.'

'If they had not been in the boat in the first place then it would not have happened at all. So he is to blame.'

Jack began to cry and his brother joined him.

'Margaret,' said Stephen calmly to his wife. 'Take the boys up to their room while I speak to Jerry here.'

'My name is not Jerry.'

As Margaret led the two boys away, Stephen said, 'From what I believe, and this comes from all of the boys, your son was in the boat before both of my sons. So who was leading who exactly?'

'We have just left him sitting in bed with a scar running down half of his face,' said Finkel quietly. 'He has had over twenty stitches. He is disfigured for life, do you understand?'

'I am sorry to hear that, really I am,' replied Stephen, suddenly filled with remorse. 'Look, Mr Finkel, I don't know what you want me to do about this. I will be punishing my boys, on that you can depend, but I cannot have you going for any of them like that.'

'You should allow me to punish them.'

Stephen laughed at him, the absurdity of the words causing him genuine mirth. 'Don't be ridiculous. If you lay a single finger on any of them, or even speak to them without my permission come to that, I will rip you apart, believe me.'

Finkel did not respond but stood glaring at him. His face as red as the roses that Descartes had placed on the tables in the dining room behind him, the sweat at his brow beginning to run into his eyes.

'I believe this conversation is now over,' said Stephen who turned around and walked away towards the stairs, not waiting for a reply.

He found his family in the boys' room, Jack lying on top of his bed and Margaret and Francis sitting on the other. She looked up as he entered the room.

'How did it go?' she asked as he sat down beside her and looked at Jack who was beginning to fall asleep.

'Not good,' he replied. 'But let's just say that that Finkel character won't be bothering the boys again.' He sighed and then lay back across the bed. 'You know what, Margaret,' he said, 'I suddenly feel rather drained. I feel I could sleep for a week. It looks like we are going to have to stay at least another day now, until the police give us permission to leave. I think it's probably best that we just stay around the hotel tomorrow.'

'Yes,' she said, smiling down at him. 'You're probably right. Come now, let's leave them both to sleep.'

They stood up and looked at their sons. Jack was now fast asleep, fully clothed on the top of the bed. Margaret leaned over and pulled the counterpane from under him and wrapped it over his body. He turned to his side and let out a soft snore before curling up into a ball. Francis, his eyes half closed, began to take off his pullover but was struggling due to the tiredness.

'Here, let me help,' said Stephen and pulled it over his head before placing it on a chair in the corner of the room. 'Get into bed, son, and we'll see you tomorrow.'

Once Francis was settled into bed they left the room, switching out the light as they closed the door behind them.

'I don't know about you,' said Stephen with a sigh. 'But I need a drink. Do we still have any of that whisky left?'

'Yes,' she replied. 'There's enough left for a couple of glasses.'

'Good,' he said. 'The first good news I've had all day!'

She stood on her toes and kissed him softly on the cheek.

CHAPTER TWELVE

The Grahams slept late and missed breakfast. Stephen knocked on the boys' door a little after ten o'clock but on hearing no reply decided to leave them to sleep. They were obviously both physically and emotionally drained from the previous day's events. Stephen made his way to the dining room and was informed by Descartes that the Finkels had eaten early then headed back to the hospital to check on their son. He found them a couple of bread rolls and told them that he would bring coffee up to their rooms if they wished. Stephen thanked him and turned to leave.

As he walked through the lobby, he noticed Cesare Roncalli sitting on an easy chair by the window reading a newspaper. He looked up as Stephen approached him.

'Hello, Mr Graham,' he said in perfect English smiling at him.

'Hello,' Stephen returned the greeting and sat down in a chair opposite with a huge sigh.

'Tough day yesterday,' said Roncalli putting his paper down onto his lap.

'You can say that again,' replied Stephen smiling back at him. 'If you don't mind me asking, what has your boy said about what happened?'

'It appears that your elder boy did a very courageous thing,' the Italian replied. 'Apparently there was some sort of argument before they took the boat. He tells me that there were some words spoken between your boy and the German boy before they got in but it was the French boy who got into the boat first. However, Marco should never have been a part of it and I have confined him to his room for the day.'

'Yes,' said Stephen Graham thoughtfully. 'It appears that they are all telling the same tale.'

'I hope they find the janitor,' said Roncalli. 'It will be such a shame if he has perished. A brave man.'

'The longer it goes without him turning up the more hope will fade I'm afraid.'

'Very true,' replied Roncalli.

They looked up as the front door to the hotel was opened. Descartes, who was busy behind the reception desk left his post and went round to meet the new arrival.

It was Henri Le Bot, accompanied by two more gendarmes. On seeing the two men sitting near the window he walked over and was joined by Descartes.

Speaking quickly in French to the hotel owner, it became apparent to Stephen that the news he was bringing was not good. Eventually he turned to Stephen.

'Monsieur Graham, the news I have is catastrophic. The body of Claude Lavoie was found this morning. The tide had dragged him out of the cove and he was found on the beach two miles to the north of here. The body has been moved to the morgue but it is clear that he has drowned.'

'Oh sweet Lord,' said Stephen and put his head in his hands for a moment. Bringing them down over his face he said, 'Does his family know?'

'We are in the process of finding his next of kin now. I am sure Monsieur Descartes here can help with this.'

'Okay,' said Stephen, standing up. 'I'd better tell the boys.'

'Yes,' said Le Bot.

Before setting off Stephen asked, 'So what happens now? With the boys that is?'

'We have their statements and if there is nothing to add to them then I see no reason why you cannot leave if you need to. As long as you leave a contact address in case we need to get in touch with you for anything more. There will be an inquest but it looks a simple, sad story to me and I cannot see the judge coming to any other conclusion.'

As Stephen set off, Le Bot caught his arm and he turned to look at the gendarme.

'Yes, is there something else?'

Le Bot grimaced. 'Your boys,' he said. 'Try not to let this destroy them. You all look like decent people and this was nothing more than an accident. They will have been correct in thinking that the boat would have capsized if Claude had tried to get into it. From all accounts he was a slow witted fellow and decided to swim back when he could have simply hung onto the outside of the boat. Why he set off to swim back when he was clearly exhausted was his own choice. Not that of the children.'

'Thank you,' said Stephen. 'I will speak to them. Do you know how the German boy is?'

'Yes,' he replied with a sigh. 'He will survive, thanks to your son. However, he has a very bad looking scar stretching from his forehead down to the bottom of his cheek. He needed a lot of stitches and he will have to live with it forever sadly. But he is in good spirits apparently and should be out of hospital later today.'

'Good and bad news then,' said Stephen and walked away.

Now that he had been given permission to go home he made a decision that they would pack their things straight away. There was a ferry leaving mid-afternoon and if they hurried they could probably make it.

Stephen Graham realised that this was the second occasion in his life that he couldn't get away from France quickly enough. He was confident that this time he would never be returning. Whenever he was here Death seemed to follow him. Someone always seemed to die. He did not know if he was being melodramatic but he vowed that as long as he lived he would never set foot on French soil again. And if his sons had any sense, neither would they.

PART TWO

JACK GRAHAM

CHAPTER THIRTEEN

Northern France, May 28th, 1940

It was the birds. That was what he could hear. The birds, softly singing above him.

Second Lieutenant Jack Graham lay in the ditch unable to move. Something hard was digging into his lower back causing him some discomfort but he ignored it as he looked up to the clear blue sky. He could see the odd white cloud moving slowly across his vision, the soft breeze blowing gently giving a sense of peacefulness and serenity. He thought he was smiling but was not totally sure. If he wasn't then he should be. How could you not smile at something so beautiful and so wonderful? Life was just that, he thought, beautiful and wonderful. At moments like this, how could anyone argue otherwise?

He could not quite remember how he had came to be there. He knew he was in a ditch and he knew that he was somewhere in northern France but that was about all he could remember. In fact he could remember nothing of his life prior to being in the ditch and had no concept as to how long he had been there. All he knew was that he had found peace, in a dry ditch in the early summertime in France.

He made another attempt to move but immediately realised that he was unable to. He seemed to be paralysed and he quite liked it that way. Looking up to the sky he listened to the birds singing and he knew he didn't need anything else. The quietness and solitude of the moment was a joy to him. Nothing else mattered right now, nothing else was important.

After what seemed like an age, or was it only a matter of seconds, he could not be sure, he was able to distinguish other sounds around him and he became aware of movement in his peripheral vision. He cursed the intrusion of these interlopers, they were not welcome and he tried to ignore them but then the sounds got louder still. Explosions, people crying and shouting and screaming out in pain and frustration, aircraft flying low overhead, the unmistakeable noise of small arms fire. All distant at first but getting ever louder the more he became aware of them. The sound of chaos all around.

Then he became aware of someone shaking him, calling out his name and a face appeared before him, only inches away from his own. A face that he recognised but the name to whom it belonged he could not remember. He did not want to remember because remembering would bring him back to the world from which he had escaped, back to that unknown world that he had somehow forgotten but he knew to be a place of only pain and death. He wanted to be left alone, there in the ditch, the place where he had found true and total peace. He did not want to re-join the real world, whatever that was, he did not want to go back to it. He was content lying there, despite the irritation of the object pressing into his back.

He closed his eyes and blocked out everything once more, filtering the things away that he did not want or need. The pain. The noise. That familiar stranger invading his space and shouting into his face.

Everything. And slowly, as he wished it, it happened. He had filtered away everything.

Well, almost everything.

The sound of the birds singing. That he kept.

CHAPTER FOURTEEN

Aldershot, England – Eleven Months Earlier

Jack Graham, Second Lieutenant of the Royal Fusiliers, knocked on the mahogany office door and waited for a reply. He had just been told by the adjutant that the major was a bit of an eccentric fellow and it was advisable for new officers to do their best not to antagonise him.

'He has his funny ways,' the adjutant had said with a wry smile. 'Bit of an odd character is old "Double H". Served in the Great War from beginning to end and was wounded about five times apparently. Some of us think he must have developed his odd traits then but who knows? Maybe he has always been like that.'

'Like what?' Jack had replied.

'Oh, don't get me wrong,' said the adjutant waving his hand. 'Don't misunderstand me. He may be a bit of a daft old bugger, but he fully knows what's what. There's no fooling him so don't even try to. He joined the army as an enlisted man and was commissioned in the battlefield and he's had plenty of opportunities for advancement up the ladder since, but has always refused. He prefers to stay close to the men apparently, says a staff job just isn't him. And despite his little eccentricities we wouldn't want any other C.O., believe me.'

Jack had thanked him and then walked the short distance to the main headquarters building for his nine o'clock meeting.

There was a booming reply from inside the office. 'Enter.'

Jack opened the door and walked in. Closing it behind him he marched the five paces required and stood before a huge wooden desk, paperwork and stationery arranged neatly upon it. Seated at the desk, concentrating on what he was doing, was Major Harding, writing on a piece of paper in a buff file. He had not looked up since Jack had entered the office. Jack saluted and awaited a response from his new commanding officer, who continued to write in the file, still ignoring him.

Eventually, Major Harding looked up. 'Very good, very good,' he said on seeing Jack's salute. 'Now sit down and stop all that messing about.'

'Thank you sir,' said Jack taking off his hat and sitting on a chair facing him. Harding went back to his writing and did not say anything, ignoring him completely while he finished off the paperwork.

Jack was able to study him for a minute or so. Major Herbert Harding, or "Double H" as he was known affectionately by his men, looked a big man. Although he was seated, it was obvious that he was well over six feet tall and he looked, to Jack, just as wide. He had a bald pate with greying hair around the sides and a huge handlebar moustache that curled up perfectly at both ends. His uniform was immaculate and he wore many ribbons upon his chest that proved to Jack that he was a well experienced soldier. After a while he put the pen down and looked up at his new junior officer.

'Facial adornment,' he said loudly.

'Excuse me, sir,' replied Jack blankly.

'Facial adornment... beards, moustaches that sort of thing.'

'Yes.'

'What is your opinion?'

'My opinion, sir?'

'Yes, do you agree or disagree?' Major Harding stood up and walked around the desk with his hands clasped behind his back. Jack could see now that his first impression of the man being huge was fully correct. Impeccably dressed, his uniform tailored perfectly to encompass his large frame, he appeared the model soldier. His tunic was pristine and the perfectly cut trousers rested at just the right height upon the most highly polished boots Jack had ever seen. Harding positioned himself behind Jack awaiting a reply.

'I have no idea. I have never really given it any thought.'

'Well, you should, my boy. It is very important to get it right. If you look young, then a well groomed moustache can make you appear older, more... dare I say it... capable... trustworthy, you know.'

'Um... Okay.'

'And if you are going grey, starting to age, then the removal of such adornment will give you a more youthful countenance don't you think?'

'Maybe. Like I say, sir, I have never given it much thought,' replied Jack.

'Take some advice and grow a moustache, my boy, you look about twelve years old.'

'I'll try to, sir,' said Jack. 'I've always found it difficult to grow stubble. I must be a bit of a late developer or something.'

'Nonsense, my boy,' replied the Major heartily, slapping him firmly on the back, knocking Jack forward in surprise. 'You are a fusilier. You're a macho man now, son.'

'Okay, sir,' replied Jack agreeably. 'I will do my damnedest to grow a good one.'

'That's the spirit,' said the Major and then went back to his chair and sat back down. He continued.

'Not only are you in the Fusiliers, you are an officer in the Fusiliers, my boy, and as such you need to look the part. To look the part, I tell you. I expect your uniform to be perfectly pressed, your boots always bulled so I can see my face in them from thirty yards and your moustache, which you will grow, by the way, to be well groomed and waxed.

'I expect you to carry yourself with back straight and chest out. Your hair, and your pistol to be well oiled and if you do happen to find yourself "well oiled" in the officers' mess and you have the need to fall over, then I expect you to fall over like a gentleman.'

'And how does a gentleman fall over, sir? If you don't mind me asking.'

'With style, my boy, with style.'

Jack tried hard to stifle the smile that he was aware was beginning to appear upon his face. This did not go unnoticed by Major Harding.

'You will find I am a "work hard, play hard" kind of man, my boy. It is a mantra to which I have lived by all my life and I will do so until God above decides he wants me to join him in Paradise, which I am assured will be my ultimate destination.'

'Yes, sir.'

'I expect you to join in with that way of thinking too.'

'I will certainly aspire to do so,' said Jack with a smile.

'Good, good. That's what I want to hear.' Harding stroked his moustache before continuing, his mood altering slightly, becoming a little more serious.

'There's a war coming my boy, have no doubt about it. Forget what the prime minister says, waving his pieces of paper at airports and the like, there's a storm coming from which no one will be able to take shelter and it will be up to men like you and I to sort it out. I was involved in the last one, but I fear that this one will be much worse, if that can at all be possible. Diplomacy cannot stop this Hitler fellow. He won't listen to reason, the irritating little man.' Harding stopped for a moment. 'It isn't going to be an easy ride, my boy, not at all. Prepare yourself for hard times ahead... Are you up to it?'

'Yes, sir,' said Jack solemnly. 'I believe I am.'

'Good, good.' Major Harding looked down at the paperwork on the desk in front of him before continuing. 'I see from your results from Officer Training School that you didn't exactly excel did you? Don't answer. But then you didn't exactly fail either. What this paperwork tells me is that I have a very average officer sitting in front of me.'

'It was an exceptional intake, sir,' replied Jack defensively.

'Maybe so… Now tell me a little of your background.'

'Yes, sir, certainly,' Jack adjusted himself in his seat. 'After leaving boarding school in Hampshire I attended Mag…'

Major Harding raised his hand. 'No, no, no,' he said irritably. 'Not all that bloody rubbish. I have that written here in front of me. Tell me about your family, that kind of thing.'

'Okay, sir, sorry sir,' said Jack, shuffling in his seat. 'My father is a barrister practicing on the south coast. He is looking at retiring in a year or so's time but if that happens I will be very surprised. I have a younger brother, Frank, who also wants to join the army. He is currently at university in London studying languages.'

'So why is it that the army appeals to you both?'

'I'm not too sure to be honest, sir,' replied Jack thoughtfully. 'Maybe it's because of my father. He was in the army during the war. Maybe it's about following in his footsteps, that kind of thing. The thing is, he never speaks of his experiences in the trenches, just occasionally comes out with a little story about what they got up to behind the lines, but never about the things he saw or anything like that.'

'That's understandable,' said Major Harding pensively. 'Perfectly understandable.'

'My mother died a couple of years ago, unfortunately. That's why I can't see my father retiring any time soon. He needs to keep busy. My brother, Frank, well he's a bit of a wild one if I'm perfectly honest. He was a very quiet child but since going to university he seems to have come out of his shell.'

'And what kind of things do you like doing, hobbies and all that?'

'I used to enjoy fishing… angling… when I was a child but haven't done it for a number of years now. I wasn't really very good at it if I'm being honest. I quite like playing tennis… and rugby of course.'

'Of course… any fiancé or sweetheart?'

'No, sir,' replied Jack. 'I never really had time for that sort of thing. Too busy you see.'

Major Harding let out a small smile but said nothing. Eventually he spoke.

'Okay. Now listen here, Graham. You will take command of number two platoon. The previous incumbent has just been promoted and moved on to B Company so a gap has come up, which you are to fill. You have a very experienced sergeant, Harry Greenwood, who will be someone you can take guidance from should you need it. The platoon also has a very promising young corporal, I believe, Cooke, I think his name is, who should have really gone to OTS like yourself, but for some reason, known only to him, he prefers life in the ranks. That's his choice and it's a free country, I suppose, so he can please himself. In short, my boy, you have landed a rather decent posting and if you play your cards right you will get on fine.'

Harding stood up as if to signal the end of the interview and Jack followed suit.

'Now, go and meet your men, young man.'

Jack saluted. 'And you can pack in all that nonsense when you are in this office,' said Harding impatiently. 'Good day.' He sat back down and looked again at the paperwork in front of him.

Jack turned on his heel and walked to the door. 'Thank you sir,' he said as he opened the door but Harding did not look up or respond.

As he closed the office door behind him some moments later, he reflected on the interview that had just taken place. As long as he was able to grow a half decent moustache then he would get on fine here, he thought. Yes, he thought, he would get on fine.

He placed his hat firmly onto his head, smiled to himself and went in search of Sergeant Greenwood and number two platoon.

CHAPTER FIFTEEN

South of Lille, France, December 1939

Jack examined the plans then looked up at the finished product as Corporal Cooke waited anxiously.

'Good job, Greg,' said Jack looking at the completed concrete pillbox that number two platoon had erected at the side of the road leading into the town. 'Give the boys the rest of the day off will you. I'll go and speak to Harry in a minute. Do you know where he is?'

Corporal Gregory Cooke smiled at his platoon commander. 'I think he's gone back to company headquarters to see the quartermaster, sir.'

'Okay,' said Jack. 'I'll pop along in a few minutes and go and find him. Tell the men that I want them back here at eight hundred hours tomorrow morning. If they are going to go out tonight then make sure that none of them gets into any trouble will you?'

'Of course, sir,' said Cooke. 'How long do you think it will be before something happens?'

'I have absolutely no idea, Greg,' replied Jack. 'There's no intelligence as yet to say the Germans are building up an attacking force and similarly we are not exactly setting up to move towards them are we?' He indicated the defences they had been building. '"Double H" is hoping it might all peter out and we can all go home, but that's just wishful thinking on his part because from Hitler's actions so far, I can't see that happening. The worry is that when it comes, it will happen fast and without warning and we have to be ready for it. I just hope we are able to stand it when it does come.'

'I'm sure we'll be ready, sir,' said Cooke encouragingly, 'I have no doubt that they'll receive more than they bargain for when they meet the British Army.'

'Let's hope so. Thank you, corporal.' Cooke stepped back and saluted. Jack offered a token salute in response and turned around to leave. Like "Double H", Jack was not keen on saluting although where his commanding officer found it an irritation, Jack found it more uncomfortable than anything else. It just didn't feel right to him.

He could justify his decision to give the platoon some rest and relaxation. They had completed the week's tasks early and had worked hard outside in the cold, without complaint, for days, to accomplish it. They had built up the last of the defences on the approach roads to the east of the town in accordance with the bigger plan to put up a brick wall against any planned German attack and Jack was pleased with the efforts of his men. They had done a fantastic job and this would reflect well on him, so they deserved their break.

"Work hard, play hard," that's what "Double H" had told him, and if it applied to the officers then surely it applied to the other ranks as well and if giving them some free time was his decision then it had been well earned.

Since joining the regiment earlier in the year Jack had tried to be a fair platoon commander. He had often leaned on the more experienced Sergeant Greenwood for advice, as suggested by "Double H", and the both of them had offered support and encouragement where needed. He had grown to like the people under his command but felt as though he was responsible for each and every one of them, like a father looking out for his sons, and he liked it that way. It gave him a sense of purpose. He had been told by Sergeant Greenwood that he had gained the respect of his men as both a man and an officer. Things could not be going any better.

However, he had an ulterior motive for allowing the platoon a free night off and that motive was Bernadette.

He had met Bernadette Reyer a little over a month ago, shortly after arriving in France. The premises he had found her in would not have been to the approval of his father, that was for certain, but Jack was a man now and a soldier, and as such was able to make his own decisions and, he understood, his own mistakes. But Bernadette was no mistake. Her profession left a lot to be desired but it was something that Jack could block his mind to because if he thought about it for too long it would drive him mad so he had decided never to think about it if he could help it.

Lieutenant Dan Wilson, the commander of one platoon, and his friend, had coerced him into travelling into Lille on one of their rare weekends off and introduced him to the delights of alcohol and women. He had been very dubious at first but on finding an establishment that offered both and indulging in what these two vices had to offer, he had not taken much persuading to go a second time. Or even a third or a fourth. Dan had told him not to get emotionally attached to any of them, to just hand over the money and walk away, otherwise it would end in tears and at first that was what Jack had done. However on meeting and being with Bernadette he realised that there was no other he wanted to be with and when she stopped taking any payment from him he realised that their arrangement was somewhat different to the other officers and the consorts that they would spend their time and money with.

Jack knew that this behaviour was not exactly virtuous, or that of what was expected of an officer of the Fusiliers, and wanted to keep it from the men and his superiors but he doubted that the major would disapprove anyway. "Work hard, play hard" was the man's motto and wasn't that exactly what Jack was doing?

As he walked towards company headquarters, he thought of Bernadette. Beautiful Bernadette. The girl whose smile melted him every time he saw it. The girl he knew he could never be with in the long haul. He knew this was a short term plan, a fleeting relationship in the story of his life, but it was the kind that was forging him into a man. What was wrong with it anyway? Who had the authority to criticise it in the whole scheme of things? It was just two young, unattached people sharing a mutually beneficial experience during a bleak time in their so far short lives. They were both uplifted by it. They were hurting no one and the only individuals in jeopardy of being damaged were themselves.

But then Jack was no fool. He knew it would come to an end at some point and that could happen at any time. At any point orders could come to move the battalion to another location. It all depended on the strategy of Lord Gort, the commander of the British Expeditionary Force. He also knew that Bernadette saw other men too, slept with them, did things with them that should only be between two people who were officially attached to each other, but he was a realist and knew her profession before he embarked to offer her his heart. And his soul if he was honest with himself. But then he felt that he was only lending it to her for a brief time and could quite easily take it back and when he asked for her to return it, he knew she would hand it over willingly and with a smile upon her face.

He found that he was whistling as he walked, tipping his cap to the civilians as he passed them, walking by or sitting outside the cafes and estaminets enjoying a coffee or other such beverage. Some smiled back but mostly they ignored him. He did not care but continued to do it anyway. They could be miserable if they wanted to be, but not him, not today. He would find Sergeant Greenwood, who would sort him out with transportation, and he would set off to spend the night with Bernadette. Just him and her, he and she, no one else. Life could not get much better.

He found Sergeant Greenwood standing in the courtyard of the building that had been requisitioned as company headquarters, with a clipboard in his hand, supervising the offloading of a wagon containing food supplies. On seeing Jack approach he put the clipboard to his side and smiled at him. Knowing Jack's thoughts on saluting he did not raise his hand.

'Hello, sir,' he said. 'How are tricks in the village?'

'Finished the approach defences with time to spare, Harry,' Jack replied. 'I've given the boys the rest of the day off. What are you up to here?'

'Doing a little bit of work for Major Harding, sir,' he replied. 'Will you be wanting me for anything once I've finished?'

'If you have time, I was wondering if you could find a spare vehicle for me. I have some business in Lille this evening.'

Greenwood could not prevent a small smile, which did not go unnoticed by Jack. However he chose to pretend he had not seen it.

'I'm sure I can do something for you, sir. Why don't you wait inside and I'll see to it once I've sorted this wagon out?'

'Thank you, Sergeant,' said Jack and as he turned away and walked toward the front door, he was sure that he heard a short snigger from his platoon sergeant.

If he had strained his ears even further, he might have heard the whispered words, 'Randy little bugger.'

*

Jack leaned onto his side and in the darkness of the bedroom strained his eyes to watch her sleeping. There was something childlike and pure about the way she slept. She hardly made a sound and he leaned his head in closer to her to see if she was actually breathing and once he was sure that she was, he leaned back. This was something he did often, like a parent with a new born baby. Bernadette Reyer lay naked under the sheets with her back to him. He looked past her to the window where the slight gap in the curtains revealed that outside the morning sun was still yet to rise and would not do so for a couple of hours yet. He turned around and felt for the cigarettes on the bedside table and after fumbling around for a few seconds he located them, along with the book of matches he had purchased the previous day.

Placing one in his mouth he sat up and lit it, causing the room to brighten briefly before returning to darkness once the flame of the match was extinguished as he shook it. The glow of the lit cigarette the only light in the room.

Bernadette stirred and said something in her sleep that Jack did not understand before turning to face him. She wriggled slightly before placing her arm above her head and her soft snores continued.

By the glow of the cigarette Jack could see the smoke gently rising to the ceiling as he blew it out, forming strange and elaborate shapes. He watched them change and dance as they ascended out of his vision and into the darkness. He compared the smoke disappearing into the shadows to his life at that moment. He had no control over either and where it was headed he did not know. Was his life, like the smoke, heading for a dark place where it would ultimately vanish and be forgotten about? Maybe living for the day, as he was doing, was a little immature, he thought, but then it was a good way of coping with the uncertainty of the path his life was taking. He stirred restlessly at the thought and tried to put such thinking out of his mind.

Sensing the movement Bernadette awoke. She tapped him on the arm and he turned to her in the darkness.

'I'm sorry,' he said. 'I didn't mean to wake you.'

'It is okay,' she said in heavily accented English. 'Could you give me a cigarette?'

Jack turned to the table and retrieved one from his pack. Lighting it with the end of his own he handed it to her as she sat up beside him.

'Merci,' she whispered as she took it and placed it in her mouth.

Jack watched her in the gloom, her body silhouetted against the curtain as she smoked her cigarette quietly. The crisp white sheet had fallen to reveal her perfect breasts and Jack took a short intake of breath at the beauty of her. The perfect woman. Long dark brown, almost black hair and bright blue eyes, a slightly upturned nose and dimples on her cheeks, a beauty spot, which may have been a tattoo, he was not too sure and her soft, naturally dark, almost Mediterranean skin. Yes, he thought, the perfect woman. He was not too sure how old she was, he had not asked her as he had heard that it was rude to ask a lady her age, but he thought that she was probably slightly older than his twenty-three years.

She turned to look at him. 'Are you okay, Jacques?'

He loved the way she used the French variant of his name.

'Could not be any better,' he replied, smiling in the darkness.

She became aware of his eyes wandering to her body and pulled up the sheet self-consciously. Jack could not help smiling to himself at this. How could she be embarrassed after last night?

'What time are you leaving?' she asked.

'I have given orders that the men are to form up at eight o'clock so I need to be back for seven so I can sort myself out before I see them.'

'Oh,' she said with a sigh. 'I was hoping that we could have spent the day together.'

Jack did not know what to say. This was the first time that she had wanted to spend any time with him other than in the bar downstairs or up here in the bedroom. This was dangerous, he thought. His heart ached to say, yes, that he would abandon his plans for the day and get word to Captain Jenkinson with an excuse that he was ill and Sergeant Greenwood would have to take over his duties for the day, but he knew that was not really an option. Even if his day was free he could not spend it with her. He knew if he did then he would never go back, that he would hide away with her until all this was over.

He looked at her. 'You know I can't do that. There is nothing that I would like more but you know that I can't, don't you?'

As his eyes adjusted to the darkness, he could see that she was smiling sadly.

'Oui,' she said softly, 'I know… But it is so sad.'

'Maybe if things were different,' he said. 'Maybe if there was no war then we could be together.'

'If there was no war then we never would have met,' she replied. 'I am grateful for the war, Jacques. I love the war.'

Jack felt his heart throb inside his chest and a cramp seemed to form in his stomach. So, he thought, this was what love felt like.

They sat in silence for a few minutes, smoking their cigarettes, each lost in their own private thoughts until Jack finally broke the silence.

'I've never asked you before,' he said quietly. 'But how did you end up here… doing this?'

'I met you downstairs last night,' she said with a giggle, pleased with her little joke.

'No,' said Jack, ignoring her attempt at humour. 'You know what I mean.'

'Oh, don't be so serious,' she said still giggling, putting her cigarette out in an ashtray at the side of the bed. Then she snuggled back down under the bedcovers, pulling the sheet over her shoulders. 'Okay, Jacques,' she said, 'what do you want to know?'

Jack took one last drag of his cigarette and then stubbed the butt into the ashtray on the small table at his side before moving down to join her. Their faces were only inches apart.

'It's all right,' he said. 'You don't have to tell me anything that you don't want to.'

'I am from the south originally,' she said. 'My father died during the Great War and my mother and I moved to Paris to stay with my aunt and her husband when it was over. Not long after we arrived in Paris my mother took and ill and she too perished.'

'I'm so sorry,' said Jack. 'You don't have to tell me any more if you don't wish to.'

'I have started now,' she said, and continued. 'My uncle was not a very nice man and when I was sixteen I ran away with a friend of mine and we lived with some older friends for a while in Amiens before that went wrong. And then one day I collected my things and without telling anyone I was leaving, I took the first train away. That train arrived in the station two miles from here and it is here I have been ever since.'

'So what happened to your uncle?'

'I have no idea and no interest,' she said. Jack could see a tear leaving her eye, which she quickly wiped away. 'He was a horrible man and I hope he is dead.'

Jack didn't need to say anything. He knew.

'And your friend, the one you went to Amiens with, what happened to him?' For Jack also understood that the friend was a "him".

'I do not know,' she said, either not noticing his use of the word or realising that he understood. 'I hope he is okay. I am sure he will be.'

They lay in silence for a few more minutes.

'Your turn,' she said after a while.

'What would you like to know?'

'Who you are. Nothing more,' she whispered.

Jack looked into her eyes. Her beautiful blue eyes.

'I am John Graham, known as Jack. I am from the south of England and was born in 1916 which makes me twenty three years old. I am the son of Stephen and Margaret Graham. My father is a barrister and was in the army in France during the last war. My mother died suddenly a few years ago, unfortunately, and my father now lives alone because my younger brother, Frank, is going through officer training in England. He's in the army too. I had a fantastic childhood and couldn't have wished for better parents, or a closer brother. I went to boarding school in Hampshire and then on to university at Oxford before joining the army. When I was a child we used to go on annual holidays to Devon and sometimes to St Malo in Brittany until an incident happened there that I do not care to remember. I have been with the Fusiliers since finishing OTS earlier this year and came to France in September.'

Jack was aware he was babbling and that Bernadette probably could not understand half of what he was saying but he was in full flow and continued anyway.

'I have done things in the past few months that I have never done before. I have trained soldiers, some older and more experienced than I. I have drunk alcohol for the first time, danced with pretty women for the first time and fallen in love for the first time.'

'Wow,' she said, interrupting him. And then she kissed him firmly on the mouth. Pulling away she said to him, 'You cannot fall in love with me Jacques, I am not good for you.'

'I will be the judge of that,' he replied.

'No you won't,' she said sadly. 'You know it can go nowhere. You know what I do and what I have been doing for a long time now. I am no good for you,' she repeated.

Jack sighed but did not reply.

'You will leave me without telling me you are going,' she went on, 'like I did to Pierre, but for you it will be different. You will be ordered to leave and I will not see you again. It will happen suddenly and it will happen totally. There is nothing either of us can do about it. In another time, another world, another life, maybe this could have worked. But, my dearest Jacques,' she said stroking his face, 'this isn't another time… or world… or life. This is the one we have, the one we have to live, even though we may wish it otherwise.'

Jack looked at her and kissed her softly on her lips. He did not say anything. He knew that every word that she had said was true but he did not want it to be so. He had already decided that he would live for the moment and telling this girl that he loved her had now complicated the affair. It wasn't living for the moment, it was planning for a future that could not be. You couldn't just declare your love for someone and then walk away from that relationship. It couldn't be done.

But it had to be.

Jack looked towards the gap in the curtain. 'I hate these winter mornings. You can never make out what time of day it is.'

She turned to look at the window with him, happy that the subject had been changed so suddenly. She did not reply.

Jack got out of the bed without looking at her and took his trousers from the chair where he had left them the night before. He dressed slowly, trying to make every moment with her last. He could feel her eyes looking at him but he could not bring himself to turn around and look in her direction, for fear of her seeing him close to tears.

When he was fully dressed and had put on his wristwatch, he picked up his cap and paused. He still could not bring himself to look at her. He turned to her but stopped, his mouth open as if to say something but the words would not come. Putting the cap on his head he walked to the door and left the room without looking back, leaving her alone and naked in the bed.

As he walked down the stairs to the exit, he knew that he would never see Bernadette Reyer again.

CHAPTER SIXTEEN

Near Arras, France, May 1940

The army was in full retreat.

Jack, from the passenger seat of the Bren gun carrier at the rear of the convoy, looked forward at the remains of the company as they travelled the long country road away from Arras. Private Wood in the driver's seat at the side of him, his head wrapped in a blood-stained bandage. In the back of the carrier, crammed into the small space that one soldier would normally occupy, were three more of his men. Corporal Cooke, who was manning the machine gun and Privates Rutter and Smalling, the latter with a bad wound to his left arm rendering it useless, sat in silence as they motored along the road.

They had remained near Lille until the German attack finally came on the tenth of May and then the regiment had been ordered to move further north, to Belgium, to assist with the defences there. However, before they had managed to get into the line they had been moved back south again to Arras to take part in the counter attack of the twenty-first of May. That was a week ago now and what a week it had been. At first the attack seemed to be going well, small gains being made and the German advance, under Rommel, had been halted.

However, these gains had not lasted very long and soon the German Seventh Division had halted the British and was now forcing them back toward the sea. It seemed that in the north, the German advance was unstoppable and the British, Belgians and French were unable to prevent the Blitzkrieg from pushing to the coast and completing a major victory for the enemy. With a fear of those in the south being cut off and total defeat a strong possibility the orders had been received telling the army, pretty much wherever they were it seemed to Jack, to retreat to Dunkirk where strong defences were currently being set up. Jack could see only one reason for this and that was the abandonment of mainland Europe to the Nazis. Behind Dunkirk there was only one way to go and that was across the Channel and back home to England.

He looked at the vehicle in front, another Bren gun carrier containing five more of his men, all looking tired and battered. He had never expected it to be like this, but then he had never really given much thought to what it would be like. He had avoided thinking about it, content with the work he had been carrying out and the sense of achievement he had felt when he had been praised for that work. It was ironic that at the first sight of the enemy all the hard graft he and his men had done in building defences was abandoned within minutes. It had all been a complete waste of time.

He watched the vehicle in front, trundling along at top speed, black smoke emitting from the exhaust and occasionally wafting into his face. The sound of the caterpillar tracks rolling along the tarmacked roadway mixed with the noise of the engines and those of the trucks further ahead, which were carrying the rest of the company including many wounded. Despite there being so many people in the small convoy the one noise he could not hear was the sound of human conversation. He looked at those in the vehicle with him and they all looked weary and defeated. It would be hard to motivate any of them over the coming days but he would have to try, he realised.

Jack thought back to five days previously when he had killed his first man. The company had been tasked with advancing on a small village where an enemy unit was thought to be in residence and his platoon was charged with attacking the right flank. As the main thrust of the attack took place, a group of around ten Germans exited the back of one of the buildings and made to escape to the wooded area where Jack's platoon were preparing their part of the assault. They didn't stand a chance as the Bren gun section opened up on them ripping them to pieces. As they walked past their bodies, to clear out the building, which looked like it had once been an inn, he averted his eyes from the carnage his men had just caused. He had not wanted to be physically sick in front of them.

As he and two soldiers of the platoon, he could not remember who they were, approached the door from where the unfortunate enemy soldiers had departed, he was aware of movement inside and managed to jump for cover just in time as a rifle shot was fired from an upstairs window. The soldier inside having seen his comrades killed a few moments ago, must have been very nervous, thought Jack, as his shot was way off target missing them all by some distance.

With his Enfield No. 2 service revolver in hand and the safety catch off he ran for the door, while his comrades fired upon the window to give him cover. He remembered the adrenalin pumping throughout his body, his breathing becoming fast, not from lack of fitness but from the sheer terror of it all. He had never been so scared in all his life. Never.

He remembered acting quickly, not allowing himself to freeze. He had taken one deep breath and then had moved swiftly into the building. Thinking back now he realised it had been a totally reckless thing to do. He had no idea if there were any more Germans in the building besides the gunman on the first floor. He should have waited for the others to catch him up and throw in grenades but all his training had gone out of the window in the heat of battle. However, he had been lucky. There had been no-one in the first room he entered and it was clear that the ground floor was empty. He quickly found the stairs leading to the first floor and as he approached them he saw something bouncing down them. It took a second to realise what it was and he had pulled back into the room he had just left as the stick grenade exploded sending dust, debris and wood flying past him. He was then joined by the two soldiers who had accompanied him outside.

'Bloody 'ell, sir, that was close,' said one of them with a nervous grin. He had a mills bomb in his hand, the pin already pulled and the hand lever clasped tight. They approached the stairs and the same soldier, Private Gray, Jack remembered now, whispered to him, 'Count to four,' and let the lever drop, arming the grenade. After a pause Private Gray threw it up the stairs and they both turned away awaiting the explosion, which happened less than two seconds later.

Before the dust could settle, Jack ran up the stairs as fast as he could and on reaching the top he could see that the German was lying on his back in the corner of an empty room that overlooked the field he had just crossed. He was obviously badly injured, blood pouring from a huge gash in his head, but he still had the strength to lift his rifle and point it directly at Jack. Without even thinking about it Jack had emptied all six bullets into the man's chest, killing him instantly.

Jack shuddered thinking about it now. He had stared Death in the face and he had not flinched. He had felt nothing as he had fired his pistol and even now he did not feel anything, no remorse. What did that make him? Tough? A cold hearted killer? Emotionless? He didn't know and in a way it scared him that he could do this and not react. But then this was war. This was his job, his duty. But it didn't feel right. Was this how his father had felt during the last one? If so then it didn't make him a bad man because his father was the most humble and honest person he knew.

Jack's thoughts were disturbed back to the present by the convoy slowing down and a minute later it had stopped completely. He jumped out of the carrier.

'Wait here,' he said to the men without looking at them, realising that it was very much a pointless thing to say as they couldn't exactly go anywhere.

Walking to the jeep at the front of the convoy he found Captain Jenkinson, who was in conversation with Dan and Lieutenant Watson from three platoon.

'What's happening?' asked Jack. 'Why have we stopped?'

Jenkinson did not say anything but indicated with his eyes to the road ahead of them.

They had reached a bend in the road, which led to a small wooded area. Blocking the road were a number of old vehicles and carts being pulled by various animals; horses, donkeys and one even had a cow tethered to it. The carts contained a large number of civilians, mainly old men, women and children together with household possessions. Jack could see one of them had an old battered piano resting precariously atop it.

'This is ridiculous,' he said. 'How on earth are we going to get past them?'

'That's what we're discussing,' said Jenkinson with a frown.

'Is there any way around?' asked Dan, running his fingers through his hair.

'We would have to turn back for that, I'm afraid,' replied Jenkinson with a sigh.

'Well, there's only one thing we can do,' said Jack looking at the crowd of refugees preventing them from progressing. The others looked at him expectantly and as he looked back to them he said, 'We'll just have to move them out of the way. Let's get the lads out of the trucks and get them to shift them to the side of the road.'

'They won't like that,' said Dan.

'So what? We need to get moving. Let's face it we have no idea how far the Germans are behind us now do we? We'll just have to shift them whether they like it or not.'

'Jack's right,' said Jenkinson. 'Get the boys off the wagons and get them to work. Drag them off the road if you have to, I don't care. We need to keep moving.'

'Yes, sir,' said Jack and Dan in unison and then turned away to carry out the order.

*

After a half hour of pushing and shoving and gesticulating and shouting, enough room was made to allow the convoy to pass. A lot of the civilians had not taken too kindly to being manhandled and pushed to the side of the road and into the woods and Captain Jenkinson had lost his patience on a couple of occasions, even pulling out his revolver at one point and waving it in the face of an old man who was not for moving.

As they drove past the civilians, some of them waved their fists in anger but most just watched them passively as they went by, their faces blank, almost resigned to their fate, whatever that fate may be.

As they passed the last cart, which looked to have got its wheel stuck in a ditch, an old man and a young woman trying desperately and ineffectively to free it, Jack felt an enormous sense of responsibility. Wasn't the whole point of them being here in the first place to help these people? And here they were, forcing them off the road and abandoning them to the approaching Germans and whatever hardships that would bring. He justified the actions they had just taken because they were combat soldiers and, as such, if they needed to get past then they should be given free passage. But was this the right thing to do? Jack wasn't sure.

'Stop!' he shouted suddenly.

Private Wood slammed the brakes instinctively, causing those in the back to jerk forward, Private Smalling letting out a small scream as he hit his damaged arm on the side of the vehicle.

'Bloody 'ell, sir,' said Wood. 'Bleedin' shit meself then. What is it?'

'Reverse please, Private.'

'What's the matter boss?' asked Corporal Cooke from the rear.

'I can't leave those people like that,' replied Jack. 'I can't leave them stuck like that when we've caused it.'

'The idiots shouldn't be taking up the road,' said Wood. 'It's their own fault.'

'Just do as you're told, Private,' ordered Jack.

Wood put the carrier into reverse and pressed the accelerator. As they sped backwards, Jack could see the convoy ahead not slowing down and getting further away with each passing second.

'What about the others?' asked Cooke.

'This won't take long,' said Jack. 'We'll soon catch up with them again.'

'Whatever you say, sir.'

Jack got out of the carrier, 'Okay, everyone apart from Smalling come with me.'

He was joined by the others and the four of them approached the cart where a man in his late sixties was attempting to pull a donkey that was tethered to it. Upon the cart sat a youngish woman with three children, a girl and two boys and at the side of them, piled high, were suitcases, occasional furniture and boxes of books and other such items. The donkey was not for moving, its feet stubbornly fixed to the spot. No amount of coaxing from the old man was making it move forward.

'Okay,' said Jack. 'Get these people off the thing and give me a hand.'

Wood and Rutter walked to the back of the cart and spoke to the woman and children but they could not understand what they were saying and looked at them blankly.

Jack spoke to the old man, 'Do you speak English…Parlez-vous Anglais?'

'Oui monsieur, a little,' he replied.

'Thank God for that,' said Jack. 'Tell your family to get off. We will help you to move it, but they need to get off.'

The man shouted to his family on the cart and they reluctantly stepped down and stood to the side. Jack and Corporal Cooke then held on to the donkey's bridle and pulled with all their strength as Rutter and Wood pushed from the rear. However, the donkey still did not budge.

'Bloody hell,' said Jack taking a break. 'Stupid bloody animal.'

He looked up to see Smalling watching from the back of the carrier, laughing hysterically at them and Jack couldn't help smiling himself. How ridiculous they must have looked. However, when he looked around at all the refugees, some now back on the road and some still standing amongst the trees, he saw that none of them found the situation at all comical.

Then he had an idea and took out his pistol. Standing slightly behind the animal he raised it to the air and fired a shot. Instantly the donkey jerked forward, freeing the cart from the hole, a look of terror on its face and braying noisily. As it did so, a lamp at the rear of the cart fell backwards, smashing as it hit the ground. Cooke grabbed the bridle and attempted to prevent the donkey from going any further. Luckily the weight of its cargo stopped it from running away and with the assistance of the old man the animal was soon calmed.

As Jack put the pistol back into the holster, the young woman approached him, holding the broken lamp. She was furious. She shouted at him in French, waving her arms wildly, her eyes bulging and her face red.

'What's she saying?' Jack asked the old man.

'My daughter is asking who will pay for the lamp?'

Jack looked at him. 'Are you kidding me?' he asked. 'Seriously?'

'Oui, monsieur,' replied the man indifferently, as though what she was asking was perfectly reasonable.

'Tell her to send an invoice to Lord Gort and if she gets no joy with him tell her that King George will gladly refund her if she presents herself at Buckingham Palace within the next fortnight. Now get out of my way you ungrateful shit before I order my men to put your bloody cart back in the bloody hole.' Turning to the three soldiers he said, 'Come on lads, we've wasted enough time as it is.'

Two minutes later they were back on the road. No one said a word but Jack could sense that all of them wanted to laugh, himself included.

After five minutes of travelling they came to a junction where the road forked to the left and right.

'Which way now, sir?' asked Wood, stopping the vehicle.

'Let me think,' replied Jack. The truth was that he was unsure. He did not have a map and he could see no military vehicles in any direction. However, further along the road to the right he could see a line of refugees, similar to those they had just passed. 'Turn right,' he said.

'Are you sure, sir?' asked Wood.

'Honestly? No I'm not, but those civvies over there are obviously going in the opposite direction to the Germans so that'll be the way we need to be going too, don't you think?'

Happy with Jack's logic, Wood put the carrier into gear and turned right. As they approached the column of refugees, Jack could make out that they were not all civilians, many of them were French and British soldiers and as they got closer he could see that a lot of them were walking wounded. The road was wide enough for the carrier to pass to the side of them quite easily and as they got nearer Jack asked Wood to slow down. They pulled alongside a group of four British soldiers and slowed to walking pace.

'You, soldier,' he shouted to the nearest infantryman who had a bloodied bandage around his head.

The soldier turned to face him. 'Hello, sir, nice day don't you think?'

Ignoring the sarcastic pleasantry Jack asked him, 'Have any trucks passed you, say, in the last ten minutes or so?'

'Couldn't tell you to be honest, boss,' he replied casually. 'Not been paying much attention. We're on our way to Dunkirk or somewhere. We think this is the right way. Just following these Frenchies 'cause they seem to know where they're goin'.'

'Which unit are you with?'

'We're a bit of a mixed bunch to be honest. I'm with the Royal Norfolks…
or was that is. Eric here and his two pals are Lancashire Fusiliers. Things have
got a little mixed up with all this fighting and stuff. Those bloody Germans
will be the death of me yet, mark my words.'

Jack tapped Wood on the shoulder and they accelerated away. Jack looked
with dismay at the rabble that was once the British army. A few short months
ago they had marched into the country with hope and confidence and all he
could see now, whenever he came into contact with them, was a shadow of
that army, a caricature of what had once been a proud and capable force. The
civilian refugees were becoming an issue, clogging the roads adding to the
mayhem in their desperate attempts to get clear of the advancing Germans. It
moved him close to tears but he forced them back and made himself look
forward. He had to find the rest of the company and he knew that he should
never have stopped to help the old man with the cart, but that was done now
and there was nothing he could do about it.

Then from behind he heard a noise, a familiar noise that shook him to the
bone and made the hairs on his neck stand up. This was a noise he had first
heard only a few days ago and it put the fear of God into him. He turned in
his seat and looked to the sky behind them and his worst fears were realised.

Already civilians and soldiers alike were jumping to the side of the road to
find cover wherever they could. Jack made a quick calculation and understood
that they had a matter of seconds and, looking at the open road ahead where
such cover for the Bren gun carrier was lacking, he made an instant decision.

'Stop!' he screamed for the second time in half an hour, but this time he
was aware that his voice sounded much different. This time it was filled with
urgency. This time it was filled with fear and terror.

Again Wood slammed his foot down on the brakes.

'Everybody out!' yelled Jack. 'Take cover.'

He turned around and grabbed the injured Private Smalling by the scruff
of the neck as the others jumped from the vehicle, half dragging him out and
onto the road where they both fell in a heap. Corporal Cooke had the presence
of mind to detach the Bren gun from the housing and Jack was aware of him
jumping into the ditch at the side of the road. He was also conscious of the
rushing of both the soldiers and the refugees, desperately searching for a place
of safety away from the approaching threat from the air.

The Junkers Ju 87B, otherwise known as the Stuka dive bomber, had
become the terror of the skies. It had played a vital part in the German
Blitzkrieg as they had advanced through France and Belgium and Jack was all
too familiar with the sound it made as it dived at an angle of eighty-five

degrees towards its target, air activated sirens fitted to the spats over the wheels, letting out a high pitched shriek to terrify those on the ground. They were fitted with two 110 pound bombs on each angled wing and a single much bigger bomb attached to its belly. Two wing mounted 7.92mm MG17 machine guns could be fired by the pilot and the rear gunner had an MG15 at his disposal to fire on any following enemy aircraft. All in all, it was a formidable aircraft, Jack thought, and when he looked up he could see, to his horror, that there were two of them.

He looked around frantically in search of suitable cover. There was only one vehicle in the vicinity and that was the Bren gun carrier they had just abandoned and this was the obvious target. As he got to his feet, pulling Smalling with him, the shriek of the Stukas became louder and he thought that his head would burst with the sheer din of it. It was terrible and all consuming, as though Lucifer himself was falling from the sky to inflict his wrath upon the people below.

And then he found that he had made it to the ditch somehow. He did not know how he had done it but he was there nevertheless. There was something digging into his back and as he attempted to move he realised that he couldn't. He was fixed, paralysed, as though the devil had grabbed him and was holding him in place, refusing to let him go. It seemed strange to him as he lay there that for some inexplicable reason he liked it like that. It was oddly peaceful.

Lying on his back and looking up to the sky. The beautiful blue sky.

And then one sound seemed to take up his thoughts until he could hear nothing else. It was the birds. That was what he could hear. The birds, softly singing above him.

CHAPTER SEVENTEEN

Slowly Jack's senses began to return. He awoke to find Corporal Cooke shouting in his face and shaking him gently but firmly. At first he could not make out what he was saying, his head still fuzzy and hazy from the concussion of the bombs, but he soon realised that Cooke was checking if he was all right, that he was not dead. Jack tried to speak, to let him know that yes, he would survive but when he spoke, his words, even to himself, seemed drawn and incoherent, as though he was intoxicated.

Slowly, as his mind began to clear, the pain set in. His body seemed to ache all over and he had a pounding in his head that caused him to squint his eyes to force back the throbbing. He tried to move but as he did so the object that he had been aware was digging into his lower back, pressed against him once more.

He shook his head in attempt to clear it. 'Here, Greg,' he said, lifting up his arm. 'Help me get up.'

Cooke gripped his hand tightly and gently eased Jack up until he was able to stand and climb out of the ditch. Before looking at his surroundings he checked himself for any signs of serious injury and, apart from a few scratches to his face and hands and a general ache all over, the worst being his head, he was happy to see that he had not been badly harmed.

'I'm okay,' he said to Cooke, 'I'll be all right.'

And then he looked.

The Bren gun carrier that they had been travelling in had taken a direct hit and was on its side burning, the tracks hanging loosely from the wheels. Carts had spilled their contents in the roadway and numerous dead animals and people lay around. Fires burned where the Stuka's bombs had hit and craters filled the road and surrounding fields. It was total devastation. He looked for his men but could not see them.

Cooke turned to him. 'Smalling's had it, sir,' he explained. Pointing further down the road he continued, 'Wood is fine. He's over there looking after some casualties.'

Jack looked in the direction he was pointing and could see Private Wood kneeling at the side of the road, applying a field dressing to an injured woman who had blood pouring from a gash in her head. She was wailing uncontrollably.

'Rutter has hurt his leg,' Cooke explained. 'I think he twisted his ankle when he jumped from the carrier. It's swollen up already.'

'Okay,' said Jack, his mind now clearing and racing, thoughts flying into his brain with every passing second. 'So basically. Three of us are fine, one is dead and the other has a bad ankle.'

'That's about the size of it sir.'

'Okay. How long was I out for?'

'About five minutes sir. That's all.'

'Right,' said Jack. He looked at the carrier on its side. 'Looks like we are walking from here I'm afraid, Greg.'

He looked around again and could not believe the sheer carnage that had been delivered to them. He could not understand or accept that the Germans could bomb a civilian refugee column and then realised that the target had been his group and the other soldiers who had found themselves mixed in with them. At once he blamed himself. If he had not stopped to assist the ultimately ungrateful family then he would still be with the company and would be closing in on the relative safety of Dunkirk right now, and these poor people may still be alive.

The noise then hit him like a hammer. The moaning and cries of the civilians as they realised that some of their family were either dead or seriously injured, combined with the groans of those who had been hit. Had it all been his fault? This pain and grief that had come down from the skies? Was it all down to the choice he had made a half hour earlier? Jack was not a believer in fate but he could not help thinking that this could have all been avoided.

The sounds filled his head until he felt like it would explode.

'Are you okay, sir?' asked Cooke, concerned, seeing Jack's face.

'Yes, yes,' replied Jack. He would need to pull himself together. He could not let this affect him because the others needed his leadership and direction.

After a moment he said, 'Come on, we need to make a move. We need to get out of here. Round up as many British soldiers as you can find and we'll pull out together. If you get any resistance then let me know. Leave the French soldiers to deal with the civvies. They are on their own now, I'm afraid. Get everyone here to me as soon as you can. I think we need to get away from civilians and it won't harm our chances of getting to Dunkirk if we all stick together. Safety in numbers and all that.'

'Yes, sir,' said Cooke and turned away to carry out Jack's instructions.

Jack sat down on the roadway and closed his eyes and his ears to what was happening around him. He needed to ignore it, to blank his mind from it all and not let it distract him. He had to function as a leader. The men would look to him as the senior person present to get them to safety. It was his duty as a British officer to look after his men.

He became aware of someone standing in front of him and looked up. It was Private Wood.

'Thank you, sir,' he said.

'For what?' asked Jack, bewildered at his gratitude.

'Look,' he replied indicating the burning vehicle that they had been travelling in. 'If you hadn't acted quickly when you realised what was coming then we'd all be dead.'

Jack stood up. 'It didn't do Smalling any good did it?' he responded.

'Don't blame yourself for that, sir,' said Wood. 'He just got unlucky and it wasn't you that dropped the bombs now was it?'

Jack could not argue with the logic of what Private Wood was saying. He was correct, it was not he who had inflicted this carnage, it had been the choice of the pilots of the aircraft that had attacked them. It was they who were to blame not him. Even if Jack and the other soldiers were a legitimate target, the pilots could not have missed the fact that there were a lot of civilians around but they had ignored this, although they must have known there would have been significant collateral damage.

After a few minutes Cooke returned with a large group of British soldiers and Jack turned to view them all. What he saw did not exactly inspire him with confidence. A more dishevelled bunch of people he had never before clapped eyes upon. There were roughly twenty-five of them, some with bandages around their heads, a couple with their arms in makeshift slings. A few were without helmets and some did not even carry any form of weapon. Those with leg injuries hung onto their friends as they hobbled slowly to form up in front of him, covered in dust and grime and none had obviously shaved in days.

Jesus Christ, thought Jack.

'Are there any officers among you?' he asked loudly. They looked about each other but no one responded. 'Okay,' he carried on, 'it looks like it's me then. Listen up. We need to get our arses out of here and to Dunkirk as fast as we can. From what I know and can understand it looks like they want us to go home and I'm sure that's an instruction that we are all quite happy to comply with right now. If we stick together then we might just make it. I have no idea where the Germans are and I'm guessing that neither do any of you and I must admit that that's a concern but we'll just have to deal with it. I want all injured men brought forward so we can assess them. We are leaving no one behind even if we have to carry them. There's nothing we can do for these civilians now, I'm afraid. So if we are going to make it then we have to look out for ourselves.

'I want a quick inventory of all weapons, ammunition, food and water. Can the NCOs please deal with that? We need to be setting off in less than ten minutes and I don't want to use the main roads if we can help it. So let's make it snappy, gentlemen.'

'Do you know the way, sir?' shouted a voice from the rear.

Jack looked over to where the soldier who had asked the question stood. 'I think we know the general direction, don't we, and that will have to do for now I'm afraid. One thing's for certain, we can't hang around here to be target practice for the Luftwaffe again and we won't be much use if the Panzers turn up either, will we? We have to move and move quickly. Okay everyone, snap to it.'

Jack stepped aside while Corporal Cooke and a big sergeant from the Lancashire Fusiliers got to work carrying out his orders. He wandered back down the road and lit a cigarette, welcoming the brief respite. He walked to where the Bren gun carrier was still burning and stopped to look. Private Smalling's corpse lay ten yards back up the road from the burning vehicle, face down in the roadway. Jack approached it and bent down, turning him over. He could see that he had suffered blast and shrapnel injuries to his chest but his face was remarkably untouched. His eyes had already clouded over and they stared blankly into nothingness. Jack closed them with his free hand. He said a small prayer in his head and then, putting the cigarette into his mouth, he dragged the body to the side of the road and placed its arms by its side. He could not leave him lying haphazard in the middle of the road, but they had no time to bury him. He hoped that the Germans or the French would give him that courtesy. He quickly snapped off the man's dog tags from around his neck and placed them in his pocket.

As he stood up, he felt a small twinge in his back and remembered the uncomfortable feeling that had irritated him whilst he had been lying unconscious in the ditch earlier and looked over curiously to where he had been. He was not prepared for what he saw.

A girl of around ten years old lay dead in the ditch, her head at an impossible angle from the rest of her body. Jack understood immediately what had happened.

The bomb blast had thrown him into the ditch on top of her, his body breaking her neck and killing the poor unfortunate child. Tears filled his eyes and he turned away swallowing back the vomit that had arisen in his throat. He could not help letting out a sob, his body's reaction to the sight he had seen and the realisation of what he had done. This was his fault. He found that he could not even blame the pilot of the Stuka that had dropped the bomb. If they had not stopped to help the refugees in the woods, they would never have been here. If he had not attempted to get Smalling out of the carrier then he could have made it to the ditch and safety and would not have been blown on top of the girl. Smalling had died anyway.

Cooke approached him. 'Sir,' he said. 'Whatever's the matter?'

With his back to the rest of the men, so they could not see his distress, Jack replied. 'I killed her, Greg?'

Not understanding what he meant Cooke replied, 'Who? What do you mean?'

'The girl in the ditch. Over there,' he pointed to the spot. 'I killed her.'

Cooke now realised what he was talking about but did not turn to look. He already knew. He had seen her when he had assisted Jack from the ditch.

'But you know,' said Jack, tears now pouring down his face. 'You knew didn't you?'

'Yes I knew,' said Cooke with a sigh. 'But what could be done, sir? You were in a bad way for a minute and there was no point alerting you to it. It was not your fault.'

'It was,' muttered Jack. 'If I hadn't tried to help Smalling then she would still be alive, wouldn't she? And what good did that do? Look at him. He died anyway.'

'You can't blame yourself, Jack,' Cooke said. 'This is war. Shitty horrible things happen in it and none of it is our fault. None of it. We didn't start it. We didn't send our army into Poland and Belgium and France and all the other places these bloody Nazis want to take over. They have to be stopped and we are trying to do that. Okay, it isn't going too well at the moment but I know that if we get back to England we can regroup and one day we'll be back. I honestly believe that. You cannot blame yourself for any of this, I won't allow it.

'And anyway, those men behind you are looking for leadership. They want to get home and they are looking at you to get them there. You are more than capable to lead them, more than capable. So wipe your eyes, compose yourself and do your job.'

Jack looked at him. He knew the man was talking sense and that he had to snap out of this train of thought. It would render him useless and would drag him down when what was needed was for him to be strong and resilient. He wiped his eyes, took a deep breath, turned around and walked purposefully back to the small group of soldiers waiting for him a few yards further up the road.

The refugees, under the guidance of the French soldiers were now starting to get better organised. Carts and vehicles were now being put back onto the road and people were salvaging what they could from the attack. There were many dead and many wounded but Jack could do nothing about that, he did not want to think about it any more. Like Cooke had just said, he needed to focus on the task at hand and that was to lead the men to Dunkirk and the boats that hopefully would be waiting to take them back to England.

He approached the tall burly sergeant from the Lancashire Fusiliers.

'Okay, Sergeant, what have we got?'

'Hello, sir,' he replied. 'Sergeant Harrison, Lancashire Fusiliers. We have twenty-three men in all, twenty-four including yourself. A mixed bag, Fusiliers, Royal Norfolk's and even a couple from the Tank Regiment. We have no one seriously wounded but have one of your boys with a twisted ankle and another two who have nasty wounds to their legs so they'll need assisting. We have a couple more with slight head injuries but they'll live and one chap's arm is in a real mess.'

'Okay,' said Jack taking it all in. 'So that's roughly twenty men who can still fight if needs be. What about weapons and ammo.'

'Most are armed, sir. We have two Brens with around fifteen mags between them and a Boys with a good few rounds too. The rest have their Lee Enfields and two or three Thompsons. The Thompsons have plenty of ammo.'

'Good, good,' said Jack. He thought for a few moments.

'Okay, Sergeant Harrison, this is what we'll do. The lads who can't fight, give their weapons to those who can or ditch them. Give out their ammo to the others. I want two men to every one who can't walk unaided and we'll rotate when they get tired. We set off in two minutes.'

'Very good, sir,' said Harrison and turned away to carry out his order.

Jack looked at Corporal Cooke. 'Okay, Greg,' he said quietly. 'Let's get the hell out of here and get to Dunkirk.'

'Yes, sir,' replied Cooke. 'A fine idea if I may say so.'

'Oh yes. And Greg,' said Jack.

'Yes, sir.'

'Thanks.'

CHAPTER EIGHTEEN

Keeping to the side roads, avoiding built up areas and crossing fields whenever necessary the group headed westward in the hope of meeting more stragglers making their way to the relative sanctuary of the coast where hopefully they could re-join the main body of the army. All the time Jack kept an eye on the skies in the fear that the Luftwaffe would return to finish off the job that they had started earlier. He was aware of the slow progress caused by those who needed assistance to walk, but he had made a promise that no one would be left behind and he intended on sticking to it. He had seen enough death and heartache over the last few days to last him forever and he did not want to see any more. Leaving those behind who were slowing them down was not an option. He had no idea how the Germans would treat them.

It was now mid-afternoon and the sun was shining brightly. He turned to look at the men as they trudged heavily along, helping their comrades and carrying equipment and supplies. They had used their initiative and were swapping the heavy equipment, the bren guns and the Boys anti-tank rifle, between each other to give those getting tired a break. As far as he could tell, their morale was getting stronger, maybe due to having a purpose now and someone in control who had an idea and was putting that idea into practice. They now had someone to follow.

Jack felt proud that these men had put their faith in him and he hoped that he would be able to repay that faith by getting them to safety. But then he needed them also, as much as they needed him. He could not do this on his own and he was grateful for having the intelligent Corporal Cooke with him and the experience of Sergeant Harrison.

As they approached the top of a small ridge, Cooke, who had gone on ahead, came back running to him. He had gone forward to reconnoitre the area over the ridge and he now had something to report, a smile on his face.

Breathing deeply from the run he said, 'There's a small village over the ridge, sir. I can't see any civilians. Looks like they've abandoned the place, but there is some military activity down there.'

'Is it ours or German?' replied Jack raising his fist in the air to signal for the group to stop where they were.

'Looks like ours, sir,' replied Cooke with a grin. 'They have a couple of Bedfords too, if my eyesight is correct.'

'Excellent,' said Jack smiling. At last, he thought, the first bit of good luck today.

'Okay, Greg, thanks.' Turning to the others he said to them, 'All right lads, it looks like there's a small village ahead with some of our boys there. I'm going ahead with Sergeant Harrison to make sure it's our lot, then Corporal Cooke here will bring you all forward when I signal him. Don't move from here until he says so, is that clear?'

They nodded in agreement and some decided to sit down in the field, dropping their weapons clumsily and taking off their packs, thankful for the break.

Sergeant Harrison came forward and stood next to him. He carried a Thompson submachine gun and checked the magazine before putting it back and cocking the weapon. He looked like he was not prepared to take any chances.

'Okay, Sergeant,' said Jack. 'Let's go.'

They moved forward and once over the rise they could see the village below, roughly half a mile away. The village was typical of the many he had seen in this part of rural France. There seemed to be one road in and one road out cutting through the heart of the village. Jack saw that there were many houses and buildings near the centre with farmhouses just on the edge and further outside, set in the surrounding fields, where cows and sheep grazed peacefully. The main square was quite large, a church could be seen opposite where Jack looked, surrounded by a high white wall with a large iron gate. To the right he could make out a row of shops with a small inn in the middle and facing that what looked like a village hall. Set in the middle was a small stone fountain with a low circular base where the sunlight reflected back as water splashed almost lazily into it.

From their vantage point they could see two Bedford General Purpose Lorries parked next to the fountain. Jack took hold of the binoculars that hung from a lanyard around his neck and raised them to his eyes. From what he could see there appeared to be no civilians and he presumed that they had fled like so many of their countrymen, fearing the advance of the Germans.

'Good news, Harrison,' he said. 'Brits. Give the signal to Cooke and let's get everyone down there.'

Ten minutes later Jack and Sergeant Harrison were in the square and they approached one of the trucks where two soldiers leaned against it smoking cigarettes. On seeing Jack walking towards them they stood up straight and threw the cigarettes to the floor.

'Who's in charge here?' asked Jack.

'Captain Rogers, sir,' replied one of the men. 'He's over there sir, in that café on the corner.'

'Thank you, private,' Jack replied. 'Is there any food around here? I've got twenty-odd hungry soldiers who need feeding. They'll be here in a few minutes.'

'I'm sure we can find them something,' he answered.

Jack did not reply. Leaving Harrison with them he walked on and entered the café that the soldier had pointed out.

Standing with their backs to him were two officers, leaning over a map that they had spread out over one of the tables. They did not turn around as Jack approached.

'I'm looking for Captain Rogers,' he said.

The man on the right turned around and on seeing Jack asked. 'Who's asking?'

'Second Lieutenant Jack Graham, Royal Fusiliers,' he replied saluting. 'I'm with a group of stragglers, Royal Norfolks, Lancs Fusiliers and some others. About twenty-five in total. We have some wounded that could do with being looked at.'

'Nothing we can do for you, I'm afraid,' said Rogers, not returning the salute. 'We're only stopping for a few minutes. Jerry everywhere and I don't have time to stop for anyone.'

'What do you mean there's nothing you can do for us?' said Jack angrily.

'Don't you understand English,' said Rogers, who looked heavily stressed. 'We've got Panzers on our tail, I believe, a truck full of wounded soldiers and no room for any more. One of the trucks has a fucked up gear box and won't get out of first gear so we're making very slow progress. The main body of my company pushed on ahead, yesterday, couldn't hang around for us, you know, otherwise we'd all be in the shit. If the Germans are as close behind us as I think, then we haven't much time and they are probably gaining on us as we speak.'

'So why have you stopped here then?' said Jack. He could not keep the contempt from his voice.

'Because,' said Captain Rogers with a sigh, 'we needed to refuel and to be quite honest, we have absolutely no idea where we are. Needed to get our bearings. You don't happen to know do you?'

Jack started laughing. This was the most surreal conversation he had had in ages. 'No, sir, we're as lost as you are.'

Jack approached the map and looked at it with them. He knew he was wasting his time. 'I've got the men coming down from the hill now, sir,' he said. 'Three of them need transportation and there's another with a really banged up arm. The rest of us are either fine or walking wounded, able to hold and fire a weapon if need be. Is there any chance you can take our wounded with you?'

Captain Rogers turned to him and looked him in the eyes. 'Lieutenant Graham. I know that we are all in this bloody mess together and all that but I cannot justify leaving some of my men behind to make room for yours.'

'No, sir,' said Jack firmly. 'You cannot justify leaving injured British soldiers to the mercy of the enemy when you have serviceable transportation to get them to safety.'

They were disturbed by a frantic knocking on the door and they all turned to see a French policeman banging incessantly upon it, a look of urgency and panic on his face.

Rogers beckoned him to enter and the gendarme spoke to him quickly in French, his words tripping over each other as they exited his mouth.

Rogers raised his hand. 'In English, my friend. English. Anglais, anglais.'

The gendarme, who could not have been older than twenty-five seemed to calm himself for a moment as he concentrated on translating his thoughts to English.

'The Germans, Monsieur, I have just passed them not twenty minutes ago. They are headed this way, the road that leads here to Abbeville. They were taking a break… resting… but as I passed them they were getting back into their tanks and trucks. They are SS, Monsieur, and I have been hearing rumours about them.'

'What rumours?' asked Jack. 'What rumours?'

'That they do not take wounded prisoners, Monsieur,' said the gendarme frantically.

'How do you mean?' asked the Lieutenant who had been standing with Rogers. This was the first time Jack had heard him speak.

'I hear that they shoot them, Monsieur, kill them. You need to leave right now.'

He turned to go to the door but Rogers grabbed him by the arm preventing him from leaving.

'Hey, hey,' he said. 'Don't rush off. I need more information from you.'

'Non, Monsieur. I need to leave. Right now.' He then continued to speak in French once more, waving his arms and trying to break the grip of Rogers, but the captain would not let him go.

'You can go in a minute,' he said. 'First tell us how many of them there are? How many tanks, trucks… John,' he said turning to the lieutenant at his side. 'Get everyone on board the wagons now. We're leaving.'

'Yes sir,' replied the Lieutenant and left the café. As he opened the door, Jack could see Corporal Cooke leading the men into the village square where he was met by Sergeant Harrison.

'Sir, what about my men?' asked Jack. He was now getting really worried. Rogers ignored him and listened to the gendarme's reply.

'There were two tanks, one of those half-tracks and three lorries full of soldiers. I think I saw a motorcycle combination also,' he replied animatedly. 'Now, Monsieur, I really must go.'

'How did you get here?' asked Rogers.

'In my police car.'

'I think you will find that it is now my police car,' said Rogers. He looked out of the window to where Harrison had led the group. 'Shit, shit,' he said closing his eyes tightly. When he opened them again after a few seconds, he looked as though he had made a decision.

Ignoring the gendarme's protestations he turned to Jack, 'Okay, Lieutenant Graham… Jack. Let's get organised. There's not a lot we can do other than buy some time for Sergeant Bentham to get the wounded out of here. If we're quick, we can set up an ambush for the krauts and delay them long enough for the wounded to get clear. Put your wounded on the second truck, as quick as you can, then get back to me here. Come on, if he's right we don't have a lot of time.'

'Thank you, sir,' replied Jack relieved at the captain's change of heart. 'Thank you so much.'

Quickly Jack ran back out into the square and called for Harrison to gather the men together.

'They are going to make room for the wounded,' Jack shouted when they had all assembled. 'There's room on the trucks for all of you with injuries and we have commandeered that car over there. The rest of us, well I'm afraid the news isn't so good. There is an SS unit about fifteen minutes from this village and they are headed this way. We need to give the guys a fighting chance of getting away because rumour has it that they are not exactly honourable when it comes to wounded prisoners.'

Jack paused. 'I can't guarantee that we will get away with them, but who knows, as long as we organise ourselves properly then we may soon be with them again. Now you wounded guys get aboard that second truck and get the bloody hell out here. See you on the beach.'

Captain Rogers and the lieutenant he had called John spoke to their men. Jack could see the disappointment on their faces. They were obviously not too happy about giving up their seats on the trucks to Jack's wounded but they dared not argue against Rogers. Once the wounded were on and the able-bodied had disembarked they all joined Jack's ragtag unit in the centre of the square to await their orders.

The three officers stood together.

Rogers said, 'Okay, Jack, John. Here's the plan. Jack, if you take one of the Brens and the Boys you've brought with you and get into those woods just outside the village on the approach road, you might be able to hit the armoured vehicles before they get chance to get into the village. I'm guessing that as soon as you start firing, the lorries will stop and the foot soldiers will get out. The Bren can give them a blast then fall back to the village.

'I'll have a group in that window there,' he indicated a three storey building at the side of the approach road, the first structure on entering the village, 'and one there.' He pointed to the building opposite. 'If they follow you down the road here then we can get them in the crossfire. I'll have another on the parallel road in case they come that way instead.'

'And then what, sir?' asked Jack calmly.

'Then we fall back to the farm at the back end of the village, the one on the road that the trucks will leave on. There's roughly thirty of us and probably around double of them but if you can hit them hard in the initial stages we may just about even up the odds. Any questions?'

The two lieutenants looked at the captain and shook their heads.

'I'm sorry, gentlemen,' said Rogers with a wry smile. 'Not much of a plan, I know, but it's the best I can do. No time to think of another.'

'Yes, sir,' they both said.

'Okay, Jack, off you go. John, take one of the Brens up to that position over there and…'

Jack did not wait to hear the specific instructions that Lieutenant "John" was receiving but turned to his men.

'Okay, Greg,' he said to Cooke. 'Get the Bren and six mags and bring the Boys and all the ammo it has. Six men and us two. Now, let's go!'

Two minutes later, carrying the heavy gear, breathing hard and sweating profusely in the afternoon sun, the eight men jogged to the positions as ordered by Captain Rogers. Three minutes after that, lying on the ground just inside the wooded area, with a clear view of the roadway ahead, Jack and Cooke loaded the Boys anti-tank rifle and waited. Approximately twenty yards to their right, hidden by bushes, were Private Wood and a private from the Lancashire Fusiliers lying prone with the Bren gun also made ready for action. They were under instructions not to open up until the German lorries had stopped and to concentrate the fire on the covered sides where the bullets would penetrate and cause most damage. Across the road from them, almost directly opposite, lay the rest of the section armed with two Thompsons, rifles and grenades.

Jack was not particularly happy with the plan as there was no exit strategy but like Rogers had said, there had not been any time to formulate anything better, so they would just have to live with it. If everything went well in the initial stages then things might just turn out fine, but he was under no doubt that the troops they were about to engage were battle hardened, experienced killers. But then again, he thought, they were not British.

He looked to his side at Corporal Cooke. As usual he was focused and, to Jack, did not look in the slightest bit nervous. He remembered what "Double H" had said to him all those months ago, was it really a year now? When he had first arrived from Officer Training School. He had told him that Cooke was officer material but for some reason had not pursued a career in that direction. Jack had quickly grown to understand what the major had meant. He had been a rock for him over this past week and Jack genuinely did not know how he would have made it to this point without him. He was curious as to his story, but, he thought, that would have to wait for another time.

And then they heard it.

They looked to their right but could see nothing, as the road ahead was at a slight rise, but they could clearly hear the sound of motorised vehicles, getting steadily louder. Jack had the now familiar feeling of blood racing through his veins as the adrenalin started to make its presence known in his body. He could feel the perspiration starting to form at his brow, neck and top lip and quickly wiped his mouth with the back of his hand. Cooke looked at him and offered him an encouraging smile but Jack could not find it within him to return the gesture. Cooke turned his attention back to the road.

Slowly, rising above the ridge, a Panzer Mark II tank appeared, followed by another. The Boys anti-tank weapon had proved effective in battle against this machine and Jack hoped that Cooke would be able to take them both out before they knew what was happening. The weapon was bolt action with only a five round magazine fitted to the top. Jack held another full one in his hand, ready to reload as soon as Cooke had emptied the first, which was fitted, cocked and ready to fire. Jack realised that this plan could only have a hope of working if both tanks were near to the front of the column and he was relieved to see that that was so. He now had to put his faith in the skills of his corporal in firing the weapon quickly and accurately.

The first tank was over a hundred yards away and closing. Behind it, leaving a gap of only a few yards, was the second followed by two lorries, a half-track and then a third lorry. Jack thought that with the men in the tanks and half-track, they were probably facing a force of around forty to fifty Germans.

He rested his hand on Cooke's shoulder. 'On my command, Greg,' he whispered. He looked over to where the Bren gun crew were lying and could just about make out where they were. He knew that they would only open fire when the time was right and that the time was only seconds away.

Then the tanks were alongside them and Jack could see clearly the tank commanders, standing tall and erect, their torsos and heads protruding from the hatches as they watched the road ahead. These men, whoever they were, were about to die, thought Jack, and they had no idea.

'Fire!' he yelled and before the sound of his voice had vanished into the ether, Cooke opened up on them.

Jack had never been this close to an anti-tank rifle when it was being fired and the noise was absolutely deafening. The recoil threw the gun backward along its barrel slide, lifting the weapon high, but Cooke had it quickly under control and was feeding another round into the breech before it was fully settled. He expertly and rapidly took aim again and fired another. Jack could not let the noise distract him and he watched as the first two rounds hit home on the lead tank. The Germans were taken completely by surprise and as the front tank began to burn, the second stopped where it was, the driver hitting the brakes. Behind it, the column stopped and then it seemed that all hell had broken loose.

The Bren gun operated by Private Wood opened fire on the two trucks that had stopped behind the tanks and Jack could see wounded and dead Germans fall from the back as the soldiers tried to scramble out. Those who were able to get out without being harmed took cover behind the vehicles only to be cut down by the four British soldiers waiting on the opposite side of the road. Jack could hear the sound of Thompson sub machine guns being fired and the crash of grenades as they exploded amongst the German troops. He could also make out the dull thuds as bullets hit human flesh.

As the first tank blazed and rolled lazily to the side of the road, Jack reloaded the Boys and Cooke began to concentrate his fire on the second tank but the commander of this one had been quick to react. As fire hit the ammunition in the lead tank, it exploded into a huge fireball, a black mushroom cloud billowing into the air above. The second tank turned off the road and headed directly towards them.

All around him Jack could hear the sound of battle and he was able to make a quick assessment of the situation. The half-track and lorry at the rear of the column had reversed back over the rise in the road and were quickly disappearing from sight. Some of the survivors from the lorries, about ten in total were also sprinting away, following the vehicles, carrying their weapons with them, all the time being fired upon from the group across the road.

Jack looked up and could see the second tank getting closer. Private Wood had now changed his target and was firing furiously upon it, the bullets from the Bren gun pinging and ricocheting off the armour ineffectively.

Then Jack became aware that Cooke was shouting at him.

'Fresh magazine, sir,' he yelled above the noise of the shooting.

Hastily Jack snapped off the spent magazine and replaced it with another. Cooke cocked the weapon and took aim against the approaching tank. The machine gun on the tank began to open fire on them, the bullets whistling over their heads and smashing into the trees around them sending splinters in all directions. Jack felt a sharp pain in the back of his neck as a splinter hit him but he quickly ignored it.

For some reason, he did not feel afraid. At this moment in his life, probably the closest he had ever been to death, he had never felt more alive, more exhilarated and he realised that he was actually smiling.

Suddenly the approaching tank stopped and began to turn on its axis. At first Jack could not understand what was happening but then realised that the driver must have been hit. The tank commander could be clearly seen looking down into the vehicle and shouting frantically in German. As it spun around, Private Wood and his comrade from the Lancashire Fusiliers emerged from the trees breaking cover. Wood holding the Bren gun at his hip and firing as he walked forward, concentrating on the tank and the commander who was attempting to duck below the bullets.

Then Jack saw the top of the German's head evaporate in a cloud of red mist and his limp body drop down into the turret. Cooke continued to fire the Boys on the vehicle until it too was burning like the other.

The brief skirmish was now over. Two Panzers had been destroyed, two German lorries were rendered useless and from a quick observation Jack was able to calculate that roughly half the German force had been destroyed. He could hear the moans of some of the wounded Germans but ignored them.

'Quick,' he said shouting to those across the road. 'Back to the village now. Fall back.'

As Corporal Cooke stood up, he said to him, 'Jesus Christ, Greg. I think that went a little too well. They were supposed to follow us back down the road.'

'I know, boss,' he replied sombrely. 'We'd best get back to the village because, believe you me, they will be back and they are going to be a slight bit pissed off.'

Jack looked around at the devastation they had caused and he suddenly felt very frightened, more frightened than when he had lay there waiting for them a few minutes earlier, and when the tank had been bearing down upon them. He knew that Cooke was right, the Germans would be back and when they did return they would be more prepared and they would be extremely angry.

As they jogged back to the village, he looked up and could see the soldiers in the window of the houses where Rogers had positioned them and wondered if they would have enough men. He also pondered if there was a much bigger force behind those that they had just attacked and, if this was the case, then what chance did they really have. He feared that they had merely hit a wasp's nest with a stick and there would be massive repercussions to come.

As he reached the square, he looked to the road opposite that led out of the village and hoped that the trucks containing the wounded soldiers had managed to put some distance between them and that they were well on their way to safety. He hoped that the coming sacrifice would all have been worth it.

CHAPTER NINETEEN

Jack stood by the fountain in the village square with Corporal Cooke and the six others who had been involved in the ambush. Captain Rogers approached him with Lieutenant "John" at his side.

'Bloody hell, Jack, that was all a bit much. I saw it from the window over there. We need to make our move now before they come back.'

'Agreed,' replied Jack. 'We need to get a shift on. When they come back it'll be with reinforcements and they'll be hugely pissed off. We need to find some sort of transport.'

'It looks like the civvies buggered off in their cars. We could do with a couple of trucks but they've been used for the wounded,' said Rogers thoughtfully.

'If I could make a suggestion,' said Lieutenant 'John'.

'Of course. Go ahead.'

'Let me take a look at those two jerry trucks. You never know they may be fine, even if it's just to put a few miles between them and us. After all, we can't be too far from the coast now anyway.'

'Okay,' said Rogers. 'Take a team out there and have a look. But be careful. Any sign of enemy activity, get yourselves straight back here.'

'Will do, sir,' he replied and walked away hastily.

Rogers turned to Jack. 'Get your men some food and water and take a rest. We've got lookouts in the two buildings so hopefully we'll see if they intend to make a counter-attack. Our priority now is to get away from here.'

Rogers left them and headed back to the building on the very edge of the village where one of the Bren gun crews had taken residence.

Jack sighed. This had been an extremely long day and he felt tired beyond words. He assessed what he had done since setting out with the company that morning. He had assisted refugees, been blown up by a Stuka dive bomber and been involved in the most frightening, high intensity skirmish since the war began. He was shattered both mentally and physically and to add to this, he knew that the day was far from over.

He leaned back against the fountain and put his hand into the water. Feeling the coldness of it he turned, cupping his hands, and splashed some into his face. He scooped some more and poured it over his head and let it run down his neck and back. He needed to remain alert, to maintain the focus and professionalism he had so far managed to display.

He became aware of Corporal Cooke looking at him. 'Penny for them?' he said.

'Oh I don't know, Greg,' he replied with a large sigh. 'What's this all about eh? How did we both end up here like this?'

'Beats me sir.'

'Me too. Can you believe we both volunteered for this? To get our arses shot at and blown up in a foreign country.'

'Yes, sir,' said Greg. 'It is all rather frightful.'

Jack started laughing. 'Rather frightful? That sums up the day I suppose. Good way to put it.'

'I'm a little bit worried, if I'm honest, sir,' carried on Cooke. 'If we don't get any transport then we are wholly likely to be killed or captured. The Germans are very close.'

'I know,' replied Jack. 'But I think from this point on we are playing it a little bit by ear. Not ideal I know.'

Jack took out his cigarettes and offered one to the corporal who took one. They both stood watching the activity of the others in the square for a while as they smoked. Private Wood and the others who had taken part in the ambush either sat or lay on the ground, smoking, drinking or eating their field rations. Wood himself was lying before them, on his back, his knees bent and his hands clasped behind his head. He had his eyes closed and appeared to be sleeping. Jack envied him this ability to switch off, to be able to put what he had just taken part in to the back of his mind and let his body unwind. He felt that even though he was so tired, he would not be able to totally relax ever again.

After ten minutes Jack heard an engine. 'Stand to!' he yelled, taking his revolver from the holster. The others jumped up, grabbing their weapons and checking their ammunition.

'It's okay, sir,' said one of the privates after a few seconds. 'It looks like Lieutenant Green has managed to get one of the jerry trucks working.'

He was right. The lorry pulled into the square, battered, bullet ridden and with the tarpaulin cover discarded. Sitting in the passenger seat was Lieutenant John Green and on the benches in the back, hanging on to the metal tarpaulin supports were the crew he had taken with him.

Rogers again came running over and arrived at the lorry as Lieutenant Green got out of the cab.

'Story?' commanded Rogers.

'Hello, sir,' he replied. 'Spot of good luck to be honest. This truck is perfectly serviceable thankfully. It's an Opel Blitz and one thing you have to hand to the Germans, they know how to build sturdy vehicles. The other one was a no-hoper, I'm sorry to say. The boys have destroyed it beyond repair.'

'How many can we get in the back?' asked Rogers.

'Well, sir,' replied Green. 'We can get three in the front, bit of a squeeze but it'll be fine and if the boys squash up a bit, with weapons and all that, we can probably get around a dozen in the back, maybe push it to fourteen if they cram up a little.'

'Okay,' said Rogers, 'and we have the commandeered police car too. We can get another five in that if we squeeze up. That's transport for twenty-two. How many of us are there?'

Jack made a mental calculation. 'I brought in twenty-three with me, but six of those went on your truck earlier. That leaves eighteen of us and however many of you.'

'Okay,' replied Rogers, thoughtfully. 'There's around ten of us. So we need to find transport for another six then… Shit.'

'Sir,' said Jack after a while, 'listen. I came in on foot and if needs be I will just have to go out on foot too. We really need to get organised because I can't see it being too long before they're back. Take the truck and the car and get as many out as you can. I'll stay back with five others and we'll see what we can find, otherwise we'll head off on foot again… Where's that policeman by the way? What happened to him?'

'He's in that bar over there,' Rogers nodded to an inn at the opposite side of the square. 'Drowning his sorrows I think. Anyway, I know it sounds callous, but he's not my concern.'

Jack did not like the idea of leaving the policeman to the mercy of the advancing Germans but knew that Rogers was talking sense. The French people now had to take care of themselves. They were a beaten army and a beaten nation and if there was a chance that the British could escape then they could live to fight another day. At the moment it was all about self-preservation.

'No point in waiting any longer,' said Rogers. 'Okay, John, let's get moving.'

Lieutenant Green shouted to the men, ordering them to get aboard and Jack could see those in the observation positions start to pick up their weapons and make their way to the waiting vehicles. Rogers clambered up into the passenger seat vacated by Green and Green himself went to the police car and sat in the driver's seat.

Jack turned to the ambush group and spoke to them as they started to rise.

'As you just heard, boys, only room for two of you, I'm afraid,' he said apologetically. 'Any volunteers to stay with me? It's going to have to be Shanks's Pony for the rest of us.'

Cooke and Private Wood stepped forward.

'Well, you're our boss and someone has to look after you,' said Wood with a grin, picking up the Bren gun and checking it.

Three others stepped forward. Lancashire Fusiliers.

'Well,' said one of them calmly, 'I suppose us Fusiliers are better sticking together.'

'Thanks,' said Jack, relieved that this had been so easy. 'Okay you two,' he said to the remaining pair, 'get in the truck and good luck.'

'Thank you, sir,' they said and then ran to the back of the truck where they were helped aboard by their comrades at the rear.

A couple of minutes later the two vehicles were ready to go. Before setting off Rogers leaned out of the cab window and called Jack over.

'Lieutenant Graham, it's been a pleasure,' he said with a smile. 'Sorry there's no room for you but if you stay off the roads then you might just have a chance. It can only be about ten miles to the coast, you can almost smell the Channel from here. With any luck I'll see you on the beach tomorrow.'

'Yes, sir, thank you.'

Rogers held out his hand and Jack shook it.

Without another word he sat back in the seat and the captured German Opel set off, followed by the police car, both vehicles crammed with British troops.

Jack watched them leave the square until they had gone beyond the buildings and were out of sight.

'Come on,' he said wearily, 'let's move.'

They filled their water bottles from the fountain and then the six of them set off at a slow jog, following in the direction of where the others had gone, Jack and Cooke at the rear.

They reached a bend in the road that led out of the village and as the front four turned into it a familiar horrific noise hit them. At first Jack could not comprehend what was happening, but Cooke was able to grab him by the collar and pull him backwards, pushing him down onto the roadway before they could follow the others around the corner.

The unmistakeable sound of a German MG34 belt fed machine gun filled their ears. Lying on the ground Jack saw a slow trickle of blood appear on the cobbles before him, obviously coming from the four soldiers that had led them out, but now he could not see. He realised immediately that none of them were making any sound and knew that it could only mean one thing, that they were dead. All four of them. There was no way they could have got to cover, there just had not been time, it had all happened so quickly and as there was no return fire, he knew his worst fears were realised.

He tried to get up, pulling the pistol from the holster but Cooke prevented him.

'There's nothing we can do for them now, sir,' he whispered. 'They're gone.'

Jack looked at him and knew he was on the verge of panicking. 'Fuck, Greg,' was all he could say.

Cooke pulled him to his feet and together they ran, crouching low, back towards the square, keeping to the walls of the buildings so as not to be seen. They could now hear more shooting and the crash of a Panzer cannon followed by an explosion and as they rounded another corner they could see, between the buildings of an alleyway, smoke rising in the air around a mile away from where Captain Rogers had headed not five minutes ago.

There was more noise behind them and Jack peered around the corner of the building and looked at the opposite side of the square. A Panzer Mark II followed by a half-track and two lorries appeared from the roadway. It was now obvious that the group they had ambushed earlier were merely a reconnaissance unit and this was the main body of the German advance. Jack could feel panic setting in. He was at a total loss as what to do. Rogers and Green were either dead or captured and he and Cooke were in grave danger.

Then he felt Cooke grabbing him once more and he was half dragged along the alleyway.

'Come on, sir,' he whispered urgently. 'We have to get out of sight.'

Before he could think what to do, Jack found himself being bundled through a doorway and fell onto a wooden floor, Cooke stumbling behind. He looked up and could see that he was in the bar that the gendarme had headed to once they had commandeered his car. To his right was a stairway and ahead of him he could see the young policeman walking to the door curiously to see what was happening outside. As he opened the door, he was hit with a hail of bullets, riddling his torso causing him to dance wildly like a drunken marionette before falling backward into the building. Jack, on his hands and knees attempted to get up but was frozen to the spot as he witnessed the murder. He wanted to cover his ears to the noise of the guns but he could not move.

As he lay there, blood pouring from his body, head and nose, the gendarme's eyes met Jack's. Jack watched as the life flickered from him, his body jerking spasmodically as he lay there on the wooden floor. Jack managed to prevent himself from being sick, but only just, swallowing back the vomit that filled his mouth and holding back the nausea that was threatening to consume him. Once more he felt himself being half-dragged and bundled along by Corporal Cooke.

'Up the stairs, sir. Quickly!'

Cooke pushed him up the stairs to the right, making him move as quickly as he could and he was soon at a long landing where he was able to finally calm himself and take stock of their situation. He bent over double and took a number of deep breaths before standing up straight and looking at Corporal Cooke. Neither of them spoke. They did not need to, there was nothing to be said.

He saw that there were a number of rooms along the landing, obviously for paying guests and Cooke tried the doors on two of them before finding an unlocked one to the rear of the inn. They quickly entered a small, basic room that had a large window with a net curtain that overlooked a few houses and the fields beyond the village. They stood to the side of the window to avoid being seen and then slowly peeked out.

They could see the smoke from the German attack on the two vehicles and Jack saw that there was only one pall and this could only mean that only one of the vehicles had been hit. Did that mean one had got away or did it mean that they had been captured or killed? He had no way of knowing.

They could now hear voices, German voices, coming from outside. Shouting, boots running on cobbled stones, vehicles engines being revved loudly. They were trapped. There was no way out.

Jack looked at Cooke.

'Should we give ourselves up?' asked Cooke quietly.

'Not an option,' replied Jack. 'Look what they did to that poor gendarme. They never gave him a chance. What do you think they'll do to us after what we've just done to their comrades?'

'Yes, but that was war,' said Cooke. 'They're casualties of a legitimate action.'

'Do you want to take that chance, Greg?' asked Jack calmly. He was now beginning to compose himself. He could feel his pulse starting to slow and could no longer hear the heartbeat that had been hammering in his chest for the past few minutes. 'Seriously? I know I don't! We'll have to hole up here for a while and hopefully they'll move out soon. We can try to get away when it gets dark.'

Cooke held his gaze for a moment longer before turning his head away to look out of the window once more.

Jack looked around. It was a simple enough room, he observed, standard for the type of area and hotel. It was of an average size, a single bed in the middle with a bedside table and lamp, a freestanding wooden wardrobe and a small washbasin against one wall.

'I'm just thinking,' whispered Jack after a while, looking at the bed. 'If they decide to stay in the village for the night, they're bound to use this place aren't they? All these comfy beds. What do you think?'

Cooke followed his gaze to the bed. 'Shit. You're probably right. We need to find somewhere else to hide.'

They crept carefully to the door and slowly opened it. They could still hear activity outside and as yet there was no indication that any of the Germans had entered the building. Jack looked down the corridor to the right and could see a door at the very end that was slightly different to the others. Remembering it was a three storey building he guessed it led to the landlord's quarters and he moved quickly, hoping the door was unlocked.

He tried the handle, Cooke behind him, his Thompson submachine gun pointed back down the corridor in case anyone should appear. The door opened to reveal a staircase leading up to the next level. They quickly closed the door behind them and walked slowly up the stairs to an apartment that took up the whole of the top floor. However, Jack still did not feel totally safe here and swiftly looked around in search of an entrance to the attic above them.

It was Cooke who located the access, a small hatch in the ceiling just outside the bathroom. Jack grabbed a dining chair from the room to the side and stood on it. Quickly he pushed against the wooden hatch and it lifted away easily. He was pleased to see that there was light inside coming from a small window that looked out to the front of the inn and that there were boards laid on the floor. It was an ideal place to hide.

He climbed through the gap with Cooke pushing his legs to assist him. Once inside the attic he lay on his stomach to help pull Cooke through, after the corporal had first put the chair back in place and passed the Thompson up. They struggled for a minute or so as the weight of Cooke strained Jack's arms but eventually they were both through and lying on the floor on their backs, breathing heavily.

Jack leaned over and replaced the entrance board. Now he felt safe. The Germans had no reason to look up here, even if they did decide to occupy the place later on. As long as they remained quiet, then hopefully they may just get away with this. He was aware, however, that with every passing moment, as every hour ticked away, they would be further behind enemy lines and the chances of getting to Dunkirk would be more and more difficult. He tried to put it out of his mind and to concentrate on what he needed to do now.

He was suddenly aware of renewed activity outside. He crawled to the window that was providing the light by which they could see and was joined by Cooke. From this vantage point they were able to look down directly onto the village square, where they could see German vehicles parked and enemy soldiers taking a break. A half-track was blocking the exit road opposite and two Opel trucks, identical to the ones they themselves had attacked earlier, were parked to the left, facing away from the centre.

He could hear the shouts of German officers coming from the left, ordering and directing their troops, but he could not see who was doing the shouting and did not want to put his face too closely against the small window. He had no idea if they could be seen from the square and he did not want to take any chances of being spotted.

The sound of many feet moving quickly on cobbled stones began to get louder and soon Jack was able to see that it was approximately twenty British soldiers, their hands clasped behind their heads, led by Captain Rogers. Jack scanned the group quickly but could see no sign of Lieutenant Green and with a heavy heart presumed that he must have been killed.

Jack and Cooke watched as the British prisoners were ordered to stand in front of the church wall to the right of the fountain where they were guarded by SS soldiers in combat uniform. Jack sighed and leaned back. He didn't know whether to feel sorry for them or pleased that they were out of the action and therefore out of danger.

Then an officer caught his eye. There was something about him that was oddly familiar, something that tugged at his memory and he did not know why.

With an arrogant swagger, a young, blond German officer came into view carrying a large pistol in his right hand that looked oversized. Jack recognised the weapon as a Mauser C96 with an extended box magazine, which he thought slightly odd as German officers usually carried smaller handguns. The German approached the fountain and put his weapon on the wall, took off his cap and ran his finger through his thin wispy hair.

Jack remained transfixed. He could not take his eyes off the man. Cooke tapped him on the shoulder, having noticed Jack's reaction on seeing him.

'Are you okay?' he whispered.

'That man,' Jack replied. 'That officer... The one by the fountain with the blond hair. Do you see him?'

'Yes, I see him. What about him?'

'I think I've seen him before... but I can't think where.'

Cooke did not reply.

And then the man turned his head to face away from the fountain and towards them.

Running down the left side of his face, from his forehead to his lower cheek was a huge ugly scar that caused his mouth to slightly rise at the corner. It made him look as though he had a permanent sneer.

And then Jack remembered where he had seen him before.

CHAPTER TWENTY

Obersturmführer Otto Finkel of the 12th Company 3rd SS Division (Totenkopf) was not having a good day. His friend and colleague Obersturmführer Torsten Grieber had been killed outside the village earlier that afternoon while reconnoitring ahead of the main body of the Division, when they had been ambushed by a group of British soldiers on the approach road. He had passed his still burning Panzer on the way into the village and could clearly smell the sweet, familiar odour of burning flesh.

He had got used to the sights and smells of the battlefield as the German army had advanced through Europe and even though his friend had now become part of the detritus of war, he could feel nothing more than this was just one of those days. A day to be forgotten. There was a bigger picture to take into consideration and one man's death could not move his sight from that, no matter how sad it was.

He had joined the Waffen-SS as a natural progression from the Hitler Youth and hoped to make a good career from it. He loved the uniform and the immediate authority and respect it demanded when he wore it, particularly away from the front line and despite the ugly childhood scar on his face, he thought he cut a fine picture of how a true German should appear. Strong, proud and powerful. His father had been robustly proud of his son when he had become an officer, parading him in front of his friends and promoting his interests wherever possible, but his mother had remained her usual subservient self. Otto put that down to her being French.

He splashed water into his face from the fountain. Although the earlier heat of the day was giving way to a cooler late afternoon, he was still very warm and was grateful of the sharpness of the cold water as it hit his skin.

He looked at the group of prisoners gathered in front of him with contempt. They looked defeated and worn out and he could not understand how they had managed to inflict such damage on Grieber and his troops. It did not seem possible that this ragtag bunch could inflict such damage on them so easily.

It had taken himself less than a minute to defeat them in the end.

The survivors of the attack on Grieber's reconnaissance squad had reported what had happened and a plan was quickly devised to circumnavigate the village and attack it from two sides. They had not expected to see the British running away in a commandeered German truck and a police car. He had laughed when he had first seen them. They had looked so pathetic.

One of the Panzers had fired a single shot at the car and hit it first time, blowing it sky-high and killing all inside. The truck had stopped immediately and not another shot had needed to be fired, the British realising that to put up any resistance would be suicide. And here they were, now, standing before him with a look of complete nervousness on all of their pathetic, ugly faces.

The two MG34 gun crews had arrived too late at their positions and had had to watch as the vehicles passed them by, but they had managed to wipe out four stragglers who had been following on foot. Their bodies still lay in the street around the corner, where he was happy to leave them to rot.

He took out a packet of cigarettes from his trouser pocket and put one in his mouth. Placing the pack next to the Mauser on the fountain wall he lit the cigarette with the lighter his father had given him for his birthday. It was embossed with a swastika on one side and an inscription on the other, the SS motto 'Meine Ehre heißt Treue' ('My Honour is Loyalty').

Otto smoked his cigarette. He was aware of the British officer, who he believed to be a captain, observing him intently. He looked over to him and their eyes met for a brief moment, the British soldier unable to hold the stare and bent his head down. Otto sneered at him with contempt and then turned away from them. He continued to smoke the cigarette in silence for a few minutes and then threw the butt into the fountain, watching it sizzle as the water extinguished it.

He shouted over to the soldiers who were guarding the British and they moved away from them, backing off with their MP40 machine pistols still pointed in their direction. They were left to stand against the wall and Otto saw that some of them were beginning to get restless at the uncertainty of what was happening.

Otto picked up his cap and put it back onto his head, collected his Mauser and cigarettes, then stepped to the side, as the tail flaps of the two Opel trucks behind him dropped down to reveal the barrels of two MG34 machine guns.

*

Upstairs, in the inn across the square, Jack and Corporal Cooke had a clear view of what was taking place below them.

'How do you mean you've seen him before?' asked Cooke curiously.

'Years ago,' replied Jack transfixed, unable to move from his position in the window. 'It was when we used to holiday in St Malo... in Brittany... years ago.'

Cooke did not reply but looked down at the German officer below as he smoked his cigarette.

'I wasn't sure at first,' continued Jack. 'I thought there was something familiar about him but couldn't quite place it. It was the scar... I was there when he got it, you see.'

'Right,' said Cooke. 'What was he like? Was he okay?'

'He was just a normal boy to be honest. We were all so young at the time. He hung around with me and my brother but then he had an accident and we didn't see him after that, we had to come home,' Jack explained. 'I've never seen him since. The last I ever saw of him was when he was carried away to hospital. I've never seen or heard of him since that day... until now.'

'Are you sure it's him?'

'Completely. Like I said, it's the scar. It's definitely him.'

'What's his name?' asked Cooke.

'Otto... something,' replied Jack trying to remember. 'I can't remember his surname to be honest but his Christian name is definitely Otto.'

'If we give ourselves up, do you think we'll be treated well by him?' asked Cooke.

'I'm not sure,' said Jack. 'I don't know the fellow now and only knew him as a child for a few days. If I remember correctly, I think his father blamed me for the scar that's on his face... but I wasn't responsible, it was just an accident. Who knows?'

'Something's happening,' said Cooke suddenly, disturbing Jack from his memories and bringing him back to the present.

They looked down into the village square and saw the Germans guarding the prisoners move away from them, leaving them standing against the tall white wall that formed the perimeter of the church grounds. The German officer threw his cigarette into the fountain, placed his cap on his head and picked up his pack of cigarettes and pistol before moving away towards the two trucks that faced away from the group of British soldiers.

'I have a bad feeling about this,' said Cooke nervously.

Jack was about to reply, to agree with him, but before he could say a word the air was filled with sound of machine gun fire as the MG34s at the rear of the Opels opened up on the prisoners.

It was clear that the prisoners had not been expecting it. None of them had time to move, to make any kind of escape before they were cut to ribbons by the bullets being fired by the SS soldiers. Jack saw Rogers being hit, his chest riddled with bullets as his body fell to the ground, jerking as the muscles in his legs contracted.

They could not take their eyes off what was happening in front of them, staring in disbelief at the murder they were witnessing.

The bullets continued to fly, ripping chunks of masonry out of the church wall as they passed through the seventeen unarmed men. Two soldiers at the edge of the group attempted to escape from the carnage, running to the right, but they were quickly cut down by the guards at the side who fired their MP40 machine pistols at them, knocking them off their feet before they had managed to get more than ten yards away.

The firing carried on for over thirty seconds, some bullets hitting the already dead corpses but it did not stop the SS from continuing and they only stopped once the ammunition ran out in the MG34s.

It was then strangely quiet.

Jack looked at Cooke who had pulled back from the window, his eyes staring ahead blankly in horror. He watched him as he turned to the side and was violently sick on the floorboards. Jack realised that he himself was shaking violently and realised that he may be in shock. He turned his head again to the window and looked down at the square below, to the men whom he had that day fought with, led and had spoken to only minutes ago. They were all dead, lying in an undignified heap in a massive pool of blood and gore only a few yards below him.

Then the odour of Cooke's vomit hit his nostrils and he too turned to the side and threw up over the floor, the vomit splashing onto his boots. He looked again at Cooke who was now sitting down with his back to the wall, tears pouring down his face.

Jack heard the sound of engines starting and peered out of the window again.

He could see the German officer, who he believed to be his childhood friend Otto, casually walk over to the group of dead soldiers lying on the ground.

And then Jack saw that they were not all dead. Two had been protected by those in front of them, the bodies of their comrades had taken the full force of the machine gun bullets and they were still alive, although badly injured. They lay on their backs, side by side on the ground.

As Otto approached them, one of them held up his hand as though putting it up would somehow protect him from what was to come. Jack stared, paralysed, as the German officer lifted the Mauser, cocked the weapon and then casually shot both of them in the head from point blank range. Again Jack felt the vomit rise as he saw the backs of their heads explode, spraying blood and brain matter against the white church wall. Otto then calmly walked over to where Captain Rogers lay and fired two more rounds into his body before stepping over it and walking to a waiting half-track.

The two Opel trucks, now with the guards on board, pulled away and drove out of the square, quickly followed by the half-track and the other vehicles, leaving a strange, eerie silence in the square behind them.

Jack looked at Cooke who stared back at him. He did not know what to say. What could he say? What could either of them say? There were no words available to them. What they had just witnessed was beyond belief, incomprehensible.

Jack sat down next to Cooke and shook his head slowly from side to side.

Corporal Cooke did not move.

CHAPTER TWENTY-ONE

It was getting dark outside. Jack was unaware of how long they had been sitting there but knew it must have been a couple of hours. They had both fallen asleep for a while, their minds had somehow emptied of all thought and slumber had taken hold of them. When Jack awoke he was momentarily unaware of where he was and had forgotten what had taken place outside earlier, but on seeing the splash of vomit on his boots it all came back to him in a sudden, horrific flash.

He nudged Cooke who woke with a start and muttered something incoherently. Jack ignored him and said, 'Come on, Greg, we need to get out of here.'

Cooke stood up, stretching his arms and legs. He looked at Jack and rubbed his eyes before moving to the window and looking out. 'Looks like they've gone, sir,' he said. 'We've got to be very careful from hereon in. We can't afford to bump into them again, otherwise the same will happen to us.'

'I can't believe what I've just witnessed,' said Jack. 'I can't believe they could be so cruel… so evil.'

'Me neither,' replied Cooke. 'I've never known anything like it. You hear stories and rumours but you can't believe they're true. They're all dead, boss. Every single one of them. Murdered. There's no other word for it.'

'There isn't. They didn't stand a chance.'

'And you knew the officer in charge? The German.'

Jack stood up. 'I knew him as a child. A very likeable child too, if memory serves me correctly. I can't believe it's the same person, but I know it is. What happened to him to turn him into a cold blooded killer? Christ alone knows.'

'One thing's for certain,' said Cooke determinedly. 'They won't take me without a fight and if I see that blond haired bastard again I'm taking him out.'

'The only thing we can do, Greg, is to get our arses to our own lines and get back to England. We can report it there.'

'What good will that do? The bloody Germans are running riot all over Europe. I don't think justice is likely anytime soon.'

Jack sighed. 'I feel your frustration Greg, I really do. But we have an immediate issue and that's to get the hell out of here and we need to make our move as soon as it gets dark. Let's try and find something to eat in this place… keep our energy levels up. For the time being we have to forget about what we've just seen and think about ourselves for a while.'

They removed the board that covered the attic exit and dropped down into the apartment below. They found some bread and cheese, which they ate hurriedly and put a couple of apples into their pockets before going downstairs to the bar area.

Jack found some orange juice behind the bar, which they drank and then checked their water bottles before moving to the doorway, stepping over the body of the young gendarme as they did so.

The light was getting fainter as the sun moved down in the sky casting shadows across the length of the square. There was not a sound to be heard, the streets and houses deserted, the residents long gone in an attempt to get away from the advancing Germans.

Jack pulled the pistol from the holster at his side and checked that it was loaded, even though he had checked it many times and knew it was. He stepped outside and looked over to where the dead soldiers lay, slightly to the right of the inn, and walked over to them. Cooke followed, the Thompson at the ready.

'Sir,' he whispered urgently. 'What are you doing? We need to get away from here.'

'I know, Greg,' he replied not looking back. 'I will only be a minute.'

Jack reached the bodies and quickly moved from one to the next, collecting the dog-tags from around their necks and trying to avoid looking into their faces, or what was left of them. The blood was congealing on the cobbles and as he moved, his boots occasionally stuck in the tacky gore, the consistency reminding him of glue, but he could hardly avoid it. However, he felt that he had to do this. The families of these poor, unfortunate souls would need to know what happened to their husbands, their sons, their brothers.

When he had collected them, he stuffed them into his pocket and turned to Corporal Cooke.

'Okay, let's get the others and then we can go.'

After retrieving Private Wood's tags and those of the three Lancashire Fusiliers who had died with him, they set off along the roadway, following in the direction that the SS troops had taken. In the distance they could see the smoke from the police car still rising into the early evening sky. Jack knew that there would be no point in attempting to retrieve the tags of Lieutenant Green and those who had travelled in the car with him, as they would have been destroyed by now. Instead, he surveyed the area ahead for a way forward that would be out of sight from the roadway. Like Corporal Cooke had said, the last thing they needed right now was to bump into the Germans again.

To the right of the roadway, about half a mile away, was a copse. He could see in the distance another.

He turned to Cooke, 'If we stick to the woods, we may have more of a chance. We won't be seen from the roadway or the air. Not much of a plan but it's the best I can do.'

Cooke did not respond but instead jogged quickly in the direction that Jack was indicating.

As the two of them moved, Jack wracked his brains frustratedly. He could not remember the surname of the German officer. He knew his first name was Otto but for some reason the surname would not come to him.

They had never really spoken about what had happened in the cove near St Malo all those years ago. His father had never again brought up the subject and it was something neither Jack, nor his brother Francis wanted to talk about either, so over the years the players of that day had largely been forgotten. He remembered there being a scruffy French boy and a quiet Italian but their names had long been erased from his memory. He had remembered Otto because he had saved him. He had pulled him out of the sea alive, but with a horrific injury to his face that he had felt bad about for years after. He had liked Otto despite not wanting to and had been extremely upset about what had happened to him and the French hotel janitor, Claude.

Yes, he thought, as they entered the relative sanctuary of the woods, he had liked Otto a lot at the time. But now times were different and their countries were once again at war. However, war did not give any man the excuse to murder people in cold blood, nothing did. That young, blond, unassuming child whom he had once felt an affinity with, a closeness to, he now hated with a passion. He felt sick to the stomach at the thought that he had turned into a Nazi murderer.

Jack wished he had left the bastard to drown.

They slowed to a walk once they reached the trees, the both of them exhausted and continued slowly to the opposite edge of the woods. They could see a road going across the top and across that road was another small copse that they thought to be in the direction they needed to be heading.

As the evening gave way to dusk and the light faded even more, they started to feel a little safer, more relaxed. They checked the roadway and could see no traffic approaching so ran across it and into the safety of the trees opposite. Once inside and out of view, they stopped and rested on a fallen tree, taking a drink from their water bottles.

'Jesus, boss, I'm drained,' said Cooke.

Jack looked at him and saw that this was obvious. His face looked as though it had aged ten years since that morning. He looked tired, haggard and beaten and Jack assumed that he himself looked the same. All he wanted to do was rest but he also wanted to get to the British lines and he knew that they could not do both. They had to keep moving.

'Lights,' said Cooke looking over Jack's shoulder and crouching down behind the tree.

Jack turned his head and could see a number of lights approaching them from the right. Trucks.

'For God's sake,' he said quietly. 'Are they ours or theirs?'

'No idea,' replied Cooke, straining his eyes in an attempt to distinguish if they were friend or foe.

As the first truck passed, Jack could see a union flag emblazoned on the door.

'Shit, they're British,' he shouted jumping up. 'Come on, quick.'

They both ran out of the trees towards the road waving their arms and shouting at the passing trucks, 'Here, over here!'

There were five trucks in total and it was the second from the back that noticed them and stopped. Seeing it halt, the remainder of the convoy applied their brakes and waited. Jack approached the nearest truck and a soldier, a young sergeant, leaned out casually.

'Who the bloody hell are you two?' he asked.

'Royal Fusiliers,' replied Jack smiling. 'Have you got room for two more?'

Seeing he was addressing an officer, the soldier sat up straighter and replied. 'Yeah, hop in the back, I'm sure they can squeeze up a bit.'

As Cooke walked to the rear of the vehicle, Jack stopped. 'If I were you,' he said, 'I'd kill those lights. There are Germans all over the place and they'll see you from miles away. Believe me, you don't want to bump into them.'

'Righto, sir,' he replied. 'I'll let everyone know. You look done in. Get in the back and have some rest.'

Jack thanked him and then walked to the rear of the truck where Cooke was already settled. He leaned out and assisted Jack into the back where he sat on a bench next to a large soldier with red hair. He looked around and could see many faces in the gloom, all looking at him for a few seconds before they turned away to think their own thoughts, none of them interested in the two new arrivals and whatever story they may have. Jack assumed that they probably had their own similar tales and, just like them, he didn't want to hear them right now.

As the truck proceeded along the roadway, he was aware that the one behind had done as requested and had switched off its lights. He rocked back and forth as the vehicle hit bumps and potholes in the road and before he knew it the fatigue took over and he had fallen fast asleep.

CHAPTER TWENTY-TWO

Jack looked around the beach and was again amazed at how many soldiers were here. There were thousands upon thousands of them, sitting quietly on the sand or standing patiently in line, awaiting their turn to go out to where the small boats came in for them to take them out to the larger Royal Navy ships that were further out to sea. From there it would be a short hop back to the safety of England. He had heard that thousands had already been evacuated from the East Mole, a perilous jetty that extended nearly a mile out to sea where smaller craft had managed to dock, despite the hazards and possibility of being smashed against the concrete foundations.

He could not understand why the Germans had not finished them off as they were pretty much sitting ducks here. He had seen RAF fighter planes flying overhead, presumably to provide support to those defending the town's perimeter but did not know why the German army was not pushing harder to capture those on the beaches.

They had arrived in Dunkirk in the early hours of May 29th. That was two days ago and he remembered it now as a bit of a blur. The group that had picked them up had been from the Durham Light Infantry, on their way to the coast for evacuation and on getting a mile from the front line had had to abandon the vehicles.

The officer in charge had ordered the trucks burned so as not to fall into enemy hands and then they had quietly and quickly, under cover of darkness, aided only by the light of the fires that burned within the destroyed town, successfully found the British lines. From there they had simply walked down to the beach, stopping only to get some food from one of the buildings nearby that had been set up as a food and first aid centre.

There had been numerous air attacks throughout that day and Jack had seen the ships and boats out at sea come under heavy attack from the Luftwaffe. A ship had also been attacked and wrecked just off the East Mole and he was unsure of how many casualties had been suffered but from what he could see he assumed it was very many.

He had made an attempt to search for members of his own company but could not find anyone, there were just too many soldiers filling every available safe building or lying out on the beach. He had no way of knowing if they were alive or dead and did not know if they were still in France. They could have already been evacuated back to England.

He had lost Corporal Cooke the day before. Jack had fallen asleep on the beach and when he had awoken the man was gone. He had searched for him for a couple of hours but had then given up, he could have been anywhere and Cooke was probably looking for him too. He surmised that the regiment would re-group on the opposite side of the Channel, so he did not give it any further thought or worry. He realised that he was alone and the irony of his situation was not lost on him. He was with thousands of people, all in the same situation as he was, but he had never felt so alone in all his life.

He was now sitting down in the sand, drinking the tea that he had collected from a nearby food station. Jack was impressed with the organisation of the troops by the senior officers and the fact that they were, in general, behaving themselves and queuing patiently where required. He had seen the occasional fracas as someone had tried to jump the line but they were dealt with expertly by the officers. On one occasion he had seen a soldier threatened with a pistol before he reluctantly took his allocated place at the rear of the line.

He could hear the sound of tank, artillery and anti-tank weapons being fired in the near distance as the battle for the town raged a few short miles away, but Jack was astonished at the absence of a full on assault by the enemy. There did not look like there was much fight left in anyone on the beach and if the Germans got their act together then they could deal the British a total defeat, but the way things were going, everyone would be evacuated before that happened.

Occasionally a German plane would fly over the beach, spraying the occupants with machine gun fire. The soldiers on the ground would fire their rifles and machine guns back at the aircraft but Jack was yet to see any of them shot down.

As he crouched there, sipping at his sugared tea, soldiers coming and going around him, he heard a voice.

'Mister Graham, is that you?'

He looked up to see a familiar face looking down at him. It was a private soldier from number one platoon whose name he could not remember.

'It is, isn't it?' he said. 'Private Sandbrook, sir. One platoon. We thought you were dead.'

Jack stood up, throwing the remains of the tea into the sand.

'Yes, private, it's me all right.'

'Bloody hell, sir, you're a sight for sore eyes I can tell you. Double H... uh Major Harding I mean, will be very happy to see you, sir.'

'What?' said Jack not quite understanding. 'They're here? The company is here?'

'Yes, sir,' he replied enthusiastically pointing down the beach. 'They're just over there. Waiting to get out of here like everyone else. We've got a slot this afternoon apparently. We're going home.'

Jack could not believe his ears.

'Okay. Lead the way.'

He picked up his tunic and stood up. He followed Private Sandbrook half a mile along the beach barely listening to him as he spoke at him at a hundred miles an hour, passing soldiers in lines and sitting in the sand until he started to see faces he knew. Looking around he spotted his friend, Lieutenant Dan Wilson, standing with Major Harding, "Double H". He walked over and when he was a couple of yards away, Harding noticed him.

'My God!' he exclaimed loudly. 'Mister Graham. We all thought you'd copped it.'

Lieutenant Wilson turned and on seeing his friend his eyes lit up.

'Bloody hell, Jack,' he said clasping him by the hand. 'Jesus! We thought you'd had it, mate. What happened to you? Where have you been?'

Jack shook his hand enthusiastically, happy to be back in the company of people he knew.

'Don't crowd the boy,' said Major Harding. 'I'm sure he has a tale to tell. All in good time, all in good time.'

'It's good to see you all,' said Jack. 'I thought it would never happen if I'm honest with you. Thought I'd never make it here. We got a little bit cut off I'm afraid.'

'Where are the rest of you?'

'Gone I'm afraid, sir,' Jack replied dejectedly. 'Corporal Cooke and I are the only ones who made it here, but I seem to have misplaced him somewhere I'm sorry to say.'

'Okay, my boy,' replied Harding gloomily. 'You can give me a full report when we get back across the water.'

'I need to speak to you privately when I get a chance, sir,' said Jack. 'I need to tell you something quite urgently.'

Harding thought for a moment. 'Okay, no time like the present I suppose,' he replied, his curiosity suddenly aroused. 'It's not as though we are doing anything right now, is it?'

They walked away from the rest of the company and finding a semi-private place some yards away Jack explained to Harding what had happened to him and the rest of his men over the last couple of days, ending with the massacre of the British prisoners of war. Harding looked genuinely shocked at the story he told him.

'So you believe you know this German then, this Hun?' he asked him. 'The one who was in charge?'

'Yes, sir, I knew him all right… when we boys though.'

'Are you certain it was him?'

'One hundred percent. I just wish I could remember his surname,' replied Jack. 'I'm sure my father will remember when I ask him.'

'Good.' Harding thought for a moment. 'Get this down on paper, Graham. As soon as you can. Today. Right now if you can find a pen and some paper. If what you say is true, and I have no reason to doubt that it's not, then I will need to report it to the War Office.'

Then Jack remembered the tags he had taken off the dead British soldiers and pulled them out of his pocket.

'Here, sir,' he said holding them out to him. 'Their dog tags. I took them off them before we left. Some still have their blood on, I'm sorry.'

Harding took them from him and looked at them.

'This is all too terrible for words. We've all heard the rumours about them but I did not expect them to murder unarmed prisoners-of-war. This needs to be reported and rest assured, young man, that is the first thing I will do when we get back to Blighty.'

'Thank you, sir,' said Jack. He was relieved that he had now shared the information he had and that the authorities would be informed about the murders. He trusted "Double H" to do as he had said and felt as if a weight had been lifted from his shoulders and he could now relax a little. He knew that the perpetators of the crime would probably never come to justice and that irked at him massively but what could he do other than report it? There may come a point, when the war was over, when Otto would have to answer for what he did the other day. Who knows how all this will turn out, thought Jack. At least the army was escaping and while there was still an army, there was still a chance.

He looked out to sea at the ships moored some distance away, the small boats going backwards and forwards, ferrying soldiers from the East Mole and the beach, taking them to safety.

Soon, he thought. Soon it would be his turn. Soon he would be on his way home and he could put this chapter of his life to bed. It was over. And then as he started to relax he remembered the name of the young German boy he had rescued from drowning all those years ago, not too many miles away to the south of where he now stood. The same boy who had put a bullet into the heads of the two dying soldiers and fired into the corpse of Captain Rogers. The same boy who had ordered the murders of close to twenty unarmed British soldiers.

Finkel, he thought. That was it. That was his name.

Otto Finkel.

He set off to find pen and paper.

CHAPTER TWENTY-THREE

Jeff Watson, the skipper of the *Margaret Rose*, the small fishing boat he had named after his eldest daughter, scratched his grey bearded chin and rested his arms on the gunwale as his craft approached the East Mole. This was the third trip of the day, ferrying troops from the stone jetty out to sea where they could board the large destroyers that would take them back to England and safety.

He had heard the call for as many available serviceable boats to make their way to assist with the evacuation and knew that this was something he could not ignore. Sailing down the east coast of England he had joined the many hundred similar vessels at Ramsgate and they had set sail two days ago to assist where they could with collecting the boys from the beaches. As his boat was too large, he could not take it directly to the shore, where he could see many thousands of them waiting in line, seemingly unconcerned about the German planes overhead as they attacked the ships and boats awaiting to take them to safety.

Watson had never been to war. He was a peaceful man and earned a decent living fishing in the North Sea and the sights and sounds of warfare were alien to him. However, he could not leave all those young men stranded, awaiting an unknown fate, particularly when he had a strong craft capable of taking so many of them back home.

Carefully, young Toby expertly piloted the boat towards the pier, avoiding the wreck of the *Fenella* of the Isle of Man Steam Packet Company that had been sunk a day or so ago whilst attempting to take troops off the East Mole, its superstructure jutting out of the sea adding to the hazards that needed to be avoided. Watson knew the dangers and felt a little guilty at having coerced Toby and his brother, Harry, to come with him on this adventure. He was hugely proud of the two of them for how they had cheerfully and competently conducted themselves since they had agreed to accompany him.

As they got closer, they could see the eager faces of the soldiers as they lined up, waiting patiently to board the vessel. Slowly they drew alongside and Watson threw a line to a group of soldiers who quickly fixed it to the mooring, and Harry, at the bow did the same. A minute later, the troops started to board, an officer on the pier counting them as they got on.

'How many can you take?' he shouted.

'I can squeeze on around sixty,' he shouted back.

The boat started to fill quickly and was soon loaded with tired looking and bedraggled soldiers, all carrying minimal equipment having abandoned most of it on the beach. He noticed that only a few still carried weapons.

Watson had to be quick. There were many other boats lining up behind him waiting their turn to collect whatever numbers they could to either ferry to the destroyers or make the journey back to England. This was his third trip of the day, ferrying troops to the destroyers lying off the shore, and he had decided that he would maybe do one more before heading back to England, to refuel and gather fresh supplies before returning the following day to go through the whole process again.

Each journey was getting more and more dangerous. He could hear the sounds of battle in the distance and the German aircraft seemed to be increasing their attacks on the shipping, including the many civilian and merchant vessels that were assisting with the evacuation. The situation on the East Mole was becoming more and more hazardous with each visit and Watson thought that it was getting too dangerous to continue the pick-ups from here and the powers that be would have to come up with another plan shortly.

Soon the limit on what he could carry was filled and the lines were thrown back on board by the soldiers who were still on the pier. The *Margaret Rose* was then turned from the pier by Toby and once again it set out to sea. Watson returned to the wheelhouse to supervise the trip back. He watched as Harry made his way through the troops, apologising as he stepped over and past them to get to the stern to look out for mines, another hazard that Watson had had to contend with.

Through the window he looked to the skies and could see the German planes flying overhead, so many targets for them to pick from and prayed that they would be left alone. Some of the men on the deck were also looking up and those with weapons had them at the ready. Being so close to safety and after going through all that they had, they did not want fate and irony to deal them such a terrible blow with England only a short journey away.

As the *Margaret Rose* gathered speed, Watson said a short prayer to himself, just like he had done many times over the last couple of days.

*

Jack stood on the deck of the small fishing craft that he had been lucky enough to get a place on and looked around at all the men who were with him. "Double H" stood to the side, quietly smoking a cigarette and Dan was sitting across from him, his back against the gunwale, his eyes closed. Others looked nervously to the sky, hoping against hope that the Luftwaffe would leave them alone and pick on another similar craft rather than the one they were on. Jack guiltily felt the same way.

Many still had their weapons and held onto them tightly, as though a Lee Enfield .303 was some kind of assurance of safety against the Stuka dive bombers and Messerschmitts that circled overhead, like vultures on the African savannah, coveting the carcass of a wildebeest, waiting for the opportune moment to swoop down and strike.

He looked into the wheelhouse where a young boy, no more than seventeen years old, wearing a woollen hat, controlled the craft. An older, bearded man was at his side, giving him advice, an arm around his shoulders. Jack was extremely grateful that they had made the no doubt dangerous journey to assist the army where they could. It made him proud of his fellow countrymen that they would make this perilous trip to save him and his comrades, despite the dangers that they would have surely faced.

As he watched them, he heard movement behind and turned to see soldiers rising, looking to the sky ahead of the vessel. Those with weapons started to cock them, making them ready to be fired and instinctively he pulled out his pistol. Then the young boy looking out for mines returned quickly to the wheelhouse, a look of horror on his face, passing through the soldiers as they stared skyward.

Coming at them, flying no more than ten metres above the waves was a Messerschmitt fighter plane. As it got closer, those soldiers who still held weapons began to open fire, their panicked shots having no effect whatsoever. Then the aircraft opened fire, the bullets hitting the sea in front of the boat before riding up and hitting the deck.

As men dived for cover, Jack let off a couple of rounds before the plane overflew and was gone from sight.

He looked at the devastation. At least three were dead and numerous had serious wounds. Comrades moved quickly, opening field dressings and applying them to the wounded where necessary in an attempt to stop the bleeding. Their cries of pain mixed with the din of the boat's engine, the whine of the aircraft flying overhead and the sound of battle that was raging all around them as the flotilla of small boats attempted to dodge the enemy aircraft attacks.

Jack was aware that the wheelhouse had also been hit, its windows smashed, leaving broken glass strewn around the deck and the shelving and maps on the back wall ripped to shreds. He was relieved to see that the three civilians had been spared and were continuing to move the craft as best as they could to get out of danger.

He holstered his pistol and turned to see if he could be of assistance to any of the injured soldiers.

He knelt down beside a man with a horrific wound to his chest, being tended to by two of his friends who were frantically pressing field dressings onto him, desperately trying to prevent him from bleeding to death. Realising there was little he could do with this one, he looked for another. However, the familiar sound of an aircraft engine getting increasingly louder filled the air once more.

Jack looked up and saw, with horror, that the Messerschmitt had circled around and was bearing down on them again, its guns blazing in an evil determination to finish them off.

PART THREE
JEAN-LUC DESCARTES

CHAPTER TWENTY-FOUR

Near Lyon, France, Mid-July 1942

Jean-Luc Descartes sat at his desk and looked out of the window of the second floor studio apartment that he owned. He lived alone and it suited him, the solitude seemed to help with his writing, allowing him to blank out the mundane and allowing him the concentration he needed for him to carry out his work. The view was the only distraction, it being so beautiful, and he often found himself daydreaming as he sat there, fingers hovering over the old typewriter, the machine waiting for the keys to be struck, for the words to make the short journey from his brain to his fingers and then onto the paper. It was not often that he got writer's block but when it happened it was only ever fleeting. When it did come he would look out of the window and stare up at the expansive, open, clear blue sky, where, on a day such as this when the sun shone between perfect white clouds, it would sometimes help to free up his thoughts and then the words would come flowing once more. He thought that if he squinted his eyes and tried really hard, he could just about make out the faint outline of the mountain range many miles to the east and this would somehow generate the stimulus he needed to overcome it. The view, he felt, could serve both as a distraction and as an inspiration, depending on the mood he happened to be in at the time.

Jean-Luc was twenty-seven years old and stood five feet ten inches tall. He was of medium build and still wore his hair unfashionably long in the bohemian style just as he had done when he was a youth. At the moment he was sporting a short moustache but he planned to remove it in the next day or so, having got bored with the look and receiving complaints from Catherine that it tickled her when they kissed. He did not care that the older generation disapproved of his appearance. He had never been concerned about other's opinions of him and he ignored the things he heard people say as he passed them, or comments he often heard being said behind his back about his unkempt and antithetic look. He did not let it bother him, in fact he found it all very amusing. He liked being the opposite of other people, in his appearance, his manner and his thoughts and ideas. In fact, he did not care what anyone thought of him and never had. If they did not like him then that was their choice and there was nothing he could do, or would want to do about it. He simply did not care at all.

He looked down at the words he had typed on the sheet of paper and sighed. Writing this book was taking an age. He had been preparing for this novel his whole life, the story forming over many years, taking shape and direction in his head until he felt he was finally ready to put it all down on paper. He was happy with the first part, which was now completed, but had read back the second and felt the opposite. It would need a complete re-write.

He was lucky enough that his short stories and articles had earned him a relatively modest income, his two children's books now in print and selling quite well. His agent and publisher in Paris had asked for more, but Jean-Luc did not want to get bogged down writing mundane stories about *Georges the Giraffe* and *The Little Sparrow* for the rest of his writing life, even if it did pay the bills and put bread on the table. The money he had been left by his mother when she died also added to the comfortable lifestyle that he now enjoyed.

However, it was getting increasingly difficult travelling between the two sectors to visit Bruno, his publisher. He tried to do most of his business over the telephone, preferring to stay away from the capital and the Germans who occupied the city. He did not worry too much about his Jewish heritage, despite Catherine's misgivings, as he had never registered himself and would never, on any account, wear the yellow star that the Germans forced everyone in the occupied zone to wear. He would not humiliate himself in such a manner and after all, he had never even been in a synagogue in his life. His lack of religious beliefs had meant that he had not once considered himself a Jew anyway or anything else religious for that matter. He did not believe in God and never had. He was a Frenchman and if truth be told, a bit of a communist too. He was the complete opposite of what the Nazis approved of and for that he felt proud of himself.

He decided that if new ideas did not appear within the next fifteen minutes then he would finish for the day and do something more productive. He picked up the pack of cigarettes to his right and took one out. Placing it in his mouth he fumbled in his jacket, which was hooked over the back of the chair he was sitting on, for the book of matches he had inadvertently stolen from Catherine a few days ago. Finding them, he lit the cigarette and inhaled.

Catherine, he thought. What was he to do with her?

He believed she loved him deeply and totally, which was a bit of a shame, for he knew that he did not love her back. He had tried to make himself feel the same way as her, to reciprocate her feelings, but no matter how hard he tried he knew it was unachievable, so had given up. He had concluded that love was one emotion he was incapable of feeling. When he thought about it, he could not remember loving a single human being his entire life and that included his mother and grandparents. He just did not have it in him.

Poor Catherine. Poor unrequited Catherine. She was better off with somebody else, someone who could give her what she wanted. But these were extraordinary times they were living in and people took comfort wherever they could get it. He knew this to be a selfish attitude, but then, it was how his life was for now and in a way they were both using each other.

Yes, he thought, these were strange and difficult times. The war was everywhere. Even if the Germans had not yet moved their troops to the south, to the parts of the country controlled by the Vichy government, their influence seemed to be apparent throughout the whole country. Those collaborators who did the bidding of that madman Hitler, allowing him to keep his troops available for other things, made him embarrassed to be a Frenchman. Whilst the English were busy booting the Nazis out of Africa and the Russians, from what he could gather, were starting to do likewise in their own country, the French had capitulated very quickly and the puppet government led by the old hero Petain was now bending over backwards to appease them.

Catherine was part of the Resistance. She had not openly admitted it to him but it was fairly obvious. She had even made a half-hearted attempt to recruit him recently, arguing that with him being half Jewish it was his duty to do something. He had told her that he was not interested and he just wanted a peaceful life, nothing more and nothing less. Although he agreed with what they were doing and admired their efforts, armed resistance was not for him. He was a writer. That was all he was. Nothing more. He saw the war as having nothing to do with him. He had not caused it and wanted no part of it.

Eventually, his mind wandering away from the passage he was attempting to complete, he stood up and put the cover over the typewriter. The sun had long since passed overhead and was now casting shadows over the buildings and fields as he looked over in the direction of the Alps and imagined their wonderful splendour. He loved this time of day, particularly in summertime when the heat of the day made way to a warm, balmy evening, the noise of the occasional car as it passed and the sounds of children being called home to their beds. It all seemed so tranquil and he often found himself smiling in contentment at such times.

He heard a knock at the door and walked across the large open room to the front door. He knew it would be Catherine and although she was a regular visitor and often spent the night with him, he had refrained from providing her with the key that she longed for. The key that would say to her that, yes, she was his girl and he was her man. For Jean-Luc, this was his place and giving her a key was too much of a commitment.

He opened the door and stood aside as she entered the room. He looked behind her and down the fire escape, which led to the front door, a habit he had taken up after realising that her activities were not confined to working in the clothes shop in the centre of Lyon with her sister. He had to make sure that no one was following her. Even though he knew he did not love her, he still cared deeply for her and was worried about her coming into any kind of danger. Content that she was alone, he closed the door and turned to look at her.

He noticed that she seemed a little agitated and frowned slightly.

'Hello, my dear,' he said, kissing her on the cheek. 'Would you like a coffee? You will have to have it black though. The milk has gone off.'

'Hello,' she replied. 'Black is fine.' Catherine hated the way he called her "my dear", as though she was his grandmother or an old aunt.

Jean-Luc walked to the kitchen area and took two cups from a cupboard and placed them on the worktop. He filled the kettle from the tap, placed it on the burner and then struck a match from a box at the side and lit the gas. Then he turned to her and looked at her properly for the first time since she had entered the apartment.

She was wearing a summer dress, a floral print in mainly green, which highlighted the greenness of her eyes. She wore plain white sandals on her feet and a flower in her hair, in an attempt to make her look prettier than she actually was. She tended to wear little make up now that they were lovers and she no longer felt that she had to impress him, but she always managed to find the time to pencil in a beauty spot on her left cheek, which Jean-Luc managed to find both amusing and endearing. Her dark brown hair was tied back in a pony-tail, which only served to enhance her slightly overlarge nose.

He smiled at her and walked over and kissed her again, this time on the lips, holding her by the shoulders. Pulling away he said softly, 'You look nice, Catherine.'

'Thank you,' she replied and smiled back, somewhat awkwardly, her eyes moving from his face and darting around the room, as though scanning the place, before resting once more upon his eyes. 'When are you going to shave off that moustache? You said you were going to get rid of it.'

'Soon,' he replied. 'Are you okay? You seem a little preoccupied.'

She moved away from him and sat down at the chair he had just vacated near the window. She looked at the cover over the typewriter and stroked it absentmindedly.

'I'm starting to get worried, Jean-Luc,' she said, unable to look in his direction, preferring to stare out of the window at the same view that he had been enjoying only minutes earlier, but not registering the beauty of the scene as he had done. 'Something is in the air and it doesn't feel right.'

'What are you talking about?' he asked.

'There is a strong rumour… amongst my friends…'

'Ah, your friends,' he interrupted. 'Would these be the friends whom you keep so secret? These mysterious friends of yours…'

She turned to look at him. 'Please, Jean-Luc, I am being serious.'

'Okay,' he apologised, holding up his hands. 'Please go on.'

She was about to continue but at that point the kettle started whistling and Jean-Luc walked to the kitchen and poured the water into the two cups. 'I'm sorry,' he said. 'It'll have to be this cheap instant stuff. It's all I've got.'

'That's fine,' she said uninterestedly.

'Go on,' he said. 'You wanted to tell me something.'

'Yes,' said Catherine. 'My friends believe that something is imminent. Something that will affect you.'

'How so?'

'Orders are about to come out to round up the Jews. Orders from the Germans.'

'The Germans are in the north. They are not here.'

'I know that, Jean-Luc, I know that. We have contacts in the police and it looks like it is about to happen very soon. You need to get away.'

'This is ridiculous,' he replied and walked over to her. He handed her a cup of steaming coffee and then pulled a wooden chair from behind him and sat down to face her. 'No Frenchman will be a part of this. I can't see the order being carried out. Why would our own police collect French people to hand over to the Germans? It makes no sense.'

She held the cup in both hands and blew across the top in an attempt to cool it. 'You think our gendarmes won't do it? If you think that then you are being very naïve. Some of them are worse than the Nazis. They can't wait to do it.'

'I'm not too worried,' he replied. 'Really I'm not. The war is not my concern. It has nothing to do with me?'

'Nothing to do with you?' she almost shouted. 'Nothing to do with you? It is to do with everyone, whether we like it or not. And it is worse for you. You are Jewish, Jean-Luc, Jewish. You know how they treat the Jews.'

'I am not anything other than a Frenchman,' he replied. 'I haven't been a Jew for a long time.'

It was true. In his own mind Jean-Luc had never felt Jewish. His father had been a Roman Catholic before a German bullet, or bomb, he had no way of knowing which, had taken his life at Verdun twenty five years before. He had never known him and had no memory of the man, only the image of him on a faded old photograph that was on the wall near to the front door. His eyes moved to it. Also in the picture was his mother who had died five years previously following a short and painful illness. She had been a Jewish orphan and had no known family so Jean-Luc knew nothing about his Jewish heritage. The only other family he had were his grandparents on his father's side who were both now very old and still living in St Malo as far as he knew. He had not seen either of them since he was a teenager, having been sent home from a holiday there following a tragic accident that really had nothing to do with him. Or had it? He could not quite remember.

'It doesn't matter whether you class yourself as a Jew or not,' went on Catherine. 'What matters is that they class you as one and as such you will be an "undesirable" to them. They will come for you.'

'I mind my own business,' he said defiantly. 'My life is of no concern to them. None at all. They will leave me alone.'

'Jesus, Jean-Luc,' she said. 'Wake up. They won't and you know it.'

'Okay,' he said finally, knowing that he was being childish and pig-headed. 'What do you suggest I do then?'

'Leave before they come for you.'

'And go where exactly?'

'My friends could possibly get you to Switzerland. Or Spain maybe.'

'And then what?'

'What do you mean?'

'What happens after I get to Switzerland or Spain, or wherever? What do I do then?'

'There are people there who are prepared to help,' she said. 'Good people who will put you up until all this madness is over.'

'Put me up?' he laughed. 'No I don't think so. I'll take my chances here I think.'

She sighed. She had known him long enough to realise that once his mind was set there was no changing it. She would be wasting her breath.

'Well, promise me one thing. Promise me that should things get too hot then you will at least consider accepting some help from me.'

He looked at her and paused before answering. 'Okay,' he said. 'Fine. If things get too 'hot' as you put it, I will listen to what you have to say. That I can do for you.'

Finally she smiled a smile that she meant. It was a start, she thought. If nothing else it was a start.

She put down her cup and stood up suddenly. 'Okay, you hairy man,' she said. 'Find that razor and let's get that horrible thing taken off your face.'

*

'Okay,' said Jean-Luc leaning out of the bed and taking a cigarette from the pack that lay on the floor next to where they had thrown their clothes. 'Are you going to tell me where you've been for the past few days?'

Catherine lay naked next to him. She pulled the blanket over her body and up to her chin. 'Are you going to give me one of those?' she asked.

He took out another and lit them both before handing one to her as she sat up beside him, pulling the blanket with her. He smiled to himself at her modesty now that the fun was over.

'Let's just say I have been away on a course and leave it at that shall we?' she finally replied to his question.

'Um… okay,' he said rubbing the stubble under his nose where the moustache used to be. 'Did you learn a lot on this course?'

'Yes,' she said laughing. 'Very practical and the instructor was quite nice too. Very handsome. For an Englishman he spoke remarkably good French.'

'Do I need to be jealous?' he asked, humouring her.

'Only slightly,' she giggled. 'Just a little bit maybe.'

He smiled at her indulgently. Jealousy was another emotion he had no comprehension of. If she wanted to sleep with other men then what business was it of his? He did not own her, after all.

'Why don't you come with me?' she said after a while. 'The next time we have a meeting. They know about you and I'm sure that you could contribute to what we are trying to do.'

'And what could I possibly contribute?' he asked.

'You are very good with words, Jean-Luc,' she replied, turning her head to look at him. 'Your ideals and politics are the same. Maybe you could write leaflets, propaganda, that sort of thing.'

147

'You know that kind of thing is not for me, Catherine,' he said quietly. 'I am a simple man wanting a simple, quiet life. That's all there is to me. I'm no revolutionary. I may have fairly leftist ideals but that's all they are, ideals. I'm not about to put up a red flag outside my window or anything like that.'

'You may not have a choice. Whether you want it or not, the war will eventually get round to involving you and from what I've been told it's imminent. Whether you consider yourself a Jew or not, other people do. Other more violent people with power. You really need to think about it and start making plans.'

He turned and looked at her and at once saw the desperation in her eyes. She was genuinely worried about him. For that brief moment he felt awkward in her presence, realising that what he was doing to her was unfair, leading her on in some way.

'Okay,' he said after a while. 'I will think about it.'

'Promise me, Jean-Luc. Please don't just say the words to appease me.'

'I promise, Catherine. I promise,' he replied and kissed her on the forehead.

'Thank you,' she whispered. 'That is all I ask.'

CHAPTER TWENTY-FIVE

Catherine left early the next morning to return to work at her sister's shop in the centre of Lyon, arranging to see him again the following weekend. Two days later, after his morning exercise, which entailed walking four miles around the town, Jean-Luc found himself once again sitting at the desk attempting to continue writing his novel, the one that he was convinced would make him his fortune and maybe even famous one day. It was hard convincing Bruno, his publisher, that he was capable of more than the short children's stories he had produced so far, but he was determined to finish the book, whether Bruno would publish it or not. He could not blame him for wanting more of the same, as the books had sold quite well and had been lucrative for the pair of them.

He had not seen Bruno Jeunier since the Germans had invaded and taken Paris two years ago and Jean-Luc had no desire to go and see him now. He had no intention of setting foot in the occupied zone. Despite what he said to Catherine he was no fool and realised that a Jew, even a half-Jew such as he, walking amongst the Nazis was not the safest thing to do. All of his business with Bruno was now conducted over the telephone and that suited him fine.

Voluntarily adopting the German Statute on Jews in October 1940 all Jews had been instructed by the Vichy government to register themselves at their local police stations, but Jean-Luc had never done so and had no intention of highlighting to the authorities his family background, particularly when being half-Jewish meant nothing to him. He was not going to walk around the places where he had grown up advertising the fact that he was somehow different to the rest of the population; that because his mother was from a Jewish family it made him somehow inferior to the rest of them. He did not feel inferior, in fact, most of the time he felt quite the opposite. He would not allow them to segregate him and he would not be treated as a second class citizen because the occupying forces in the north deemed it so. He knew he was walking a potentially dangerous path, but so far it had not affected him in any way and the police had not been knocking on his door. Not yet anyway.

Catherine was genuinely fearful for him, of that he was sure, and although he dismissed what she had been saying he had not totally ignored her. He still felt safe. He still felt that if he just stayed where he was and kept his head down, that all this would pass him by. But she was convinced that something was imminent and when he thought about it he realised that she would know better than he did. She was in the Resistance, the Maquis, and had only recently been with them on some sort of training course with a British spy. Surely, therefore, it made sense to listen to what she was telling him and to heed her warnings. Maybe, he thought, it was time to take his head out of the sand.

He sat looking at the typewriter and took off the cover. He leaned to his side and lifted the window to allow some fresh air into the room and as he did so he spied a police car on the road outside his building. Two gendarmes got out of the vehicle and one of them looked up and caught his eye. Jean-Luc instantly recognised his old schoolfriend Henri Cheyrou, who, on seeing Jean-Luc started to raise his hand in greeting before thinking better of it and lowering his arm.

Thinking nothing of it, Jean-Luc turned his attention back to the typewriter and inserted a piece of paper before thinking carefully about what he was about to write. For some reason his mind was not quite on the task, the way that Cheyrou had lowered his arm and the aprehensive look on his face made Jean-Luc feel slightly uneasy.

He rose from the desk and walked towards the door. As he did so, there was a loud knock upon it, which stopped him in his tracks. He became aware that his heart was now thumping loudly in his chest and his mouth had gone dry. Before he could move there was another more violent knock on the door and a voice shouted, 'Police, open up.'

Taking a breath, Jean-Luc turned the key that was in the lock and opened the door.

Standing before him were two gendarmes, his old friend Henri Cheyrou and an older, more serious looking sergeant. Before Jean-Luc could say anything the sergeant brushed past him and into the room. Jean-Luc stood aside to allow Cheyrou in also, who passed him with a grim smile upon his face.

'I am Sergeant Paul Rodier and this is my colleague gendarme Henri Cheyrou, we need to ask you some questions.'

'Why don't the two of you come in,' said Jean-Luc sarcastically. 'Make yourselves comfortable.'

Rodier, a short, wiry man with a thin moustache looked at him and frowned. Ignoring Jean-Luc's attempt at humour he said, 'Are you Jean-Luc Descartes?'

'I am.'

'Then I will get to the point, monsieur,' said Rodier authoritatively. 'We have reason to believe that you are Jewish and as such should be registered with us.'

Jean-Luc looked from him to Cheyrou, who had his head bowed in embarrassment.

Thinking quickly Jean-Luc replied, 'And where did you get this ridiculous information from, may I ask?'

'No, you may not,' replied the policeman. 'Just answer the question.'

Jean-Luc took a breath.

'Who the hell do you think you are?' he said firmly. 'Barging into my home uninvited and accusing me of these things and not even having the courtesy to tell me where you have gained such information.'

For a brief second Rodier's hand hovered over the pistol that was holstered at his hip. 'You will find that I have the authority to do whatever I so please, Descartes. I do not need your permission. Now answer the question.'

Jean-Luc turned to his old friend. 'Henri,' he said, ignoring the sergeant, 'Why are you here? Why are you involving yourself in this disgraceful behaviour?'

Cheyrou looked up and Jean-Luc could see in his eyes that the man was troubled with what he was being made to do.

'It is my job, Jean-Luc,' he replied. 'I have no choice.'

Jean-Luc did not reply but stared at him until Cheyrou was forced to bow his head once more.

'So you two know each other do you?' said Rodier contemptuously. 'How nice. Now Descartes, answer the question.'

Jean-Luc turned back to Rodier. 'No, monsieur Rodier. No I am not a Jew. I have never been a Jew and I have no intention of ever becoming a Jew. I can see that your brain is obviously a little on the small side and so I will say it again so you may understand what I am saying. No... I... am... not... a... Jew. I hope that is clear enough for you.'

'Jean-Luc...' started Cheyrou but was instantly cut short by Rodier.

'You arrogant shit,' he replied viciously, spittle appearing at the corners of his mouth. 'You jumped up arrogant shit. How dare you speak to me like that!'

'This is my home and I will speak to you any which way I see fit while you are in it without my permission,' replied Jean-Luc.

'Jean-Luc… please,' pleaded Cheyrou. 'You are not making this easy.'

'I don't intend to make anything easy.'

Regaining his composure, Rodier continued. 'Monsieur Descartes, we have reason to believe that you are Jewish and that you failed to register your ancestry when you were legally obliged to do so. You are hereby ordered to accompany us to the police station where you will be processed and if necessary handed over to the relevant authorities for transportation to Paris.'

'I will do no such thing, you little rat,' replied Jean-Luc. He could feel his heart now straining in his chest, as though it was going to vibrate out of his body. He was aware that he was sweating, despite the cool breeze flowing through the apartment between the open window on one side and the open door on the other.

Rodier drew the pistol from the holster at his side and pointed it at Jean-Luc. 'Who do you think you are talking to, Jew-boy?' he said menacingly. 'I will put a bullet in your head if you carry on in this way.'

Jean-Luc looked to Cheyrou. 'Henri,' he said calmly. 'Tell this idiot that there has been a mistake. You were at school with me. You know I am not a Jew.' Turning back to Rodier, he said, 'Where is the paperwork to prove it? Do you have any with you? If you are about to take me away to God knows where, the least you can do is show me the proof.'

Rodier moved forward and thrust the gun into Jean-Luc's face. 'Open your mouth,' he ordered.

'What?' asked Jean-Luc not comprehending what the man was wanting, unable to understand what exactly he was about to do.

'You heard me, open that dirty fucking mouth of yours,' repeated Rodier slowly and firmly.

Jean-Luc looked to Cheyrou. 'Do you think this is correct Henri?' he asked, ignoring the little sergeant's demand. 'Do you think what this prick is doing is the way to treat innocent, law-abiding people?'

Henri Cheyrou turned away in embarrassment. It was obvious to Jean-Luc that his old school friend was extremely uncomfortable with the whole situation.

Jean-Luc looked back to Rodier.

'Very well,' he said and opened his mouth.

Rodier forced the pistol into his mouth and moved his face closer. 'How does that feel eh, Mister big man? Do you like the taste of it? Not easy to talk with a gun in your mouth is it? Just give me one reason to pull the trigger you arrogant arsehole, just one, and I will take great pleasure in spraying your brains all over this Jew hovel you are living in.'

Cheyrou stepped forward. 'Sergeant Rodier, please. Is this really necessary? What if he is telling the truth?'

Rodier looked at him but did not say anything. After a couple of seconds he withdrew the gun from Jean-Luc's mouth. Relieved that the immediate danger of having his head blown off was over, the metallic taste of the gun metal still in his mouth, he swallowed hard. However, he did not say anything.

'We are acting on information gained from a third party,' said Rodier. 'We can sort all that out at the police station.'

'So you have no proof then?' said Jean-Luc, regaining his composure. 'You are acting on a scurrilous rumour from someone who may have some kind of vendetta against me? This is ridiculous.'

For the first time in the conversation, Rodier seemed to hesitate. Pressing the new advantage in the exchange, Jean-Luc continued, appealing to his old friend.

'Henri, listen to me. You know I am not Jewish, don't you?'

Cheyrou opened his mouth nervously but before he could answer Jean-Luc carried on, knowing that his whole future, his whole life depended on what was said in the next minute or so.

'Can I suggest that you return to the gendarmerie and check your records? I did not register because there was no need for me to register. I am about as Jewish as you are and if you take me away now you are making a terrible mistake that I fear you will not be able to reverse.'

Cheyrou turned to Rodier. 'Maybe he has a point, Sergeant Rodier,' he said. 'We would not want to arrest an innocent man. Maybe it is best to do as he suggests.'

'Yes,' said Jean-Luc. 'Listen to him. I am going nowhere. I will stay here while you check whatever it is you have to check. May I also ask you to check the reliability and credibility of your source because whoever it is, they are either very much mistaken or very much vindictive. There was really no need to put your gun in my mouth. I have done nothing wrong.'

Rodier lowered the weapon, holding it loosely at his side. 'I see no reason why you cannot accompany us to the station while all this is checked out once more. Get your shoes on and come with us.'

'No. I totally refuse. I am a Frenchman and I will not be treated in such a manner.'

Cheyrou turned to his superior. 'Look, sergeant,' he said, 'I have known this man since I was a child and I can pretty much vouch for his honesty. I have no knowledge of his ancestry but I see no reason for him to lie. Maybe if we re-check our sources we could come back later. There is no need for any unpleasantness.'

Jean-Luc knew that everything was now on a knife edge. He turned from them and wiped the sweat from his brow before turning back.

Rodier was deep in thought, now outnumbered in his argument. He looked at Jean-Luc who was taller and bigger built then he was and Jean-Luc thought for a moment that maybe the man was a little worried that should he put up any kind of resistance to the arrest, Rodier may not come out of it pain free.

Cheyrou looked at him and something passed between the two of them. An understanding. The both of them knew that Jean-Luc was half-Jewish yet Cheyrou would not abandon his old friend. He was clearly troubled that his career in the gendarmerie had made him a puppet, through the Vichy regime, of the Nazis in Berlin and it clearly did not sit right with him.

After a moment's more deliberation, Rodier said, 'Very well. We will re-check what we have and then we may return later. Do not leave this building until you hear from us.'

Trying not to make his relief too obvious, Jean-Luc replied, 'Thank you, Sergeant Rodier. It is common sense. There has been a mistake made and I thank you for being reasonable. I will remain here as you say.'

Rodier holstered the pistol and without another word he walked from the apartment and down the steps back to the car.

Cheyrou hesitated. 'Jean-Luc,' he said. 'I can do no more for you. You need to get yourself away because he will be back, believe me. And when he comes back he will be with more than just me. And he will be mad as hell.'

'Don't worry, Henri,' said Jean-Luc. 'I am going.'

'This is terrible,' said Cheyrou, turning towards the door to leave. 'This is terrible for me, but I have no choice but to go along with them.'

Suddenly Jean-Luc felt a growing anger. He stopped him.

'Henri, you are one of my oldest friends and you come round here with that little bastard to take me away. To a place you know not where, but let's face it, we all know it's a place from which I would have been unlikely to return. The man puts a fucking gun in my mouth and threatens to kill me, for God's sake. And you want me to feel sorry for you because of it... because you have to do it... that you have no choice? We all have choices, Henri, we all have choices. So fuck you, my old friend, fuck you!'

Cheyrou looked at him for a moment longer before turning and following Rodier down the steps.

A minute later Jean-Luc heard the sound of the engine starting and the car being driven away. He stood without moving for a couple of moments and realised that he was in a state of mild shock. In the space of a few minutes, his whole life had been turned upside down. Catherine had been right. He had always known what she had said to be true but he had never wanted to believe it, stubbornly choosing to ignore it. His life had been simple and he had liked it that way, but now, due to circumstances beyond his control, it was changed forever.

He looked around the apartment that he had called home for so long, the apartment that he had grown to love and at once understood that he would probably never see it again. He would have to abandon it and all the possessions that he had built up over the years, including the heavy typewriter that had provided him with so much pleasure and was the source of his income.

He would have to leave and leave quickly. He moved to the bedroom and hastily packed a bag with clothes and other essentials, stuffing in as much as he could. Throwing it over his shoulder he moved to the door and on seeing the picture of his parents adorning the wall at the side he stopped for a moment to take one last look at it. For a second he was tempted to make room for it in his holdall and he started to take the bag down from his shoulder. But then he stopped himself and instead touched it with his fingertips, a final gesture of farewell to his previous life.

He opened the door and walked down the steps, not once looking back at the life he was leaving behind.

He had to get to Catherine. She would know what to do.

*

Two hours later, after withdrawing all of his money and closing his account at the bank in the centre of Lyon, Jean-Luc entered the shop owned by Catherine's sister, Monique. Luckily there were no customers, it being early afternoon, and Catherine looked up from behind the counter as he walked in.

Seeing his bag and the somewhat distraught look on his face she instantly walked to the door, locked it and put up the closed sign.

'I need your help,' he said simply. 'They came for me this morning.'

'My God,' she said shocked. 'Come through to the back quickly and tell me what happened.'

Following her, she led him to a small stock room at the rear of the shop where Monique was standing, preparing coffee. She looked up as they entered, a puzzled look upon her face.

'Monique,' said Catherine. 'This is Jean-Luc.'

'Ah, the elusive Jean-Luc,' she replied. 'Pleased to meet you finally.'

It was clear to Jean-Luc that Monique was not exactly pleased to meet him. He understood instantly that she did not have much time for him, the sarcastic tone in her voice quite evident. This was the first time that they had met, despite him having a relationship with her sister for over a year now. Many times he had been invited to meet Catherine's family and many times he had found a suitable excuse. The truth was that although he thought a lot about her, the relationship was not serious enough, in his view, for him to warrant getting close to her family. Obviously Monique thought that he was not treating her sister with respect.

Catherine indicated for him to sit in a chair beside a rack of dresses and he sat down sheepishly, placing the holdall at his feet. He realised he looked a forlorn figure, totally lost as to what to do, his life and future now in the hands of others. He had never felt so insignificant in his life.

As she knelt before him, her arms resting on his knees, he quickly told her of the morning's events and his flight to the city to find her, all the while her sister observing from a few feet away. When he had finished, Catherine stood up and went to speak to Monique.

He was able to observe Monique as her sister whispered hurriedly with her, both of them trying to keep their voices low so Jean-Luc could not understand what they were saying. He found that he did not mind. He realised that he was intruding on them, putting them both in danger by just being there but there was nothing else he could do. She was slightly taller than her younger sister with darker hair and eyes. She too had the large nose that was an obvious family inheritance but overall she was far more pretty than Catherine.

It was clear that Monique was arguing with Catherine, letting her know that just by having him in the building was extremely perilous for them all. At one point he felt like walking out as their backs were turned, getting away from them and leaving them alone but he quickly removed that thought from his head. He would have to wait and see how this played out before he abandoned himself to his fate outside.

After a few minutes they turned and Jean-Luc was surprised to see that it was Monique who approached him, Catherine going back into the shop.

'My sister seems to love you, Monsieur Descartes,' she said, standing before him as he looked up at her. 'Although I do not understand why, it appears that she does and so, for her, I am compelled to help her.'

Jean-Luc did not say anything, merely nodding in embarrassment.

'So here is what we will do,' she continued when she realised he was not going to reply. 'You will stay hidden here until it is time for the shop to close and then we will call some friends to come and collect you. We will continue working here today as though all is well, as though we know nothing of what has happened to you. Catherine has gone to open the shop again. I have no doubt that at some point the police will arrive here to ask about you and if we have closed the shop for no apparent reason then they will want to know why.'

Jean-Luc shifted nervously in his chair.

'I cannot profess for having any time for you, Monsieur, but my sister does and so be advised that I do this for her and for her alone.'

'I understand,' said Jean-Luc quietly. He was not going to argue with her and tell her that he loved her sister or anything as dramatic as that, particularly when he would not mean it. He was not going to lie to her. After all, he pretty much gathered that Catherine knew exactly about his feelings toward her.

'You cannot stay with either of us,' continued Monique. 'It is too dangerous for us. I know what Catherine does in her "spare time" and the less attention she can draw to herself the better. You will stay with our friends and they will decide what to do with you.'

Abruptly, she turned and walked back into the shop, leaving him sitting there, on the chair in the stock room, like a naughty schoolboy who had just been disciplined by the headmistress.

It was not very often that Jean-Luc Descartes felt inferior to anyone. Even when, as a Jew, the state told him he was and did everything to adopt the conqueror's insane policies, he always felt their actions achieved the opposite and actually made them inferior to him. Now this woman, who had spoken to him as though he was twelve years old, had finally achieved it and for some odd reason he found that he was smiling.

CHAPTER TWENTY-SIX

'So tell me everything that happened to you. The whole story.'

They had come for Jean-Luc at six o'clock. Three of them, all wearing mechanics overalls. They had taken him out of the back door to the alleyway where the deliveries were made, before bundling him into the back of a box van and placing a bag over his head. They had driven for only ten minutes before backing the van into a building, which smelled of engine oil and grease and had guided him up some stairs and then sat him on a chair before removing the cover from his head.

Jean-Luc looked around and observed the scene. Three of them, two young men of around his own age and one slightly older. The two young ones were very scruffy, with uncombed hair and grubby hands, which he presumed were from working on car engines all day. The older one, who seemed to be their leader, was sitting behind a desk facing him, staring at him intently. Upon the desk was a telephone and a pile of disordered paperwork with a number of sets of car keys. It was clear he was in an office above a vehicle repair shop and he could hear traffic outside, which indicated to him that he was probably on the outskirts of the city. He was aware of someone behind him, in the shadows in the corner of the room, and turned to see who it was but was immediately interrupted.

'Face me, Descartes,' said the man who had spoken to him from behind the desk. 'Do not look around. Concentrate on me. Nothing else is of your concern.'

'As you wish,' replied Jean-Luc. He was not altogether too happy with the way he was being treated. He was no criminal and did not like being treated as such.

'The whole story, please,' repeated the man. 'From beginning to end. Leave nothing out.'

Jean-Luc sat up in his chair. 'They came for me this morning... the police.'
'Why?'
'They say I am Jewish.'

'Are you?'

'It's not important to me.'

'It is to them. Are you?'

'Half. My mother was Jewish, my father Christian.'

'To them, that's Jewish. And you know it. Why did they not take you?'

'I knew one of the gendarmes. I was at school with him. He helped me to persuade the other one, Rodier he was called, to check their records again and that I would wait.'

'Yet he knew you to be Jewish. This friend of yours knew you were lying yet he assisted you.'

'He did.'

'His name?'

'Henri Cheyrou. I wasn't that friendly with him at school. In fact I had few male friends at school.'

The man opposite began to write. No one else spoke. Jean-Luc turned his head slightly, to get a glimpse of the mysterious figure that he sensed in the corner, but as he did so the man looked up and he stopped.

'How do we know that you are not a spy?' asked the man calmly.

'Excuse me?'

'How do we know you are not a spy?' he repeated calmly. 'It is a simple question.'

'I suppose you will have to take my word for it,' said Jean-Luc agitated. 'I'm not sure I care for the inference.'

'I will need more than your word.'

'What can I say to you? I do not know what to say. If you cannot or will not help me then let me walk out of here and I will work my situation out for myself.'

'There is a warrant out for your arrest, Descartes,' said the man. 'If what you say is true then you will be picked up by the morning and on a train to Drancy before you know it.'

'So, are you going to help me?' asked Jean-Luc with a sigh. 'All this cloak and dagger bullshit. Is it really necessary?'

'It is necessary, yes. Just answer the questions,' came a voice from behind him. The person in the shadows. There was something about the man's voice that Jean-Luc thought different. It did not sound quite right. Then he realised that the man was not French but a foreigner. He half turned but again was rebuked. 'Face forward. Do not turn around.'

Was this the handsome English spy that Catherine had alluded to? He had a strong feeling that it was.

'Listen,' said Jean-Luc resignedly. 'I just need your help. My friend Catherine, whom I know to be one of you, part of your little gang, has told me that you can help me. Believe me, I am on your side, I believe in what you do. But all I am is a simple writer of children's fiction, minding my own business in life, just plodding through it. Do you think that I need all this? My life has been turned upside down in the space of a few hours and I am really annoyed about it. Truly I am. If you do not want to believe me then that is up to you and fine by me. Just get me out of here. But if you can help me and want to help me then please cut out all this nonsense and let me know what you can do for me.'

The man behind the desk looked at him. 'Descartes,' he said. 'Our mutual friend, Catherine, speaks very highly of you. I cannot see it myself, but she does. We have to be certain you are what you say you are before we are willing to help you. Your name is on no Jewish register, but I suppose it is clear why not,' he conceded.

The man looked over Jean-Luc's shoulder, at the mysterious foreigner in the corner of the room as if waiting for an instruction. Then there was the sound of a door opening and closing and Jean-Luc presumed the man had just left the room.

'We will keep you here for a few days,' said the man looking back to him. 'We will make some checks and then we will let you know what we have decided. Walk freely about the building but keep out of sight of anyone outside. If you make any attempt to leave then it won't be the gendarmerie you will have to worry about because I will shoot you dead myself. Is that understood?'

'Yes,' replied Jean-Luc. 'I understand. Thank you.'

'In that case let me introduce myself to you. I am Claude Benoit, my two colleagues are Michel Trouvier,' the man to Benoit's right nodded to Jean-Luc, 'and this scruffy bastard to my left is Pierre Buque. They will be your chaperones for the next few days. Treat them with respect and do as they say.'

'Thank you, gentlemen,' said Jean-Luc. 'I really appreciate what you are doing for me.'

'We haven't done anything for you yet,' said Benoit with a small laugh. 'So I would hold back on your thanks for now if I was you.'

*

Jean-Luc spent the next few days attempting to keep himself as invisible as possible in the garage while he waited for the decision to be made as to what they were to do with him. He was made to wear a pair of old, dirty blue overalls that were stained and smelled of engine oil, in case a customer or anyone passing happened to look in and see him. He would hopefully be mistaken for a mechanic who was supposed to be in the building and not for the fugitive that he was. His new "friends" also made him cut his hair in an attempt to assist with the blending into the background process, along with growing some stubble to finish off the hiding of his normal appearance.

For the time being Jean-Luc was quite happy to let his life be controlled in this way. He had come to realise that ignoring the dangers that had faced him had nearly ended in his deportation and possible death and although he did not necessarily like it, he had to start listening to people and to even act upon their advice. He had seen Catherine only once since his change in circumstances and that was just a flying visit to see how he was doing two days ago. She had re-iterated what Benoit had told him and for the first time in a long while he was able to appreciate how strong a character the girl was.

However, he doubted he would see her for some considerable time as everyone thought it safest if she stayed away in case the police had any suspicions about her involvement with him. They had made enquiries with her about his whereabouts but she had been able to convince them that she had not seen him for some time and their relationship had ended many months ago. This visit had scared her, someone had obviously told the police about her involvement with him. Trust no one was all that she could say to him, for you never knew who was capable of stabbing you in the back.

Jean-Luc had not seen or been aware of the mysterious foreigner, whom he presumed to be an English agent, since the night of his arrival and surmised that the final decision on what was to happen to him would be made by the Englishman, whoever he was. Michel and Pierre, who he discovered to be cousins, had spoken in hushed tones about a "Grey Man" and Jean-Luc worked out that this was probably the stranger's code name. He was curious as to the story of this man but knew better than to ask questions about him, fearing his protectors may take his curiosity for something rather more sinister, which, of course, it was not.

He was growing to like his two babysitters. Pierre, the elder, was the obvious superior to his slightly younger relative and Michel seemed to hang onto his every word. Whenever Pierre asked Michel to do anything, like passing him a spanner or making a coffee, he would drop whatever he was currently doing in order to carry out the task. However, the banter between the two of them was quite endearing and Jean-Luc would occasionally find himself smiling at the fun they were having without really realising it. Pierre would often ask Michel to do ridiculous tasks and then wink at Jean-Luc to indicate he was having fun with him. This show of trust made it clear to him that they no longer saw Jean-Luc as a threat and had come to the correct conclusion that he was a fugitive from the authorities and therefore an ally and could be trusted.

Claude Benoit was the leader of this little group and as such had an authority over them that was respected and treated seriously. A short, stocky man of around five feet five inches who always seemed to have a rolled up cigarette between his very thin lips, Benoit had a dominant presence that guaranteed that respect. He was also the owner of the repair shop, so as well as being their leader, he was also their boss. Jean-Luc had not spoken much to the man since their conversation a few nights previously as he spent most of his time in the office on the telephone or with his head in paperwork, and he did not come across as the most approachable of people.

In the evening Jean-Luc slept in the basement, on a mattress on a cold concrete floor. He would often be joined by the black cat that spent its days roaming around the workshop watching the comings and goings of the mechanics as they worked on the cars, vans and other vehicles, sometimes getting in the way of the men as they worked to which they would hurl insults and the odd mistimed kick. Jean-Luc welcomed the warmth of the animal on his legs as he attempted to get whatever sleep he could.

On the morning of the fifth day he was asked by Pierre to go to Benoit's office as he had some news for him.

Benoit had his back to him as he entered the office, filing some paperwork into a large metal cabinet, standing on his toes in order to reach the back of the top drawer. Upon hearing Jean-Luc enter he turned his head, a cigarette hanging from his bottom lip as if glued to it and said, 'Sit down, please, I will be with you in a minute.'

Jean-Luc sat down in the same chair he had occupied on the night of his enforced fleeing, facing the still untidy desk. Eventually Benoit finished what he was doing, shut the drawer noisily and then turned to him.

'We have a little problem, my friend,' he remarked.

Jean-Luc was pleased to hear himself referred to in this somewhat endearing way. It gave him faith that these people now trusted him.

'Why is that?' he asked. 'Do I need to be worried?'

Ignoring the second question Benoit replied, sitting down to face him, 'We were hoping to have some things in place to have you moved but it may be some time before this can happen now. Things beyond our control I'm afraid.'

'So what do you suggest?'

'We have had a chance to make enquiries and to study you,' admitted Benoit casually. 'We believe you may have some qualities to offer our organisation.'

'I have told Catherine before that this war has nothing to do with me. I want no part of it.'

'Do you think we do?' asked Benoit, sitting back in his chair. 'Do you think any of us want to do any of this? Living constantly in fear of our lives? We cannot ignore it and as Frenchmen we are not willing to allow those in Vichy to tell us to bow down to the Nazis, particularly when the Nazis are not even here. You claim to be a patriot, Jean-Luc. As a patriot you cannot sit back and watch this happen. You also admit to being a Jew… Okay a half-Jew and say this means nothing to you. Well, maybe not. Maybe it does not mean a thing to you, but it means a hell of a lot to the Germans and for that reason alone you need to be worried. You know of the rumours and have seen it first-hand. Otherwise why are you sitting before me now?'

Jean-Luc found that he could think of no argument to counter what Benoit was saying.

Benoit continued. 'They are rounding up all the Jews they can find, Jean-Luc. How long do you think you will last out there on your own? They are rounding them all up, our own police force, our own people and shipping them out to a holding area in Drancy, near Paris. Giving our own people to the Germans. Can you believe that?'

'Okay,' said Jean-Luc after a while. 'What if I agree to join you? What could I do for you? I am a man on the run. A man with a price on my head, so to speak. Wouldn't I be a dangerous person to have around?'

'You are also a man with nothing to lose. You have already lost everything.'

Benoit stubbed out the cigarette he had been smoking and then picked up a cigarette case from the desk in front of him and took out another. He offered the case to Jean-Luc but he shook his head. Benoit shrugged and then placed the new cigarette into his mouth and lit it from a lighter he took from his pocket.

'Okay,' he said, blowing out smoke and leaning back in his chair once more. 'Here's the deal. Here is what we will do.'

Jean-Luc remained impassive. He was prepared to hear what they had to say and if he was totally honest with himself, he knew that he did not really have much of a choice. They could not let him just walk out and take his chances on the streets. If he was picked up, he knew the identities of their group and there was a chance he could betray them, if tortured. He knew that Benoit would not allow that to happen and would probably have him killed.

'Go on,' he said eventually. 'I am willing to listen to you.'

'I believe you are very good with words,' said Benoit.

'It has been said,' replied Jean-Luc. 'I have had some things published.'

'I also hear that you are a patriot and something of a communist.'

'A patriot, yes. A communist is a matter of opinion.'

'Okay,' said Benoit. 'I would like to offer you a job. We are a fairly new group and have only recently had training. You may have been aware of an Englishman with us when we brought you here.' Jean-Luc nodded. 'Well, that Englishman was sent here to train us and brought with him some equipment. Weapons, explosives and a radio. He is our contact across the Channel. We do not know of his real name but we know him as "Francois" or the "Grey Man". Why, I have no idea.

'If you were to accept the job then we would take you to a location away from here where we would pass on our knowledge to you. Call it a training course if you want. You would be required to assist with producing literature to further our cause and to occasionally assist in operations.'

'What type of operations?' asked Jean-Luc.

'As yet I do not know. Everything we plan has to be approved by Francois back in London before we can take any kind of action. He takes his direction from the Free French and the Allies.'

'And what if I decide not to take you up on your kind offer?'

Benoit offered a small smile. 'Then you will stay hidden here until we decide what to do with you.'

Jean-Luc laughed humourlessly. 'I don't really have much choice then do I?'

'You always have a choice, my friend,' said Benoit grimly. 'There are always choices to be made, we all have free will. What matters is will you make the right one?'

Jean-Luc sighed and stood up.

Benoit rose from the chair and took the cigarette from his smiling mouth. He then held out his free hand and as Jean-Luc shook it he could not prevent the feeling that he was entering a game that he was not altogether too confident about winning.

But then, was not Benoit correct? He had said that he was a man with nothing to lose and he could not argue with that. He had nothing and no one, he was a non-person, a loner, unsafe in his own country. He needed a purpose to his life and maybe what this man was offering was just that. Maybe he was making the right choice. Time would be the judge of that, he thought, and he sat back down as Claude Benoit took a bottle of cognac and two glasses from the desk drawer for them to toast their new agreement.

CHAPTER TWENTY-SEVEN

Lyon, France, April 1943

Jean-Luc kept the engine running as he waited outside the apartment block, a revolver hidden under a newspaper on his lap. Catherine sat in the passenger seat beside him smoking a cigarette and blowing the smoke out of the window that was half open. Occasionally she would turn to him nervously and he would smile at her encouragingly, offering what support he could.

At times like these, waiting for something to happen, the inevitable action that was imminent, he found himself completely relaxed and at ease. He had thought that he would be nervous, that his heart would beat frantically and his hands would shake with the fear that he presumed he was supposed to feel, but he had always been remarkably calm, his head clear and in total control of his wits. He was able to function. Catherine, on the other hand, always looked the opposite and he had recently lost his temper with her after a mission because she could not stop shaking, stuttering over her words and he had been fearful that they would be compromised because of it. Maybe she was not up to this after all, he had thought, but then she had always played her part perfectly, despite the emotions she showed.

She ignored his smile and turned back to look out of the side window, keeping watch for any passing German or Milice patrols that may inadvertently stumble across them as Pierre and Michel carried out the operation, which had been meticulously planned over the previous two weeks.

The target had been selected carefully. A high roller in the Milice, a collaborator who was fair game and deserved something much worse than the bullet he was going to receive this evening. For him it would be quick, unlike the unfortunates who he gladly handed over to his Nazi puppet masters. People like that made Jean-Luc's skin crawl and they deserved everything that came to them.

He sighed to himself and looked out of his side window where he saw a young boy across the street wheeling along a bicycle with a flat tyre, tears staining his grubby cheeks as he took it home. He noticed that the child's knees were grazed and he smiled to himself. Children, he thought. What strange creatures. He could barely remember ever being one. But then he could hardly remember anything about his life up to just over six months ago when everything had changed. What happened before that was as though it had happened to somebody else.

After he had agreed to join the circuit he had been spirited away by his new friends to undergo basic Maquis training in the hills to the south of Lyon. He had learned how to handle the various weaponry that the British had provided: handguns, grenades and the rather awkward Sten gun Mark II with its side magazine. They had taught him how to plant bombs to cause maximum damage to whatever target the leadership saw fit to destroy and how to handle himself if he was caught and interrogated. He found that he had enjoyed it all despite his initial misgivings. He felt that he had finally found a sense of purpose and belonging with this little group of likeminded patriots and he could not decide whether this was the happiest he had been for some considerable time.

It was a far cry to writing children's fiction or the novel that he had left in his apartment, half completed, when he had been forced to flee his previous life. Although he had been recruited for his writing abilities, he had not once been asked to pen a single line and had been employed instead as a lookout, courier and driver. However, he was quite happy with this arrangement as they also provided him with a place to live, hot meals and even a few francs when he assisted them in the repair shop.

He had briefly met the Englishman twice now, this Francois or "Grey Man" as he had initially been referred to, and was taken with his professionalism and the fluency of his French. He had not actually spoken to him himself, merely being able to observe him for a brief time when he last visited. If he had not known the man to be a foreigner, he would have easily believed that he was a native of France. He even looked French if that was at all possible, his hair combed back and a small thin moustache over his top lip. He had come over to France just that once more, not long after Jean-Luc had joined them and he remembered standing in the field with other volunteers with a torch in his hand as the Royal Air Force light bomber circled overhead, waiting with them to see the white canopy in the moonlight as the agent dropped down, followed by three canisters of supplies for the circuit. The Englishman had brought with him more weapons and ammunition and quite a large sum of money, which he had strapped to his body and was extremely reluctant to part with. This "Francois" was the undoubted leader of the circuit, the handler who sorted out their supplies and logistics, passing on information and instructions from the leaders in London, leaving Benoit in charge when he had to return to England or had business elsewhere. Jean-Luc was aware there were many such circuits in the area, all remaining independent of each other, probably for security reasons, the only link between them being this English agent.

His new friends and colleagues had managed to get him forged papers in the name of "David Pascal" and all traces of Jean-Luc Descartes were now gone, as though he had been wiped off the face of the earth like so many other Jews that they had heard about. In a way the Nazis had succeeded in killing Jean-Luc Descartes. For the moment anyway, he simply did not exist.

Catherine had been totally correct when she had said that the Germans would not leave the south of the country unoccupied for very long and on November 8th, just over five months ago, they had swooped south to take the control away from the collaborators at Vichy. It had not taken them long to establish strongholds in all the major cities, particularly here in Lyon where German troops seemed to be everywhere. The Gestapo, led by the Nazi Hauptsturmführer Klaus Barbie, now had a large presence in the city, taking over the six storey Hotel Terminus on the Cours de Verdun Rambaud, near the railway station, to use as their headquarters, actively seeking out Jews, Resistance members and any other "undesirable" for transportation to the camps in the east. Stories were emerging of torture and sadistic practices taking place within the hotel, which, if true, did a lot to convince Jean-Luc that his small contribution to the Maquis was not only worthwhile and just, but also very necessary.

And then there was this newly formed Milice, with its dirty little bastards that he hated more than anyone, more than the SS and the Gestapo combined. They were Frenchmen; made up of the misfits, miscreants, halfwits and thugs that would have been laughed at, ignored and deemed insignificant before the war. They actively assisted the Nazis in rounding up Jews and harassing the general population, walking about openly in their ridiculous blue jackets and berets, using torture on any Maquis they caught to gain information to help them capture more and disrupt Resistance activity, which was growing stronger in the area. Jean-Luc often dreamed of the day when he would see them all hanging from the nearest tree or lamp post, when the rest of the French people, the good people of France, took their retribution.

Catherine turned her head and looked at him, the cigarette shaking slightly between her fingers. 'What is taking them so long?'

'Stop worrying,' he replied calmly. 'The apartment is on the fifth floor and they will be using the stairs on the way down. You didn't need to come on this one anyway. We could have managed without you.'

'Of course I am going to come,' she said irritably. 'I just can't understand why you are always so calm all the time. Nothing seems to bother you.'

'Maybe that's just the way I am,' he replied. 'Don't worry about it.'

She flicked the cigarette butt out of the window and took another from the pack on the dashboard. As she lit it, he said, 'Smoking all those cigarettes will not be doing you any good.'

'What do you care?' she snapped. 'You don't care about anything or anyone in this world, not even yourself half the time.'

He did not reply but turned his head to look out of the window once more.

After a few moments Catherine said softly. 'I'm sorry. I didn't mean that. It's just that operations make me nervous. I just want this to be over. The whole thing. It's all starting to get me down.'

Jean-Luc took her hand and kissed it. 'We'll be fine. Just concentrate on keeping lookout. Do your job.'

She pulled her hand away a little too sharply and turned her head back to the task. She wound the window down with the handle and adjusted the wing mirror slightly.

Jean-Luc smiled to himself. Poor Catherine, he thought. He would never love her and she was coming to understand that now. It was not because there was something wrong with her, it was just that he was a man incapable of love, incapable of passionate emotions of that kind. He had strong views on politics, he knew what was right and wrong, that sort of thing, and he was very much capable of hate, but love, love was something alien to him and he did not know why.

A minute of silence passed and then Catherine said sharply, 'Here they are now.'

Jean-Luc did not turn around but heard both the rear doors open and close and felt a shift in weight within the vehicle.

'Okay,' he heard Pierre say. 'Let's go, my friend.'

Jean-Luc put the car into gear and pulled away from the kerbside, entering the traffic at a normal speed. He did not want to attract any undue attention, so stuck to the speed limits, driving calmly and steadily. He looked in the rear view mirror and saw Michel wiping sweat from his brow after placing the Sten gun that he had been carrying under his overcoat into the footwell in front of him. His cousin sat calmly, lighting a cigarette as he gazed disinterestedly at the passing scenery.

He took a circuitous route on the way back to Benoit's garage in case anyone was following them but after a few minutes he was able to determine that this was not the case and they had got away unobserved.

'How did it go?' asked Catherine after a while, turning in her seat to look at the two men.

'It is done,' said Pierre calmly.

Michel was more enthusiastic. 'We did not give him time to beg for his life,' he said. 'When he opened the door, he did not know what hit him, the little shit, standing there with a glass of wine in his hand. I punched him in the face and then Pierre here dragged him into the bedroom and put a bullet in his neck. All very quick and we saw no one going up the stairs and no one coming down. A perfect hit. It…'

'That's enough, Michel,' said Pierre calmly. 'Like I said, it is done. We do not need to go into any details. Leave it now.'

Michel looked at Catherine sheepishly but did not say anything further. Catherine turned back around.

As they drove along, they came to a junction and stopped at a red traffic light. As they waited for the lights to change, Jean-Luc became aware of a large vehicle that had pulled up alongside them, to their left. He turned his head slightly and realised that it was a troop carrier, a German Opel with the tarpaulin cover removed revealing two rows of combat soldiers with MP40 machine pistols strapped across their chests. Some of them looked casually across at the black Citroen he was driving.

Turning his head slightly he said quietly, 'Make sure that your weapons are concealed… Don't look or panic. They do not suspect anything.'

He could see that Catherine had begun to shake.

'Catherine,' he said calmly, 'Take control of yourself. Relax.'

He turned his head back and saw that the passenger in the cab was looking directly into the car, directly at Jean-Luc. The soldier's face was impassive and uninterested, bored with the journey he was taking and Jean-Luc understood that he was merely looking at them for somewhere to place his eyes and nothing more than that. As long as they all remained calm, they would be all right.

After a few moments, the man turned his head to face forward before the lights turned to green and they carried on with their journeys, Jean-Luc turning right and the Opel continuing ahead.

'Oh my God,' said Catherine. 'Jesus Christ. Do you think they suspected something?'

'For Christ's sake,' said Jean-Luc. 'No I don't. You are going to have to stop behaving like this or we will have to keep you away.'

Catherine was furious. 'You have no right to decide what I can and cannot do. I take my orders from Claude, not you.'

'Take it as advice then.'

She turned to look at Michel and Pierre. 'What do you two think?'

'Keep us out of this,' replied Pierre, closing his eyes. It was obvious that he was embarrassed having to witness the breakdown of the relationship of the two lovers in the front of the car. 'We will discuss it when we debrief later.'

'This is ridiculous,' said Catherine sulking down into the seat. 'Ridiculous.'

A few minutes later Jean-Luc pulled into Benoit's vehicle repair shop and cut off the engine. Michel and Pierre jumped out of their seats and pulled the roller shutter doors down behind the Citroen using the chains at the side and when it was fully closed, they returned to the car to assist Jean-Luc and Catherine in taking the weapons from the rear of the vehicle where they wrapped them in hessian sacks and then stored them beneath the floorboards at the bottom of the vehicle repair pit.

Five minutes later they were in Benoit's office each with a cup of coffee in their hands, Claude sitting behind the desk smoking one of his roll-ups.

When they had debriefed the mission, which had gone exactly to plan, the conversation moved to other things.

'When can we start killing Germans?' asked Michel. 'It is all well and good knocking off collaborators but we need to begin proper action.'

'Patience my dear Michel,' said Benoit, relaxing back into his chair. 'The time will come for that. I have spoken to Francois about it and not just yet. Apparently something happened in Prague last summer and they do not want a repeat of that here. So it is just the Milice and any other collaborators for the time being. The Germans do not care too much about them.'

Jean-Luc leaned forward. 'What about the infrastructure? Are we going to get a chance to use those explosives you have got stored in the back?'

Benoit looked at him and smiled. 'Jean-Luc… David… whatever you are called now… my Jewish friend. Again, patience. We await direction from our English colleagues.'

'Why should the English dictate what we do?' said Catherine. 'They are not here on the ground.'

Benoit sighed and blew out some smoke into the air above their heads.

'The English are not here, that is true,' he said calmly. 'I applaud your enthusiasm, my friends, believe me I do. But we must take direction from others for the time being. They have a plan and we must carry it out. For the time being we will disrupt them by hitting a few collaborators and blowing up the odd radio mast when they ask, but until they say otherwise, we keep away from killing Germans. Don't get me wrong, there is nothing more I would like than to engage them in open war, but that is not possible and so we must remain patient, vigilant and steadfast. I have nothing more to say on the matter.'

Benoit looked at Jean-Luc. 'Are you ready to advance my friend?'

Everyone turned to look at Jean-Luc who frowned. 'What do you mean?'

Benoit smiled at him. 'The next target, I am sure you will find interesting. I have picked him out just for you and I want you to carry out the operation. You will be the gunman.'

He slid a folded piece of paper across the desk and Jean-Luc picked it up. He unfolded it and read it, raising his eyebrows slightly as he did so.

'Can you manage that, do you think?' asked Benoit. 'Do you have the stomach for it?'

Jean-Luc looked at him, deep into his eyes. 'We will find out won't we?'

CHAPTER TWENTY-EIGHT

Two weeks passed without anything significant happening within the circuit. Business was good at the repair shop, keeping them all busy and after work they often shared a couple of bottles of wine in the local bars. Jean-Luc was beginning to like the way his life had turned. The sense of belonging to something significant had now become strong within him and he had grown to like and respect the people around him.

His relationship with Catherine had steadied. She had not been to see him for over a week now and he was beginning to think that she was moving on from him. He was not quite sure but he had the feeling that she was now seeing someone else. He did not know how he felt about this. He did not know if he was a little jealous or a little happy for her, he could not be sure. In the end he put it down to indifference. He did not really care one way or the other.

When she did see him, she would answer his questions with one or two word answers and their conversations were now restricted to pleasantries and small talk, a far cry from how they had been a few months ago when they used to share a bed together.

He had gone with Benoit the previous week to take a look at the new target's place of residence, a small modest house that he shared with his wife and two children in the suburbs to the north of the city. There was a chained and padlocked exit leading to an alleyway at the rear that could be used as a getaway route. However, Jean-Luc had expressed his reservations about carrying out the mission at the man's home, preferring to keep the family out of it if at all possible, so they had hit a stalemate with what to do. Benoit had continued with the surveillance of the man but was so far unable to come up with an alternative plan that did not include his family being involved.

'There is only one way of doing it, Jean-Luc,' he said. 'We go in the evening as it is getting dark. We will have to do this pretty soon otherwise, with the nights getting shorter and it getting dark later, we may miss the opportunity.'

'I don't believe we really have an opportunity,' said Jean-Luc. 'Not with doing it at his house anyway. Why can't we make this as simple as possible?

We could just do it in the street. I could walk up, pop him and then we get away in a stolen car or something.'

'In other words, with no proper plan?' laughed Benoit. 'That is the surest way of it going awry. Too many witnesses, too many chances for it to go wrong, which leads to the risk of being caught being far too great. I will not compromise this group, my friend. We may have to abandon this one if you are not prepared to go to his house to do it.'

Jean-Luc sighed. 'No,' he said. 'I want this one to happen. I concede to you, Claude. Whatever you think is best. Formulate a plan and then let's do it.'

So, two days later, Jean-Luc found himself, along with Pierre, exiting the back of the black sedan they had stolen the previous night, driven by Michel with Catherine in the passenger seat acting as look out once again. This time, Benoit had joined them and was sitting in a small white Fiat parked at the corner of the street. He would sound his horn if any patrols came their way, to warn the two carrying out the mission of their presence.

'Good luck,' said Catherine as he exited the vehicle and when he looked back at her he noticed that her face was tinged with sadness. He realised then that she was still in love with him, despite all that had happened and however much she tried to fight her feelings for him, she still loved him.

Both he and Pierre wore long overcoats, which looked slightly out of place in the late April dusk, but they were necessary to hide the weapons they both carried. Pierre, with a cocked and ready Sten Mark II concealed under his, would be able to bring it up and fire from a magazine of thirty-two rounds if necessary. Jean-Luc, a British army service revolver in his pocket, gripped tightly with his right hand. He too could pull the weapon out of hiding immediately if the situation required it. Both walked confidently to the target's house.

Jean-Luc was still not happy with the plan. He did not want children to witness the killing. The man's wife was fair game as far as he was concerned, but children should remain out of it. However, Jean-Luc could not help feeling that the man had it coming and deserved what was about to happen to him. He was not altogether comfortable with gunning down a man in cold blood but he balanced that misgiving with the knowledge that this man, who was about to meet his end, had willingly assisted in the rounding up of French Jews on behalf of the Nazis. He had not cared about what would happen to any of them, men, women and children but knew that they would be transported to their probable deaths. Yes, thought Jean-Luc, the bastard had it coming to him and should take the medicine that he was about to receive.

The plan was simple. As soon as they were in the house, they would rip the telephones from the walls and Pierre would round up the family in the front room. Jean-Luc would then take the target to the kitchen, or another room away from the family, where he would carry out the job and then they would run back out to the waiting car and get away. If they heard any sounding of car horns, they were to presume that a patrol was nearby, so would either abandon the plan or get out as fast as they could, depending on how far they had gone.

The house sat back from the road slightly but the front door and garden could be seen from the houses either side, which gave him cause for concern. It was a modest two storey building with an attic room to the centre of the roof where Jean-Luc observed a lamp in the window, providing light for the room as the night drew in. He noticed a small shadow moving about in it and presumed this would be one of the two children that they knew lived there.

They approached the green front door and Pierre used the brass knocker upon it, slamming it hard three times. Jean-Luc pulled down the ski mask with his free left hand and watched as Pierre did the same.

'Ready?' asked Pierre quietly and Jean-Luc nodded. Again he was surprised at how he felt nothing. No fear, no sense of excitement, no adrenalin being pumped around his body. Was there something wrong with him? He could not work himself out. He did not seem to care what happened, no thought for his own safety. He could understand why Catherine got so frustrated with him.

The door was opened by a short plump woman with dark brown hair who was in her mid-forties. On seeing them both standing there wearing ski-masks she took a step back and was about to let out a scream until Jean-Luc jumped forward and grabbed hold of her firmly and placed his hand over her mouth.

'Keep quiet, madame,' he whispered into her ear. 'We are not here for you or your children.'

The woman was clearly petrified, her face red and tears immediately started to pour down her face. She let out a low whimper, which Jean-Luc did well to stifle.

'Who is it, Edith?' came a man's voice from a room to their left.

Pierre instantly lifted the Sten gun from under his overcoat and marched purposefully to the room where the voice had come from. Jean-Luc followed close behind, pushing the woman ahead of him, his hand still firmly over her mouth.

They entered the room to see a young boy of around ten years old sitting quietly on a sofa reading a book. The man they had come for was on a chair at a writing desk still in the uniform of a sergeant of the Gendarmerie and Jean-Luc recognised him immediately. He rose from the chair, dropping the pen he had been using onto the floor, his mouth agape as he tried to comprehend what was happening in his own home.

Jean-Luc pushed the woman forward towards him and she ran into the gendarme's arms, burying her head into his shoulder. The man instantly moved towards his son, dragging her along with him. The boy, for some reason, moved his head from his book for a brief moment before carrying on reading, indifferent to the scene in front of him. It must be a good story, thought Jean-Luc, smiling to himself behind the ski-mask.

'What do you want?' demanded the gendarme defiantly. 'Take what you will but leave my family alone.'

'We have not come for your things or for your family,' said Pierre, waving the sub-machine gun around. 'You have another boy. Call him down now.'

'He is asleep upstairs,' said the man, stroking his wife on the back in a feeble attempt at calming her. 'Leave him out of this.'

'Very well,' said Pierre. Turning to Jean-Luc he said, 'Okay my friend, it is time.'

This was the cue for Jean-Luc to complete his part of the mission. He quickly moved forward grabbing the woman from the gendarme's arms, but she clung on tightly, letting out a low wail. She was clearly clever enough to understand what the masked intruders intended.

'Let go, Edith,' said her husband. 'You will make matters worse. Let these men take what they want then they will go and leave us in peace.'

Eventually she let go of him and he stepped away from her. 'Sit with Andre,' he said to her. 'This will soon be over.'

Jean-Luc moved forward and grabbed the man by the arm, thrusting the pistol into his neck. He forced him ahead, back through the hallway and dragged him unceremoniously to the kitchen on the opposite side of the building. He knew the man was small but was still surprised at how easily he could manhandle him.

'Take what you want, I have told you. Just leave us alone and go.'

'Get on your knees,' said Jean-Luc calmly.

'What... what?'

'You heard me, you little weasel bastard, get on your knees.'

At last the man began to realise what was happening. He now understood that these were not robbers who had simply come to take away the family silver. They were Maquis. They were here, in his house, and they intended something a lot more sinister than robbery.

Realising he was in mortal danger the gendarme began to plead. 'Please, monsieur, there must be some kind of mistake…'

'On your knees, I won't tell you again,' repeated Jean-Luc, forcing him down.

'My wife and children are here. You cannot do this here, in my home. There must be some kind of mistake. There is no reason for this.'

'You are guilty of treason,' said Jean-Luc coldly. 'You have assisted the enemy in rounding up our countrymen and women… and children… to send them off to their deaths.'

'I have done no such thing,' said the man as Jean-Luc forced him to his knees, pressing the barrel of the gun against the base of his neck. 'You are mistaken, I am a friend of the Maquis. I am a patriot.'

'Liar!' said Jean-Luc venomously. 'You don't recognise my voice do you, Rodier?'

The man hesitated slightly as Jean-Luc took off the ski-mask to reveal his features. He had changed his appearance since they had last met, his hair now short and his face full of stubble but Rodier recognised his eyes. Jean-Luc could see it. 'Do you recognise me now?'

Rodier looked into Jean-Luc's eyes and he could see that there was no point in lying or begging any more. He knew that his words would be wasted. 'You!' he said, the terror evident in his voice. 'You! I knew you were lying to me, you Jew bastard. I fucking knew it… and so did that fool, Cheyrou. Do you know where he is now, eh? Do you? Well I'll tell you, you little…'

He was cut short by Jean-Luc who had moved the revolver to the man's lips and forced it inside his mouth, knocking painfully against his teeth in the process.

'Oh shut up,' he said calmly. 'You nauseating little man. I can guess what you arseholes have done with my old friend. But to more immediate matters. Do you remember when this role was reversed, Rodier? When you put that gun in my mouth thinking you were the big man. Well, not so funny now is it?'

Rodier tried to mumble something but Jean-Luc was not interested in anything the man had to say.

'Well, Rodier, a piece of advice for you. If you are going to put a gun in a man's mouth, don't waffle on, thinking how big it makes you feel. Pull the trigger. Oh, and by the way, you were right. I am Jewish.'

With that, Jean-Luc squeezed the trigger, firing a bullet into the man's brain. It exited at the back of his head, spraying blood, brain matter and pieces of skull across the room, splattering against the far wall. The sound was muffled slightly but it was still loud enough to be heard in the front room, where Pierre stood guard over Rodier's wife and son and Jean-Luc heard the woman let out a shriek and begin to sob uncontrollably, calling the pair of them bastards and much worse.

Jean-Luc was again surprised at his lack of feeling for what he had carried out. He felt as though he had just killed a spider, or a rat, and the feeling of compassion for the man or his family was simply not there. Maybe he did have a heart of stone as Catherine had told him on many occasions.

Pushing all other thoughts from his mind, he pulled the ski-mask back over his face and moved quickly to the hallway where he was met by Pierre. He could see beyond, into the living area where Madame Rodier and her son sat on the sofa. She was sobbing, clinging onto her son.

When Jean-Luc thought back later of what happened next, he remained surprised at the speed of it all. It seemed to happen so quickly that he found it hard to process when he later had to recall it.

There was a sudden noise coming from outside. The sound of a car horn being pressed. Three times. It was the signal from Benoit that things were not as they should be in the street. Jean-Luc moved to the hallway window and saw the white Fiat, being driven by Benoit, moving down the street and across the front of the house where it then turned the corner and disappeared out of sight. He looked further up the road and saw that the stolen black sedan was still where it should be and he wondered how Catherine was coping. He prayed that she and Michel did not panic and leave Pierre and himself stranded.

Pierre joined him at the small window and they both saw a truck carrying German troops appear, driving slowly down the roadway. 'If we stay where we are for a few minutes, they will pass by. They have no way of knowing that we are here,' he said and Jean-Luc nodded in agreement.

Suddenly there was a noise from behind them and they both turned around to see a boy of perhaps twelve years old coming down the stairs that separated the living area from the kitchen. What made the situation particularly bad was that he was carrying a small pistol in his right hand and was pointing it at the pair of them. Maybe he had heard the commotion downstairs and taken the gun from his father's room, Jean-Luc had no way of knowing, but he presented a very real threat, particularly with the enemy just outside the house. He remembered thinking that they had made a huge mistake in not getting the family together before they carried out the execution, even if the young boy seemingly posed no threat to them at the time.

The boy pointed the weapon at Pierre and fired a single shot, hitting him at the top of his thigh, forcing his leg to immediately give way and for him to collapse onto the parquet floor, sliding down the wall as he did so.

Before Jean-Luc could react to prevent it from happening, Pierre raised the Sten gun and let off a short burst. The bullets hit the young boy square in the chest, throwing his body back up the stairs before it settled and then slowly slid down to the bottom, coming to rest in an untidy heap at the foot of the stairs.

For a brief moment nothing happened. Nobody moved. Jean-Luc looked at Pierre who was clearly in shock, both from the wound in his leg and the reaction to what had just taken place. 'What have I done?' he whispered, his eyes staring vacantly at the corpse of Rodier's son. 'God forgive me… what have I done?'

Hearing the noise and fearing the worst, Madame Rodier came racing out of the room and on seeing her son lying dead at the foot of the stairs she started to wail uncontrollably, moving towards the two Resistance fighters, flailing her fists at them as she did so.

Ignoring her and the blows that she was raining down on them, Jean-Luc turned his head to see that the truck had stopped at the front of the property, the driver and the passenger from the cab getting out and looking at the house curiously. They had clearly heard something and were about to investigate.

'Shit,' said Jean-Luc as another blow hit him, the woman inconsolable and trying to peel the ski-mask from his face.

He raised his pistol and hit her on the side of the head causing her to collapse unconscious to the floor. It was surprising how quiet the house now became.

He again cautiously looked out of the window and saw the two men at the gate, talking together, deciding whether they were going to approach the property and investigate the noise they had just heard. He also noted that the car containing Michel and Catherine had now left and he hoped that they would do as was planned should anything like this happen, and pick them up from the street to the rear of Rodier's house.

'Can you walk?' he said to Pierre who was still staring vacantly at the boy he had just killed.

'Can you walk?' Jean-Luc repeated more strongly and Pierre was broken from his trance.

'Yes… I think so… with a little help.'

'Okay,' said Jean-Luc. 'Let us pray that our friends have not abandoned us. We need to get out at the back.'

Jean-Luc became aware that they were being watched. It was the younger of the two brothers who was standing looking at them from the doorway to the living room.

'Go back and sit on the sofa,' urged Jean-Luc. 'Wait for the police to come.'

The boy looked at him for a brief moment and then walked back into the room and sat down, just as Jean-Luc had ordered.

'Come on, Pierre,' said Jean-Luc, putting the revolver into his pocket and retrieving the Sten from the floor, where it lay in a pool of Pierre's blood. 'Lean on me.'

There was a loud knock on the door behind them as they hurriedly passed through the kitchen towards where they could see the back door. Thankfully there was a key in the lock and Jean-Luc turned it and opened the door.

The back of the house led to a long yard with a number of ostentatious stone statues of Greek and Roman gods. At the far end was a tall wall with broken glass embedded at the top to deter intruders, with an iron gate in the middle that led to an alleyway and Jean-Luc was grateful to see the black sedan waiting for them, Catherine at the wheel. Michel was out of the vehicle holding a set of bolt croppers with a second Sten gun strapped to his side. He quickly broke the chain that secured the gate, threw the tool to the side and then opened the gate to allow Jean-Luc and Pierre through. He pointed the gun in the direction of the house.

Jean-Luc was aware that the front door to the property was being forced open. No doubt the Germans had looked through the window and seen the carnage that he and Pierre had just left behind.

Michel stepped behind them, into the yard, and fired a short burst. Jean-Luc did not look back to see what he was firing at as he was concentrating on getting the wounded Pierre into the car and to safety. Opening the back door he bundled the bleeding man into the back of the car and, leaving the door open, he turned to assist Michel.

The two Germans had managed to take cover and return fire. Jean-Luc found cover behind the large wall, but Michel had managed to get himself trapped on the wrong side, and had been forced to lie on the ground behind one of the statues.

'Shit,' shouted Jean-Luc. 'We need to get out of here, the others will be coming. There are at least fifteen of them.'

He leaned to the side and fired a quick burst towards the back door and was immediately met with a return of fire from the kitchen window, which one of the German soldiers had smashed with the butt of his machine pistol.

'Michel, Michel!' he shouted and fired another burst towards the window. He was aware that the spare magazines were in the back of the car and he had no way of getting to them before the Germans would be on top of them. 'Michel!' he shouted again.

He risked taking a look around the side of the wall and saw instantly that Michel was hit. He could not tell if he was dead but it was a head wound and there was blood forming in a pool in front of him where he lay motionless his body resting over the Sten gun.

Jean-Luc made a decision.

He went to the car and shouted at Catherine who was sitting with her hands clinging tightly to the steering wheel, 'Move over, let me drive.'

Throwing his weapon into the rear with Pierre, who by now was lying across the back seat, a look of agony and despair on his face, he pushed her into the passenger seat and got behind the wheel. He put the car into gear and then pushed his foot down hard on the accelerator, the car lurching forward.

'What about Michel?' asked Catherine. 'What about Michel?'

'Michel's gone,' answered Jean-Luc. 'Reload the Sten. Hurry!'

The urgency in his voice and the aggressive tone made her react. She leaned over to retrieve the weapon and Pierre handed her a spare magazine from the bag that was on the back seat. She quickly reloaded it and cocked the weapon, making it ready to fire.

'Where are you going?' she said desperately on seeing the route he was taking. 'This is going to take us back near them.'

'I know,' said Jean-Luc and steered the car around a bend and braked hard. 'Wait here.'

He grabbed the weapon and opened the door. 'I will be very quick. Stay here,' he shouted behind him.

As he walked quickly around the corner, he could see the German truck ahead of him. All the passengers, the German soldiers, had now disembarked the vehicle and were pouring into the house and to the houses and gardens around it. They were clearly not yet aware that they had fled the scene.

Moving slowly and deliberately, he aimed the weapon at the truck and fired the complete magazine into the engine block and front tyres. As he turned away from the destruction he had caused, he could see the front of the cab start to burn as the soldiers nearby dived for cover.

He jogged back around the corner to the sedan and got behind the wheel. 'Okay,' he said calmly. 'Let's get the hell out of here.'

CHAPTER TWENTY-NINE

Dusk had given way to darkness as they returned to the garage and as they pulled into the repair shop Jean-Luc could see a light in Benoit's office. As he and Catherine got out of the car and moved to the rear to assist Pierre, Benoit joined them.

'What the hell happened? Where's Michel?'

'Michel is dead,' said Jean-Luc without turning around.

'What?'

'He's dead. The Germans shot him in the head in the back yard. We had to leave him there. There's nothing else we could do.'

'Jesus Christ,' sighed Benoit, shocked.

'Come on, man. Give us a hand with Pierre. We need to get him to a doctor.'

Catherine stood to the side and let the two men carry their injured friend up the stairs and into Benoit's office, where Jean-Luc used his forearm to wipe everything off the desk, knocking paperwork, stationery and dirty cups across the room. Catherine followed them in and sat on one of the chairs in the corner, quietly weeping.

As Pierre lay on top of the table, semi-conscious and moaning quietly with the pain, Benoit took the first aid kit from the far wall and took out a pair of scissors. He proceeded to cut Pierre's trousers to reveal a large bloody hole in the man's leg.

'He's lost a lot of blood,' explained Jean-Luc. 'He needs professional medical attention.'

'And who do you expect me to take him to?' asked Benoit. 'What the hell happened out there? This was supposed to be a simple job.'

'We would have been fine if those bloody Germans had not turned up,' replied Jean-Luc. He did not wish to admit that it had been a small boy that had caused the trouble, a small boy who should have been collected from upstairs before they carried out the mission. It was their own fault, his and Pierre's and nobody else's. Had they retrieved the boy when they entered the house then none of this would have happened. The German patrol would have carried on its journey unaware of what was taking place inside the house and Michel would still be alive.

And then Catherine spoke. 'What happened in the house? We heard Pierre's gun go off. That's what alerted the Germans. What happened? Why did he shoot?'

From the desk Jean-Luc turned and looked at her, aware that Benoit too was waiting for the response.

'We were surprised by one of Rodier's sons. He managed to get hold of a pistol and shot Pierre.'

Catherine started to sob and shake. 'So what did he do? Did he shoot the child?'

Jean-Luc did not reply but instead looked at Benoit who watched on, lost for words.

Taking the silence as an admission, Catherine began to sob louder. 'For God's sake how could we let this happen?'

'There was nothing he could have done,' explained Jean-Luc coldly. 'We have to move on from this. We need to sort Pierre out.'

Benoit sat down on his chair and looked at Pierre forlornly. Pierre had now lost consciousness and the blood was still dripping from his leg, forming a small river across the desk and dripping onto the floor.

'You are right, Jean-Luc,' he said resignedly. 'Pierre needs proper medical attention. We must take him to a hospital or call for an ambulance.'

'If we call an ambulance, we might as well walk over to the Hotel Terminus now and hand ourselves in,' said Catherine desperately. 'They will have to report a gunshot wound.'

'We may need to put our contingency plan into operation,' said Benoit, looking at the face of his now unconscious friend draped across his desk, Jean-Luc frantically trying to halt the flow of blood with a towel he had found on a chair.

'Catherine, please get off your arse and help me, will you?' shouted Jean-Luc. He was beginning to get irritated with the lack of concern for their fellow Maquis.

'We need to make plans,' continued Benoit, ignoring Jean-Luc as Catherine got off the chair and stood with Jean-Luc in front of him.

'If we have been compromised,' he continued, 'we will need to get away and get away tonight. We might have to leave our friend here.'

'No way!' said Jean-Luc. 'We have already left one of them. I am not prepared to leave another.'

Benoit sighed. 'We may have no choice, my friend. How long will it be before they realise who they have? We are not even sure if Michel is dead or alive are we? If he is alive then he will talk. He will betray us.'

'He won't betray us,' said Catherine angrily and then broke down into more sobs.

'We will all betray each other if it comes to it,' replied Benoit. 'We are all human and the human body can only take so much suffering. We have all heard how Barbie operates. So, believe me, we will all eventually betray each other when it comes to it.'

'What do you suggest we do?' asked Jean-Luc. He could see the sense in what Benoit was saying and he felt a tinge of sadness as he watched this man whom he had grown to respect, gradually being destroyed in front of him. The man was clearly devastated as he came to realise that the group that had gathered together to fight against the invader, to fight for what was right and just, was disintegrating before his very eyes. Michel was probably dead and if not, he would betray them all, but Benoit bore no grudges for he knew that if he was in the same situation he would probably do the same thing eventually. It all depended on how much punishment each of them could stand before they finally gave in. And Pierre was dying on his desk in front of him.

'There is only one thing that we can do,' he said. 'We must flee. We need to get to our brothers in the south and get in touch with Francois when we are able. We will have to leave Pierre to take his chances with the Germans. He will surely die if we try to move him.'

'How will we do that?' asked Jean-Luc. He had moved away from the desk leaving Pierre lying there, his eyes closed and his breathing shallow and erratic. He had tended the leg as best he could with the limited supplies that were available to him and he knew that what Benoit was saying was their only option.

'Catherine,' said Benoit calmly. 'Go to your family and warn them. Book yourself into a hotel this evening and then take the first train to St Etienne in the morning. I will send the distress message to London and then me and Jean-Luc will travel tonight and meet you in the café at the station when you arrive. We will decide what to do from there.'

'But...'

'Don't argue, Catherine, now go!'

Catherine stood up, glad that someone was taking charge and that she now had instructions what to do. She walked around the desk and threw her arms around Benoit, kissing him on both cheeks. As she walked past Pierre, she bent down and kissed him on the forehead and stroked his face. He stirred, mumbling something unintelligible and then returned to his slumber.

Finally she approached Jean-Luc. She took his hands and put them to her face before standing on her toes and kissing him firmly on the lips.

'Sometimes I think that you find it hard to express your feelings, Jean-Luc,' she said quietly, almost whispering. 'I know that you don't love me and that you have found it hard to love anyone, but that is no matter to me. You see, I love you, I always have loved you, from the very first moment we met. So it does not matter, you see, you being unable to love me. Because I do it enough for the both of us.'

She kissed him again and then stepped back. Looking from one to the other she said firmly, 'Good luck gentlemen,' and then turned around and left the room without looking back.

The two men stood in silence for a few moments, both of them looking at the door that Catherine had just exited.

'Okay,' said Benoit finally. 'We have work to do, my friend. Let's get on with it.'

CHAPTER THIRTY

Benoit and Jean-Luc sat near the window of the station café, sipping at the coffee that they had purchased and watched the entrance to the platforms where two ticket collectors stood waiting for the morning trains to arrive. A German soldier stood with them.

They had arrived in the town late the previous night and had slept in the car before abandoning it two miles away and then walking the remaining distance to the train station. They were aware that they both looked worse for wear, the strain of the previous evening, the flight from Lyon and the disrupted sleep all taking an effect on their bodies.

After Catherine had left they had taken the radio from the hiding place in the pit and transmitted the pre-defined message, alerting London that their operation was now compromised and they were abandoning the garage and heading to meet up with colleagues in the south. They were unsure of how to make contact, but Benoit had a friend not too far away who he trusted and hoped would put the three of them up for the time being, until they could get themselves organised again.

Then they had filled the boot of the car with the radio and weaponry before telephoning for an ambulance and then heading off in the car. They had found a suitable place, not far from where they had abandoned the vehicle and buried the equipment, keeping a pistol with three clips of ammunition each, which they now had cocked and ready in their coat pockets.

They had not engaged in much conversation, preferring the quietness of their own thoughts. It was clear to Jean-Luc that Benoit was totally devastated at how things had turned out. He had had to abandon his life, for the time being anyway, and go on the run. He'd left behind his business and his friends and Jean-Luc thought that the only saving grace for him was that, like himself, he had no family to worry about. His wife had died before the war and his son was with the Free French somewhere with the Allied forces.

Catherine, on the other hand was a different matter, she had her mother and her sister to think about. There was no doubt that the Gestapo would have them both in for questioning and probable punishment based on what she had done and it was only right that Benoit had sent her to warn them to 'disappear' for the time being.

For a brief moment they had contemplated ending it for Pierre, to simply put a bullet in his head and be done with it. The man was bleeding to death anyway. However, Benoit was not the sort of man to abandon his friends and consequently was certainly not the type to put a bullet into the head of one to save his own skin. Neither was Jean-Luc. The only chance Pierre had of survival was for proper doctors to take care of him and it had been extremely urgent that he had attention as soon as possible.

They had both therefore decided that the only option was the course they had taken and they had no regrets about what they had done.

There was also the uncertainty that Michel was still alive and, like Benoit had said, they would all give each other up eventually if they were pushed. They would not want to and they would all deny that they would ever do such a thing, but the man was a realist and had heard the rumours about the ruthlessness of Barbie and his cronies. There was no shame in it, he had said. After all they were all human and had their limitations and at least they had been part of the few that had actively resisted the occupier. For that they should all be proud.

Benoit took out his cigarettes and offered one to Jean-Luc.

'No thanks,' said Jean-Luc with a smile. 'They stink.'

Benoit smiled back. 'Yes I suppose they do. But I like them. They keep me sharp and alive.'

'Can't be good for you,' replied Jean-Luc, 'All that shit going into your lungs can't be doing you any good.'

'Well I like them,' Benoit said with a shrug. 'They're my only vice.'

'What about the cognac you keep in your desk drawer?'

'Ah yes,' he laughed. 'That too.'

They sat in silence for a few moments and Jean-Luc looked again towards the platform. A few people were now starting to arrive and depart and the café they were sitting in was starting to get busier. He could see through to the first platform where he observed two German soldiers pacing up and down, rifles over their shoulders. He also noticed that now standing with the ticket collectors and the German guard, was another man in a long leather overcoat and homburg, which was the obvious, and somewhat comical, uniform of the Gestapo.

Benoit had followed his gaze. 'Look at them, the Nazi pricks,' he said. 'God I hate those arrogant bastards.'

'Me too,' said Jean-Luc, not averting his eyes. 'One day this will all be over my friend. One day these goose-stepping idiots will be kicked out of France and I just hope I'm around to see it happen.'

'Me too,' replied Benoit and then sat back in his chair, blowing smoke above his head.

'You know what,' said Benoit after a while. 'I don't think I could stand being taken by them. I don't think that I could do it.'

'We are adaptable,' replied Jean-Luc. 'Whatever happens, we adapt. It is human nature.'

'Well I don't think I could do it, that's all.'

There was movement on one of the platforms as a train arrived. The hiss of the steam as the brakes were applied could be clearly heard in the café and they both looked towards the platform again.

'This is the train,' said Benoit. 'All things being well she should be on it. We will be away from here in a few minutes, Jean-Luc.'

Jean-Luc turned his head to look at the platform exit where people were now starting to pour through to the concourse, heading for the exits and on to their final destinations. He watched as each person passed, all of them unaware that the two men who sat in the corner of the station café were in fact Resistance members, fighting for their freedom against Nazi occupation and tyranny.

After a minute or so, Benoit said, 'There she is. Thank God.'

Jean-Luc looked to where he indicated and sure enough, he saw Catherine walking purposefully towards the café door. Benoit was smiling at her but Jean-Luc looked beyond her to see if anyone was following.

She entered the room and on seeing them in the corner, headed directly towards them and sat down without saying anything. Jean-Luc now turned his head to face her.

He took one look at her and stood up. 'Benoit,' he said. 'Let's get out of here.'

'What do you mean?' he asked, looking up at him. 'All in good time.'

'No,' he said. 'Right now. She's betrayed us.'

'How do you know?' he said confused. Then he looked at Catherine who was softly weeping.

'They have Monique,' she whispered. 'What could I do?'

Jean-Luc did not wait another second and marched hastily to the door. As he exited, he could see two men in the long leather coats that always gave them away for who they were, striding towards the door to the café. They were flanked by two SS soldiers who had machine pistols at the ready.

Jean-Luc moved immediately to the left and walked as quickly as he could to the exit onto the main street, hoping that they had not seen him amongst the crowd of passengers, but almost straight away he heard one of them shout. 'You. You in the long coat. Stop there.'

Without looking around Jean-Luc pushed through the crowd now leaving the station and once out onto the street, began to run.

*

Inside the café Benoit had not moved. Whether this was out of fear or a resignation to accept the inevitable, he was not sure. He was happy to see his friend leave the building, hoping beyond hope that he would get away. Then he looked at Catherine who was wiping the tears from her face and still muttering, 'What could I do? They have my sister. I did not know what to do?'

As the door opened and an SS soldier walked in with a Gestapo officer, Benoit looked at Catherine. 'Do not weep, my dear,' he said softly. 'I told you that you would betray us didn't I? We would all do it if the situation was the same.'

'On your feet,' came a high pitched voice to his side, but he ignored it. He could sense that the man was holding a pistol and it was pointed at his head.

'Catherine,' he said. 'How did they get to you?'

'It must have been Michel. He was not dead.'

'I said on your feet, scum!'

For the first time Benoit turned to look at the Gestapo officer to his left. 'Can I help you?' he said calmly. He was aware that the other customers were now hurriedly leaving the café, not wanting to be a part of, or witness to, what may happen next.

'You are to come with us,' replied the man venomously. 'Or do you want me to put a bullet in your head right here.'

Benoit stood up. 'Okay,' he said calmly. 'Lead the way little man.'

He could see outside the café that there were a number of German soldiers and more Gestapo officers gathered in a large group. They were clearly taking no chances with the arrest, they were after a group of killers after all, and child-killers at that. He could see that some of them were moving very quickly towards the exit to no doubt aid in the pursuit of Jean-Luc and he smiled. Jean-Luc Descartes. He was a lot more intelligent than he had initially given him credit for. He had seen straight away that Catherine had been compromised and had acted very quickly in getting out of the station before the Germans could get to him. He prayed to himself that Jean-Luc would make it to safety.

'Empty your pockets,' demanded the Gestapo officer. 'Quickly!'

By now more soldiers had entered the café and had their rifles and machine pistols pointed in his direction. He knew the situation was hopeless for him. There was no way out.

Calmly he took out his wallet and some loose change and placed them on the table in front of Catherine.

'I'm sorry, Catherine,' he said, giving her one last smile. 'Say a prayer for me.'

With one quick movement he brought up his right hand from the coat pocket, clutching the small automatic pistol, knocking off the safety catch as he did so. He knew there was one round in the chamber and it was ready for firing. Before any of the soldiers or the Gestapo officer could react, he placed the weapon in his mouth and pulled the trigger.

The bullet exited the back of his head spraying blood and brains onto the window and counter behind him. Some of the blood sprayed into Catherine's face and she began to scream uncontrollably.

'For Christ's sake,' yelled the Gestapo officer, who had also been hit by the human detritus; blood hitting his face and coat. 'Jesus Christ! What is wrong with these people?'

Turning to the soldiers around him he shouted. 'Get this stupid bitch out of here and clean this mess up.'

He quickly marched from the café to join the others on the station concourse.

*

Half a mile away, Jean-Luc was still running.

He had discarded the long coat as it was too heavy and was restricting his movements, throwing it into bushes as he ran by, after first taking out the automatic pistol and placing it in his trouser pocket. It was only after a minute that he realised he had left the spare clips in the coat but there was no way he could go back to retrieve them.

He was aware that people were looking at him as he flew past them but not one of them attempted to stop him. At no point did he look back. At first he could hear the shouts of his pursuers but as he jinked and ducked through the side streets, running on instinct and adrenalin, he gradually heard their shouts diminish until, at last, he could no longer hear them.

He turned a corner and came across a small pavement café. He sat down at one of the tables near to the doorway and picked up a menu. He needed to gather his thoughts, to weigh up all his options. He still had the false identification in his wallet, which was in his trouser pocket, along with a few hundred francs that they had taken from Benoit's safe the previous night.

He checked the wallet and counted the money. They had taken and divided the emergency stash and he had a considerable amount that he hoped would be able to get him to safety, wherever that may be.

He had no idea where he was to go. None at all. He was in a city that he had only ever been to once before, as a child with his mother, and all the streets were unfamiliar to him. He knew no one here. Not a soul. It was Benoit who had the contacts and he was more than likely in the hands of the Gestapo by now, along with Catherine.

The waiter approached and he ordered a coffee and some breakfast.

'Are you all right, monsieur?' asked the young waiter as he wrote down the order on his pad. 'You look rather flushed.'

'I'm fine, thank you,' he replied. 'Just a little under the weather. Can you point out the bathroom.'

'There is one inside, monsieur,' he said, indicating the building behind him. 'Just go through. It is on the right.'

Once in the sanctuary of the bathroom, he looked in the mirror. The waiter was right, he looked a mess. His eyes were baggy and his face was very red and sweaty from the exertions of his flight from the train station. He splashed cold water into his face and took off his jacket and shirt and washed himself down with the cold water from the tap in an attempt to cool himself. He dried off as best he could with the paper towels provided and then returned to the table and sat back down.

He looked around. People were going about their business and the traffic that passed did not give him any cause for concern. After a couple of minutes the waiter returned with his coffee and croissants and placed them in front of him.

As he sipped at the coffee, he was able to finally think about Catherine. Poor Catherine, he thought. Not a lot had gone right for her and by default her bad fortune was being passed onto him. He did not blame her for what she had done. She had betrayed her two closest friends in order to save her sister and he could see the rationale in that, even if it did place him in a very difficult position. Whatever was going to happen to her now she had to deal with on her own. He could not think about it.

He moved on to contemplate his own situation. He was a Maquis whose circuit did not exist any more. His colleagues were either all dead or would soon be all dead. He knew that both Benoit and Catherine would go the way of Michel and Pierre who he presumed to be dead already. To make his own situation worse, he was also Jewish with no one to turn to for assistance. He thought about contacting Bruno, his publisher, but thought better of it. He did not want to involve anyone else. Bruno had a young family and he did not want to put any of them in any kind of danger.

As he ate the breakfast, he made a decision. He needed to get out of St Etienne as quickly as possible. The SS and Gestapo would be searching for him, he was sure of that, and they would not stop until he was caught. But did they know what he actually looked like? How could they? They had only caught a passing glance at him as he had ran from the station and that was why he felt some confidence sitting at the pavement café, hiding in plain sight. He would steal a car and drive south where he would abandon it and then make his way to Marseilles on the coast, where he would try to find someone who would smuggle him to Spain. From there he could either wait the war out or he could continue on to England and join the Free French. It was not much of a plan, but a plan it was nevertheless and with making this decision he was able to feel a little more hopeful. He had a purpose once more.

He finished his food and suddenly had a feeling that he was being watched. He looked up, and, standing across from him ten yards away on the pavement, stood a tall, well-built gendarme. Their eyes met for a brief second and for some reason, Jean-Luc suddenly felt very nervous and looked away, almost too quickly he realised.

The gendarme approached him.

Jean-Luc looked up. 'Can I help you?' he said.

'I feel I know you,' said the gendarme. 'I have seen your face somewhere before but I cannot place it.'

'I'm sorry,' said Jean-Luc as calmly as he could. 'I do not know why.'

'Yes,' said the gendarme more confidently, 'I have definitely seen your face somewhere before monsieur—what is your name?'

'Pascal, David Pascal.'

The gendarme thought for a few moments and then said, 'No, the name does not ring any bells. Can I see your papers please?'

'Certainly,' said Jean-Luc in as helpful a tone as he could muster. He felt in his pocket for his wallet and then handed the documents to him. He put his hand back into the pocket and gripped the pistol tightly.

The gendarme took the identification papers from him and then examined them closely before handing them back. 'Sorry to have bothered you, Monsieur Pascal,' he said stepping back.

'No trouble at all,' he said smiling, letting go of the pistol and taking his hand out of his pocket. 'Not a problem.'

The gendarme continued on his way and Jean-Luc observed him as he walked along the road and turned a corner, taking him out of sight.

He suddenly felt a huge feeling of unease. The incident with the gendarme had unnerved him and he now wanted to be on his way again. He suddenly did not feel safe there any more. He thought about the pistol in his pocket and rather than it be a protection for him, he now wondered if it was a hindrance. If the gendarme had been more suspicious and had asked him to empty his pockets, then the situation could have very easily escalated into something a lot more worrying.

He made a decision that he needed to get rid of the gun and he needed to do it straight away. He rose from his seat, placed some money on the table in front of him and walked swiftly back to the bathroom. Once inside the toilet cubicle he closed the door and took the gun from his trouser pocket. Using his sleeve to wipe off any fingerprints and then using the same sleeve to hold the weapon, he took the lid off the cistern and placed it inside before flushing the toilet and washing his hands in the sink. Again he threw cold water over his face and dried himself.

As he left the entrance to the café and stepped onto the pavement terrace, he was suddenly aware that all was not as it should be. Facing him was the same gendarme talking to the waiter who was pointing back to the building where Jean-Luc now stood. More worryingly were the four SS soldiers and two Gestapo officers standing with him.

And they were all now looking at him.

Jean-Luc decided to brave it out. He could not run, there was nowhere to go. He walked casually to the exit, towards them and as he approached he said, 'Excuse me gentlemen, can you let me pass?'

A short Gestapo officer wearing a homburg and round glasses stepped forward, blocking his way. Jean-Luc was reminded of Heinrich Himmler, probably the look that the idiot was going for, and he very nearly laughed in the man's face.

'Papers,' said the man sharply.

'Excuse me?' said Jean-Luc calmly, pretending not to understand.

'Papers,' he repeated, more strongly. 'Show me your papers. It is a simple request.'

Jean-Luc looked at the gendarme. 'I have just provided this man with my papers not five minutes ago,' he said feigning confusion. 'I'm sure he found everything in order.'

The gendarme turned his head away, unable to meet Jean-Luc's gaze.

'I am asking you for your papers, not him.'

'Very well,' said Jean-Luc taking out the necessary documentation from his pocket.

The Gestapo officer studied the paperwork closely and Jean-Luc could feel that he was starting to sweat again. He hoped that his nervousness would not be apparent to the armed group in front of him.

'David Pascal,' said the Himmler lookalike and then looked up from the paperwork. 'What is your business in St Etienne, Herr Pascal.'

'I am here on a business trip.'

'A business trip? What is your business?'

'I buy and sell antiques.' Jean-Luc had no idea where that came from.

'And do they sell good antiques in this town?'

'That's what I am here to find out.'

The man smiled humourlessly. 'You seem nervous, Herr Pascal. Why is that?'

'Because you are making me nervous,' replied Jean-Luc. 'You are questioning me for no reason I can think of and I am wondering why.'

'Have you been to the train station today?'

'Yes,' Jean-Luc said. He thought it better to base his lies on partial truths. 'I arrived on the train from Lyon this morning.'

'Do you have your ticket stub?'

'No, I discarded it in one of the bins outside the station,' he replied.

'Did you see anything or anyone that gave you cause for suspicion?'

'No. But I did see a lot of soldiers on the platform and concourse. What was all that about?'

'I will ask the questions… Pascal. Now can you empty your pockets for me?'

Jean-Luc sat down at the table to the side and did as he was told. The more the conversation dragged on, the more he felt uneasy. This idiot was not going to let him go quickly. What irritated him most was that had it just been this Himmler clone and the gendarme, he felt confident enough to handle the situation with a certain degree of violence, but the SS soldiers who accompanied them put all chance of an escape out of the question. He would have to talk his way out of this one, there was no other way.

He became aware of activity behind him and turned to look in the direction of the café and then saw that all hope was now lost.

Standing on the step at the entrance, only a few feet away, stood an SS soldier who must have gone into the building while the Gestapo officer was interrogating him. Dangling by the trigger guard from the index finger of his right hand, his arm raised in the air, was the pistol he had just placed in the toilet cistern. He turned back to the Gestapo officer who raised his eyebrows at him.

'Well?' he said. 'Have you an explanation for this?'

'That has nothing to do with me,' replied Jean-Luc.

'So we will not find your fingerprints on it, should we check?'

'Seeing that I have never seen it before in my life and therefore never touched it, then no, you won't find my fingerprints on it.'

The Gestapo officer sat down across from him, flanked by two SS guards who now pointed their weapons at Jean-Luc's chest.

'Help me out here,' he said condescendingly. 'Help me to understand what is happening here. We are searching for a man who matches your description. By your own admission, you were at the station this morning the same time as we know he was. We are told that you arrived here from the direction our suspect fled, all sweaty and red of face. This gendarme here recognises you from somewhere and you provided him with papers that although are very good forgeries, are forgeries nonetheless. And then we find a pistol in the same toilet that you have just visited.'

Jean-Luc smiled at him. 'Would you believe me if I told you it was all a terrible coincidence?'

'You are smiling at me,' he said in disbelief. 'You are smiling at me as though this is funny.'

'It's not the situation I am laughing at,' replied Jean-Luc. 'It's you and your cronies with their pathetic little faces thinking you are the master race. Well, where's your blond hair and blue eyes? And where's little Adolf's blond hair and blue eyes, tell me that? And he's not even German! You're all crazy.'

'Remarkable,' replied the Gestapo officer indignantly. 'Utterly remarkable.' Turning to the soldiers to his side he spoke in German and the next thing Jean-Luc knew he was being manhandled and thrown into the back of a truck where the SS guards joined him.

As he sat on the wooden bench in the back, his hands now manacled together, he could see the waiter and the gendarme who had given him up watching as they drove away and as they turned a corner, he saw them both go about their business as though none of what had happened had taken place.

The waiter wiping the table after first pocketing Jean-Luc's money and the gendarme walking slowly on his beat in the opposite direction. Both of them seemingly without a care in the world, indifferent to what they had just done.

The only thought that now crossed his mind was a feeling of inevitability. Whether they were taking him to his death he had no way of knowing, but if they were then so be it, he thought. So be it. At least he would go to his grave having tried to do something about what was happening and that should count for something.

He thought back to a few months previously when he had been resisting Catherine's attempts for him to join the Maquis and smiled to himself again. The last few months he had spent as part of Claude Benoit's small outfit, living in the garage with men he was proud to call his friends, playing his small part in resisting the occupation, had been the happiest days of his life. If that was all now to end in front of a firing squad, then he was happy to make that short walk, happy to have the bag placed over his head and happy for the sound of the rifle fire as the bullets would smash into his chest taking his life from him.

Yes, he thought, as the truck drove along the St Etienne streets, taking him back to Lyon and to the inevitable torture and probable death at Gestapo Headquarters at the Hotel Terminus, he had never been as happy in his whole life. It had all been worth it.

CHAPTER THIRTY-ONE

The cell was cold and dark. The room had once been used to store cleaning equipment and although there was still the odour of bleach and other such chemicals, it was, however, filthy, the smell of dirt and excrement mixing with it to produce an ironic contrast to its previous use. It was pitch black inside with no window to offer any kind of light but he knew the room to be very small having caught a glimpse of its dimensions as they had first thrown him into it a few days previously. He also knew there was a bucket in the corner to be used as a toilet should he have the energy to stand up and there was a wire framed bed with no mattress that filled the rest of the room but he preferred to lie on the floor when they allowed him the luxury of solitude.

His body ached from head to toe. He could not find a single part of himself where he felt no pain. He had almost grown accustomed to it, could almost ignore it if he tried hard enough, but whenever he attempted to move, even to lift the metal cup that contained the meagre amount of water they gave him, the pain would shoot through his spine all the way to his brain and he would yell out in agony, the act of screaming out providing him with a release valve for his suffering.

They had brought him back to Lyon a few days ago now, he could not remember exactly how many, and had got to work on him straightaway. He had decided on the journey that he would tell them the entirety of what he knew, there was no point trying to cover or lie now as all the circuit were either dead or captured. The only thing he would not admit to was the fact that he was actually Jean-Luc Descartes, the fugitive Jew, and not David Pascal, the name on the false identification that he had been provided with. He would also try and refrain from mentioning anything about Francois, the English agent, but then there was nothing he could tell them about him anyway. He knew absolutely nothing about the man other than his codename.

But they had wanted more than he could give. More information about things that he simply did not have, that he simply did not know. They wanted to know about the other cells in the area and their plans. They wanted to know the names of any other members and although he had obliged them with Pierre, Michel and Claude Benoit they had not been interested in any of them. They were all dead now anyway, he had been told. All of them. They had asked about Catherine and he had explained that she had little involvement, was merely a courier that did it out of love for him. She was no threat to them and had done little wrong, he had argued, but they had ignored him. He had no idea what had happened to her or where she was or even if she was still alive. He feared she was dead like the others. Or soon would be.

They had started the expected way. They had tied him naked to a wooden chair in an empty basement room where a large SS man with a shaven head and tattoos on his neck and arms had gone to work on him with a rubber cosh, breaking his nose with the first strike. The man had been an expert with the thing, using the weapon like an artist would use a paintbrush, skilfully and purposefully, only this man was not producing a work of art that could be displayed anywhere other than in a chamber of horrors. As he struck the blows, the Gestapo officer who was trying to look like Heinrich Himmler asked the questions and wrote any answers he gave on a clipboard he held in his left hand.

After a while he had lost consciousness and had been roused with a bucket of freezing cold water thrown into his face and chest to allow the torture to commence once more.

After that first session, Jean-Luc had been dragged unceremoniously down the corridors and thrown onto the hard floor of the cell, his already swollen head, crashing down sharply on the stone floor with a resounding clunk. He remembered hearing the sound but did not feel any further pain as his brain had shut itself off to what was happening.

He knew that his face had swollen considerably as he could barely see out of his right eye, which had closed up to a narrow slit. He had no idea how long he had lain like that, it could have been hours or it could have been minutes, he had no way of knowing, but they were soon back for him to repeat the process all over again.

He could by now barely speak to deny the charges, admit the things they wanted him to admit, give names and addresses that he simply did not know or answer any other question they had for him. At one point he thought that he had begged them to shoot him if that's what they intended to ultimately do, to simply get on with it, but he could not remember if he had dreamt that or whether it was real.

On the fifth day they took on another tack. He was dragged from the cell by two SS guards and, his feet dragging along the ground as they held him up, was taken to the usual room and once more strapped to the wooden chair. Without saying a word, the guards left him and closed the door behind them.

As he sat there, his head hanging limply forward, his chin resting upon his chest, he became aware of the presence of a man in the shadows in the corner of the room to his right. Someone new. He tried to lift his head to see who it was but the pain and exhaustion forced him to give it up. He presumed it was the same Gestapo officer who had overseen his visit to the Hotel Terminus thus far.

'Look at me,' came a voice from that corner, a voice belonging to someone he had not met before. A softly spoken voice that seemed out of place in this nightmare he was living in, yet a voice that demanded a certain respect, demanded to be heard. This was someone who had a lot of power, a lot of authority in this place.

Jean-Luc attempted to lift his head once more to take a look at the man and as he approached, he was able to observe him closely.

The man was impeccably dressed in the uniform of a Hauptsturmführer of the SS and wore a cap upon his head although indoors. Jean-Luc could not make out exactly how tall he was as he had placed a chair directly opposite him and was by now sitting upon it, only a few feet away. He had a somewhat narrow, yet handsome face, with thin lips and sharp cheekbones. But it was the eyes that shocked him. He had never seen eyes that looked so evil, so utterly malevolent. The man was clearly amused at what he looked upon; this poor, defeated man who was stripped bare before him, all dignity and hope gone, beaten out of him by the thugs he commanded. He looked at Jean-Luc and liked what he saw.

'Look at me,' he said once more and Jean-Luc was now able to steady his head for a while. Although he did not at first appreciate who he was looking at, he understood that it would be in his best interests not to antagonise the man.

'Good,' said the man, taking out a cigarette from a pack in his pocket and lighting it. He blew the smoke into Jean-Luc's face.

'Are you enjoying your stay in our wonderful hotel?' he asked and then laughed to himself at his little joke. Jean-Luc did not reply. 'I know it is not exactly the most prestigious hotel in the region, but we like it. It is good for us.'

He let Jean-Luc sit in silence for a while.

'Do you know who I am?' asked the German eventually. 'Do you know of me?'

'I think I know who you are,' replied Jean-Luc exhaustedly. Every word demanded the greatest effort.

The Nazi raised his eyebrows. 'I am Hauptsturmführer Klaus Barbie and I run this little show. I am sure that you have heard of me.' He did not wait for an acknowledgement but continued, 'You may also know that I am, what you might call, a hands on type of operator. I like to get involved with these little interviews, particularly when my colleagues are not getting the answers that they seek. It would be in your best interests to speak up, to let us know what you know. It can prevent a lot of unnecessary pain and heartache, believe you me.'

Through his swollen lips Jean-Luc replied, 'I have told them everything I know.'

'Do you think you are brave, lying to me?' asked Barbie calmly. 'Does it make you feel courageous? Does it? Trust me, you need to stop this.'

Once more Barbie blew smoke into Jean-Luc's face before continuing, 'Does it not disturb you that one of your own countrymen betrayed you? That gendarme could have simply carried on walking but he chose not to. He chose to hand you in.'

'Maybe he is still a policeman. Maybe he just thought he was doing his job.'

'Do you not feel any animosity towards him?'

'Don't get me wrong,' replied Jean-Luc weakly. 'If he was here right now then I would rip his stinking heart out.'

Barbie smiled, 'That's the spirit.'

The Nazi stood up and walked behind Jean-Luc, out of his sight.

'Now,' he demanded, 'tell me who you are.'

'I am David Pascal. I...'

'What have I just said?' snapped Barbie sharply. 'I distinctly remember just telling you not to lie to me and yet here you are, immediately telling me an untruth before I have even managed to finish my question. Now, I will ask you again. Who are you?'

'I don't know what you want from me,' said Jean-Luc quietly, the effort of speaking taking too much of what little energy he had left. 'I am David...'

He suddenly felt an immense pain in the left side of his already swollen head and his body was forced to the side. Unable to prevent it, the chair toppled over to the right, taking him with it, and once more he lay upon the cold floor wishing that they would just end it all.

He became aware of Barbie shouting and then others entering the room. He was untied from the chair, hauled to his feet and before he knew what was happening he was being dragged into another room where he was aware of more people, he knew not how many, waiting for him. He noticed a large metal bath filled with water in the centre of the room and before he could do anything to resist it he was thrown face first into it.

The water was freezing and the shock of the temperature caused his whole body to stiffen. He had not had time to take a breath and as rough hands held him beneath the surface, he tried as hard as he could not to breathe, not to suck the icy water up into his lungs. When he realised that they had no intention of dragging him out, he started to panic and struggled against their efforts to hold him down, but they were too strong and his body had no choice but to search for oxygen. He felt the water enter his body and at this point he gave up.

He gave up on the life that he had clung onto despite the best efforts of these Nazis to take it from him, and for some reason, as he accepted that he was about to die, he felt only one regret. That he had never known what it had been like to love another human being with all your heart. There had been people in his life that he had been supposed to love, that he was expected to love, but the emotions he had been told of, that he had read about, that he had even written of in the work he had been forced to abandon, he had never at any point in his life actually felt himself.

Suddenly, as he was about to succumb to the inevitable, he was hauled out of the water and instantly his body attempted to take in oxygen. He had no control as he sucked in the stale rank air around him and instantly started coughing and vomited in front of him as the icy water exited his lungs onto the floor. He felt disappointed that they had not finished off the job and let him die.

He was aware of the sound of laughter and as he lifted his head up he could see that it was Barbie, laughing along with two other officers as they observed him.

'That is disgusting,' laughed the Nazi, 'truly repellent.' Turning to the two thugs who held on to Jean-Luc he ordered. 'Sit him back down.'

A chair was brought from the side of the room and once more he felt himself being forced to sit on it.

'Has that awoken your memory?' said Barbie, now serious once more. 'Are you going to tell me who you are now? Or do you want another little swim?'

Jean-Luc looked at him and met his eyes. He did not care what happened to him any more. There was no more they could do to him. 'Fuck you,' he said boldly. 'Fuck you and all these bum boys of yours.'

Barbie's face changed completely. He was suddenly overcome with rage, his face reddening instantly. He marched over and struck Jean-Luc as hard as he could, smashing his fist into his already swollen eye. He was held in place by the two Nazi guards and his body was not allowed to fall to the side, his face taking the full force of the blow.

Jean-Luc had never felt anything like it. The pain was too intense for him to endure and for a few seconds he passed out because of it.

Unable to prevent it from happening, he once again found himself being forced into the icy water of the bath and being held underneath. This time it seemed to last twice as long and again he was forced to accept the death that by now he welcomed.

But they would not let him die. They took him to the edge of death once more but they would not let him succumb to it.

He did not remember too much about that afternoon when he looked back on it later. He was barely aware as parts of his body were wired up to a generator and thousands of volts applied to it. He was also vaguely conscious of them working on his hands with hot needles as Barbie laughed on, watching them take his nails off one by one and at one point he thought that the Nazi leader himself had taken an active part. By this time they did not seem to care about any information that he may or may not have. They were now doing it for their own simple sadistic pleasure.

He awoke shivering to find himself on the familiar cell floor. He had no idea what time of day it was, how long he had been there or remembered them taking him there. He instantly felt pain in his left hand that overtook the agony he felt in the rest of his body. He managed to lift his hand to his face and could see that at least three of his fingers were broken and he had no nails on any of them, including his thumb. Blood, mixed with dirt and grime, covered the tips of his fingers and when he looked closely he saw that the tip of his little finger was missing and he could see the white of the bone beneath the congealed scab. He had no recollection of this being done and realised it must have taken place after he had lost consciousness.

He put his hand back down to his side and moaned. He had never been a religious man in any sense of the word, but for the first time in his life he willingly prayed. He prayed to the God he claimed not to believe in.

He prayed for one thing and one thing only.

He prayed for death.

*

He was left alone for a full day apart from a couple of minutes when a guard came into the cell to force him to take on some water, which he guzzled greedily, spilling some of it down his chest.

The following morning he was once again taken to the room and placed in the chair to face his tormentor.

'We may not know who you really are,' said Barbie calmly. 'It is quite pathetic really that you have held onto this information for so long and put yourself through this unnecessary ordeal. In fact, when you think about it, it is all rather comical.'

Jean-Luc found no reason to smile with him. If there was a singular person upon the earth that he hated, then that man was facing him right now. He chose to say nothing.

'I believe that the reason for this is that you are probably a stinking Jew,' said Barbie calmly. 'And, to add to that, you are a member of the Maquis, or whatever it is you idiots call yourselves. A double hit so to speak. Two crimes for which to be punished.'

'Then take me out and shoot me,' replied Jean-Luc. 'Take it from me, you will be doing me a favour.'

'And for that very reason and that reason alone I will do no such thing,' replied Barbie. 'I have something ultimately better for you. You can join the rest of the vermin. For I know what awaits you at the other end of the journey I am going to send you on. It is nothing more than you deserve.'

Jean-Luc sighed and looked down at his deformed hand, the bones of his fingers starting to set at awkward angles.

Barbie noticed his gaze and laughed at him. 'Oh dear, I wonder how you are going to get along with that,' he said and stood up. Without looking back he left the room, obviously bored with the conversation and Jean-Luc presumed he had now gone to seek out another victim for whom to have some fun with.

Two hours later, having been dressed in the clothes he had been arrested in, he found himself being taken on the first leg of a journey that he knew he would never return. They had even given him back the false papers under the name of David Pascal but something had been added. The word JEW was now emblazoned across them. He almost laughed at the irony of it.

He did not know what would happen to him and at that moment he did not particularly care, but he had a fair idea, and for the moment he was just happy that he had seen the last of Hauptsturmführer Klaus Barbie and the Hotel Terminus.

He did not hold out much hope for the future.

CHAPTER THIRTY-TWO

Drancy Deportation Camp, Paris, Early June 1943

The old man stood at the entrance to Stairwell Number Seven. His right eye, slightly discoloured, showed the signs of a recent beating that was struggling to heal. His emaciated frame, not having received a decent meal for a number of weeks now, was getting thinner and weaker by the day and he knew that if this place was to stay open for much longer then he would either die here or be deported with so many others he had seen come and go in the few short weeks he had been here. His once thick and shiny black hair had become grey and noticeably thinner over the course of a very short period of time and he was well aware that the looks that used to turn heads not so long ago had now totally abandoned him. He looked down at his left arm, with the newly acquired black band that gave him a certain amount of authority as Chief of Staircase, enabling him to move about the camp with relative ease, and he sighed to himself. He had acquired it due to the misfortune of another, who had been deported to the east only a couple of days previously and he felt a certain amount of sadness for that. At the end of the arm was his withered and destroyed hand that made him pretty much useless for any type of work other than organising the comings and goings of the sixteen rooms in the block, in conjunction with the Chiefs of Rooms.

The old man was close to his twenty-eighth birthday. His real name was Jean-Luc Descartes but everyone here knew him as David Pascal.

His mind wandered back to the day he had been taken from the Hotel Terminus and delivered by the SS to the camp. He had been shocked to see that the place was being run by the French gendarmerie with very little help or administration from the occupier and it had made him sick to his stomach. At the time he had been so very weak and once processed, which was very quick due to his lack of possessions, he was allocated to a second floor room off the stairwell he was currently standing in front of. He remembered little of the first few days but what he could recollect was of someone applying water to his head with a dirty rag to keep him cool and feeding him a very thin cabbage soup that he now realised was the staple diet of the camp, along with very weak coffee and a minimal ration of bread.

That man was named Edward Bernheim, a man of around fifty-five years old, the then Chief of Staircase Number Seven who had witnessed him being dragged into the block and had taken it upon himself to look after this stranger for no other reason than it was in his nature to assist a fellow who needed help. Edward had nursed Jean-Luc as best he could and before too long he was back on his feet, although unsteady and weak due to the wounds that had not healed correctly and the lack of proper nutrition.

Over the course of those few weeks, Jean-Luc had grown close to this kindly man and saw him as a kindred spirit. They had shared memories of life before the war and their hopes for the future when all this was over, for they both believed it would all end one day. Edward had no idea where the rest of his family were but presumed they had been taken away before his arrival, deported to the work camps in the east. Although they both knew that deportation almost certainly meant certain death, they refrained from admitting it to each other, preferring instead the idea that the children of the camp had dreamed up; that they were going instead to "Pitchipoi", a fictional, made up place where things would be better, and they were not being sent to be worked to death in a foreign country. Although they all went along with this premise, they all knew the reality of the situation.

And then had come that fateful day a week ago when Edward had found his name on the list of deportees. He had been very philosophical about it, almost to the point of resignation.

'Ah, David,' he had said. 'It was only a matter of time, after all. We both knew that this would happen sooner or later.'

Jean-Luc had woken early on the day of the deportation and had carefully watched from the window as the hundreds of deportees were taken from the departure staircases, numbers one, two and three and then lined up in the courtyard below. He had been careful not to be seen as Hauptsturmführer Rothke, the Camp Commandant, did not allow anyone to watch from the windows and anyone caught doing so was severely punished. Below him, the movement of so many people, divided into groups of fifty to make up each train carriage, caused black dust and dirt to rise up from the broken pebbles of the gravelled courtyard, partly enveloping them in a black mist as though a portent of what was befalling them. They had formed a pitiful line as they trudged away, some holding hands and others quite lost as to what was happening, unable, or unwilling, to comprehend that this could be happening in a civilised country. They were jostled along by both gendarmes and SS guards as they slowly walked the path between the barbed wire, and then on to the waiting buses that would take them away along the Route Des Petits Pont to Bobigny train station for onward transportation to a different hell.

Jean-Luc had so far been lucky regarding deportations. As a Frenchman, he was being overlooked, the deportations being mainly those of foreign nationals or people of foreign backgrounds, but he knew that they would eventually get round to him. He was sure they would get round to everyone eventually. From what he could pick up from others, the war was not going very well for the Germans but it was far from over just yet, so he had a sense of inevitability regarding his ultimate fate.

As he stood there, in the shade of the late afternoon sunshine, he looked about the camp. Located approximately twelve kilometres north east of the centre of Paris, Drancy deportation camp comprised of a large U-shaped building of four storeys. The East wing, in front of which he now stood, was separated from the West wing by the large courtyard used for the logistics of the deportations and for the morning roll calls. The two wings were connected on the north side by Block 3 where those with certain privileges were housed. Various staircases, ten on each wing, led to the rooms, four on each floor, which housed the unfortunates who happened to find themselves prisoners here. Each room was supposed to house fifty people, but often there would be many more, living in cramped and disgusting conditions. For every room there was a water system to be used for cleaning clothes, utensils and people and to provide them with drinking water. Consisting of a long trough controlled by one tap that allowed cold water to flow along a pipe with seven or eight outlets that were too high, water would constantly spray over the trough ensuring that the concrete floor was always wet and slippery. There was no heating system and during the long, cold nights the prisoners would attempt to get what sleep they could on dirty, straw mattresses that had worn to virtually nothing if they were lucky, or just lay on the cold concrete floor, huddled up to the person next to them for warmth.

Jean-Luc turned to his left to observe the constant stream of people entering and leaving the latrines, or the "Red Palace" as they were otherwise known. Beyond these two buildings, that were too small for the number of users, was the barbed wire fence and beyond that, civilisation. Four gun towers occupied each corner to prevent anyone from trying to escape and outside the perimeter could be seen a number of high rise buildings, a gendarmerie and other administration blocks.

He was disturbed from his thoughts by someone calling to him. At first he paid no attention but then realising that he was not using his real name he looked up.

'David, David.'

He turned around and looked back inside the stairwell where he spotted Andre Goldman coming down the stairs and heading toward him. Andre was forty years old but, like Jean-Luc, looked a lot older. He was a room leader on the second floor. As he approached, Jean-Luc could see that he was in some distress, so he stepped inside the building to meet him.

'Yes, Andre,' he said when the man was with him. 'Whatever is the matter?'

'Another has passed, David. It is old Monsieur Dray.' And then he added, his voice tinged with sadness, 'I thought he could not last much longer.'

Jean-Luc sighed. Dray's name had been on the list for the next deportation, which was to take place in two days' time. 'That means that some other unfortunate will now have to take his place,' he said to Andre.

This was true. The deportation had to number one thousand and if one dropped off the list then another had to take their place.

'Maybe Pitchipoi will be better than here,' said Andre optimistically. 'Maybe there will be more food and better conditions.'

'Yes, maybe,' replied Jean-Luc half-heartedly. He did not want to destroy the man's optimism. He found that many of the prisoners said things like this. Whether they actually believed it was a matter of debate, but nobody wanted to talk about what the probable reality of it all was. And who could blame them? Things were bad enough in this place anyway without adding to the depression.

He followed Andre up the stairs and entered the room. Sitting and lying about on the filthy floor and straw mattresses were a mass of humanity in different states of health. Some, the newer ones, looked well enough but it was their eyes that made them stand out. They had not yet got used to the daily mundane routine and the lack of food, and were still shocked that they had ended up in such a place as this, that human beings could treat other human beings in such a way. However, those who had been resident for a while looked more resigned to their fate and consequently due to the length of time without proper nutrition, they looked the more desperate. He had by now become used to the stench of the rooms. Despite the best efforts of the prisoners, keeping clean was a virtual impossibility, one bar of soap for every ten people and no changes of clothing, if they had not been allowed to keep any on admission. The place was a human cesspit.

Andre led him to Dray's almost skeletal body, which was lying on its back on the concrete floor. Dray's face was drawn, the cheeks sucked in, making his huge pointed nose appear even larger. His eyes, not yet fully clouded over, stared vacantly at the ceiling above and his mouth was wide open revealing a number of missing and blackened teeth. Those around watched on indifferently, immune to what was taking place as they had seen it so many times before.

'Come on,' said Jean-Luc without stopping for any pleasantries with those in the room who had seen him. 'Let's get this over with.'

Putting his forearms beneath the corpse's armpits, careful not to use his damaged hand that was in perpetual pain, he unceremoniously lifted the old man as Andre grabbed the legs and together they carried him from the room and down the stairs.

Once they were outside they got the attention of a passing gendarme who, with a disgusted look on his face, led them outside the wire where they were ordered to dump the body, without any ceremony, onto the dirt, where it was left for collection later.

'I don't think I can take much more of this,' remarked Andre once they had returned to the stairwell. 'This is all getting too much for me. I cannot go on much longer.'

'You will be surprised at what a human being can endure,' replied Jean-Luc. 'Look at me. I am no hero by any stretch of the imagination, but I spent a few days under the interrogation of the Gestapo and Barbie, yet here I am, still breathing, still hoping that I will come through this.'

Andre looked at Jean-Luc's withered and deformed hand. 'I had no idea,' he said quietly. 'I apologise for my self-pity.'

'Think nothing of it,' replied Jean-Luc. 'We are all allowed to feel sorry for ourselves once in a while. Especially in a place like this. Come, let us go inside.'

They entered the building and found a spot on the stairs where they could sit and talk. Usually Jean-Luc preferred solitude. He liked being on his own and always had. Maybe this was the reason he had never been able to commit himself to anyone his whole life. The reason why he had never had strong feelings for his mother or his grandparents and the reason he could not give his life to any woman. He knew that people had found him intriguing and he had managed to form the odd friendship or two and even felt sadness once in a while, but he had never found anyone yet that could touch his heart and he could not understand why.

The people he had seen in this place had made him think. Despite being put through unbearable hardship by the Nazis, and some Frenchmen, people who hated them for no other reason than their religion and race, they still endured. He had seen the greatest acts of kindness amongst the greatest acts of evil. They accepted it with a quiet reluctance.

'If I may be bold?' said Andre and Jean-Luc looked at him, nodding for him to continue. 'You are a bit of an enigma to us, David. You do not say much, you have had maybe only one friend, Edward, but you do not mourn him. You seem to just get on with things without complaint and we can see by your injuries that you may have more cause for complaint than anyone.'

'I have no cause for complaint for anything that happens to me,' said Jean-Luc. 'What will be, will be. I have no control over any of it. None of us have.'

'No, it is more than that with you. What happened to you to make you so cold, so unfeeling?'

'Edward knew what was to happen to him,' said Jean-Luc. 'He knew as well as we all do that eventually it will be our turn and we can either accept it and go with it or we can die here, like old man Dray out there. If we die here it just means someone else takes our place on the train. So by surviving to the train, we are all saving a life for however short a time, until it is their turn to do the same.'

'Like I said,' laughed Andre humourlessly, 'What happened to make you so cold?'

Jean-Luc turned to look at him. 'My life has just seemed to happen,' he said after some thought. 'I only had one ambition in my life and that was to be a writer, which I achieved to a certain degree. I was not concerned with anything else. But then I have now come to realise that my nature will not allow me to be any good at it. I may be able to write the odd children's story but not anything of any substance. I have not had the experience for it... the emotional experience. I have never loved and if truth be told, I have never been loved, not really. Although, someone thought she did once.

'I have done things on impulse all my life. I remember as a boy when on holiday in St Malo, I witnessed two English brothers having an argument over fishing... angling... and had I not stepped into a rowing boat a man may not have drowned and a young boy may not have been left disfigured. But at the time I did not care about it and I have not thought about it too often since, and when I have, it has never really bothered me. Maybe I just made the wrong choices somewhere along the line.'

'You are a strange one,' said Andre, looking at him. 'No offence.'

'None taken. For it is true,' replied Jean-Luc softly. 'It is so very true, my friend.'

As new prisoners arrived, they were likely to be processed and deported within days of their arrival. Under Rothke the deportations were averaging at almost one per week. A thousand people, men, women and children shipped out to the camps in the east to face more hardship and probable death at the end of it, to satisfy the Nazi lust for Jewish corpses. It was mind-boggling in its enormity.

If there was anything that could affect Jean-Luc, turn him from the virtual apathy that he was feeling, it was the children. How could grown men send infants and youngsters to their deaths without any feeling of remorse or sense of wrongdoing? He could not understand it at all; it was totally alien to him as a human being, despite the attributes he personally lacked.

A few days after Dray's death one such group arrived in the camp and he observed them being taken to a stairwell across from him. A group of young children mixed in with the adults, some of them extremely young. He asked a passing gendarme, one whom he knew to be sickened by the job he was doing, who they were and where they had come from.

'They are a group of orphans,' he replied, stopping to watch with him. 'I fear that they will not be here very long.'

'Disgraceful,' said Jean-Luc boldly. 'Utterly and totally disgusting... Aren't you afraid?' he added after a while.

The gendarme turned to look at him. 'Why would I be afraid? It is not me who will be on the deportation trains.'

Jean-Luc smiled at him. 'The Germans will lose this war, have no doubt about it. And when they do, those who are suffering now will come looking for those who have caused it. I see also that you wear a crucifix around your neck. Now I am not a religious man, in fact I am not even fully Jewish, despite what my papers may say, but if you are religious then do you not fear what will come to you beyond this life?'

'We have no choice in what we do,' replied the gendarme.

'We always have choices. But then you do not have to justify yourself to me. You can save that for when you meet your God.' Without waiting for a reply he turned and went into the stairwell.

That night, lying in the cramped room on the filthy mattress he shared with two other men, Jean-Luc could not get the sight of the orphans being led up to the rooms in the West wing out of his head. He wondered what conditions were like over there and what they were feeling right now. Orphans with no adults to take care of them, some of them not much older than three or four years old. It sickened him so much that he felt vomit in his mouth and quickly swallowed it back, the acidic taste burning his throat as he did so.

He remembered what he had said to the gendarme about having choices and answering to God. If there was a God, then would Jean-Luc be able to justify that he saw this happen and did nothing about it? That he had merely observed and had the attitude that it was nothing to do with him? Could he justify that attitude, if not to the God he did not believe in, could he justify it to himself?

He made a decision that the very next day he would go across the courtyard and take a look at what was happening over there.

*

The following morning he was awoken the usual irritating way. Waiting patiently for him to open his eyes was Georges Travers, a middle aged carpenter from the Parisian suburbs who was finding it extremely difficult to give up smoking. Tobacco was banned inside the camp and most people who had smoked before their incarceration had been able to simply give it up. However, there were a few that had found it too much and would attempt to get cigarettes, almost to the point of obsession, making it the sole purpose of their existence within the camp. Travers was one of them.

Jean-Luc kept his eyes closed, knowing Travers would be there, sensing the idiot's eyes staring at him. When he could stand it no longer, he opened them. Before he had chance to stretch out or bring himself up onto his elbows he was greeted with the familiar high pitched voice.

'Pascal, Pascal,' said Travers desperately. 'Pascal, can you do me the utmost of favours?'

Jean-Luc rubbed the sleep from his eyes with his good hand and then looked at him. He had tried to feel some sort of compassion for the man but over the course of the short time he had spent in this place and the hardships and deprivation he had seen, someone not being able to have a cigarette was something that he simply had no time for.

'Good morning, Georges,' he replied pleasantly. 'Good morning. Now what can I do for you?'

The man sat down on the cold concrete floor next to Jean-Luc. 'Please, Pascal,' he said conspiratorially in a hushed voice, as though wishing to keep others out of earshot. Jean-Luc looked around and noticed, as he expected, that nobody could care less about this man and his obsession with getting his next smoke. 'Please Pascal, if you get a chance, can you speak to Brutus and see if he can get any cigarettes for me?'

Jean-Luc yawned. Brutus was one of the gendarmes that had made a tidy little profit out of selling single cigarettes to those prisoners, such as Travers, who found themselves in the position of being unable to drop the habit. They had preyed on them and taken everything, what little there was, that they had been allowed to bring into the camp with them.

'What have you got for him?' asked Jean-Luc casually, stifling another yawn. 'I cannot simply ask him unless you have something of value to barter with. He will just tell me to piss off otherwise.'

'But you are a Chief, Pascal,' said Travers desperately. 'You wear the armband.'

'That does not make me one of them,' said Jean-Luc irritated. 'Far from it my little friend. Do not compare me with any of those bastards.'

'I am sorry,' said Travers, now looking worried. He did not want to upset the one man he felt could help him. 'I meant no offence.'

'Look around you,' said Jean-Luc, indicating the room, full of human misery. 'Look around you. Do you think anyone here gives a shit if you have a cigarette today or not? No they don't, and that includes me. I saw a group of children… including those barely walking, being taken into the rooms across the courtyard yesterday. Young orphans with no one to help them, confused and lost. And you want me to spend my time today, using what little influence I have in this place, and by little I mean none, attempting to find a cigarette to satisfy your nicotine craving. Well guess what?'

'We all have our own issues to deal with,' interrupted Travers, clearly upset with Jean-Luc's tone of voice.

'Yes, we do,' agreed Jean-Luc, 'that much is true. But, as I was saying… what I meant was… I have other things on my mind today. You will have to sort this out yourself, like most of the others have done.'

Without another word Travers stood up, and, on the verge of tears, walked away to sit on the other side of the room.

Jean-Luc lay back, glad of the respite from Travers' inane babblings. So what if the little idiot was upset with his attitude. Jean-Luc did not particularly care, there were worse things happening in the camp than not being allowed to smoke.

In the early evening, after eating the pitiful ration of thin cabbage soup that along with the measly portion of bread was the only thing available to them, he walked across the courtyard and approached Stairway Number Fifteen. Andre had decided to accompany him and together they entered the doorway and were greeted by the Chief of Staircase, a short balding man of perhaps fifty years old who looked at them suspiciously.

'What do you two want?' he asked, stepping in front of them.

'Which floor are the children on?' asked Jean-Luc. 'The ones who arrived yesterday.'

'Third floor,' replied the man. 'What do you want with them?'

Ignoring him, Jean-Luc pushed him aside and walked to the stairs leading to the upper floors, Andre following him after first smiling apologetically at the man who looked perturbed that his authority in his own stairwell had been disregarded.

'You can't just come in here and… and…' the man shrugged and then gave up as it was clear that the visitors were not listening. He leaned against the wall and turned his attentions back to what was happening outside.

On reaching the third floor, it was clear immediately which room the children were being kept in. He could hear the cries of small children coming from the first room to the right and he opened the door and stepped inside, followed by Andre. He looked around the room and even though he thought that he had pretty much seen everything, he was still shocked at what he saw.

The room was filled to bursting point with children of all ages. There must have been over a hundred of them in a room supposed to house fifty. Some very small, below the age of three, stood naked and filthy, bemused at what was happening to them, whilst others around the room cried pitifully. Some lay sleeping on the thin straw mattresses that were stained with excrement and urine, whilst others stood around, staring aimlessly into space. Over against the far wall two women were at the water trough, scrubbing furiously at soiled underclothes in an attempt to get them clean enough for the infants to wear again. Their job was made infinitely more difficult due to the lack of hot water and soap, yet they tried their best anyway. A handful of other women attempted to comfort the little ones whilst trying to mend torn and worn rags that they used as clothes, as well as preventing them from scratching at the scabs on their bodies caused by bedbugs and lice.

And then the stench of the room hit him. It was the odour of human excrement and urine and it was strong enough to make him move backwards a step. He had never smelled anything so bad in all of his life. Never before, in his whole life, had Jean-Luc seen anything so utterly pitiful and disgusting. How human beings could treat innocent children so badly was beyond his understanding, beyond his comprehension, his brain unable to process the evidence in front of his eyes.

He became aware that he was standing in the doorway with his mouth agape and was disturbed from his sudden trance by a young woman sitting a few yards from him, two very young boys on her knees.

'Can I help you, monsieur?' she asked, looking up at him with some suspicion.

'I am sorry... I... I...' he stuttered. Then he took control of himself and said. 'I am sorry Mademoiselle, I wanted to see if I could help with anything here.'

'And why would you want to do that?'

He followed her gaze to his armband and then looked back at her. 'Do not be suspicious of this,' he said, raising his arm slightly, 'For it means nothing. I saw a group of children arriving yesterday... without adults... and wondered if I could do anything to help.'

'There are many children here without parents,' she replied. 'And I suspect that they won't be here for much longer. They will be going to Pitchipoi very soon. Following their parents.' She sighed heavily. 'We do what we can for them. We tend to their sores, clean their filthy rags and collect their food. But most of all we pray for them. That is all we can do I am afraid.'

'I cannot be here,' said Andre from behind him. 'I cannot witness this, I am sorry, Pascal. I have to leave.'

Before he could say anything, Andre was halfway down the stairs and Jean-Luc wanted nothing more than to follow him out of the building but for some reason he could not leave, something was compelling him to stay.

To the left of the doorway, where he still stood, was a group of around ten children of differing ages. They were better clothed and looked more healthy than the others.

'They are the new ones,' said the woman. 'Give it time and they will be as bad as the others. That's unless they are deported first. It is disgraceful.'

One of the children caught his eye, a young girl of around four or five years old, standing slightly apart from the others. She was wearing a green coat with a red dress underneath, had on black shoes and her straight blonde hair hung loosely down her back. The girl was staring at him with the most beautiful blue eyes that he had ever seen and for some reason she was smiling at him. He was to remember this moment for the rest of his life, for his heart skipped a beat inside his chest. It was a physical thing, something real and unexpected, something that he had never experienced before.

Then he noticed that she was clutching a book to her chest and when she saw him look at it she held it out to him, as though asking him to take it and read it to her. He felt his heart skip a beat once more and involuntarily took a sharp breath for it was a book that he recognised. It was a copy of a book that was on his shelf back home in Lyon. It was one of the books he had written.

'Monsieur, are you all right?' asked the woman, a look of concern on her face. 'You look like you have seen a ghost.'

'Maybe I have,' he whispered and walked into the room, heading for the group of newcomers and the girl in particular.

As he approached her, he crouched down on his knees to be at her level and took the book from her. The smile had never left her face all this time.

'And what is your name?' he asked quietly.

'Emilie,' she replied in a soft voice. 'And what is your name, monsieur?'

He could not help smiling at her. 'My name is David, but you can call me Jean-Luc,' he said as quietly. He had no idea why he had given her his real name, maybe it was that he could not lie to her wholly.

'Do you know where my mama and papa are?' she asked. 'I would like to see them. I have not seen them for a long time.'

'You will see them very soon,' he lied, for he did not know what else to say to her. 'But in the meantime, you will have to make do with little me.'

She smiled again and looked at the book in his hands. He looked down at it. *The Little Sparrow*. He had written it some time ago and it was part of a series of books that Bruno had been rather pleased with. It was a very simple tale with lots of colourful illustrations to delight the intended young audience.

'Will you read it to me, Monsieur Jean?' she asked. 'My papa reads it to me but I do not know where he is.'

He sat down and leaned his back against the wall. 'Of course I will read it to you,' he said smiling down at her. 'But very soon your papa will be able to read it to you again.'

'Do you promise?' she asked, settling down beside him.

'I promise,' he lied.

He noticed the young woman looking at him and caught her eye. She smiled encouragingly and then returned her attentions to the children on her lap.

What am I doing, he thought to himself. What in God's name am I doing?

CHAPTER THIRTY-THREE

Jean-Luc visited Emilie every evening for the next two weeks, reading *The Little Sparrow* to her and any of the other children who were within earshot. Each time she would settle herself on his knee and ask the same questions. 'When am I going to Mama and Papa?'; 'Are they at Pitchipoi?'; 'When are we going to see them?' and each time he would give the same answer.

'Very soon, my little sparrow, very soon,' and she would laugh at his use of the book's title when addressing her.

He looked forward to each evening when he would see her and as he became more familiar there he was greeted by the women volunteers with smiles and appreciation. He had given the children something to look forward to each night, something to take their minds off their circumstances, the horror they were forced to live out and the fact that they all missed their parents very much.

But as the days wore on, they could see a change in him. Jean-Luc was getting weaker and thinner as the time passed. He was saving his bread ration and giving it to Emilie every evening, making her eat it when no one else was looking, attempting vainly to keep her health and her spirits up. But with each time she asked about her parents and his responding lies to her, he felt a piece of his soul being chipped away leaving him feeling a lesser being than he was previously. But there was nothing else he could say to her.

One morning in mid-June, the camp was ordered to form up in room order in the courtyard. Thousands of people crammed shoulder to shoulder awaiting an announcement. With so many people gathered together the black dust that was generated from the broken pebbles at their feet was causing those with any kind of chest problem, and that was a significant amount of people, to cough and splutter, spitting out black phlegm into the ground before them. Jean-Luc, standing next to Andre in the throng, struggled to see what was happening but could make out a group of SS officers setting up a table at the far end, facing the mass of prisoners. He thought for a moment how easy it should be for the crowd to rush the Germans and kill them all. It would be very easy to do, but, as usual, he knew that he was in a minority of people with such thoughts of retaliation and retribution.

For the whole of the day, as they stood there, each prisoner was interrogated by a short, skinny SS officer with eyes that showed no expression. Word got round that this was SS Hauptsturmführer Brunner and he would shortly be taking over the running of the camp from Rothke. Why he would want to interview every single person held within the walls was a mystery and as the murmurings and speculation in the crowd grew, the gendarmes were quick to strike out at the prisoners to keep order and quiet.

Eventually, on the second day, June 19th, Jean-Luc stepped forward.

There were four of them facing him. Two seated and two standing. Brunner, who held a pen in his right hand was writing on a piece of paper and did not look up as Jean-Luc approached.

'Name and stairwell,' he ordered without looking up.

'David Pascal. Stairwell Seven.'

Brunner looked down the list as his seated colleague, a fat and rather ugly officer in Jean-Luc's opinion, scrambled through a box file, eventually pulling out a card. He handed it to Brunner who read what little there was on it before looking up at him.

'David Pascal, Jew from Lyon. Suspected Maquis,' he said in a monotone. 'Why are you not dead?'

'Maybe God is looking out for me,' replied Jean-Luc.

'There is no God in this place,' said Brunner. 'There is only me.'

Jean-Luc did not reply and Brunner looked back down at the card. 'Chief of Staircase? Do you think having that armband will save you?'

'I do not need to be saved,' replied Jean-Luc boldly. 'I fear it is you who needs that.'

Brunner's mouth smiled but his eyes remained emotionless. 'Off you go Pascal… or whoever you are.'

Jean-Luc did not wait to be told twice and moved quickly away, leaving the next in line to occupy the space he had vacated in front of the four SS officers.

As he made his way back to the stairwell, he could not help thinking that the slimy little man who had just interviewed him would be the worst thing that could have happened to the camp since he had been there. He felt a cold shiver run down his spine and for the first time in a very long while, he felt truly scared.

*

On June 23rd, a thousand prisoners were deported. These were the ones picked by Brunner from his interviews and Jean-Luc was surprised that his own name had not appeared on the list. The prisoners were gathered in the deportation staircases the previous night and taken out to the courtyard at six o'clock in the morning for processing. They were gone by eight o'clock, all traces of their existence having gone with them.

Although there had been weekly deportations under Rothke, there was something a little more sinister about the arrival of Brunner. He took over the running of the camp on July 2nd and immediately evicted the gendarmes, replacing them with SS guards. The Germans had now completely taken over the camp.

Casual beatings, at an alarming rate, now became normal practice. Prisoners were punished for the most trivial of things and even, on occasion ordered to carry out the punishments on each other for no other reason than that it amused their captors.

Jean-Luc continued to visit the children across the courtyard each evening, taking what little extra food he could find to give to Emilie whom he could see deteriorating before his eyes. Her clothes had become tattered and dirty, despite the best efforts of the female volunteers who had taken it upon themselves to look after them. Although he gave her part of his own rations, he could see that it was still not enough, even for a child as small as she was, and her face was becoming more drawn and noticeably thinner as each day passed. However, she always had a smile for him. Her eyes would twinkle and her face would light up whenever he entered their room, but gradually he could see the smile had left her eyes and she was merely smiling so as not to upset him.

Each day the same question to him: 'Monsieur Jean, when are we going to Pitchipoi to see Mama and Papa?'

He would offer the reply that she wanted, the same lie day after day: 'Soon, my dear, very soon.'

He knew that she did not believe him but she still smiled and accepted his answer nevertheless. He would then put her on his knee and read his book to her, the book that she clutched so tightly to her small, scrawny chest. And other children would gather around to hear the same familiar words that they had all grown to love. He would leave each evening with the promise that he would return the following day and he always kept his promise. He was determined that he would give them something to look forward to each day;

this little thing that he did, even if it gave them only a few minutes of pleasure, then it was worth it.

He was beginning to feel extremely ill and one day in mid-July Andre found him lying on the concrete floor in the room they shared with so many others. Jean-Luc had not been aware that he had collapsed until he was being roused by his friend.

'I'm fine, I'm fine,' he insisted when Andre eventually woke him up, his head hazy and fuzzy. 'Honestly, my friend. Do not worry.'

Andre handed him a metal cup containing water and he drank from it roughly, spilling half of it down his chest.

'You do not look fine,' said Andre. 'You can't go on like this, giving your food away. It will kill you.'

Jean-Luc looked up at him. 'What can I do, Andre? Please tell me. I cannot let these people make her suffer. She has done no one any harm. No one. Yet here she is in this hellhole. She is four years old for God's sake. Four years old.'

'You can't help her if you are dead, David,' replied Andre. 'You can't help her then can you?'

Jean-Luc did not reply but drank again from the cup, finishing the drink. He handed it back to Andre who shuffled away quickly to get him another.

Andre handed him the refilled cup and sat down beside him on the cold damp floor. 'You were saying some very strange things when you were out of it just now,' he said.

'Like what?' asked Jean-Luc curiously.

'Something about a boat and to "get him out of the water". Maybe you are having flashbacks. And then you started mumbling about a Catherine and a Claude... and Michel is dead, yes that was it, "they've killed Michel".'

Jean-Luc looked at him and smiled. 'Do not worry yourself about it, my friend. I often have strange and vivid dreams so it will be nothing.'

Later when he was alone and feeling a little better, Jean-Luc thought about what Andre had told him about the things he had said in his delirium. He thought back to all those years ago in the boat in the cove at St Malo and the way it had all turned out. He wondered that had he not got into the boat and picked up the oar then maybe his and the lives of others may have turned out differently. Life was about the choices you made, he realised, that was all it was about. If you made the correct ones then you would walk a happy path, but if you made the wrong ones then the road and the destination would turn out to be different. He had made many choices recently that had led him to the situation he was now in. If he had listened to Catherine and ran away to Spain or Switzerland then he would not be here now, dying in the cesspit that was Drancy. But then, he thought, he would not have met Emilie and what would have become of her? He came to the conclusion that all the choices he had made had been the right ones. They had to have been.

*

The new list was out.

As Chief of Staircase, Jean-Luc had been given the papers by the Personnel Bureau and, without looking at the names upon it, he pinned it to the noticeboard at the bottom of the stairwell. Unlike the others, he did not want to see immediately if his own name was upon it.

Soon the camp was in its usual frenzy as the prisoners clambered to see if their names were on the list, all of them wishing beyond hope that it was not. Desperate to stay in the place that was slowly killing them anyway, their bodies and their spirits slowly dying, yet they preferred this depraved existence to deportation and the transport they would undergo to the fictitious "Pitchipoi" which in reality they knew to be certain death.

Andre found Jean-Luc sitting on the stairs halfway up the stairwell, showing no interest in what was happening around him.

'David,' he said as he approached and Jean-Luc looked at him and smiled half-heartedly.

'Am I on it?' he asked calmly.

'You are,' came Andre's muted reply. 'I am so sorry my friend.'

'It was bound to happen sooner or later,' he replied calmly. 'It was just a matter of time, let's face it. And you, are you are on the list?'

'They have decided to spare me this time, it is just Category B prisoners, by the looks of it,' he replied embarrassed at his good fortune.

'Oh, the irony,' said Jean-Luc half laughing.

'Irony?'

'Yes, my friend,' he replied standing up. 'You see I am not a full Jew so I should not be in Category B. It is all down to Barbie that I am, but then I did piss the man off slightly.'

'You are a man of mystery,' said Andre, shocked at what he was hearing. 'You really are.'

'I am a very simple man, Andre. There is nothing mysterious about me. Really there isn't... you look a little troubled, my friend. Please tell me what is the matter. It is something else too, isn't it?'

Jean-Luc could see that Andre was agitated.

'There is more,' he said, tears welling in his eyes. 'It is the children across the way... the ones you visit every night... they are on the list too.'

Jean-Luc could not speak. The words would simply not come. He knew what this meant. There was no way these children would be going to the east to work. They were too young, unable to hold and use tools. There could be only one reason for their names to be on the list for deportation.

He had seen other children being taken away before but had always ignored it, preferring not to think about it. He knew that if he had done, then it would have made him go mad, lose his mind. But this time it was different. This time he had a connection to those that the Nazis were shipping out to their deaths. His own life did not matter but that of the children and Emilie in particular, did.

He sat back down on the stairs to prevent himself from falling over and put his head in his hands. He felt his friend's hand on his shoulder as he attempted a token of comfort and became aware that he was sobbing. He could not remember ever crying before in his whole life, yet here he sat, a broken man crying his heart out for children that ultimately were not really his responsibility.

After a few minutes he raised his head and wiped the tears from his eyes on the back of his sleeve.

'I need to get with them,' he said quietly. 'I need to be in their carriage with them when they go.'

He arose and left the stairwell, ignoring the pleas of Andre behind him and marched purposefully across the courtyard. He could see others in other parts of the camp reading the lists that had been put up by the other chiefs and SS guards and saw some of them weeping, collapsing onto their knees and wailing. One or two were being dragged by SS soldiers and he saw an old man beaten over the head with a rifle butt, for what he knew not, but Jean-Luc ignored them all.

Entering the children's room he was met by Anna, one of the volunteers. He could see by her red eyes that she had been weeping.

'They're taking them all, Monsieur Pascal,' she said, breaking down in front of him. 'They are taking all of them.'

'I need one of the adults to swap with me,' he said calmly, holding her by the shoulders. 'I need to get on your room list so I can travel with them.'

'No one will swap,' she replied. 'No one will abandon them.'

'I need to be with Emilie,' he responded. 'She needs me now more than ever.'

'I will ask,' she replied. 'But I cannot promise you.'

He felt a tug at his coat and turned to look down. Emilie looked up at him with the soulful blue eyes that he could not resist.

'Monsieur Jean,' she said with her usual innocent smile. 'Is it time? Are we going to Pitchipoi?'

He knelt down and took hold of her shoulders. 'Yes, my dear, it is true. But do not worry because I will be coming with you.'

'Then why are you looking so sad?' she said softly. 'There is no need to be sad, Monsieur Jean. We are going to be with Mama and Papa. Papa will like you I am sure. And you can both take it in turns to read *The Little Sparrow* to me.'

'And I am sure that I will like him also,' replied Jean-Luc. 'We will be going in three days' time so you need to make sure that you are ready for the train journey. Listen to the nice ladies and they will tell you what you need to do. Now I have to go but I will be back later to read to you.'

She leaned over and placed her lips on his cheek. 'Thank you, Monsieur Jean,' she said sweetly and then turned to seek out her friends, leaving him still kneeling watching her.

'I will see what I can do,' said Anna behind him and he rose and turned to face her. 'I promise,' she said.

CHAPTER THIRTY-FOUR

Jean-Luc's opportunity to get in the group of fifty with the children came a day later when one of the volunteers decided that jumping to her death from the fourth floor onto the spiked railings below was a better option than taking the three day train journey to the unknown. There had not been much fuss made about him switching carriages; he presumed the SS did not care too much as long as they all left and he found himself, the night before the deportation, resting with them in a room off Deportation Stairwell Number Two, close to the camp exit.

There were fifty to a room and the idea was that each room would take up a railway carriage. Twenty carriages meant a total of one thousand Jews were to be deported early the following morning by train from Bobigny. They had been allowed to take what meagre possessions that they still had and these had been taken by "porters" and arranged on the courtyard below. All the adults had had their heads and beards shaved, to get rid of and prevent lice was the reason they had been given.

As Brunner had ordered building work to be done, including the concreting of the courtyard, the space outside was now quite limited, meaning that they would be crammed together when they had to report down there in front of the Red Palace at six o'clock the following morning, July 31st, 1943.

He had found Emilie and had gone through the ritual of reading *The Little Sparrow* to her and her friends and, when finished, had handed the book back to her. She slept with the book cuddled up to her chest, as though it was a teddy bear or some other such cuddly toy and not the worn and battered hardbacked book that it actually was. He found that he could not sleep himself and spent the night watching the children and the adults who had volunteered to look after them, as they all tried to rest their bodies in anticipation of the journey that lay ahead.

*

Jean-Luc held onto Emilie's hand as they were ushered out of the buses that had taken them to Bobigny railway station where a very long train stood awaiting its human cargo.

The processing at Drancy had gone remarkably quickly. They had been arranged in room order and a roll call was taken. Those children who could not understand what was happening had been lifted up and answered for by the adults and soon they were all loaded, with their luggage, onto the buses. A short journey to the train station had followed and this was where they all now stood. There was an enormous sense of gloom and despondency about the group and some of them, both men and women, had wept softly at what was befalling them. The children had remained remarkably calm.

As they were roughly shepherded towards the platform, all around them SS guards stood menacingly, clinging onto rifles and machine-pistols, their officers pacing pompously in front of them. They were being forced forwards, towards the train and some of the prisoners began to get agitated.

'What about our luggage?' he heard one of them shout. 'Our things are still on the buses.'

He was hit in the back by an SS guard with a rifle butt causing him to collapse to the ground. He was quickly dragged to his feet by two of his friends. It was clear that they would be taking nothing more than the clothes they stood up in.

Jean-Luc picked up Emilie and held her tightly to his chest. He could feel the sharp edge of her book digging into his shoulder but he ignored it as he edged forward with the crowd to the carriages. He could see, as he approached, that the carriages were not those designed for carrying human passengers. Each one of them had its door wide open revealing a bucket in one of the corners and straw upon its floor. It was clear that comfort was of no concern to their captors.

The group to which Jean-Luc belonged was ordered to stop as the nearest carriage was filled. Anyone complaining was dealt with quickly and brutally, two SS guards with pick-axe handles striking anyone who was too slow to move or made any comment they did not appreciate. Jean-Luc could see an old man with blood pouring from a large gash on his head being dragged into the carriage by those around him, pulling him away from any further beating. He felt sick to his stomach and forced Emilie's face into his shoulder to prevent her from witnessing the scene.

As his group stood watching what was taking place, his eyes wandered to a figure standing a few metres to his right.

An SS officer, dressed in black stood observing the platform and the loading of the people onto the train. What caused Jean-Luc to look closely was the deep red scar that ran down the left hand side of his face. The man took off his hat to wipe the sweat from his brow, pushing his fingers through his thin blond hair before putting the hat back onto his head. He wore a large, oversized sidearm at his hip.

Jean-Luc felt his heart skip a beat as the feeling of déjà vu completely took over him. He found that he was shaking from head to foot, despite the heat from the morning summer sun beating down upon him.

He could not quite place where he had seen the man before, or if indeed he had ever seen him, but there was something about him that was strangely familiar, something that he could not quite place. Maybe it was from a dream, he thought, maybe from an imagining or a character he had maybe dreamed up for a story that had never got written.

For a brief second their eyes met but the German did not hold the stare, turning to talk to two of his subordinates who then turned and ran away to do his bidding. He found that he kept staring at him, kept looking over in his direction as his brain tried its best to place the man. To process where he had seen him before.

And then Jean-Luc remembered. It was the scar. The scar that he himself had probably caused because of an impulsive action all those years ago. This Nazi who stood before him he remembered as a quiet, thoughtful boy and he had to shake his head in order to accept this thought as the truth.

The group were now approaching the train and he was able to work out that the next empty carriage would be the one in which he and the group of children would occupy. He turned again to seek out the stranger but could not see him, but as he turned his head back to face the train he was shocked to see the man standing just in front of him, at the entrance to the carriage. And he was looking directly at Jean-Luc.

'You seem to have an interest in me,' he said in perfect French, staring into Jean-Luc's eyes.

'No,' said Jean-Luc. 'I have no idea what you mean.'

'That is very odd,' replied the German, his eyes not straying from Jean-Luc's face. 'You have stared at me since you pretty much got off the bus. What do you find so interesting?'

'Nothing, I assure you.'

'So you find me uninteresting do you?' smiled the blond, scar-faced Nazi.

The man was getting on Jean-Luc's nerves and despite the situation he was in he replied boldly, 'In fact I do, yes,' he replied. 'I have seen hundreds like you and you are all pretty much the same to me.'

To his surprise the man laughed. A deep humourless laugh.

Behind him people were bumping into him as they were herded like cattle to the train by the SS guards behind them. Jean-Luc handed Emilie to one of the women who had managed to get on the train and as he moved forward to step on himself, the German held onto his arm, preventing him from boarding.

'Do I know you?' he asked curiously. 'Have we met before?'

'I don't think so,' lied Jean-Luc. 'I am certain I would have remembered you. Also I am very much older than you.' He was relying on the fact that his appearance belied his real age.

The German let go of his arm. 'Okay, Jew,' he said. 'Off you go now.'

But Jean-Luc did not immediately move onto the train.

'How can you do this?' he said. 'How can you send these people… these children, away to their deaths? How can you do it?'

The German turned back to him. 'This is easy for me. I have been in Russia and you will not believe the things that I have seen there. So this is very easy, believe me.' And then he was gone, marching down the platform to supervise the loading of the next carriage.

As Jean-Luc watched him go, an SS guard stepped forward and pushed him brutally from behind. He stepped up onto the carriage and the SS guard's colleague pulled along the sliding door and locked it, closing the world to them all.

Despite the sunshine outside, the carriage was very dark, the only light coming from the cracks in the wooden planks that made up the side walls and from a hole in the roof to the rear of the carriage. Some of the children began to cry and they were immediately comforted by the few adults that occupied the carriage with them.

Half an hour later the train was full and they could hear the sound of the engine getting louder as it made its final preparations before setting off. Jean-Luc forced his way to the side where, through a gap in the wooden planking, he could observe those remaining on the platform.

He soon spotted the Nazi whom he remembered as a boy in St Malo. He thought the boy's name had been Otto but he was not too sure. The surname he could not recall at all.

As the train slowly moved away from the station, Jean-Luc's carriage passed where the man stood, watching it go with a certain amount of satisfaction on his face at a job that had been carried out efficiently.

As the carriage drew closer to him, Jean-Luc put his mouth to the gap and shouted as loudly as he could, 'You may be sending us away to our deaths Otto, but it is you who is doomed, not us. It is you who is truly cursed.'

He looked out and could see the shock on the face of the Nazi at hearing his name and as it passed, Jean-Luc was able to draw back phlegm into his mouth and spit it out through the gap, hitting the man on the shoulder, the white of the spittle standing out against the harsh blackness of his uniform.

Jean-Luc leaned back into the carriage as the train gathered speed and in the gloom was able to make out Emilie standing alone against the side wall. He moved over to her and found a space in the corner where they both sat down. He cuddled her to his chest and before long he could sense that she had fallen asleep. He closed his eyes and let the fatigue and the previous night's lack of sleep take over him and before long, the chugging of the train having a soporific affect upon him, his snores slowly began to merge with hers.

*

For three days the train journeyed, stopping periodically to change tracks or for water and food stops, where the doors would be flung open and a few meagre loaves of bread thrown in, causing a scramble within each carriage, as people fought each other for whatever food they could get hold of. During these stops Jean-Luc could see bodies being dragged from other carriages and dumped in a heap at the side of the tracks; those who had either given up or had taken their own lives rather than continue on in the overheated train. Occasionally he could hear aircraft overhead and hoped that it was the Allies on a bombing mission to Germany.

The hardest thing was keeping hydrated. The heat in the carriages was intense. It was the middle of summer and the temperature was becoming unbearable inside as the sun shone down on the overcrowded train. He could hear shouts and screams from the other carriages as the prisoners pleaded for water or for God to come and take them away, to put them out of their misery.

Things were bad in their own carriage. The stench was getting unbearable as the smaller children often soiled themselves, diarrhoea and urine soaking their clothes and the adults unable to clean their clothes for them. All they could do was strip them down and leave them semi-naked in the gloom. Each evening, Jean-Luc would read Emilie's book from memory as it was too dark to see the words. Whenever he missed out or forgot a word, Emilie would remind him and then he would continue with the tale. They would all sit quietly, transfixed by the soft tone of his voice.

On the night of the third day they felt the train slow to a stop and heard movement outside as SS soldiers jumped down from the train. There was a sudden sense that they had arrived at their destination. That they were finally here at Pitchipoi, wherever that happened to be. They could hear the sound of carriage doors being pulled back and the ugly sound of German soldiers loudly ordering the prisoners from the train.

A few moments later their carriage door was opened roughly and two SS guards stood before them shouting and screaming at them to get off the train, waving their machine pistols menacingly.

Jean-Luc jumped down and then turned back and took Emilie from the carriage. Holding her hand they followed the throng of people as they were marched along the side of the train and up a long ramp to the side.

It was dark but there was lighting along the ramp and Jean-Luc could see many SS soldiers and officers watching and ordering them along. Anyone who took their time was dealt with violently, kicked and punched, forcing them on their way. He could see ahead of them two buildings with tall chimneys and to his right, behind what looked like rows of barrack blocks, the chimneys of two more, each of them spewing out hot ash and smoke that filled their nostrils with a nauseous, horrific odour. He could see the terror on some of the faces of his fellow travellers as they finally realised that what they had feared most was actually happening to them. At first he found it hard to process what was taking place but he soon realised that the fears that they had all had at Drancy were completely founded and undeniably true.

'What is that smell, Monsieur Jean?' asked Emilie innocently. 'It doesn't smell very nice.'

'I don't know,' he replied and looked down at her. He knew, by now that there was nothing he could do to prevent any of this. He had never felt so hopeless.

'Are Mama and Papa here?' she asked innocently. 'Will I see them soon?'

Fighting back tears he replied. 'Yes, my little sparrow, you will see them very soon now.'

They were ordered to halt and as they stopped a man wearing a white coat stepped forward and shouted. 'All women and children step to the left. Form a line over there.'

He indicated to his right where a group of SS soldiers, some of them with Alsatians on leads, stood waiting for them. Mixed in with the guards, Jean-Luc was surprised to see, were many Jews wearing striped uniforms.

'We need to get you all showered before you are allocated your accommodation,' went on the Nazi doctor. 'Then we can get you some food

228

before you can retire for the night. I am sure that you could all do with a good night's sleep.'

The women took their children and moved away to where the man had indicated, some beginning to cry, whilst their husbands and some of the men encouraged them to do so, telling them that everything would be fine. Jean-Luc looked up at the chimneys and suddenly felt desperate. He knew the man was lying. He knew that they were not going to be showered and fed and he was not the only one to realise this.

One or two of the men clung on desperately to their wives and children and the SS guards were forced to break them apart. Ahead of them one of the men stepped out to plead for his wife's life and was immediately shot in the head by an SS officer, his body crumpling to the ground, blood shooting in a fountain from the hole in his head.

'What is happening?' asked Emilie. 'Monsieur Jean, I am frightened.'

He bent down and spoke to her. 'Do not be afraid,' he said. 'You need to be a brave girl now. Everything will be all right.'

But he knew that everything would not be all right. Everything was far from being all right. Anna, who had travelled in the carriage with them, took hold of Emilie's hand and walked across the space to the line of women and children, followed by more of the orphans of Drancy. Jean-Luc clung onto her hand for as long as he could before an SS guard stepped forward and struck him across the chest with a pick-axe handle, knocking him back into the line. He felt no pain as he watched them go and even at this late stage, he tried to look for some kind of hope. Hope that this time the SS doctor ahead of him was telling the truth. Hope that all this was a bad dream from which he would awake. Hope that the God he had never believed in would finally show up and put a stop to this evil, to this madness.

SS officers were walking up and down the line now, looking at them, tapping some on the shoulder and ordering them to join the other line, parallel to them, to join the women and children who were now being made to walk towards the buildings with the huge chimneys. They appeared to be singling out the older of the men, leaving the younger ones alone. One of the officers approached Jean-Luc. He had his withered hand in his pocket, shielding it from him and the man walked by and on to someone else, to tap them and order them across.

As the line of women, children and old men started to move away, he found that he was weeping, that the tears were now pouring down his face. He searched the line for Anna and when he found her, he again spotted little Emilie who had her eyes fixed upon him, still believing that she was being taken to be reunited with her mother and father. In a way, thought Jean-Luc, that was exactly what was happening.

Then it dawned on him that the love that had eluded him all of his life he had now found, and he had passed on all of it to this little, scruffy, orphaned girl that looked across at him, still clutching the book he had written close to her chest, as though it was a puppy or a kitten that needed the warmth of her body to survive. And as she walked away, following the others, he found that he was on his knees and sobbing, unaware that he was screaming and unaware of the SS officer behind him who was taking his pistol from the holster at his hip.

PART FOUR

MARCO RONCALLI

CHAPTER THIRTY-FIVE

Rome, Italy, September 1943

September 8th, 1943 – Proclamation by General Eisenhower on United Nations Radio:

> This is General Dwight D. Eisenhower, Commander-in-Chief of the Allied Forces. The Italian Government has surrendered its armed forces unconditionally. As Allied Commander-in-Chief, I have granted a military armistice, the terms of which have been approved by the Governments of the United Kingdom, the United States and the Union of Soviet Socialist Republics. Thus I am acting in the interest of the United Nations.
>
> The Italian Government has bound itself to abide by these terms without reservation. The armistice was signed by my representative and the representative of Marshal Badoglio and it becomes effective this instant.
>
> Hostilities between the armed forces of the United Nations and those of Italy terminate at once. All Italians who now act to help eject the German aggressor from Italian soil will have the assistance and support of the United Nations.

In the piazza the priest sat alone, a cup of coffee on the table in front of him as he looked up to the clear blue sky. The sun was shining brightly, the heat had been rising steadily over the last few hours to a point where it was quite unbearable unless you were in the shade. This was the third cup he had consumed since arriving and he smiled to himself as he thought of his sister and her inability to be on time for anything. He had found a seat in the corner, the shade from the awning preventing the intense heat from burning into him and he cursed the black clothes that his vocation forced him to wear.

He had been unable to return to his duties with Bishop Beresi in the Vatican Archives since the Germans had occupied the city four days previously. They had posted troops around the perimeter, preventing anyone going in or out without their permission. He had refrained from any attempt to get in as their aggressive attitude since they had arrived had disturbed him greatly, no doubt brought on by the Italian surrender, which had been announced by General Eisenhower on the radio the previous week.

These were troubled and worrying times. The whole city seemed to have an uncertain nervousness about it, which was apparent wherever he went. No one knew what the future held, neither immediate nor long term. They knew that the Allies had taken Sicily and had now landed in the south of the country, and it was probably only a matter of time until they defeated the Germans. But as those Germans were still here and in control of the capital then anything was possible. The fear of revenge, and retribution for the Italian capitulation, which the Germans saw as an act of treason, was evident in every face he looked at. It could be seen in every anxious stare and every mother who clung onto the hands of their children tighter than ever before.

Rome was now no longer the open city that it had been for a while. German troops seemed to be everywhere and military hardware could be seen moving through the streets on its way to be deployed to the south to combat the threat of the British and American armies that were pushing northward. The priest tried to avoid coming into any kind of contact with them and he was surprised at how wearing the dog collar could grant him certain special privileges, the Germans preferring to leave him alone rather than give him any trouble, even on occasion standing by to allow him to walk past. He was not sure whether it was something subconscious within them, as though hassling priests was somehow out of bounds and would be punishable by a divine being when the great reckoning came, or something else. Either way he was relieved that he was able to live his life with only the minor disruption of not being able to get into the Vatican for the time being. He had decided that he would use the enforced holiday to do other things.

He looked up and saw a nurse approach.

He waved as she got nearer and she raised her hand in acknowledgement, a smile beaming across her face on seeing him.

He always seemed to be amazed when he gazed at his sister's natural beauty. Her long black hair was held above her collar by a number of clips and a nurse's hat rested firmly upon her head. She had deep brown, almost black eyes that glowed brightly every time she smiled and her skin was constantly tanned. She had a very petite, slim figure and despite what she ate, she never appeared to put on any weight. The priest was aware that men stared after her as she passed but largely ignored it as he could not blame them for looking. She was so very attractive and they were only human after all.

He stood up as she got to the table and pulled back a chair for her.

'Sorry I'm late,' she said apologetically sitting down. 'Do you forgive me?'

He smiled at her affectionately as he sat back down. 'Of course I do. I haven't been waiting long.'

She placed her hand on his, which was resting on the table. 'It is wrong for a priest to lie, you know.'

He smiled back at her but did not reply.

He caught the eye of a passing waiter and asked for two more coffees and a couple of menus. The waiter nodded and then disappeared back into the café.

'So how was your morning shift?' he asked.

'Not too busy to be honest. I am glad I have a couple of days off now though. I feel really tired. What are your plans? Have you been able to get into work?'

'I haven't tried,' replied the priest. 'I just don't know what to do for the best. I may try tomorrow.'

She took her hand away and smiled at her big brother.

Marco Roncalli was twenty-seven years old and had been a priest for the last five years. He had always wanted to take over at his local parish in Turin, the Church of the Blessed Sacrament, but old Father Lazzari had clung onto the position for the last thirty eight years and it seemed that God still did not want his company just yet. When the chance had been offered to work at the Vatican, Marco had taken the opportunity enthusiastically. It would be a chance to see his nation's capital and to enjoy a bit of Rome life while being at the heart of the Catholic Church. He had grown to love the city and its people and found that leaving the comforts of his home life with his elderly father and wonderful mother, although a wrench to his heart, had been worth it in the end. He travelled home whenever he could to see them and could see the pride in their eyes as they looked at him in his cassock and dog collar.

At one point he had considered enlisting in the army as a chaplain. He felt that he would be able to give his fellow countrymen the spiritual guidance they may need when facing all the horrors of war. He had been persuaded against it by his sister and father, who were both anti-Fascists and did not believe in their country's alliance with the Nazis. They saw it as a pact with the devil and when it had been announced that the Italian government had surrendered and the Allies had landed on the mainland, Sophia had danced around his apartment joyfully. She had been convinced that life would now be much better but had not envisaged the Germans returning so quickly to the city and in such numbers, with a steely determination to fight on.

'Never mind,' she said. 'Maybe it's better to wait and see what happens.'

'Maybe,' he agreed.

Marco sat back in his chair and pushed the hair out of his face and back over his ears. He had maintained the good looks that he had had throughout his youth, the looks that once made every young girl in the village where he grew up turn their heads and blush whenever he caught them looking at him. He had the same dark eyes and hair of his sibling but tried to tone down his appearance by wearing thick rimmed glasses that he neither needed nor found comfortable. Sophia used to laugh at him every time he wore them but had now grown used to seeing him in them and had come to realise that as a priest, it was better for all if he toned down his handsome features.

'Are you still okay for tonight?' asked Sophia as the waiter reappeared with their coffees.

'Of course,' he replied. 'Let's face it, I don't have anything else to do.'

'You make it sound like a chore, Marco. You know how I feel about them.' She looked a little upset by his remark and he suddenly felt extremely guilty.

'I'm sorry.' He sat forward and took her hand. 'I didn't mean anything by that. Please forgive me.'

She smiled again. 'I have bought Franco some new boots. Those he wears are all tatty and falling apart. I hope he likes them.'

'I'm sure he will. I'm sure they will be perfect.'

Marco looked at his sister and smiled to himself. He adored her. From a child he had watched her grow into the wonderful and selfless person that now sat before him. She truly took more pleasure in handing out gifts to her friends than she ever did on receiving them. Throughout their childhood she had always been the same and he put that down to the way that they had both been brought up in such a happy and loving household. Their parents had made them want for nothing and had always included them in all that they did. They were a family and his father, Cesare, instilled in them that family was all important. He taught them to be grateful for the things that God had given them, be humble in all things and to love each other unconditionally. These virtues came naturally to Sophia, he thought, her inner beauty was something that she was born with, it could not be taught.

'Why are you smiling?' she asked him as she sipped her coffee. 'You look silly.'

'No reason,' he replied. 'Other than I love being with you. You brighten up my day.'

'What time are we going tonight?' she asked him, ignoring his response.

'Anytime you want to. Maybe we could go for a glass of wine before we set off, what do you think?'

'Maybe,' she replied. Then she paused for a few moments, her mind seeming to drift off. 'I'm getting seriously worried about them, Marco. I really think they should get out of Rome. I've heard that more Jews from the north have arrived in the city after the announcement, heading to the south. Why they have stopped in Rome I don't know, but they can't be safe now the Germans are back. I fear they will be rounded up and Signor Trevini, Pia and Franco will be taken with them. We have all heard the rumours of how the Nazis treat the Jews.'

'Yes we have,' he replied sombrely. 'But that's all they are. Rumours. I cannot believe they can all be true. Shipping people away to camps in the east to force them to work or even worse. I know the Nazis have proved to be terrible over the past few years but after all, they are human. All humans are capable of compassion, we have to believe that. However, that said, I am worried also and think we need to speak to them tonight. I think we can take no chances.'

A tear formed in Sophia's eye. 'There are too many rumours for there not to be some truth in them don't you think? About the camps?'

They sat in silence for a while looking at the menus, avoiding taking the conversation any further for fear of upsetting each other more.

Sophia Roncalli had joined her brother in the capital the previous year after her parents had persuaded her to spend some time with him after the break-up of her engagement to Alessandro.

Alessandro Sartini had been the love of her life. Caring, handsome, thoughtful and respectful to her and her family at all times. Until suddenly one day he had told her that he could not cope with her saintliness and that he was not worthy of her and they should be apart. At first this news had floored her, it had broken her heart. However, she later heard from others and had grown to understand that he was probably not as virtuous as he had portrayed himself to be, and that the only truthful thing he had ever told her was that he indeed was not worthy of her.

At the time, worried about her state of mind, they had contacted Marco and he had added his opinion that a break from Turin as well as Alessandro would be a good thing for her. She would be able to enjoy the sights and culture of Rome and be able to have fun with the brother she loved. She had finally relented and agreed to go for a month but that month had turned into much longer and she had shared his small apartment now for just short of a year. She had gained employment at the city hospital and made new friends and had started to enjoy life again, despite the privations of war.

She had met Signor Trevini at the beginning of the year when she had witnessed him being hit by a car crossing the Ponte Palatino. The driver had not stopped to see if he was all right, only slowing down so he could shout abuse and wave his hands in fury at the old man, as though it had been his own fault for merely being there. Sophia had gone to his aid and when he had refused to go to the hospital she had insisted on helping him to his home, which was a small apartment in a five storey building on the Via del Portico d'Ottavia. His injuries had only been minor, a few cuts and bruises and a very sore right leg and after he had been cleaned and patched up she had stayed and enjoyed the hospitality that he had offered.

At first she had not been aware that he was Jewish, it had never crossed her mind, even when taking him to his home through the Jewish quarter. To Sophia it did not matter what particular religious persuasion people were, she could not comprehend how people could discriminate against each other based on their social class, religion or colour of their skin. The whole concept of it was alien to her.

As she had sat there enjoying the old man's intelligent and often witty conversation, they had eventually been joined by the rest of his family, his wife Pia, and their fifteen year old grandson, Franco, who shared the small apartment with them.

It had been immediately obvious to Sophia that Franco had fallen instantly and completely in love with her the first moment he laid eyes upon her face. She was aware that men found her attractive and had become used to the way some of them stumbled over their words when they spoke to her, so she found it endearing that this boy, ten years her junior, reacted in the same way. After attempting to compose himself he had made some coffee on the instructions of his grandfather and had handed the chipped enamel cup to her with an obvious shaking hand and an even more obvious red face.

Signor Trevini had laughed at him and winked at her. 'I don't think he has ever met an angel before,' he said and Sophia had found herself blushing at the compliment.

The one thing that she had noticed about this small Jewish family, living in the heart of the Italian capital was that despite their obvious closeness and love for each other, something did not seem right in the household. There seemed to be an air of nervousness and fear that permeated through the brick walls from outside, affecting all those within. She had noticed it also when she was helping him up the stairs to the apartment and it gave her a cold feeling throughout her body. She was no fool and knew that to be a Jew in Europe during these dark days was not exactly the safest thing to be and she cursed the war for the way it affected these normal, gentle people and all those like them. When she had finally said her goodbyes to them it was on the promise that she would visit them again.

And so, over the course of the last few months she had grown to love this small close family. She had never at any point asked about Franco's parents, feeling that if they wanted to talk about them and what had happened to them then it would be up to them to bring the subject up. She had seen a framed photograph on a shelf in the small living room of a young couple and presumed it to be them and would often catch Franco looking at it sadly. Whenever he caught her observing him he merely offered her a small smile but said nothing. However, the eyes did not smile.

She had brought Marco to visit them a couple of weeks after their first encounter and although they were slightly taken aback with his attire and his "job" (she had not told them he was a Catholic priest), they soon warmed to him and he too had come to regard the Trevinis as the closest friends he had in the capital, after his sister.

They did what they could for them, bringing them food and essential items that they were unable to obtain for themselves. Anti-Semitism was certainly not as strong here as in other places but it was still prevalent nevertheless and Sophia and Marco felt bound to assist them wherever they could, especially now that the Nazis were in the city and rumours were rife about them being taken away.

The waiter returned to the table and asked if they were ready to eat. They ordered sandwiches and a glass of wine each and sat back. Although the news of the previous week had left them both feeling elated, hoping beyond hope that the war would soon be over for Italy, the truth was that now the Germans were back in their midst, angry and aggrieved, they genuinely feared for themselves and their fellow countrymen more than ever before. There was only so much optimism available and Marco felt that it was fading fast.

CHAPTER THIRTY-SIX

As Marco and Sophia sat quietly eating their lunch, the waiter who had served them stood in the doorway next to their table looking out into the piazza, his hands clasped behind his back. Many of the tables were empty, only a handful of customers enjoying a drink or a bite to eat in the afternoon sunshine.

At once Marco became aware of him moving forward quickly as if in panic and looked to him to see what had caused this sudden disturbance, breaking the peaceful demeanour he had up until then been keeping.

He observed a small group of German officers approaching the café and the waiter guided them to a free table in the sunshine where he proceeded to pull out chairs hurriedly, inviting each of them to take a seat. Ignoring him, they brushed past and found a table under the awning on the opposite side of the doorway to the Roncallis. The waiter, now somewhat flustered, quickly followed them and again attempted to assist with the chairs but was pushed away as though he was merely an insignificant irritation. He retreated indoors to fetch menus and was out moments later placing them in the middle of their table. He stood to the side awaiting their instruction and when one of them waved him away he retreated to the shade of the doorway where he continued to observe them, his earlier relaxed demeanour now replaced by a tense nervousness.

There were four soldiers and Marco was horrified to see that they all wore the SS insignia on their collars, one of them wearing the black uniform of the Panzer Corps with a Knights Cross at his throat. He turned his head away to avoid making eye contact with any of them as they made him feel uneasy. He hated being in the presence of Nazis.

With her back to them and sensing her brothers awkwardness, Sophia turned slightly to view the table and immediately caught the eye of the German in the black uniform who tipped his cap to her and smiled before taking it off and turning to speak to his colleagues. Sophia turned back to her brother who frowned at her before taking a bite from his sandwich.

The Germans began to talk and laugh loudly at each other's jokes and comments and Marco looked at Sophia before saying quietly, 'If you feel uncomfortable, we could leave.'

She half turned to the table adjacent and replied. 'No Marco. This is our country and if we want to spend some time here then we will. They do not intimidate me.'

'Well, they do me,' replied Marco seriously. 'But, as you say, we should not be made to feel uncomfortable by them.' Smiling, he added, 'Let us pretend that they are not there.'

As the waiter walked by, Marco attempted to get his attention to order more drinks but, obviously flustered, the man did not notice and continued into the café to prepare whatever it was that the Germans had requested. He frowned at his sister who did not respond.

Marco was conscious that as their own conversation was becoming more and more stilted that of the Nazi officers was becoming quite the opposite. As the minutes passed, their behaviour gradually became more boisterous and they had started to shout and make comments at pedestrians as they passed, laughing loudly at each other's remarks. Marco could not understand what they were saying but could see from the response of each other that they were probably of a lewd nature. Two of them stood up to see better the current unfortunate who was the butt of the joke told by one of their seated friends, turning and laughing with them at what was obviously a very witty remark.

He caught the eye of one of the soldiers, a young man of perhaps only twenty years old, and on seeing Marco's stare, he sat back down awkwardly, before turning his head quickly to look again out into the piazza and once more join in on the banter.

Noticing his friend's reaction to whomever was sitting at the table behind him, the officer in the black uniform, who seemed not to be joining in as much as the others, merely indulging his friends, turned his head and looked at the Roncallis. He stared briefly into the eyes of Marco and for that fleeting second something stirred in the priest's memory, something that he could not quite determine but nevertheless gave him a very awkward feeling. Despite the heat of the day Marco suddenly felt cold, as though he had looked into the eyes of the devil himself.

The German's gaze quickly turned to Sophia and without breaking his deadpan expression his gaze lingered on her for a number of seconds. Sophia was aware of him staring but did not look at him, instead pretending that she did not realise that she was under his scrutiny.

Marco was aware that the man's colleagues had gone quiet and when he glanced at them he saw that all four of them were now staring at his sister, only at that moment noticing her as she had been sitting with her back to them.

Marco had summoned up enough courage and was about to say something to them when the waiter returned carrying a tray of drinks and placed them on the table in front of the soldiers. They all turned back and resumed their conversation, at once breaking into a hearty laugh at something the soldier in black said quietly.

'I think it may be best if we made a move soon,' he said. 'I don't like the way they are behaving and I don't like the way that they were looking at you.'

'Maybe you're right,' replied Sophia. 'They are beginning to make me nervous now. I don't feel comfortable at all.'

'There is something about the one in the black,' said Marco thoughtfully. 'Something I can't quite place. I feel as though I have seen him somewhere before but I don't know where.'

Sophia turned to look at him. The man was facing away from her, now smoking a thin cigarette. He had thin straight blond hair, cut very short at the back and when she managed to catch sight of his eyes as he turned his head to the side she saw that they were a very pale blue. Then she noticed a scar that ran down the left hand side of his face from the temple, almost to his lip, which caused the left side of his mouth to rise slightly. Involuntarily she drew a short intake of breath. She had not noticed it until now as the scar had been on the opposite side to where she could see.

The man became aware of Sophia looking at him and smiled humourlessly back at her. She quickly turned to face her brother, aware that she was now flushing after being caught out staring at him.

'Do not worry, I do not bite,' he said to her in perfect Italian.

Shocked at hearing him speak the language, she turned back to him. 'I am sorry,' she said. 'I did not mean to stare.'

'Oh this,' he said, raising his hand to the scar on his face. 'An old wound from my childhood. Do not worry, it makes me look a little more sinister than I really am.'

Taking the cigarette from his mouth and stubbing it out in an ashtray he turned to the Roncallis and pulled his chair toward them without rising from it. Remaining in his seat he held out his hand to Sophia. 'Hauptsturmführer Otto Finkel. And who do I have the pleasure of addressing?'

Sophia took his hand and was surprised to find it cold and clammy. She struggled to maintain her composure as all she wished to do was to pull her hand away from him.

'Sophia Roncalli,' she replied. Indicating her brother she said, 'And my brother, Father Marco Roncalli.'

'Pleased to meet the both of you,' replied Finkel releasing her hand. 'You must forgive my friends here, they can sometimes get a little boisterous but they mean no disrespect.'

'That's fine,' she replied noncommittally.

Finkel turned his attention to Marco. 'My apologies if we have offended you in any way, Father Roncalli.'

'Not at all,' replied Marco, smiling at him. 'Not at all.'

Marco again looked at the man. There was definitely something about him that he had seen before and the more he struggled to recall what it was, the further away the memory seemed to go. And the name. Otto Finkel. That too evoked memories that disturbed him.

'Is there something wrong, Father?' said the German. 'You seem to be staring at me rather strangely, if I may be frank.'

Breaking his trance Marco shook his head. 'It is my turn to apologise. However, I feel that I have met you somewhere before. Even your name is familiar to me but I cannot place where.'

'That is odd,' said Finkel frowning. 'This is the first time I have been to Italy so unless you have been to the Russian front recently then I can see no reason why our paths would have crossed.'

'No, no,' replied Marco. 'I feel it is from further back than that.'

The German squinted and looked hard at Marco before turning his gaze to Sophia. 'I am sorry but I really do not recall you. Either of you.'

'May I ask how you got that scar?' asked Marco. 'I do not wish to pry but you said it was a childhood injury.'

'It is,' replied Finkel. 'I got it in France when I was quite small. A boating accident. In fact I nearly drowned but was saved by another young boy. It is all so very long ago now... Are you okay?'

Marco had gone cold. It all came flooding back to him in an instant and he remembered clearly the events of that afternoon in the small cove in St Malo. Following the janitor, whose name he could not remember, to a small secluded cove where the fish were supposed to be abundant. The excitement of the young English boy whom he thought may have been named Jack or John... or George, he was not sure. He also remembered being extremely bored as the English boy had tried to fish and the way he bickered with his younger brother who had looked as uninterested as Marco had felt.

He remembered getting into the boat. He had not wanted to but had felt at the time that he had to. To join in with the other boys and not to look cowardly in front of them. His mind was filled with images of the young blond German boy falling and hitting his head and then slipping into the sea as they all watched, unable to react. Of him sinking beneath the waves and the English boy going in after him. Jack. Yes Jack. That was his name. The young German boy who had now grown up and was sitting at this very moment facing him. The young German boy who seemed very friendly, compassionate, intelligent and well mannered. That same boy right here, right now and in the uniform of the SS. The hardened killers who had all the opposite attributes to that young boy he had known very briefly in St Malo over fifteen years ago.

And then he remembered the hotel janitor in the water attempting furiously to save the lives of the two children in the water. The man who they had not allowed into the rowing boat for fear of it capsizing, who had eventually abandoned the attempt and swam back towards the shore. Marco knew that the man had been reported as missing but did not know what had ultimately happened to him, his father dealing with the police and the authorities and never mentioning the episode again. Marco had never found out the full story.

'Are you okay, Father?' repeated the German, Otto Finkel, an expression of what looked like concern now appearing on his face.

'Yes… I think so… I will be…' Marco stammered.

'Are you sure, Marco?' asked his sister leaning across the table and placing a hand over his. 'You look like you've seen a ghost.'

Marco swallowed. 'I think I have,' was his whispered reply.

After a few moments he was able to compose himself. He looked into Otto Finkel's eyes and searched for the boy that he had once known, for some trace of that young innocence that the boy Otto had owned back then. He could not see it. The eyes were now void of all compassion, the innocence of childhood left behind, probably in the waters of the English Channel over fifteen years ago.

'I do know you,' he said almost mechanically. 'We have met before. It was in St Malo in the summer of 1928. I was in that boat with you.'

Hauptsturmführer Otto Finkel did not say anything. He merely raised his eyebrows and stared deep into the priest's eyes.

'There were five of us in the boat,' continued Marco. 'I remember it as though it was only yesterday. Two English brothers, a French boy, who, if I remember correctly was some relation of the hotel owners where we were staying, myself and you. I remember watching you fall and hit your head on the side of the boat and then slip into the sea. The older of the two brothers went in after you and was assisted by someone who worked for the hotel in getting you back into the boat. It was one of the worst experiences of my life.'

'Good God,' said Finkel quietly.

The remaining three Germans were now very quiet. It was clear that they did not understand the conversation taking place before them but they could see from Finkel's expression that the time for merriment and frivolity was now over.

Sophia looked at her brother, unable to say a thing, totally lost for words.

Then Finkel smiled and stood up. 'Then, my friend, Father Roncalli,' he said heartily, 'that means that you are one of those responsible for saving my life that day. Without your efforts getting me back to shore then I certainly would have perished.' He held out his hand to Marco.

Marco stood up and took the German's hand somewhat reluctantly. Finkel shook it vigorously, clapping him on the shoulder as he did so. He looked into his eyes and spoke in German. His colleagues immediately stood up and walked over to the table, taking it in turns to shake the priest's hand.

Finkel pulled his chair closer to the Roncalli's table and clicked his fingers. The waiter came rushing over, eager to please his new customers or, more likely, eager not to upset them in any way.

'A bottle of your finest wine and three glasses,' he ordered, without looking at the man. The waiter rushed off into the café to carry out the order.

Marco raised his hand. 'There is no need. Really.'

'Nonsense,' said Finkel smiling. 'It is not every day something like this happens. We shall drink to the re-acquaintance of old friends. All three of us.' He looked at Sophia who smiled back at him politely. 'What do you say?'

'Very well,' said Marco. 'Just one glass I'm afraid. We have an important function we need to attend later.'

'That is fine,' said Finkel. 'But for now we can enjoy a nice glass of wine together.'

The waiter returned with the wine and three glasses. He opened the bottle and poured some into a glass for Finkel to try.

Without looking at him the German said irritably. 'Just pour it.'

The waiter quickly filled all three glasses before putting the bottle on the table and withdrawing to the sanctuary of the café, relieved that his part was now over.

'Tell me,' said Finkel, 'what has happened to the pair of you over the years. I must admit that I still cannot remember your face. Maybe it is the glasses. I can only remember there being five of us in the boat but can't really remember who those other people were. I had got quite friendly with the two English brothers but, to be honest, I feel nothing for them now. Had not the elder one, Jack, I think his name was, insisted on using the boat then I would not have this scar and that janitor would not be dead. But then he did save my life, I suppose.'

Marco took a deep breath. He had often wondered what had become of the man who had jumped into the water to save them and had been suspicious that his father had kept something from him. So the poor man had died. He made a sign of the cross and kissed the crucifix that hung around his neck.

'Oh,' said Finkel surprised. 'You did not know? Yes, unfortunately he drowned. They found his body the following day.'

Marco replied, 'I did not know. I thought it may have happened, that my father had kept the truth from me. I will pray for his soul.'

'You know what,' said Finkel, taking out a cigarette from a pack from his tunic pocket, 'I don't really blame them for what happened. The English boys. I feel more aggrieved at that scruffy French boy. He got into the boat first. If anyone is to blame then it is he.'

'I don't see it that way,' replied Marco. 'It was one of those unfortunate occurrences that happen once in a while. We were just boys back then… children. We did not know what we were doing. No one is to blame really.'

'No?' replied Finkel. 'Every time I look in the mirror I am reminded of that day. Someone has to be accountable.'

'If there is any guilt then it will be up to God to decide where it lies,' insisted Marco. He felt a short kick under the table from his sister.

Not noticing Marco flinch Finkel replied, 'Maybe so, Father, maybe so. But I will put my faith in justice with the Führer, and this.' He patted the holster at his side that contained what looked like a large sidearm. Marco felt a chill run down his spine and almost physically shivered. He picked up the glass of wine and drank half of it before putting it down again. As Finkel looked around, Marco indicated for his sister to drink her wine. He was now feeling very uncomfortable and needed to get away.

Sophia picked up her glass and did likewise.

Finkel looked back. 'My God, you Italians can drink,' he said on seeing their half empty glasses. 'So, go on. How have you filled the years until now?'

'Not a lot to it,' said Sophia sipping at her wine nervously. 'Marco here entered the priesthood and got a job at the Vatican. I have become a nurse and am working at the city hospital. Very normal uneventful lives.'

'Okay,' said Finkel realising that Sophia did not want to tell him much.

Marco drained his glass and then said, 'Apologies, Signor Finkel, but we must be getting along. I am sorry to have to leave but needs must.'

Finkel pushed back his chair and stood up. 'No problem, Father Roncalli,' he said, extending his hand once more, which Marco took. 'I too have many things to do before the sun goes down. However, I am free tomorrow evening and would love to meet up with you again. It would be a shame for this to be our only meeting after all these years and the bond that connects us. Maybe it is fate that has brought us together after all this time.'

'I don't know....' replied Marco hesitantly.

'But I insist. My treat. There is a restaurant on the corner over there that looks quite nice. I will meet you there tomorrow evening at half past seven. What do you say?'

Unable to think of a suitable excuse, Marco replied, 'Fine, Signor Finkel. Half past seven.'

Finkel turned to Sophia. 'And you must join us too, Fraulein. It would be my pleasure.'

'Unfortunately I will be on duty tomorrow evening. At the hospital. I am very sorry.'

'No worries,' said Finkel. 'Maybe another time then.'

They said their goodbyes and Finkel took the bottle of wine from the table and rejoined his fellow officers where they started again with their laughter and boisterous behaviour.

As they walked away from the café, Sophia said, 'Are you going to go tomorrow?'

'I think that I have to.'

'No you don't.'

'It may be good to have someone like that close to us for the time being,' replied Marco thoughtfully. 'The man is obviously not the same person as the boy I knew briefly all those years ago. Did you see his eyes? He is SS and we know what they can be like. We may be able to get information from him that can help with the Trevinis. This may be a good thing.'

'I cannot see how this can be a good thing,' replied Sophia. 'He gives me the creeps. His eyes are evil. God knows what he has done in this war.'

'Yes,' replied Marco as they turned a corner and were now out of the piazza. 'God does know. And if he has been involved in anything bad then it will be God who will punish him.'

They walked a few moments in silence.

'And by the way,' said Marco, a small smile appearing on his face. 'I think that it is time that you went to confession, young lady.'

'Oh,' replied Sophia turning to him. 'And why is that? What sins do you think I have committed?'

'Telling lies for one,' said Marco. 'You and I both know that you are not on duty tomorrow evening.'

Sophia could not help giggling.

'And no remorse either, I see,' laughed Marco. 'How do you expect to get absolution?'

'I don't think that lying to Nazis counts,' said Sophia. 'Anyway if you insist, I will say three Hail Marys before I go to sleep.'

Marco looked at her and smiled. 'That should cover it,' he said. 'And add a little prayer for your brother too. It's me who is left lumbered tomorrow evening having to entertain him on my own.'

'Sorry,' she replied, the smile still firmly fixed to her face.

They continued the rest of the walk back to their small apartment in silence. Marco thought of the words that Otto Finkel had said about fate and how, after all these years, it had brought them back together. He wished now that he had kept his mouth shut and not mentioned St Malo to the German. Maybe it was better to let sleeping dogs lie.

Then he sighed. What was done was done. He would go to the restaurant and he would engage with the man. Maybe he could learn something about the plans the Germans had for the Jews of the city and maybe he could help in some way in keeping their friends safe and well.

But, as he walked through the streets of the city that he loved, he could not get rid of the awful feeling that the fate Finkel had spoken of would not bring anything good to his life, but totally the opposite.

CHAPTER THIRTY-SEVEN

The apartment occupied by the Trevinis was to be found at the junction of the Via del Portico d'Ottavia and the Via del Tempia, a five storey building facing a cobblestoned square not far from the Tempio Maggiore di Roma, The Great Synagogue of Rome. The roads leading to it were narrow, tall apartment buildings of between four and six storeys lined the route and it was down these narrow avenues that Marco and Sophia walked later that evening.

They could sense a distinct difference in the atmosphere of the place since the Germans had occupied the city a few short days ago. No longer could they see children playing on the cobbled stones or men sitting at tables smoking pipes, enjoying the heat of the autumn sun that they may have witnessed before. It was as though the occupants were waiting for something to happen, something momentous that they had no control over, something that would change them all forever and not for the good. It gave both of them a feeling of unease and, for the first time, Marco felt that his presence in this part of the city was not a good thing, it now did not feel quite right, he did not feel in any way comfortable.

They walked up the two flights of stairs to the apartment on the third floor and Marco knocked on the simple wooden door, which a youth – around fifteen year old, opened. He was of average height for his age, with blue eyes that lit up when he saw Sophia and his black hair was slicked back with oil. His clothing was not exactly elegant, a grey oversized pullover with holes worn in the elbows and he wore stockings on his feet that had also seen better days, his big toe poking through one of them.

'Hello, Franco,' said Sophia, smiling brightly at him.

'Hell... hell... hello, Sophia,' he stammered, somewhat high pitched, ignoring Marco completely, his face flushing red. It amused Sophia that the boy always struggled with his words for the first few minutes when she was in his company but she never said anything to him about it. She found it very endearing.

Marco hid a smirk with his hand before hearing a familiar voice shout from inside.

'Don't stand there stammering, boy, let them in.'

Franco stood aside and held the door open, allowing Sophia and Marco to pass into the apartment.

They continued down a short hallway and entered a small room at the end. It was a modest apartment, sparsely furnished due to the family having to sell most of their household items to make ends meet, but there was still sufficient seating to allow them to rest their feet. The main window, which overlooked the cobbled street below, had no curtain, allowing some natural light into the room. The walls were bare, all the pictures having been sold over the past couple of years and the only one that was still on display was positioned on a small sideboard, a photograph that was clearly of Franco's parents.

'Come in, come in,' said Signor Trevini who was sitting at a dining table to their right as they entered. 'Please sit down my friends, it is so nice to see you both again.'

'And you too, Signor Trevini,' replied Marco with a smile.

Sophia approached him and kissed him firmly on the left cheek, placing the brown paper bag she was carrying onto the floor behind his chair. 'Ah,' he said with a sigh, 'The Angel of the Palatino. Here in my home. Life is good, life is good.'

'You flatter me,' said Sophia softly, kissing him again.

Signor Trevini was over seventy years old. A short man with a bald head with thin, grey, almost transparent hair at the back and sides. He may have once been quite stocky but the lack of a good diet over the past few years had left him thin and drawn. His skin was of a pallid complexion and the lack of weight in his face had left his quite large nose appearing even more prominent than it would have been.

'Not at all,' he said holding up his hand. 'If it was not for you, I would probably still be lying out in the street where that idiot left me.'

Franco, who had now composed himself and was standing behind the Roncallis, said, 'Can I get either of you a drink. We do not have much coffee left but I am sure that we can manage a couple of cups.'

Marco, who had himself been carrying a bag, now held it out to him. 'There's a few bits in there for you Franco,' he said, 'including some coffee. We can all have some. There's some other things in there too that I am sure you can make use of.'

'Thank you,' said Signor Trevini. 'You are so kind to us. You are both beautiful people. Franco take the bag through to the kitchen and give it to your grandmother.'

Franco left the room to carry out his grandfather's bidding and Marco and Sophia sat at the table across from the old man.

'How are you?' asked Sophia. 'How are you all?'

'Worried,' he replied quietly, not wanting his wife and grandson to overhear their conversation. 'We don't know what will happen now that the Germans are back. We are a little scared if I am honest. All of us. Not just us three but the whole community.'

'We have been talking,' said Marco, also keeping his voice low. 'It may be prudent for you all to get out of Rome, or to find somewhere else to live until they are gone. I can only see the Allies winning this and it won't be long before they are here.'

'That may just be wishful thinking, Marco,' replied Signor Trevini with a frown. 'Who knows what is to happen?' He sat up straight in his chair and continued. 'I know what you say makes sense but Pia will never leave this place if she has any choice in the matter. She has lived here all her life and despite the dangers, she is not for moving.'

'Maybe you need to be a little more forceful,' said Sophia, who had now sat down at the table next to him. 'Maybe you need to speak to her and make her listen.'

Trevini started to laugh. 'And do you think she will listen to me? I don't think so. Maybe you are right though. Maybe the Allies will be here in the matter of a couple of weeks or so. It may be that this all just passes over and we are forgotten about.'

'And maybe they will come for you like we are hearing they are doing in other places,' said Sophia, a tear forming in her eye.

Trevini looked at her and smiled at her sadly. 'Please do not upset yourself, my dear. We will be fine. I am sure of it. What harm have we ever done to anyone? What threat are we to them? Look at us. We are simple people trying to live a simple life. They will leave us be, I am sure of it.'

'Marco,' said Sophia turning to her brother. 'Speak to him. Please. Tell him that they need to get away.'

'I fear that my sister is right, Leo,' he said solemnly. 'We cannot trust the Nazis. They are unpredictable at best, but one thing that you can rely on with them is their cruelty and their willingness to carry it out. I would feel better if you made some attempt to get out of the city or to at least hide up somewhere away from the Jewish Quarter until they move on.'

Signor Trevini was about to speak again but was interrupted as his wife, Pia, and Franco returned from the kitchen carrying cups of coffee with them, which they placed on the table.

'Thank you so much for your gifts,' Pia said to the Roncallis. 'It is so generous of you both. You really do not need to do this for us when we have no way of repaying you.'

'Think nothing of it,' said Marco. 'Maybe one day you can do the same for us.'

Pia Trevini was two years younger than her husband and although she was very small, she seemed to generate a larger presence when she was in the room. She stood barely five feet in height and because of her stoop, due to a slightly twisted spine, she seemed much shorter, almost childlike. Her grey hair was cut quite short and pushed behind her ears giving her face a bird like appearance. She did not appear to lift her feet as she walked and seemed to glide along the floor as she moved.

'So what are you three talking about?' she asked inquisitively.

'Nothing to concern yourself with, my dear,' responded her husband loudly. 'Nothing to worry about.'

'I'll be the judge of that,' she replied dismissively. 'What have you said to make Sophia so upset? Look at her. The poor girl looks terrible.'

'She can never look terrible,' he replied. 'She is one of life's beauties.'

Sophia wiped her eyes and smiled at Pia Trevini. 'I am just so worried about you all, that's all.'

'Oh don't worry about us. We will be fine, I promise you.'

Sophia was suddenly overwhelmed with a feeling of deep compassion for her. She stood up and walked over to Pia. Wrapping her arms around the old woman she said, 'Please take our advice, Pia. Please take yourselves away somewhere safe until all this is over. I don't trust the Germans. I don't trust them to leave you alone.'

Breaking the embrace, Pia replied, 'I have lived here all my life. I am not prepared to be chased away from my home by those people. Anyway, they will be too concerned about the British and Americans to be bothered with us. They will leave us. There is no benefit in them using their resources to pester us.'

Sophia sat back on the chair. She felt drained, exhausted. She knew that she was wasting her breath. The Trevinis would not leave this place until it was clear in their heads that it was absolutely necessary and as yet they could not see that it was. No amount of coaxing or persuading would get them to budge. Then she remembered the other reason they had come to see them.

'Franco,' she said. 'Come here. I have something for you. Marco, would you be so kind as to pass me that paper bag?'

Marco leaned over to retrieve the bag she had placed behind Leo Trevini's chair. He handed it to Sophia across the table.

'Yes,' said Franco expectantly.

Sophia looked at the young man and smiled at him. He instantly reciprocated. 'I have a little something for you. A small gift.' She handed him the bag.

Pulling out a pair of brand new brown leather ankle boots, Franco's face lit up. Beaming, he looked at her. 'Why? It is not my birthday for a couple of months yet. I don't understand.'

'I have seen the state of your current footwear, young man. Any friend of mine needs to be wearing the finest boots, you should know that.'

'I don't know what... don't know what to say,' he stammered.

'Then don't say anything.'

'Thank you, thank you,' he said, sitting down on a dining chair to try them on.

Pia Trevini smiled at him and then turned to Sophia. 'You spoil him, young lady, you really do. I don't know how we can ever repay you all the kindness you have shown us, I really don't. The both of you.'

'We are just glad we can help you. It is our pleasure,' said Marco.

'Come,' said Leo Trevini clapping his hands. 'Let us take our drinks out on to the balcony. This is truly a wonderful day. Let us enjoy the evening.'

*

A half hour later, standing on the small balcony that overlooked the narrow cobbled street at the front of the apartment block, Marco stood alone with Leo. All seemed quiet below them and no one else, from where they could see, was outside, the stillness and tranquility of the night belying the more sinister reason the streets were empty.

'We are like virtual prisoners in our own homes now,' Leo Trevini said suddenly. 'The Germans are everywhere you look. I think you may be right and it may be a matter of time before we get them knocking on our doors.'

'Then you should do as we have suggested,' replied Marco. 'Get your family out while you still have a chance. Go somewhere else.'

'Where?' replied Leo calmly. 'To the north? That's more dangerous than here. Then to the south? Why? The Americans and British are on their way. I think the safest place to be right now is probably right here. At least here we know the environment. We know where to hide should the Germans decide to come for us.'

Marco sighed. He knew, like Sophia, that he was probably wasting his time and energy in attempting to get their friends to move away. If they were to be stubborn and obstinate then there was little more they could do.

Marco turned to look inside the apartment and could see Franco and Sophia talking happily to each other, occasionally laughing at something one or the other was saying.

Leo noticed his gaze and said, 'I worry about him. After what happened to his mother and father he is more lonely than he lets on. He is so young and has his whole life ahead of him and at the moment there are no prospects for him. I cannot see how he can make a happy life for himself.'

'Just promise me one thing, Leo,' said Marco. 'Will you do that for me?'

'And what is that?'

'If I find out that things are going to happen. That I feel you are in clear and immediate danger, then promise me that you will act on what I say. You will leave when I tell you that it is absolutely necessary for you to do so.'

'And how will you get to know of such things, Marco? With respect, you are merely another Catholic priest in a city full of them. What makes you so special?'

Marco sighed to himself. 'I am not special in any way, Leo. Not special at all. Like you say I am merely one of hundreds of Catholic priests living in this great city. However, I may have a friend... no not friend... let's say associate... who may be able to provide me with some information should I be bold enough to ask for it.'

Leo Trevini looked at his unlikely friend and paused. He did not ask the question he wanted to ask. He merely said, 'Okay have it your way, priest. If that moment comes then I will act upon it. I will do as you say.'

'Do I have your word?'

'I am a Roman and a Jew, my friend,' he replied quietly. 'I never lie.'

'Thank you,' replied Marco. He thought of Otto Finkel and decided that he would meet him the following night, as arranged. He had considered not turning up, of breaking his promise to meet him. He had not wished to converse with a Nazi officer even if they had known each other for a brief time as children. Times had changed and the world was a different place now. But, he thought, maybe knowing him might not be such a bad thing right now. Maybe Finkel could provide him with the information that he may need. Yes, he thought, he would go to the restaurant and meet him, no matter how much he did not want to.

Behind them, in the sitting room, they could hear Franco and Sophia again laughing loudly at something one or the other had said. They both turned and saw Franco dancing around the room in his new boots, kicking his feet out and showing them off.

Both men smiled at the sight and then smiled at each other.

'Come my friend,' said Leo, 'Let us join them once more.'

CHAPTER THIRTY-EIGHT

Otto Finkel was waiting for Marco at a table in the corner of the busy restaurant, smoking a thin cigarette. In front of him sat a bottle of red wine, a glass poured. The restaurant was typical of those in the piazza, offering traditional Italian food and wines and decorated modestly, the pictures on the walls showing scenes of Rome and Venice.

Marco had no problem spotting him as he was the only German soldier in the room, his black uniform standing out against the more brightly clothed Italians. He could sense the mood of the other customers was somewhat subdued, especially those seated at tables near to him, their voices stilted and hushed, obviously due to having an SS officer in their presence.

On seeing the priest enter he stood up and signalled to him, smiling brightly. Marco walked over and sat down, aware of the stares of the others in the room. An SS officer dining with a priest was an obvious unlikely pairing.

'I am glad you could make it,' said Otto sitting back down after shaking Marco's hand. 'I thought that you may not bother.'

'I said that I would and I am not allowed to lie,' said Marco with a wry smile. 'I wouldn't be much of a priest if I did not practice what I preached.'

'True,' said Otto. 'Very true.' He took a pack of cigarettes out of his jacket pocket and offered it to Marco who shook his head.

'No thank you,' he said. 'I stopped smoking a couple of years ago. I realised that I did not like it.'

'These are very good,' said Otto. 'They are very hard to get hold of though. They're Russian. I developed a taste for them when I was over there.'

Marco looked at the Knight's Cross at Otto's throat. 'Is that where you won that?'

Otto looked down. 'Yes it was. A dreadful business I can tell you. A truly horrible place and I won't be going back if I can help it. Anyhow, enough talk of Russia, let's order some food. I took the liberty of ordering the wine. Red. I hope it is to your liking.'

'I'm sure it will be fine.'

'Good, good,' replied Otto, pouring Marco a glass.

The waiter approached and they ordered two salad starters with a pasta dish to follow.

'You know what,' said Otto thoughtfully, 'This is the first time I have been to Italy and I have to say that it is a wonderful country. The weather is excellent, even for so late in the year, and the food is the best I have tasted in a long time. Your women are also very beautiful.'

'I like it,' replied Marco. 'It is just a shame that we are not living in happier times.'

'We cannot control history unfortunately,' said Otto.

'No. But now that Italy has surrendered we should be out of the war. It should be over for us.'

Otto leaned back in his chair and laughed loudly, causing the majority of the other customers to turn and look at them with curiosity. Otto ignored them.

'Don't be so naïve, Marco,' he said. 'Do you think the Führer is simply going to order us all out? Quite the opposite my old friend, quite the opposite. If your fellow countrymen no longer have the stomach for the fight then it will be up to us Germans to carry it on. And make no mistake, if we have to fight Italy too then we will not step back from that.'

Marco could feel his temper rising but took a breath to control it. He prided himself on his humility and his ability to remain calm and he also did not want to antagonise the man. He may have been a quiet thoughtful child, all those years ago in France, but now he was an SS officer, experienced in war and he could be very dangerous, very dangerous indeed.

Otto could see that Marco was not comfortable. 'I can tell by the look in your eyes that you see me as the devil.'

'No you are wrong, Otto. I see what you do as evil but I still remember the boy in the rowing boat.'

'Evil?'

'Yes. I see no other word for it... What you are doing to the Jews for example.'

Otto drew deeply on his cigarette and sat back in his chair before responding. 'We both have reason to hate the Jews.'

'Why so? I have no reason to hate anyone.'

'They destroyed my country. They murdered the son of God.'

'Was not the son of God himself a Jew... The King of the Jews, remember?'

Otto smiled at him mirthlessly Marco was under the impression that he was being mocked.

'All Christians should hate the Jews,' said Otto calmly.

'You consider yourself a Christian, Otto?' asked Marco.

'I consider myself a ridder of the evil you accuse me of being. We are doing the work others are scared to do. Open your eyes Marco. The world needs to be rid of these vermin. We are making the world a better place.'

It was Marco's turn to smile. 'Now who is being naïve?'

'Ah this talk is silly. We are friends are we not? Come let us eat.'

The waiter returned with two plates of food and set them in front of the two unlikely dinner companions.

After he moved away Otto said, 'Do you think it strange we are sat here together? The Nazi and the priest.'

'We live in strange times, Otto. This is no longer 1928 and we are no longer children.'

As Otto put a forkful of salad into his mouth, he said, 'Yes, we have all grown up now. I wonder what happened to the others… the others in the boat. What do you think?'

Glad of the change in the conversation Marco replied, 'I really have no idea. To be honest I cannot remember too much about them. I remember there being two English boys, yourself and a very quiet French boy but if they walked into this room right now I fear I would not recognise them.'

'You say that but you recognised me.'

'Eventually and only because of the scar on your face. I was there remember, I saw it happen. You did not recognise me though did you?'

'No, I did not, you are right.' Marco sipped his wine before topping up the glass from the bottle in front of him. 'I suppose we could speculate that they have all grown up and are somehow involved in this war, somewhere. If they are not dead, of course.'

Marco did not reply.

'So tell me Marco, what made you decide to become a priest?'

'It was always going to happen if I am honest,' he replied. 'I have only ever had one true friend outside of my family and that was God. With him everything is simple, everything makes sense.'

'You are a good looking man, were you never tempted by women? A life of celibacy has got to be difficult surely,' Otto was genuinely interested.

'Maybe when I was younger, yes,' replied Marco honestly. 'But once the decision was made then it is a very small thing to have to give up. I take my vices elsewhere. I used to smoke and I enjoy the odd glass of wine, but that's about it. The love of God and my family is all that I need.'

'Not a life I could live my friend. No, not for me,' said Otto.

'You have asked me why I am a priest. May I ask you why you are a Nazi?'

'I am not ashamed, if that is what you are looking for in me,' replied Otto seriously. 'I have been a member of the party from as soon as I was able to be. I joined the SS before the war. It is a path I have chosen and one on which I am happy to walk forever. The Führer is my leader and he will remain so until the day I die. His words speak to me in a way that your God could never do.'

'My God is a god of peace. You follow a man whose life is built on a foundation of hatred,' said Marco. 'I know which the path of righteousness is. Your path can only lead to doom.'

For the first time Otto looked annoyed at his dining companion and for a second Marco felt even more uncomfortable. Had he gone too far? After all he did not know what this man was capable of.

'Think what you will, priest,' said Otto matter-of-factly. 'It is of no concern to me.'

'I'm sorry if I have offended you.'

'Ach. Think nothing of it. People have said worse to me over the years, believe me. I have a very thick skin. Anyway, how is that beautiful sister of yours? When will I get a chance to meet her again?'

Marco felt a small shiver run down his back. There was no way he was going to let this Nazi anywhere near his sister. 'I don't know. I hardly see her myself these days as she is so busy,' he lied. 'I will try and see if I can arrange something.'

Otto looked into Marco's eyes for a moment. 'Very well, it is of no matter.'

Marco wanted the meal to be over. He wanted to get away from this man. He could feel the odd stare of those in the restaurant and was aware of muttered conversations and all at once he felt very paranoid. What would happen when the Germans left? Would sitting here having this meal with this man make people think that he was some sort of collaborator? Would his dog collar give him immunity from those types of thoughts and potential reprisals in the future? He thought not.

Maybe having this man close to him might prove useful in getting the information that he needed but he could not involve his sister in any of this. He could not let this man near her for two reasons. The first being that he just did not want her in the presence of evil and his no doubt lustful intentions towards her and secondly he could not allow there to be any misled repercussions against her when the Germans were eventually kicked out of Italy, which Marco firmly believed would happen.

'So,' he said boldly. 'What are you doing in Rome?'

'I have been detached from my unit and been given a little task,' he replied candidly. 'I am doing some groundwork for a colleague. Theodor Dannecker. Have you heard of him? He will be in Italy next month.'

Marco felt sick. 'I am aware of his reputation, yes.'

Otto raised his eyebrows but said nothing. 'I don't expect to be here long. I know that they want me back in France shortly, I have just come from there, so this job will not take up too much of my time. I am having a break from combat operations for a while. I think I have seen my fair share of bullets and bombs.'

Marco nodded. 'It is good that you are out of harm's way,' was all that he could think to say.

They ate the rest of their meal in relative silence. The conversation turning to small talk of each other's families and the work that Marco did in the Vatican.

'So, when are you returning to work?' asked Otto pleasantly.

'I have been avoiding going back due to all your troops surrounding the place,' he said honesty.

'Oh don't worry about that,' said Otto dismissively. 'As long as your papers are in order then you will be able to come and go as you please. After all, this is your country, is it not?'

Ten minutes later, their meal finished, Marco took out his wallet.

'No, no, Marco,' said Otto rising from his seat. 'My treat remember. It is the least I can do after what you did for me all those years ago. Getting me safely back to shore and all that. I insist.'

Marco was not prepared to argue with him. He just wanted to get away.

As they left the restaurant, Otto said, 'I really enjoyed our little get together this evening. Maybe we can do it again soon. And make sure that you bring your sister next time, I would love to see her again. How are you fixed for the same time next week?'

Marco forced a smile. 'Yes,' he said, 'that would be nice.'

'That's settled then. Until next week.'

They shook hands and Marco said goodbye before turning and walking away. He could feel Otto Finkel's eyes burning into his back as he walked down the street, Finkel leaning against a wall as he lit another of his Russian cigarettes.

A few seconds later Marco turned a corner and was finally able to breathe freely again. He had never felt so uncomfortable in all his life. He felt that he had been conversing with the devil himself. Although Otto's manner was somewhat lively and brash, his eyes had looked like those of a corpse, devoid of life and bereft of any compassion or humanity.

As he walked along the street in the warm, balmy evening, Marco realised that it was now totally necessary to have Otto as an associate, no matter how much he was repulsed by the idea. He had been told by him that he was working on behalf of the Gestapo under Hauptsturmführer Theodor Dannecker. Marco did not know much about the man but what he did know scared him to his very core. The rumour was that he was responsible for the rounding up and deportation of Jews in France and other countries and the man was soon to be in Italy. So with what Otto had just told him, the rounding up of the Roman Jews could not be very far off and it was Otto himself who would play a significant part in that process.

Time was now critical and somehow he and his sister needed to persuade their friends to get to a place of safety. Whether they liked it or not, they no longer had a choice.

CHAPTER THIRTY-NINE

Fifty-five year old Bishop Paulo Beresi looked at the paperwork on his desk and frowned. The backlog was getting a little too much and he felt like leaving it where it was and going for a long walk. He always enjoyed walking around the grounds as it gave him time to think, to be alone with God. He could feel His presence all around and it always gave him comfort in trying times, particularly times such as these.

He had not seen his assistant in nearly a week and he had decided that if he did not turn up today then he was going to have to pay him a visit that evening at the small apartment he shared with his pretty sister. There was more work than he could possibly handle on his own and not having Marco there put a bigger burden on his own workload. If he had been born a less tolerant man then he presumed that something like this would have not made him happy.

But then he could understand why Marco had not shown up. Unlike himself, Marco lived outside the Vatican walls and would have had to endure the gauntlet of the Wehrmacht troops who, for some reason incomprehensible to Beresi, had circled the city when they had occupied Rome the previous week. He could not understand why they had done this. The Vatican posed no threat to them, surely, no threat at all. If anything, he was ashamed to think, they had turned a blind eye to all that was happening, the Holy Father choosing to maintain a noticeable silence on the matter.

Yes, he thought, it was true that he had made a veiled mention against the actions of the Nazis in his last Christmas speech, but it was hardly a speech that was going to make them stop what they were doing and it was made some time ago. The world had revolved a lot since last December. It did not sit right with Beresi, as a man of God, that stronger words were not coming from senior church officials. It was something that he thought may one day come back to haunt them all. These were truly momentous times that they were living in and how they conducted themselves during this period would be a matter of historical record and subject to the scrutiny of scholars in years to come.

Bishop Beresi just hoped that they would not be seen as lacking in judgement, wanting in action or most importantly, compromising in faith.

He heard the door handle turn and looked up to see Father Marco Roncalli enter the office, looking tired and harassed.

'Ah, Father Marco,' he said standing up to greet him. 'I am so glad to see you.'

Marco held up both of his hands in apology. 'I am sorry, Bishop Beresi. I have been neglecting my duties, I know. However, life is a little difficult outside these walls. There are foreign troops everywhere.'

'Don't apologise, my boy,' replied Beresi comfortingly. 'Please take a seat and tell me what's happening.'

Marco sat down opposite his superior, crossed his right leg over his left and adjusted the black cassock where it clung to his knee. He enjoyed working with the bishop, who he admired and respected very much. He was a good boss, compassionate, humble and gentle. However, the man was not scared in sometimes voicing his opinion to whomever he felt needed it and often Marco was made to feel a little awkward when the man criticised others behind their backs.

Beresi stood well over six feet tall and his presence dominated any room he walked into. He wore a purple cassock and had a skull cap upon his mass of thick grey curls. His deep brown eyes dominated his highly tanned face and Marco felt that they could penetrate minds should anyone look directly into them for too long. He was possibly the most intelligent man Marco had ever known.

Marco gave him a brief resume of what had been taking place outside the Vatican walls since the arrival of the German army. Whereas Marco had chosen to stay away and not attempt to come into the city, Beresi had opted for the opposite and had stayed within the grounds, not leaving once.

Marco felt that he could trust Beresi but at the same time he did not want to burden him with the news that he had met an old friend who had changed dramatically over the past years. He did not wish the man to think ill of him and possibly make the incorrect assumption that he was fraternising with the Nazis. When he thought of this, he wondered why he was doing it anyway. Common sense said that he should walk away, never cross the man's path again but he knew that it was a choice that he could not take. He knew that if he did, then he may lose an opportunity to get information that could affect his friends on the Via del Portico d'Ottavia.

'You look very troubled, my young friend,' said Beresi softly. 'Do you want to tell me more?'

'There is nothing more to tell of any importance,' said Marco. 'I am just a little worried about my friends. The Trevinis. I think I told you about them.'

'The Jews? Yes, you told me of them,' replied Beresi. 'How are they coping now that the Germans are here?'

'Not good, I'm afraid,' said Marco. 'My sister and I are trying to persuade them to leave the city, to go somewhere safer but they will not listen. They are too stubborn and we genuinely fear for them.'

Beresi stroked his chin thoughtfully as he leaned back in his chair. After a few moments he said, 'Listen Marco... Make sure that you never repeat to anyone what I am about to tell you now. Your friends, they do not need to leave the city, they just need somewhere to hide until these evil monsters have gone. I will make enquiries but I know that some of the old monasteries are hiding some of them. I will try to find something out for you and we may be able to do something practical to help them. I'm afraid praying for them has not done a great deal of good so far. For some reason God does not appear to be listening too intently.'

'Thank you so much, Bishop Beresi,' said Marco. 'I am so worried that they will be taken away to the camps we hear about in the east. If the rumours are true then I must do something to help them, even if they do not wish to help themselves. They seem to be burying their heads in the sand over this.'

'As are some of those within these walls,' said Beresi. 'Just be careful who you speak to, even here. Do not trust everyone. In fact, do not trust anyone, it will be safer. These are very troubled times, my young friend, and when judgement day comes, we do not want to be found lacking where this period of history is concerned. These are dark times, dark times indeed.'

'I have been told that I am naïve, Bishop Beresi,' said Marco, 'and maybe I am a little. Or am I just optimistic? I really don't know. When I heard Eisenhower's announcement that Italy had surrendered, I thought that it was the end. I genuinely thought... for a couple of days anyway... that it was over for us. We actually danced, can you believe that? We actually danced around the apartment. Me and Sophia, like a couple of children.'

'Do not be embarrassed by that, my friend,' said Beresi smiling at him. 'Do not be embarrassed about having hope. Our hope and our faith are the two things they can never take from us no matter what they throw at us. Come, let us walk. It helps me to think.'

They left the office with the mountain of untouched paperwork still lying on the desks and walked through the ornate and majestic corridors, passing priests, bishops and other church officials going about their business in what seemed a hurried manner, until they stepped out into the sunshine of the Vatican gardens to the rear of St. Peter's Basilica.

Marco could understand why Bishop Beresi liked to walk out here. It was truly beautiful. An intricate system of pathways led in all directions through well-manicured lawns, which were bordered with bright flowers of every colour of the spectrum. Ornate statues and water features added to the lavish surroundings, which were all maintained by a small army of gardeners. The sound of the water as it trickled down rocks and spouted from fountains added to the relaxing ambience that they had created. Marco looked back at the dome of the Basilica that rose high behind him and felt that this was possibly the most peaceful place on earth, this little space in the heart of Italy's capital, a refuge from the pain and heartache that was taking place for so many outside these walls. In here, God was truly present.

There were not many others in the gardens that morning and they found a small bench on which to sit.

They had not spoken since leaving the office, Marco observing the bishop in his peripheral vision, walking with head bowed, deep in thought, almost in meditation, and he did not wish to interrupt his thoughts in case he was in prayer.

At last, as they sat on the bench, the bishop spoke.

'You are a good man, Marco,' he said softly almost whispering. 'A good man with a good heart.'

'Thank you,' said Marco, not knowing what else to say.

'You are selfless and thoughtful and put other people's happiness before your own. In short, you are a very virtuous man.' The bishop looked straight ahead. It was as though he was expressing his thoughts without actually realising he was doing so and Marco felt it wrong to interrupt him, or to engage him in conversation, so he chose to listen.

Beresi looked about him, taking in the surrounding scenery and sighed. 'One day I want to die here. Here on this very spot. I cannot think of a better place for it to happen, a better place from where God can take me. It is so beautiful don't you think?'

'Yes,' replied Marco, looking around. 'It truly is.'

'Anyway,' said Beresi sharply, sitting up straighter, 'Enough of this melancholy talk. We have an issue that we need to address and we need to get on with it.'

'What do you mean?'

'I know of a man. An old friend, you see. A virtuous and honest man whom I know will be able to assist us with our situation. He has already organised sanctuary for a lot of Jewish people. I will speak to him and we will have your friends added to his list. He has been working tirelessly to save as many as he can. He will be able to assist us.'

Marco smiled. The bishop had referred to it as "our situation". He was involving himself and it comforted him to know that he was getting support from someone other than his sister, someone who could actually help. He felt a huge relief, as though a weight had been lifted from his shoulders and he physically relaxed back into the bench.

Beresi turned to him. 'Do not fear,' he said. 'Do not despair. I will speak to my acquaintance and we will spirit your friends to safety. We need to do something to help these people and if just providing them with shelter during a storm is all we can do, then we must do it, no matter what the consequences are to ourselves. How can we live with it otherwise?'

'Thank you so much, Bishop Beresi,' said Marco. 'I do not know how I can repay you.'

'Don't worry about that. I will go and see him this afternoon and then I will let you know of what is to be done. Do not breathe a word of this to anyone. The less people who know the safer it will be for all of us.'

'Rest assured that I will be discreet,' said Marco sincerely. 'You can rely on that. I really hope that this will all end well.'

They sat in silence for a few moments, allowing the sunlight to warm their faces, a soft breeze blowing against them as the morning slipped away towards midday.

After a while Beresi said, 'Do you hear that?'

Marco closed his eyes and listened. He could hear the soft splashes of the water from the small fountains and water features. He could also hear the faint sound of traffic from afar and as he strained his ears he could also make out the distant rumbling of a lone aircraft. He did not know what Beresi was referring to.

'The birds,' said the bishop. 'Do you hear them?'

Then Marco could hear. It was all around him. The unmistakeable sound of wild birds singing and chirruping in the trees. He was surprised he had not noticed it sooner.

'Yes, I hear it,' replied Marco.

'The birds singing,' said Beresi softly. 'When the birds are singing then there is always hope.

CHAPTER FORTY

For the next three weeks Marco met with Otto Finkel in the same restaurant and each time he failed to bring along his sister who had insisted that she did not wish to have anything to do with the man. Respecting her wishes, Marco had gone alone and every week saw the disappointment in the German's face when he saw that once again Sophia would not be joining them.

'I am beginning to think that your sister does not like me,' he said one evening whilst lighting a cigarette.

'Not at all,' lied Marco awkwardly. 'She is just very busy at the moment at the hospital.'

Otto looked into and Marco's eyes who quickly looked down at his plate at the remains of the chicken he had just consumed. Otto said nothing but Marco knew that he had not been convincing and the German knew that he was lying.

'Maybe I will pop along to the hospital one day and surprise her,' tested Otto.

'She would like that,' lied Marco for the second time.

'Anyway, my old childhood friend,' said Otto sitting forward suddenly. 'What business do you have at the Portico?'

Marco looked up sharply. 'I'm sorry. What do you mean?'

'I believe I caught sight of you the other day walking along the Via del Tempia. You seemed in a little bit of a hurry.'

Marco swallowed and tried to remain calm. It was true, he had been on the Via del Tempia two days previously, attempting once again to persuade his friends to make the move to the monastery that Bishop Beresi had told him of. The monks had agreed to take in the three Trevinis and Marco had gone to their apartment to make the necessary arrangements. Moving them would not be easy. The Germans were everywhere and Beresi was under the impression that certain places were being observed by the Gestapo, including, possibly, the very monastery they were to be transferred to. It had been extremely difficult for them to be persuaded, the main resistant being Pia, but now that the Germans were starting to appear in greater numbers it was becoming apparent to them that the dangers Marco and Sophia told them of were real and very close to happening.

The Allied advance in the south had reached as far as Naples, the city being taken the previous week, but had now slowed due to more organised German defences. Although they were fighting fiercely, defeat for the Germans was just a matter of time, thought Marco, and the liberation of Rome would soon be a reality.

However, if Otto had seen him entering or leaving the Jewish ghetto then this surely meant that the Germans were about to act. It would be very soon now and moving the Trevinis would have to happen almost immediately if there was any hope of saving them.

'Are you all right, my friend?' asked Otto matter-of-factly. 'Have I said something to disturb you?'

'You must be mistaken,' said Marco. He was aware that in his nervousness, his voice had raised an octave or two. He was also aware that he had started to sweat.

'Come, come,' said Otto, a humourless smile on his lips. 'We both know that not to be true now, don't we?'

Marco did not reply.

'I am no fool, my Italian friend, so do not presume that I am. I know it was you and I can guess why you were there so do not insult my intelligence.'

'What do you want from me, Otto? What is it?' asked Marco quietly. 'Let's face it, we knew each other for a brief moment when we were children and even then, if I recall correctly, I don't think that we actually spoke to each other. Yet you insist on us meeting up each week to discuss trivial matters, as though we have been friends for years when the opposite is true.'

'Maybe I am a little lonely and nostalgic and seeing a friendly face each week helps me to cope with it,' he replied. Marco was unsure if he was being sarcastic or whether he actually meant it. 'Think nothing of it. However, you have not answered my question.'

'Frankly, it is none of your business.'

'On the contrary, the Jewish ghetto is very much my business. It is the sole reason why I am here.'

Marco felt physically sick and swallowed hard to force back down the meal he had just eaten that was threatening to make a re-appearance.

'You see,' continued the German casually, 'I have a certain skill that my superiors think may be useful here. I am a good organizer... in fact, I am a great organiser. When something needs doing where our Jewish brethren are concerned then I am quite the expert, believe me. I have had experience of these "Untermensch" in Russia and France. They are a purely evil and pathetic race and they need to be wiped out. It won't be long now until my work here is done and I can move on.'

Marco felt cold, despite the heat of the evening.

'So,' continued Otto after a while, 'I will ask you again. What were you doing in the Jewish ghetto?'

'If you must know, I was delivering some food to some of the unfortunate souls that you and your countrymen seem hell bent on destroying. I am not ashamed, so don't look at me that way. In fact I am very proud that I have been doing this. You can sit there with your smarmy attitude and condescending tone but you are not who you think you are, Otto Finkel.' Marco surprised himself at the boldness of his words.

However, Otto looked amused at the Italian priest's change in attitude. 'And who do I think I am?'

'You and your kind are not the master race,' replied Marco. 'Far from it. If you continue with the course you have taken then I can see nothing other than damnation for you all.'

'Bold words.'

'Maybe, but true words nonetheless.' The more Marco talked, the more his confidence grew. 'Let's face it Otto, the Allies are not far away now. Naples has already fallen. Your army is running scared and it won't be long before the Americans and British are driving their tanks along the Via del Corso. The war will be over very soon and then people like yourself will face a reckoning. First from the victors and then ultimately from God.'

'What has God to do with any of this? If he is so righteous and we are so wrong, then why has he done nothing to stop us? He has been remarkably quiet. Or are you going to quote free will to me now?'

'God gives us all free will. How we choose to behave is our own choice and not that of God, but we all have to answer to Him in the end.'

Otto sneered at him, the scar on his face adding to the grotesque picture before him. 'So if you believe I have sinned then all I need to do is attend confession and then you will simply hand me a few prayers to say.'

It was Marco's turn to laugh. 'You think that's how it works Otto? That you can simply admit in the confessional what you have done, God will forgive you and then you are on a clean slate? That you can simply walk away and do it all again? It does not work like that, not at all. In order to receive absolution then you have to be truly repentant. Not merely say the words, otherwise it doesn't work. But then some of the sins you Nazis have perpetrated cannot be forgiven by mere men such as I. You will have to wait until Judgement Day for that when God Himself will hand out your penance.'

'Have you quite finished, priest?' Otto said, his face impassive although Marco could see in his eyes that his words had annoyed him.

'Yes I have,' he replied. 'I have finished with you, Otto. I have finished pretending that I am enjoying our little rendezvous each week and rest assured that this will be the last time we ever meet like this.'

'Very well,' said Otto raising his hand. 'If that is how you feel. But now that our little friendship is at an end I must tell you that if you are seen in the area of the ghetto again, then it will my duty to bring you in to question you formally on your business there.'

Marco stared at him. It was not in his nature to hate anyone and it was an emotion that he had never felt in his life before, but right now, in this little restaurant in the city he loved, he felt a growing sense of what it must feel like. Before he could say anything else Marco stood up and threw his napkin onto the table.

'I will leave you now, Signor Finkel,' he said and started to move away.

'Oh, before you go,' said Otto, leaning back in his chair. 'I have one more thing to say.'

'Go on,' replied Marco impatiently.

'Your sister.'

'What about my sister?' he frowned.

'I wish to meet with your sister. It is the only reason why I have been wasting my time with you each week.'

'You know it won't happen. She cannot stand the sight of you.'

'That is of no importance, my friend. I wish to see her and I will see her. I could have her arrested any time I see fit, believe me. I could also send my troops into the ghetto to have words with your friends… what are they called again?… The Trevinis. Yes, that's it, the Trevini family.'

Marco raised his hand to his mouth to stop the vomit from escaping and swallowed hard.

'Tell her to expect me soon,' he said and raised the glass of red wine to his lips that sat on the table before him.

Marco stood in silence before him, totally unable to speak or move.

Taking the glass away from his mouth and putting it back on the table Otto looked up to him and said, 'You can go now, priest. Go on, off you go. Shoo.'

Marco turned around and almost ran from the restaurant.

On getting outside he turned to the right and repeatedly vomited into the gutter. Just when he thought that everything was out of him he retched some more. People passing gave him curious looks and a young man approached to offer him assistance but Marco waved him away.

'It's okay,' he said, 'I'm all right. Thank you.'

The young man turned away and walked on, occasionally turning his head to look back, out of concern for the priest who looked clearly ill.

As Marco righted himself, he looked back into the restaurant and caught a glimpse of Otto Finkel speaking to the waiter. He appeared to be ordering a dessert. Then Otto turned around and for a brief second their eyes met once more. Otto raised his glass in a mock salute and smiled.

Marco quickly turned and hurriedly walked away. He felt that he had stared into the eyes of Lucifer and he needed to pray, to purge himself of the evil that he had just encountered. He set off along the pavement, in search of a church where he could exorcise himself of the demon that had just attacked his soul.

CHAPTER FORTY-ONE

Marco headed straight for the Church of St Augustine on the Piazza di Sant'Agostino whose doors he knew were always to be found open, offering sanctuary to any passing soul in need of shelter or spiritual sustenance. He often went there to pray, preferring it to the larger churches where he always felt small and insignificant. Here at St Augustine, he felt God was more accessible, closer even. He crossed the small piazza and walked quickly up the small flight of stairs that led to the front door of the white fronted building and went inside. Fortunately, he found he was alone in the building, not wanting to face anyone at that moment, and looked for a suitable pew before kneeling down, facing the statue of Our Lady of Childbirth. He started to pray quietly offering his life once more to the service of God. The only thing he asked for in return was for his family and friends to be left in peace, free from the dangers and evils of the world. He understood that this was a selfish act but reconciled that it was not too much to ask of a god that he knew to be compassionate and just. He prayed with sincerity and humility, calling upon Him to grant him this one request, this one favour.

He was able to take his mind away from what had just happened with Otto Finkel and absorb himself in the act of prayer, almost to a meditative state. When he was capable of doing this, he was able to feel at one with God. It was as though nothing existed, only Marco and Him, and the ills of the world vanished and faded away into insignificance. It always gave him a sense of rebirth, of newness and personal fulfilment as if his soul had been taken from him, cleansed, and then replaced back into his body. It even made him feel healthier, brighter and more alive, as though the sun was shining down on him, no matter what the weather.

After half an hour he was finished. He made the sign of the cross, rose from the pew and walked back to the door and exited into the piazza. He looked up to the sky and smiled, a brief thank you to God for the moments he had just shared with Him.

Then he looked out across the square and noticed two German soldiers walking together, both wearing steel helmets and carrying MP40 machine pistols strapped across their chests. He could just make out their voices talking in that gruff language that Marco always found to sound aggressive, no matter what they were saying.

He was instantly brought back to reality and realised that the praying had done nothing to make him feel any better about the situation he found himself to be in. God had not listened to his prayers so far, so why would he do so now. He had left the chapel feeling alive and positive, almost optimistic, but now, barely a minute after leaving the building, seeing the two sentries marching across the piazza, he was left feeling empty and more sullen than he had felt before he had entered the church.

As he walked the streets, again unsteady on his feet, he was aware of those he passed looking at him. Whether they assumed that he was drunk as he tottered along, puke adorning the front of his cassock from the earlier vomiting, or whether it was out of curiosity he was not absolutely sure. However, one thing that was for certain, not one person, apart from the young gentleman who had offered him aid when he had first left the restaurant, approached him and asked him if he was okay, or if he needed help in any way. Marco did not blame them for this. These were dark times and people thought better of getting involved in things that did not ultimately have anything to do with them. Keeping a low profile seemed the key to survival.

*

Sophia heard a knock at the door and placed the book she was reading on the small wooden table to her side. She smiled to herself, realising that Marco had forgotten his key again. He was always the same, she thought, always forgetting his keys, or where he had put this and that. It did not irritate her as it may have done others, instead she found it endearing.

She walked to the front door and opened it. She was about to playfully admonish him when she realised it was not he but someone else, someone that she had hoped never to see again.

'Fraulein Roncalli,' said Otto Finkel. 'Or may I call you Sophia?'

Taken aback Sophia said nothing but stood with her mouth agape, unable to utter a response.

'You look surprised to see me,' he said, smiling brightly, the scar on his face almost dragging his left eyelid down as he did so. It was a shocking sight to see, she immediately thought, an ugly face to match an ugly character. He was the only person she had ever met whose smile looked anything but a smile. 'May I come in?'

Before she could reply he pushed the door wider and stepped into the hallway.

'Is Marco home?' he asked.

Gathering her composure, Sophia replied, 'No, I thought he was with you?'

Otto scrunched his face. 'Hmm, yes,' he said, 'He was. However we did not part on the best of terms and I was hoping we could talk a little more.'

'Well, in that case, I have no idea where he is.'

He looked at her and she could see in his eyes straight away that he was playing with her. 'Is it okay for me to wait for him then? In here? I will be quiet as a mouse.'

'Well, Signor Finkel…'

'Call me Otto… please.'

'Signor Finkel,' Sophia continued, ignoring him, 'I have no idea when he will be back and I really must retire for the night. I have an early shift in the morning and need to get to bed.'

'Ah, yes,' he said, smirking at her. 'You work at the hospital, do you not? They really must be working you hard there.'

'We are busy, yes, but I am not sure what you mean.'

'For the last few weeks when I have been meeting up with your brother, you have always been on duty. Even tonight, at this very moment, you are supposed to be there. Yet here I find you. Very strange.'

Sophia looked at him, her heart starting to accelerate.

'I have the distinct feeling that you have been avoiding me, Fraulein Roncalli,' he said quietly. 'But surely that cannot be true. We are childhood friends after all, are we not?'

'I hardly know you, Signor Finkel,' she replied. 'I don't even remember you.'

'No?' he raised his right eyebrow, the left held in place by the scar. 'So you have been avoiding me then? Whatever for? I was hoping that we could be friends.'

Sophia steeled herself and became bold. 'That can never happen. I have absolutely no interest in you… or your countrymen for that matter. I just wish that you would all leave us in peace.'

Otto suddenly lurched forward and grabbed her by the throat, pinning her against the wall. Her hip hit a sideboard, knocking a vase to the stone floor where it broke into three large pieces.

'What are you doing?' she gasped, her hands moving to his arm in an attempt to free herself from his grip. It was no use, he was too strong.

'Listen to me,' he said menacingly and she could smell the strong odour of garlic on his breath, from the meal he had not long ago consumed with her brother. It added to the nausea she was beginning to feel. 'I do not understand why you would avoid me. Is it this?' he raised his free hand to the side of his face, indicating his facial wound.

'Please,' she whimpered, 'let me go… you are hurting me.'

He ignored her. His face was now only inches from hers. 'All my life, ever since I got this, people have looked at me with repulsion, as though I am some kind of freak. People who for some reason think they are better than me because their faces are so perfect. But they are not.'

'Please, Signor Finkel… Otto,' she said, gasping for breath, his grip getting ever tighter. 'You are really hurting me.'

Again he ignored her, either not aware of what she was saying or not caring, she was not altogether sure.

'You Italians. You never learn. Always the victims. Your army is nothing short of useless and to be quite frank, I am quite glad that they have switched sides. It means that I can shoot them without feeling any regret.'

He relaxed his grip slightly, allowing her to speak.

'Please let me go. You are hurting me, I can hardly breathe,' she muttered, tears appearing in her eyes.

'Don't think I don't know what you and your brother are up to, Fraulein,' he said. 'You two Jew lovers. I have followed you on more than one occasion and know that you spend a lot of your time in the ghetto with those vermin. But do not worry, you won't be doing it for much longer, believe me. Oh no.'

'What do you mean? What are you going to do with them,' she gasped in frustration.

He released her and stepped back.

'I have said too much,' he said.

'What do you mean, Otto,' she said loudly. 'What are you planning to do?'

He stepped forward and struck her hard across the face, the pain and shock of it forcing her to her knees. 'How dare you speak to me like that, you little bitch?' he hissed. 'Do not question me. I came around here to do you and your brother a favour. Anyone helping these people will suffer for it, believe me. I was hoping to persuade you to stop.'

Suddenly he became calm and said quietly, 'I was hoping that you and I could be friends, Fraulein. That maybe we could spend a little time together.'

Sophia, still on her knees, her hand to the side of her reddening face replied, just as quietly. 'That can never, ever happen. You are deluded if you think that you and I could ever be together. I would sooner die.'

Without another word Otto turned around and walked to the door. He opened it but before he walked out he turned to her and said, 'Very well, Fraulein. Have it your way. Just be careful what you wish for.'

With that he walked out of the door, slamming it behind him, leaving Sophia Roncalli on her knees on the hallway floor.

*

Ten minutes after Otto Finkel had left the apartment Marco returned home. Sophia could see immediately that he was extremely upset. She led him to the living area and sat him down on a soft chair, where he leaned forward, putting his head in his hands.

'Whatever is the matter?' she asked.

Marco took his hands away from his face and looked at Sophia. He wiped his cheeks, which were wet with tears, with the back of his hand. 'Can you get me a glass of water please? I need to calm myself.'

Once Sophia had placed a glass of water in his hand and he had taken a few sips he took a breath and told her of the night's events. As he spoke, Sophia sat in silence, absorbing every word. She did not interrupt only to hand him a handkerchief when the tears started again.

'He is a very dangerous man,' he concluded. 'If we are not careful then I have no idea what will happen. I don't think it's just the Trevinis who are in danger but us both as well.'

Sophia looked to the ceiling, not knowing what to say. 'I know,' she said quietly, 'I know.'

It was only then that Marco noticed the mark on her face. The left hand side glowed red, and he could see that it was not the rouge she occasionally wore, as he knew that she only used make up sparingly.

'My God,' he said. 'What has happened? Here I am babbling on and I have not even noticed your distress. Please forgive me.'

'He has been here,' she said softly. 'Do not look at me that way. I am not harmed. He left ten minutes before you got here. He was looking for you initially but then he became… how can I put it… angry.'

'What happened?' he repeated, almost robotically. 'What has he done to you?'

Sophia sat down next to him and took his hand.

'He came to the door and at first I thought it was you and you had forgotten to take you key with you. He told me how surprised he was to see me here as he had been told that I was working at the hospital.

'I told him that he was not welcome and that he should leave but he ignored me and said that you and he had had crossed words before you broke for the night. He said that he wanted to come round to apologise but I had the feeling that it was me that he had really come here to see.'

'What makes you say that?' asked Marco, listening intently.

'The way he looked at me. The way he told me that he wished for me and him to become friends. In the end he revealed that he has been following us and that he knows of Leo, Pia and Franco and our relationship with them.'

Marco stood up. 'Let me get something for you. Something for your face.'

'Do not concern yourself,' she replied, smiling at him. 'There is no need. It stings a bit but it will go in time. I do not need anything.'

'If you are sure,' he said sitting back down. He took a breath. 'We need to think now, Sophia. We need to act and to act quickly.' He sat back in the chair for a few moments and then came to a decision. 'Here's what we will do.' He leaned forward in the chair and she sat down on the floor in front of him. Taking her hands in his he continued.

'Tomorrow, first thing in the morning, you will take a train to Turin. You will go back home to mother and father and stay there until all this is over.'

'Marco…'

'Do not interrupt me, please. It has now become too dangerous for you. You will go home and I will go and see Bishop Beresi tonight. We get the Trevinis out as soon as we can and get them to the monastery. I will urge him of the importance of it now. Then once that is done, I will go back to the Vatican and I will stay there, where it is safe, until the Germans are out of the city. You have no need to worry about me.'

'I cannot leave them, my brother. Or you.'

'I must insist, my beautiful Sophia. Really I must. It is too dangerous for you in Rome now. You have to leave.'

Sophia began to cry quietly. Marco leaned forward and kissed the top of her head. 'Please do not cry. I will make sure they are safe. And me too. Try not to worry.'

'I will visit them before I go,' she said. 'Tomorrow morning. I will go and see them first and then I promise you that I will go to the train station and do as you say.'

'I would prefer that you just left, Sophia,' replied Marco. 'It is not safe in the ghetto any more. For us or them. We cannot be seen there. If Otto finds us there then we could be arrested. Please do as I say and go straight to the train station.'

Sophia smiled at him and he knew that his words were falling on deaf ears. He knew that she could not leave without saying goodbye, particularly to young Franco.

'I will go and see Beresi tonight,' he repeated. 'I may spend the night there as there is so much to organise. So please lock the door, pack your bags and I will see you first thing in the morning. I will come home as day breaks.'

'Very well,' she said. 'Very well,' and kissed him on the back of his hand.

Ten minutes later, Marco, having changed his dirty clothing, walked briskly through the streets, heading for Bishop Beresi's quarters in the Vatican. Despite the feeling of desperation he had felt earlier, he now marched forward with a sense of purpose. Matters had been taken out of his hands and now he had to act. He had to be a man and stand up for what he believed. He hoped beyond hope that all would be well. That all the people he loved would get through these times and live to know happiness once again. He would do his best and with God's help it would be enough.

CHAPTER FORTY-TWO

Bishop Beresi had retired for the evening when he heard a banging on the door of his quarters. He switched on the lamp at the side of the bed and sat up, turning to the side to put on his slippers before standing up. The knocking continued without breaking. It took a lot to irritate him but the impatient, incessant banging was beginning to grind him.

'Okay, okay,' he said under his breath, 'I'm coming.'

He opened the door and Father Marco Roncalli almost fell into the room.

'Marco, my dear boy,' he said, holding his hands out to him. 'Whatever is the matter? Come in and sit down.'

Marco sat himself down on an old wooden chair that was pushed up against a wall facing the bed.

'I need your help, Bishop Beresi,' he said, his voice shaking. 'I have run all the way from my apartment... I am quite out of breath.'

'Well, take a couple of minutes to compose yourself. I will get you something.'

Beresi turned from him and walked to a small cupboard on the opposite side of the room. He opened a door and from a shelf took a small bottle of cognac and two glasses. Pouring a large measure into both, he returned to Marco and handed him one.

Marco gladly took it and sipped at the strong liquor, letting its warmth flow down his throat and into his stomach. It seemed to instantly calm him. He looked at the bishop. 'We need to move them as soon as possible.'

'It is planned for tomorrow night, Marco, do not fear. We will get them to safety,' replied Beresi calmly. He looked at Marco and could tell that there was something else. 'What is it Marco? Tell me everything.'

Marco took another sip of the cognac and then relayed the night's events to his friend and mentor.

When he was finished, Beresi said, 'It appears that your friendship, if you can call it that, with this Nazi has somewhat backfired, my young friend. From what I can gather, he has been using you to get access to your sister, who is quite the beauty. If he has been following you both then neither of you can return to the ghetto.'

'I know that she will go and see them in the morning,' replied Marco. 'I know it. She loves that family and she will need to say her goodbyes.'

'Do you believe she will follow your instructions and leave the city?'

'Yes. She is not stupid and knows it is what she must do.' Marco paused. 'But I also know my sister and know her heart. It is the purest I have ever come across and I am not saying that because she is my sister, I am saying it because it is true. She will not be able to face herself if she does not say goodbye to them before she leaves. It may be the last time she will ever see them.'

'Then let us pray that she is discreet in her visit.'

Marco drained the glass and handed it back to Beresi. The bishop raised his eyebrows as if to ask if he wanted a refill but Marco shook his head. 'No thank you, Bishop Beresi,' he said. 'I think one is quite enough for me.'

Beresi stood up. 'Well, I'm having another,' he said emptying the glass's contents into his mouth before returning to the bottle on the cupboard to fill it once more.

'Have you heard anything?' asked Marco. 'About the German plans?'

Beresi looked at him and frowned. He sat on the edge of the bed and took a sip of the cognac before replying. 'It seems that Dannecker is about to make his move very shortly. They're using the lists Mussolini had drawn up. They know where the Jews are and are going to round them up shortly. God knows what they are going to do with them.'

'The rumours are all about the east. To camps.'

'Those are the rumours, yes,' said Beresi solemnly. 'Whether they are work camps or something worse I do not know. Either way, we must save as many as we can. It is our duty as human beings.'

Marco let out a loud sigh. 'Do we know when this will happen?'

'The source I have tells me it is somewhat imminent, my boy,' he replied. 'That is why we must move your friends tomorrow night and not a moment later. I have a couple of friends who will collect them. Is there anyone who will be able to get a message to them to be prepared? I was hoping you could go tomorrow but it is now too dangerous for you to do that. It may be better that you stay here for the time being.'

'No,' replied Marco. 'I need to make sure my sister has left tomorrow. I will go and see her in the morning and when I know she is safe, I will return here as you suggest.'

'Okay,' replied Beresi. 'My two friends will go tomorrow evening to get them. If you could write a note to the Trevinis telling them to do as they say, then it might make collecting them a little easier.'

'I can do that,' replied Marco.

Beresi stood up. 'You look done in, my friend. Here, have my bed and get some sleep. I will wake you as day breaks and you can go and see your sister.'

'I cannot take your bed, Bishop,' he replied. 'I will sleep on the floor at the side of you.'

'Nonsense,' said Beresi. 'Get in the bed and do as you are told. I will get some blankets and I will sleep on the floor. It is no hardship to me.'

'But, Bishop…'

'Just do as you are told for once, Marco,' interrupted the bishop sharply. 'I don't mind the floor. It brings me closer to God. If a stable was good enough for Jesus, then the floor of this beautiful building is certainly good enough for me!'

Reluctantly, Marco did as he was told, after first composing the letter Beresi had asked for. He climbed into the bed and within two minutes of his head hitting the pillow, he fell into a deep and dreamless sleep.

CHAPTER FORTY-THREE

October 16th, 1943, Morning

Marco woke with a start. Beresi was shaking him violently.

'Marco! Marco, wake up!'

Startled and unable to comprehend what was happening and not realising at first where he was, he was only able to mutter, 'What... where...'

'Marco, you must wake up, my friend. It is happening this morning. Today.'

Marco sat up in the bed and rubbed his eyes. He could see that Beresi was very agitated. He stood before him, wringing his hands together and almost hopping from one foot to the other.

'What has happened, Bishop Beresi?' Marco asked sleepily.

'I have just had word from my contact. The Nazis are moving into the ghetto this morning. They are using the lists that the fascists organised some time ago, the ones I told you about. They know exactly where they are and they are going to take them this morning. I fear we may be too late to save your friends.'

Marco was instantly awake and alert. This was unexpected. It wasn't supposed to happen yet. Not now that they were so close to getting the Trevinis out of the ghetto and away to safety. This could not be happening. And then his mind switched to his sister. If she was going to ignore his advice and go to the ghetto to say her goodbyes, then she could be walking into danger. Very real danger.

'I have to go,' he said. 'Sophia.'

'Go to your apartment,' said Beresi. 'Go now. Maybe she is still there and you can stop her from leaving. You must not go to the ghetto.'

Marco jumped from the bed, all tiredness now gone from him, the urgency of the situation causing his senses to sharpen immediately. He did not wait for another word and ran to the door to exit the building.

'Be careful, my friend,' shouted the bishop as he left.

With Beresi's words still hanging in the air behind him, Marco ran as though his life depended on it. He had to get to the apartment, which was a good fifteen to twenty minutes away, before his sister left. He thought about going straight to the ghetto, to intercept her and for a brief moment he did not know what was to be done for the best. However, he carried on running towards his home, the heat of the morning sun beginning to beat down on him, causing him to sweat profusely and to pant like a dog chasing after a stick. He cursed his lack of fitness.

Minutes later he arrived at the apartment. Flinging the front door open he immediately knew that he had missed her, that she had already left. He could sense the emptiness of the place and knew she was not there. He called her name anyway, rushing to the small bedroom that she used and on opening the door he could see that the bed was made in the very neat way she always did it. At first he thought that it was very much like her, to leave the room in this tidy and ordered way, but then he realised that the bed had probably not even been slept in.

He walked back to the living area and saw an envelope on the table that he must have passed without noticing in his haste to get to her room. Marco's name was written on it in Sophia's fine handwriting.

He picked it up and felt a cold sweat overcome him. He did not want to open it, he did not want to read the words that the small missive would contain, but he knew that he had to. He needed to know what his sister had done.

He took out the small note and read:

Marco, I have gone to see them. Do not worry, I will spend the night there and then go straight to the train station first thing in the morning. I will write to you when I am safe in Turin. Please do not worry.

Your loving sister,

Sophia x.

He put the letter down on the table and sighed. She was already there. She must have left only minutes after he had the previous night, against his wishes. However, he knew that she could not have left without going to see them first, no matter how much he begged her not to. There was no way she could have known that the Germans would choose today of all days to make their move on the Roman Jews.

Time was now very important. If he ran to the Portico, he may be able to get there before the Germans did, or if not, if he was too late, then he may be able to persuade them not to take his friends. Sophia was in very real danger now and he had to do something.

He moved quickly to the doorway and left the apartment, not bothering to close the door behind him.

Father Marco Roncalli ran like his life depended on it.

*

In the apartment on the Via del Portico d'Ottavia, Sophia Roncalli was awoken by a strange sound. At first she was not sure where she was but then she remembered her walk the previous night through the darkened streets, to the ghetto and to the residence of her friends, the Trevinis. Leo and Pia had been surprised to see her so late and on hearing her voice, Franco had stumbled from his room rubbing his eyes, as her visit was totally unexpected and he had earlier gone to bed for the night.

She had explained that she was leaving the city and that her brother was organising for them to be taken to a place of safety, probably the following day. They had accepted this without complaint, the old couple now resigned to the fact that the ghetto was no longer a safe place to be. They had all shed a few tears, understanding that this could very well be the last time that they were to speak for a long while, until the war was over more than likely. Ever the optimist, Sophia told them that she would be back very soon and they would all be rejoicing in the demise of the Nazis. The future, she had told them, would be very bright.

Franco had given up his bed for her, the Trevinis insisting that she take it and he had moved to the sofa in the living area. She had then slept a deep and heavy sleep, the events of the evening finally catching up with her. She had been exhausted both mentally and physically.

She lay in bed listening for a few moments, wondering what it was that had disturbed her from her slumber and then, suddenly, with a mighty blow she realised what the noise was.

Outside she could hear the unmistakeable sound of truck engines and boots running on the cobblestones of the square. She strained her ears and could also make out the sound of orders being barked sharply in the language she now detested. A sudden and encompassing fear took over her and she jumped from the bed, still fully clothed, not having bothered to undress the previous night, and moved to the window.

She could see German soldiers, many of them, running to the apartment block across the road. They had already started dragging out the occupants, men, women and children clinging tightly to their mothers' hands. Some of them carried belongings that they had hurriedly gathered together; battered old suitcases, overcoats, children's toys. One old man was even carrying a desk lamp. Those that did not move quickly enough were struck on their backs with rifle butts, all the time being forced down the street, herded like cattle towards the trucks that were waiting to take them away. Sophia saw an old woman stumble and fall, her husband bending down to assist her to her feet. An SS soldier stepped forward and smashed her in the face with his rifle, knocking her back down. The horrible sound of her nose crunching beneath the blow carried to the window and Sophia recoiled in horror. The husband moved forward to protect his wife but the soldier grabbed him by the hair and dragged him to the centre of the road where a colleague stepped forward and fired his pistol at the man's head from point blank range, his body collapsing in a heap in the middle of the road.

Vomit arose in Sophia's throat as she witnessed the murder. She forced it back down and turning from the window, not wishing to see what would happen to the woman whose husband had just been gunned down, she ran from the room and into the living area, where she found Franco, clothed and tying the laces of the brown boots she had bought for him only a few short weeks ago.

'You all have to hurry,' she said frantically. 'They are here. They will be at the door any minute.'

Leo and Pia entered the room. 'What is happening?' said Leo sleepily. 'What is all the noise?'

'They are here,' repeated Sophia. 'The Nazis are outside. They are taking everyone. You need to hide, to get away.'

Leo looked at her and smiled grimly. 'And where would we hide, my love? Where would we go?' He sat down on a chair opposite her. 'We are too old to run. We would not get five yards before they would get us. We will have to do as they say and take our chances with them.' He turned to his wife. 'Pia, let us throw as many things as we can into the old suitcase under the bed. It is probably better not to resist them.'

'You have to do something,' said Sophia, the tears streaming down her face in frustration. 'You can't let them take you. I won't allow it.'

Outside they heard more gunfire, causing her to flinch in terror.

'See,' said Leo passively. 'If we resist, they will shoot us. It is happening right now to those poor fools who do not do as they say. We have no choice.'

Realising that her arguments were proving futile she turned to Franco who looked at her with a more confident expression. 'Well,' he said. 'I'm not waiting to be taken and shot. I'm getting out of here.'

'What are you planning to do?' asked Sophia.

'I'll use the fire escape and get out across the rooftops. I'll find somewhere to hide, don't you worry about me.'

He stood up and ran to his grandparents. He kissed them both on the forehead quickly and then turned to Sophia. 'I must go,' he said. 'I love you, Sophia.'

Before she could reply, the fifteen year old boy kissed her fully on the lips and then turned away. Without looking back he made for the door and was gone before any of them could say a word.

Leo and Pia moved to the bedroom to collect what they could and Sophia went to the window. People were still being dragged from the buildings and the street was now full of Jews being forced from their homes. The old man who had been killed lay in the roadway, the body of his wife now lying over the top of him, as if she had been trying to protect the corpse until she too had been murdered. Tears were now pouring down Sophia's face. She made no attempt to wipe them away.

Another truck pulled up to the right of the apartment building and more SS troops got out, jumping from the tailgate, their rifles and machine pistols in their hands at the ready, as though they were about to go into battle against a formidable enemy and not to force innocent civilians from their homes. She was about to turn from the window when the officer getting out of the cab caught her eye. She recognised him immediately.

As he stood at the side of the truck, raising his silver lighter to a cigarette he had just placed into his mouth, he looked up, and for a brief second their eyes met. Sophia was not sure, but she thought that he may be smiling, actually enjoying this. The scar down the left hand side of his face adding to the grotesqueness of both his appearance and the situation he was overseeing.

For the second time in as many minutes she recoiled from the window and leaned to the side where she was now physically sick, unable to hold it back any longer, the vomit splashing onto the threadbare carpet beneath her feet. She wiped her mouth with the back of her hand and became aware of the sound of boots on the stairwell leading to the Trevini's apartment. She could hear the thumping of fists on apartment doors on the floors below. German voices could be heard shouting aggressively and the sound of weeping could also be heard as the Trevini's neighbours were evicted by the SS thugs.

A minute later Leo and Pia stood before her, a suitcase in Leo's hand. They looked at each other in silence, waiting for the violent knock that was about to come, waiting for the devil to make his appearance.

Less than ten seconds later it came.

*

Marco raced as fast as he could to the ghetto. Despite his exhaustion and the increasing heat of the sun as it rose higher in the morning sky, he did not stop until he got to the Pontico where he was horrified to see German soldiers everywhere. It looked like they had formed a cordon around the whole of the ghetto, not permitting anyone in or allowing anyone to even attempt to escape. Occasionally he could hear the sound of a rifle being fired, or the short burst of a machine pistol and he shivered, despite the heat, as he realised what he was actually hearing was an innocent life being snuffed out.

However, he found that the only thing that concerned him was the safety of his sister whom he knew to be somewhere inside.

He approached an SS sergeant. 'I need to go in,' he said to him. 'My sister is in there. She is not Jewish.'

The soldier looked at him blankly, not understanding a word he was saying and then turned his head away, ignoring him.

'Please,' said Marco frantically, pulling at the man's arm, 'you don't understand. I need to get my sister.'

The soldier pushed him away violently, causing him to stumble backwards and then turned to him, pointing his MP40 machine pistol at his chest. He shouted something aggressively in German that Marco did not understand, and two soldiers to the side of the sergeant also raised and pointed their weapons in Marco's direction.

Marco understood that the soldier had not taken too well to being physically handled and knew that he was now in real danger. He raised his hands in supplication and pulled up the crucifix that hung around his neck before kissing it and placing it back on his chest.

'I am a man of God,' he said softly. 'I mean you no harm. I just need to get in there and find my sister.'

This action seemed to calm the situation and the men lowered their weapons. Despite what was happening in the ghetto behind them, they clearly did not want to get involved with an unsavoury incident with a Catholic priest. Marco indicated behind them and reluctantly the sergeant stood back and allowed him to pass. As he walked by, the German he thanked him and made the sign of the cross in the air in his direction. The man turned away, ignoring the blessing.

Marco ran through the streets in the direction of the Trevini's apartment building, passing rows of Jews as they were shepherded onward by the SS soldiers. No one seemed to take any notice of him, even the soldiers who were concentrating on their task, the sight of a Catholic priest running by them of no interest. Occasionally he passed a body lying on the pavement or in the gutter but like everyone else, he disregarded them, his focus on his sister and getting her out and to safety.

CHAPTER FORTY-FOUR

Leo walked calmly to the door and opened it. Immediately the soldier on the other side pushed it savagely forward, forcing Leo to step back. The soldier rushed past them all, searching the other rooms for anyone who may be hiding and when he was happy that there was no one else in the apartment he approached them. Pointing his machine pistol from them to the door, he indicated for them to leave the building.

'She is no Jew,' Leo said, looking from the soldier to Sophia. 'You cannot take her.'

The man did not understand and pushed the three of them towards the doorway, forcing them out of the apartment.

As they entered the stairwell, they were joined by others from the neighbouring apartments and Sophia was relieved to see that Franco was not among them. Maybe, she thought, just maybe, he had escaped and would be safe.

Eventually they were outside and the heat of the morning sun hit them. Leo, struggling with the weight of the suitcase, was lagging behind and a soldier hit him on the back with the butt of his rifle, forcing him to his knees on the pavement near the front door.

'Leave him alone,' Sophia screamed at the soldier. 'He is an old man. Leave him alone.'

The soldier grinned at her as she assisted Leo to his feet and she stared at him with as much hatred as she could muster.

Suddenly she felt someone grab her arm and pull her to the side, away from the line of Jews that Leo and Pia were being forced to join.

'I do not believe this to be your neighbourhood, Fraulein Roncalli.'

Sophia turned and stared into the face of Otto Finkel.

'If you are not careful, Sophia, you may end up going with them and we cannot have that now, can we? A good Catholic girl like yourself. What would your brother say to me if that were to happen?' Then he added condescendingly, 'Be a good little girl now and run along home.'

'Please, Otto,' Sophia pleaded. 'Stop this madness. These people have done nothing to you. They are harmless. Please let them go.'

'Listen, Jew lover,' he hissed back at her sharply, 'I am trying to do my best by you. I could quite easily have you thrown on the trucks with these disgusting vermin. Do you want that? I don't think you do. The best thing you can do is to leave and to leave right now.'

With Otto Finkel's hand clasped firmly around the top of her arm she looked down the street, seeking out her friends but she could no longer see them. They had been taken around a corner and were now out of sight. She looked again at him. 'Please, Otto,' she said again, 'Let my friends go. They are no threat to you. I will do anything you say, anything.'

Otto spun her around until she was looking directly into his disfigured face and she was instantly repelled by the look in his eyes. She had never seen eyes like them, so devoid of humanity, so lacking in compassion. She realised then that this animal, this thing before her, was incapable of love. Or anything like it.

'You really are quite stupid,' he hissed at her. 'You had your chance with me but you chose not to take it. I have only a few days left here before I leave again for Paris. I am doing what I came here to do and you are now starting to get in my way. It is only out of the memory of our time in St Malo, all those years ago, and your brother's assistance in getting me to safety that day, that I am now stopping from having my men shoot you where you stand. Now get the fuck out of here before I change my mind and shoot you myself.'

With that he threw her violently away from him and she fell to the ground, grazing her hands and knees on the rough pavement. He turned to his left where two soldiers were standing close by, watching the scene, and spoke to them in German. 'Take this Jew loving whore away. Throw her out of the ghetto and don't let her back in. If she resists then hand her over to the Gestapo.'

Otto Finkel turned and walked away, leaving Sophia Roncalli on her hands and knees on the ground. As she tried to stand up, the two SS soldiers grabbed an arm each and frog-marched her away.

She was not aware of where they were taking her and looked back over her shoulder in the direction of where Leo and Pia had gone, hoping to catch a glimpse of them, but she knew it was pointless. Her mind drifted away, as though intoxicated, her brain not able to compute properly what had taken place in the last few minutes, not wishing to accept it.

She let herself be dragged away, to where she hoped she would be left to grieve in peace but soon became aware that the two soldiers were not taking her to the cordon, but to a building opposite that of where the Trevinis had been living up to this day. She looked at the two men, her face moving from one to the other, the soldier on her right, who gripped her arm like a vice, ignoring her, his mind focused on what he and his comrade were about to do.

However, the man to her left was not so impassive. He stared at her and she could see in his eyes what their intentions were. It was beyond doubt.

As they took her into an empty ground floor apartment, kicking the door shut behind them, Sophia, for the first time that day, began to fear for her own safety. She started to struggle, attempting to free herself from their grip but could not break away, the two hardened SS killers were just too strong for her.

She decided, there and then, that if they were going to do this to her then they would both have to fight for it, just like she would battle with all her might and with every ounce of strength that she had remaining, to resist them. She would not surrender.

CHAPTER FORTY-FIVE

Passing the building where the two SS soldiers had dragged Sophia, Marco arrived at the apartment block where he had spent so many happy times with his sister and their friends. Ignoring the looks of some of the troops, he ran past a couple of soldiers at the door and into the block. As he entered the building, he nearly barged straight into Otto Finkel who was coming down the stairs, his head turned back, barking orders to his subordinates who were searching the rooms on the upper floors. He held an odd looking handgun in his right hand.

Before Otto could say a word Marco blurted, 'Where is she? What have you people done with my sister?'

Otto stopped and looked at him, genuinely surprised to see him. 'My God,' he said with a half-laugh, 'You Roncallis, you turn up in the strangest of places.'

Ignoring him Marco pulled at the German officer's arm. 'Tell me, you Nazi bastard, what have you done with my sister?'

Otto pushed him away and raised the Mauser. Pointing it at the Italian priest he said calmly, 'Do not ever touch me again, priest. I have let things pass between us that for others I would have had shot. Your cassock and dog collar cannot protect you forever and you should be thankful for my leniency. Make no attempt to prevent me from carrying out my duties. Now what are you doing here?'

'May God forgive you, Finkel.' Throwing his arms wide to indicate what was happening around them Marco carried on. 'Your duties? So it is your duty to ship out innocent people to their deaths? Is that what it is? What about your duty to humanity? Your duty to God? Your duty to your very soul?'

'Do not lecture me on morality, you hypocritical half-wit. You have not seen the things I have seen or experienced the things I have. You know nothing of real life, cooped up in your churches and those ridiculous clothes that you wear. Now get out of my way before I have you stripped and put on the trucks with all these other rodents. Now get out of here right now before I have it done.'

Otto turned away from him and shouted in German up the stairs and was met by a reply from one of his men. A few seconds later a number of SS soldiers, their faces red with the exertions of what they had been doing, came hastily down the stairs and passed Marco, barely looking at him.

Otto moved towards the door following them out but before he could leave, Marco said quietly, almost whispering. 'Please, Otto, I beg you. Do you know where my sister is? For all that we went through all those years ago, I beg you to let me know what has happened to her.'

Otto Finkel stopped and looked at him. For a very brief second Marco thought he could see something else in the man's eyes, something he had not seen since they were both young boys all those years ago, on holiday in France. He could not confirm in his mind whether it was a glimpse into the past, an echo of the person Otto used to be, or whether it was a tiny bit of compassion trying to escape a tortured soul. Whatever it was it made Otto pause.

Otto Finkel, Nazi officer and Jew hater, stood before him in his pristine black uniform, his cap firmly placed upon his head and a Mauser machine pistol in his hand. He then spoke quietly, almost gently, to the Italian Catholic priest leaning dejectedly against the wall before him. 'She was here earlier. We have taken her Jew friends and I ordered my men to escort her to the cordon. I hope she went quietly because otherwise they have orders to hand her over to the Gestapo. I am surprised you have not passed her on your way here. Now, Roncalli… priest, I have to ask you to leave. For your own safety get the hell out of here.'

With these last words, Hauptsturmführer SS Otto Finkel turned and walked away, leaving Father Marco Roncalli, slumped on his knees in gratitude to God, smiling amidst the horrors taking place around him, believing his sister Sophia to be safe and well.

After two minutes of praying to the God whom he loved, the God who had decided to spare his sister from this madness, he stood up and slowly walked out of the building and back onto the street. He looked upwards, to the sky and let the sun warm his face.

He was now able to focus some of his attention to what was happening in the streets around him. It was total madness. SS soldiers dragging people along, hitting and kicking at them if they were not moving quickly enough. Children crying loudly, their mothers attempting to shield them from the terrible sights all around. Old men and women attempting to keep up as best they could, all of them passing the bodies of those who had either put up some resistance or been shot on the whim of the SS.

Marco realised that there was nothing physical he could do for these people now. All he could do was bear witness and be a part of bringing the perpetrators of these crimes to justice in the future. Marco was in no doubt as to who would win this war, no doubt at all, and when it was over there would be a reckoning. That is when these people would get their comeuppance.

However, the time for justice would come later. It would come after all the shooting had stopped. The sanest thing he could do right now, at this minute, was to take the advice of the German whom he had grown to hate, an emotion he had never experienced before.

Marco realised the irony of his emotions. He hated Finkel for making him feel this way, for making him hate him.

He turned and walked away toward the cordon, heading for the safety of the wider city where he hoped to be reunited with his beautiful sister.

*

Sophia lay in a heap on the bedroom floor, her clothes dishevelled where they had been ripped and pulled at by the two SS soldiers. She was semi-conscious having been punched viciously to the side of the head, her face battered and bruised. She ached all over, every muscle and bone producing pain like she had never felt before.

They had won. The two of them had achieved what they had set out to do but she had not succumbed quietly. She had shown how Italian women could fight when they needed to. She had left the pair of them knowing that they had been in a scrap, the skin from their faces still under her nails and the blood from one of their hands starting to dry on her chin where she had bitten down on it like a wild cat.

However, they had won. They had taken from her, her virtue. Robbed her of the innocence she valued above other things. They had forced her to do things that she had not even allowed that bastard Alessandro Sartini do, even when she thought that she was madly in love with him.

She did not want to cry but knew that she was now weeping. Her body reacting in a way that made her feel embarrassed. Not for what had taken place, she had no control over that, the two of them being too strong, but embarrassed for the fact that she had felt instantly ashamed. As though this was all her fault when she knew full well that it wasn't. None of it was her fault, yet she wept with shame anyway.

The door had closed behind them a minute earlier but she did not want to wait a moment longer, for them to be gone. She needed to get away, to get back to the apartment she shared with her brother, away from this madness, this hell that she had found herself in.

Then she remembered Marco. Poor innocent Marco who loved her beyond anyone or anything else in the world. Marco who would die for her. Probably kill for her too if need be. She thanked God that he had been spared being a witness to all of this. She had to get back to him, to show him that despite what had taken place, despite what had happened, that she would be okay. Sophia Roncalli, his younger sister, would get through this and be fine.

She stood up and arranged her clothes as best as she could so that people looking at her would not be able to work out what had just happened. She smoothed down her bedraggled hair and made for the door. She took two steps and then collapsed, a sudden rush of pain in her lower abdomen hitting her like a truck. She had never known anything like it. And then to add to it she found that she was bleeding. For the first time since it had taken place she let out a wail of agony and despair.

She found in that instant that the first stages of the aftermath, of feeling a sense of bravery and resolve had now given way to hopelessness and anguish. Her friends had been taken away, probably to their deaths, Franco was on the run, she did not know where her brother was and she was now in great pain.

She made another attempt to stand and walked slowly to the door, leaning against the wall for support, to stop herself from falling over once more. She let out a small whimper and quickly wiped the tears from her eyes, the pain becoming intolerable.

She opened the door and struggled through the entrance hallway to the exit. She was aware of the cacophony outside, of troops running about, civilians hurrying along to the waiting trucks to be taken away to God knows where, but she could not think of them right now. She had to get away. To get away to some sanctuary where she could be taken care of.

As she entered the street, she was approached by an SS soldier who shouted something unintelligible into her face, his own face contorted with rage and adrenalin, pushing at her with his rifle attempting to make her join the others. Ignoring him, she leaned back against the brick wall and slowly slumped down until she was sitting on the pavement. The man cocked the rifle, raised it to his shoulder and pointed it at her head.

Sophia looked at him and for that brief second, with her life about to be extinguished, she found that she did not care.

Marco made his way quickly across the road, heading away from where he had just met with Otto Finkel. Very soon he would be reunited with his sister and they could decide on the next course of action together.

The situation had now changed. They could no longer help the Trevinis, there was nothing they could do for them any more other than to pray for them. He would still send Sophia back to Turin, to their parents, where hopefully she would be safe until the Allies arrived and liberated them. This madness could not go on forever.

As he got to the other side of the road, he became aware of a soldier shouting at someone to his left. At first he was going to ignore it, but something, he knew not what, maybe an intuition, made him look to the side.

Suddenly he was filled with horror. He stood still with shock at what he was about to witness, petrified, unable to move.

Slowly lowering herself to the ground, her back against the wall, all the time being yelled at by a burly SS soldier, was his sister, Sophia. She looked in a total mess. Her hair bedraggled and messy, her face showing signs of swelling and blood, and her clothes ripped and torn. She looked up lazily at the man who was about to put a bullet into her head.

Breaking his sudden paralysis, Marco ran forward towards the scene. He could not let this happen. Waving his arms quickly he yelled at the man, 'No. Stop, stop.'

The man turned from Sophia and pointed the weapon at Marco but upon seeing his clothing he paused and lowered the rifle slightly.

Marco got up close to the man. 'No Juden, no Juden,' he shouted.

When he realised the man was not going to use his weapon, he pointed at his sister and said more quietly, 'No Juden. Catholic. No Juden.'

The soldier responded in German but Marco had no idea what the man was saying. 'Hauptsturmführer Finkel... no Juden,' said Marco.

Upon hearing his commander's name the soldier muttered something else that Marco did not comprehend and then turned on his heel and carried on down the street leaving them alone together.

With the immediate danger now over, Marco bent down and took hold of his sister. It did not take a genius to understand what had happened to her and he could see instantly that she was in immediate need of medical attention. If he could just get her out of the ghetto and across the bridge to the hospital, then they would both be fine, he thought. They could deal with what had taken place later.

At first Sophia had not realised who had saved her but on seeing her brother's face she held out her arms. 'Marco... Marco... They have taken them... Pia and Leo... They are gone.'

Assisting her to her feet Marco replied gently, 'I know, my darling, I know. We need to get you to safety... we need to get you out of here.'

'I'm sorry, Marco,' she continued, starting to sob. 'I'm so sorry.'

'Whatever for?' he asked. 'You have no need to apologise to me.'

'You said not to come and I came anyway. I couldn't leave without saying goodbye to them, Marco, I simply couldn't.'

'I know you couldn't,' he said holding onto her tightly, making her lean against him as they struggled to the corner. 'Do not apologise to me for having a pure heart. They are hard to find in this madness. You are one shining light in all of this darkness.'

Sophia leaned against her brother as they walked along, her feet shuffling slowly and it took all Marco's strength to keep her on her feet. It was slow going and occasionally the soldiers would look at them but on seeing Marco's cassock they shied away from approaching them, leaving them to carry on slowly out of the ghetto.

After a couple of minutes Marco could see a number of SS soldiers ahead, heaping corpses unceremoniously into a pile against the side of a building. He could not see how many but they were of various ages, both men and women. He turned his head back to his sister and was relieved to see that she had her head bowed, looking down at the pavement in front of her and not at the grim scene they were approaching.

As they passed, the pile of corpses getting ever higher to their right, Marco could not help himself and found that he had to look. Something inside him was making him bear witness to the atrocity that was happening this morning.

And then he saw them.

Amongst the pile of corpses a pair of feet protruded slightly from the bottom.

A pair of feet wearing shiny brown boots. Boots that were somewhat out of place amongst the tattered and worn footwear worn by most people in the ghetto.

Boots that he had seen before on the feet of an excited fifteen-year-old boy who had been so grateful to receive them from the beautiful young woman on whom he had an almighty crush. The same woman who Marco now held tightly as they shuffled by.

'What is it?' asked Sophia quietly, sensing the change in her brother's demeanour, noticing the intake of breath he had just made.

'Nothing, my darling Sophia,' he said turning his head to her and away from the scene. 'Look at me. Do not turn your head from me. Look at me.'

Sophia was too tired and in too much pain to argue with her older brother and did as he said.

'You have seen enough for one day... for one lifetime,' said Marco, all the time not taking his eyes from hers to make sure that she did not look in the direction of the bodies being dumped by the SS soldiers.

'Let's get you to the hospital,' said Marco gently. 'Let's get you looked after.'

'Please do not take me to the hospital,' she replied suddenly. 'Please just take me home.'

'We need to get you looked at by a doctor,' Marco said. 'You really need to be in a hospital.'

'No, no,' she pleaded. 'I cannot have my colleagues seeing me like this. Seeing what those monsters have done to me. Please just take me home.'

'Okay,' he replied softly, not wishing to distress her any further. 'If that is what you wish. Once you are safe in your bed I will go out and fetch a doctor. Is that good enough?'

'Yes,' she replied between sobs.

Marco continued with his sister beyond the cordon, where the SS guards simply stepped aside and let them pass, looking curiously at the odd couple shuffling along the street. One or two made a passing comment, which the others laughed at, but Marco did not understand and did not want to understand.

They walked along in silence, all the time Marco's mind wandering to what would happen next, what the next step would be. The more he thought about what had taken place that morning, to his sister, to the Trevinis, to poor Franco who now lay dead in an undignified heap on a Roman street and to every other poor soul who had been dragged from their homes and either shot or put on transportation to take them away to their doom, the more his ire grew.

He became determined that no matter what was to become of himself, no matter what they would do to him, he would have his justice, he would have his retribution. They would answer for this. All of them. All those evil swine who had murdered innocents, killed for the sheer pleasure of it or under the excuse of some misguided, ridiculous and evil ideology. They would all be punished and not only in the next life but in this one too.

He looked at his sister and his determination grew stronger. He would not let them get away with this.

CHAPTER FORTY-SIX

Two hours later Marco found himself walking the streets of Rome, on his way to the Vatican to find Bishop Beresi. As he passed the citizens going about their business, seemingly oblivious to what had taken place a few short streets away, he felt sick to the stomach. How could these people simply let this happen? How could they stand idly by and let foreign troops enter their city and take their fellow countrymen away to their deaths, without raising an arm in protest? How could they let these men rape and murder innocent people? People who had done no one any harm in their entire peaceful lives.

He had left Sophia sleeping in her bed. They had eventually arrived home after a long and difficult walk and had bumped into their neighbour, Signora Nespola, as she was returning from the shops. Together they had assisted Sophia into the apartment where Signora Nespola had run a bath and bathed her. She had then tended to the wounds as best she could and with Marco's gratitude ringing in her ears, she had placed Sophia in bed where she had fallen asleep almost instantly. Signora Nespola had advised that the girl really needed to be in a hospital but Marco explained that was not what Sophia wanted and he would go and find a doctor. The old woman had promised to look in on her periodically, while Marco set off to do just that.

Marco had gone straight to Doctor Neli's office and explained what had taken place. Neli, an old man who always looked troubled and harassed, promised to meet Marco at the apartment in a couple of hours' time, suggesting that it may be best to leave Sophia sleeping for a while before they disturbed her any more. With that, Marco left the man's office and went in search of Beresi. He wanted to make an official complaint and felt that the bishop's advice would be needed.

Marco found Beresi in the Vatican garden, sitting alone on the bench where they had both sat some days before.

As he approached, Beresi looked up, sorrow in his heavy eyes. 'Ah, Marco,' he said softly. 'It is so good to see you, my friend. Were you in time?'

Marco sat down beside him and leaned forward on the bench, his arms on his knees, looking down at the gravel pathway.

'I'm afraid not, Bishop Beresi,' he replied. 'In truth, I am somewhat distraught.'

'Tell me what has transpired.'

Marco put his head in his hands and began to sob. Beresi placed his hand upon his back in an attempt to soothe him but it did not help. All the pain, anguish and feeling of helplessness came pouring to the fore and Marco cried. He cried like a baby, unable to speak for a matter of minutes, all the time with Beresi's hand on his back. Other clergymen passed, looking down on him and at Beresi, but the bishop waved them away with a placid smile.

Eventually Marco stopped and sat up. 'They're gone,' was all he could say.

'Tell me,' said the bishop. 'Tell me, if it helps.'

Marco glanced at this huge man to his side, this enormous man with the gentle manner and massive heart and instantly felt a calmness come over him. He was always amazed at how the man could evoke tranquillity in times of crisis, always finding a way to make something bad almost understandable and endurable.

'Franco is dead,' Marco replied. 'Pia and Leo have been taken away.'

'And what about your sister?'

'She is alive… just,' he replied and felt the tears well up again. He forced them back and turned to the bishop. 'They had their way with her, beat her and then threw her on the street like an old rag. She is at home sleeping right now. I am meeting the doctor there in an hour or so.'

'My God,' replied Beresi looking at him. 'My God.'

'The man responsible is known to me. He was there. Otto Finkel of the SS.'

'The one you told me of?'

'Yes. He seemed to be in charge. Or at least in charge of some of them. I want to make a complaint.'

Beresi shifted in his seat. 'And what do you think that will achieve?'

Marco replied, 'I have to do something, Bishop Beresi. I can't sit and do nothing. I can't let them get away with it.'

'Do you think for one moment these thugs will take you seriously?' asked Beresi. 'This is their policy. This is what they do. This is the kind of thing that they have been doing for years. Listen Marco, you have my every sympathy but if you want my advice too then please take it. Do not draw any more attention to yourself… or to your sister. Their time will come, don't worry about that. Whether it happens in this world or the next.

'The Allies will be here soon and these people will be gone. It may take a while but peace will return to this city. Write down everything that happened this morning... everything. Miss nothing out. There will be people... Americans... British... maybe even Italians... good people who will follow them. They will be seeking out these criminals and they will make them pay. They may be able to run but they will not be able to run forever. It will be they who are quaking, waiting for the knock on the door that will seal their fate, just in a similar way to what they have been doing to their unfortunate victims. Yes, write everything down and pass it to those people when they eventually get here.'

'I feel so helpless,' said Marco after a while. 'So useless and insignificant.'

'You are by no means insignificant,' replied the bishop. 'You are a witness to what has happened, to this atrocity. Your voice will be heard. But not right now, my young friend, not right now.'

Marco knew that the bishop was right. After what had taken place that morning and with the SS soldiers, even Finkel himself, prepared to put a gun to his head, it may be better to bide their time until the arrival of the Allies. When he thought of the blond German officer with the grotesque scar down the side of his face, he thought that there was no way the man could hide when the war was over and he would be held accountable for his crimes.

He sighed and then stood up. Offering his hand to the bishop he said, 'Thank you, Bishop Beresi. For all you have done for me. I must go now and be with my sister.'

Beresi stood up and took Marco's hand. 'What will you do now?'

'I cannot stay here,' Marco replied. 'I will care for my sister and when she is able to, we will travel to my parents and stay with them until this is over. Then I will assess what to do, but, I fear, it may be a while before I am back here, if at all.'

'I fully understand,' said the bishop. 'It is the right thing to do. Now, go with God, my young friend.'

Marco turned around and walked away, leaving the bishop looking after him as he went. He did not look back. In that moment, Marco decided that looking back served no purpose. No purpose at all.

*

Marco entered the apartment building and was met by Signora Nespola in the entrance hallway. She had tears on her cheeks and was extremely agitated, wringing her hands together and stepping from one foot to the next.

Marco started to shake, a feeling of dread and foreboding instantly overcoming him. Something was very wrong, very wrong indeed.

'What… what… whatever is the matter Signora?' he stammered, the words sounding like they were being spoken by someone else, someone far off.

'I have sent for the police and an ambulance,' whimpered the little old woman. 'Signor Nespola is in there with her now.'

Marco made an attempt to get past her to the stairs but she stepped in his path, blocking his way. 'Please come into my apartment, Father Marco,' she said. 'Please wait in there with me.'

Without replying Marco pushed her aside and stepped onto the stairs. Ignoring her shouts from below, he took the stairs two at a time as he raced up to the apartment. His heart began to beat at double speed and a coldness spread throughout his body. He felt sick, as though he was going to vomit, his stomach beginning to cramp up, but it did not hinder his progress as he drew closer to the door of the apartment, which was half open.

Outside, on the landing, he stopped. He did not want to go in. He did not want to see what he knew would be inside. He doubled over and let out a loud moan and then became aware of someone watching him. Downstairs he could hear the soft sobs of Signora Nespola and for a brief instant he found himself above, looking down upon himself as he leant against the wall for support.

Signor Nespola, the old lady's husband, had stepped out of the apartment and was observing him. Marco looked up and into the man's eyes. Neither of them spoke, Marco could see in the man's eyes all that needed to be said, confirming his fears.

He stood up straight and took a deep breath. He moved to the doorway but this time his path was blocked by Signor Nespola.

'Please, Father Marco,' he said softly. 'Please… '

Again, for the second time in a minute, Marco found himself pushing a Nespola aside and he entered the hallway.

He could see instantly that she was dead.

She was hanging from the beam that stretched across the whole of the room, a noose fashioned from the cord that belonged to her dressing gown. The chair on which she had stood lay fallen on the floor beneath her swinging feet where she had kicked it away. Her eyes, those beautiful brown eyes, now bulged hideously from their sockets, her tongue purple and swollen, protruding grotesquely from her mouth. What was once the most beautiful face that anyone could have laid eyes upon was now deformed into a picture of ugliness and horror. Marco later remembered thinking at the time that this is what they had done to her, they had turned something warm and wondrous into something cold and malignant.

Also around her neck was the set of rosary beads he had given to her on her last birthday and the top of a bible could be seen in the pocket of her nightdress.

Marco stood, transfixed, staring at what was his sister, feeling empty and alone, lost within himself. He found that his mind was blank, no thoughts emanated other than he was aware that his heart had emptied of everything. It was either that or it had broken into a million pieces inside his chest. Either way, his heart did not exist as it used to any more, now only serving to pump blood around his body and for nothing else.

He became aware of someone behind him.

'I tried to cut her down, Father, but I haven't the strength,' said Signor Nespola nervously. 'I am so sorry.'

Marco moved to the kitchen and took out a carving knife from the drawer. Moving back to the living area he righted the chair she had used and stood on it.

'Here,' he said to the old man. 'Please give me a hand.'

Together they cut her down and gently laid her on the floor. 'Can you help me carry her to the bedroom?' Marco asked softly. 'I would like to put her in the bed.'

'Of course, of course,' said the old man and took hold of her legs.

They carried her to the bedroom and lay her on the bed. Marco placed her hands over her chest, feeling the coldness of the body and took the bible from her pocket and put it in her hands.

Signor Nespola stood in the doorway. 'I have called an ambulance, Father. They will be here soon.'

'It's a bit too late for that,' replied Marco. 'Thank you for your help. You can go now.'

Relieved to have been dismissed, Signor Nespola turned but before he walked away he said, 'If you need anything, you know where we are. Anything.' And then he was gone.

Now alone, Marco began to weep.

'Oh, Sophia,' he said, 'my beautiful Sophia. What have they done to you?' He kissed the top of her head, his tears dripping onto her forehead and cheeks. 'What have they done?'

The feeling of loss was all consuming. It penetrated his soul and ripped it apart within him. He could never be the same again. Never. He knew in that instant that his life had changed completely and irreversibly.

Then he noticed an envelope on her bedside table, next to the lamp. It was addressed to him.

Picking it up he took it to the living area and took out the piece of paper within it. Before he could start reading, two men appeared in the room with him. He looked up and could see that they were ambulance men. Marco nodded his head towards the bedroom door and without saying a word they both headed to see her.

Marco began reading the letter:

My dearest brother, it began, *please do not be mad with me. I cannot go on any more. What those people have done has broken me and I see no other way out. They have taken everything from me. My friends, my dignity and most of all my hope. In my heart I know that Leo and Pia will never return from wherever it is they have been taken and despite your best efforts to avert me from it, I saw what they have done to poor, innocent Franco. Although you tried to shield me from it, I saw. Please remember that I love you and mother and father. Light a candle and say a prayer for me.*

Your loving sister,

Sophia.'

His hand shaking, Marco dropped the note to the floor.

He did not know what to think, what to feel. Suicide was a mortal sin and according to the church to which he was part of, it denied that person a place in the kingdom of Heaven. How could that be, he thought angrily? How could a place in paradise be denied to someone so pure and gentle? To someone who had never caused any harm to anyone throughout her whole life.

Marco felt sick to the stomach. He held one man responsible for all this. One man. He had been advised to leave it alone, that those responsible would someday be brought to justice. But what if that never happened? What if they ran and got away with it to live a free life? That could never happen for his sister now, or for him. He would always be a prisoner.

The Church. The great all powerful Catholic Church. What had it done about any of this? A few words a year ago from the Holy Father. Words that packed no punch, no power whatsoever. As far as Marco was concerned, the Church he loved had done nothing to prevent any of this from happening and had not offered too many words of criticism either. Granted, there were individuals doing their own private things, like Beresi and the few others who were attempting to do something to practically help those in need. But those at the top? The Cardinals and the Pope himself? And those all-powerful

Church leaders would agree that his own sister, Sophia, could not be allowed to take a place in Heaven, because she had run out of hope.

Marco stood up and ripped the dog collar from his throat and threw it to the floor. He pulled the cassock over his head and dumped that in a heap to his side before taking the crucifix that hung around his neck and dropped that too. He then walked into his room and took a clean white shirt from his wardrobe and put it on, fumbling as he buttoned it, his hands shaking with grief and rage.

Then he went to the kitchen and took from a drawer, a small, sharp knife that he used for filleting fish and put it up his sleeve. It was the sharpest one that he owned.

As he left the kitchen, he bumped into the two ambulance men. They were about to say something to him but he brushed past them and walked out onto the landing.

He had decided what he was going to do. His mind was made up.

He was going to find the Nazi he held responsible and he was going to kill him. Mortal sin or not, he did not care. He was going to kill him anyway.

CHAPTER FORTY-SEVEN

Marco headed quickly back towards the ghetto, ignoring the strange looks he received from those that he passed. He was aware that the look on his face, eyes red through tears and expression hard with determination, generated looks of concern and curiosity as he walked, but he did not care. At that moment in his life he did not care about anything. The consequences of what he was about to do meant nothing to him. The only thing he cared about was to get to Otto Finkel and thrust the knife he held up his sleeve into the man's heart. He wanted to look into his eyes as the Nazi bastard realised that there was a consequence to his actions, there was a price to be paid for what he had done today.

As he approached the ghetto, he could see that the Germans were still there, searching the buildings for anyone who may still be hiding from them. He could also sense in the air the odour of what smelled like burning pork but he came to realise that they were burning the corpses of the people they had murdered, no doubt Franco Trevini being one of them. He felt nauseous and what was now a common feeling of vomit rising in his throat occurred once more and again he was forced to swallow it back.

He was fully focused on his task. Nothing was going to stray him from it.

He reached the cordon and saw that the sergeant who had let him through earlier was still there. Marco approached him and the man held up his hand to stop him, not recognising him from when they had first met a few hours earlier.

'I wish to see Hauptsturmführer Finkel,' he demanded.

The SS sergeant looked at him and frowned, half recognising him now. He responded gruffly in German, not understanding what Marco had said. From his actions Marco realised he was being told to go away.

'Hauptsturmführer Finkel... Finkel,' insisted Marco. 'It is urgent... urgent. Please go and find him. I need to speak to him.'

The sergeant looked at him and frowned. Hearing his commanding officer's name had caused a reaction. He turned to one of his soldiers and spoke at him. Marco heard him mention Otto's name and the soldier ran away in the direction of the ghetto. The sergeant turned back to Marco and spoke again gruffly and he realised that he was being told to wait.

Marco did not know how he was going to do it. As he waited on the edge of the cordon, German soldiers standing only yards away, he contemplated his next course of action. He decided that he would let fate take control; he would see what happened when it happened.

It took only a minute before he saw Otto appear, strutting around the corner in his perfect black uniform, the cap now missing from his head, his blond hair glowing in the sunlight. The Mauser machine pistol was now in its holster at his side. He was clearly irritated at being disturbed from whatever he had been doing.

At first he did not recognise Marco, as he had only ever seen the man in priestly attire and it was only when he was a few yards away and outside the cordon that he realised who he was.

'Marco,' he said, shocked at seeing him. 'I thought I'd seen the last of you. Can you not take a hint? It is in your best interests to leave right now, before you do something that both of us will regret.'

'She's dead,' said Marco simply, surprised at himself at how calm he was.

'I don't understand,' replied Otto, baffled. 'Who's dead?'

'My sister, Sophia… Sophia's dead.'

Otto was clearly confused. 'I don't understand what you mean.'

'It's simple enough, you piece of shit,' said Marco venomously. 'She took her own life not an hour ago. After you had your men rape and beat her.'

'I did no such thing,' replied Otto, shocked at the accusation. 'I had her removed from the ghetto for her own good. I gave no such order.'

'I don't believe you,' said Marco, tears of frustration starting to form in his eyes.

'Believe what you like, you damned fool,' said Otto dismissively. 'Do you think I care what you believe? Well I don't. It was a mistake ever making your acquaintance so if you will leave me in peace I have work to do.'

'Work!' shouted Marco. 'You call this work? This barbarism? You are one evil bastard, Otto Finkel, and you will pay for what you have done.'

The soldiers around Otto began to shift nervously, sensing something was about to happen. They looked from Marco to Otto who shook his head at them, as though telling them it was nothing to worry about.

'Like I have just told you, I had nothing to do with what happened to your sister and if I find out who is responsible then I will punish them, but I must insist that you refrain from this attitude toward me, especially in front of my men.' With that, Otto turned around and started to walk away.

'Don't you turn your back on me,' shouted Marco, pulling the knife from his sleeve. He lunged at the German's back but was instantly intercepted by the sergeant and another SS soldier.

The soldier hit him in the face with the butt of his rifle and Marco knew that his nose had been broken, blood instantly pouring down onto his chest and soaking red into his white shirt. He fell to his knees but he felt no pain, his senses numb to all that had happened and was happening around him.

Otto turned around and looked at him.

'You fool,' he said calmly on seeing the knife lying on the ground at the side, the sunlight reflecting back off the blade. He unclipped the holster and took out the Mauser. 'You damned fool.'

Marco kneeled before the Nazi, all dignity gone, all hope lost.

He heard the sound of the pistol being cocked as Otto fed a round into the chamber and at that point he looked up. The sun shone down slightly behind the German's head, causing the blond hair to glow slightly, almost like a halo.

Marco said a prayer and closed his eyes.

PART FIVE
OTTO FINKEL

CHAPTER FORTY-EIGHT

Germany, Near Munich, Late May 1945

Major John Redford of the United States Army was starting to get annoyed. He had been kept waiting in the reception area of the headquarters building for over an hour, having to watch soldiers and secretaries bustling through the area, bouncing from office to office with various pieces of paper, files and clipboards gripped firmly in their hands. Telephones constantly ringing and raised voices could be heard adding to the hubbub all around. He sat alone quietly in the corner of the room, having been told to wait there by the pretty corporal in front of the office that was occupied by the man who he was meant to report to.

As he sat there, forgotten in the pandemonium that was happening all around him, he was getting more and more agitated. He had work to do, accommodation for the night to find and he had not eaten a thing since his breakfast almost eight hours ago. He had a folder that had been prepared by the British, which had been couriered to him the night before and he had read every word of it on the ride in. He knew exactly how he would conduct the interrogation and he really wanted to get started. Redford spoke fluent German and it was for this reason that he had been selected for the job.

It was getting late in the day and although the nights were now starting to fall later, he wanted to find somewhere to lay his head before it got dark. But that was a few hours away yet and as long as the Colonel did not keep him waiting much longer then he should be all right. But he had had enough waiting, so stood up and approached the desk where he spoke once again to the young corporal seated there.

'Can you let Colonel Walker know that I'm still waiting? I would like to speak to the prisoner today if at all possible.'

The corporal, a pretty brunette with her hair clipped to the top of her head looked up and smiled. 'He knows you're waiting, Major, I'm sure he will be with you shortly.'

'Can you remind him anyway?' he asked, getting more impatient. 'I've a lot to do today and I can't spend my time sitting around here all afternoon.'

Sighing audibly, the corporal picked up a black Bakelite telephone to her side and dialled a number. Redford returned to his seat as she relayed his message to the office behind her.

Redford had found out two days previously that a man of particular importance to his office, and that of their allies in British Intelligence, had been captured just south of Munich a week ago. The German, a suspected Hauptsturmführer of the SS, had been found hiding in a barn with three other men by a patrol of United States Rangers. He had been dressed as a sergeant of the Wehrmacht and had only come of interest due to his attitude and the way he appeared. It had been clear, even to the casual US infantryman that this guy was more than he was letting on. It had not taken long for him to be identified as probably being Otto Finkel, a wanted war criminal. The deep scar that ran down the side of his face was the giveaway.

Wanted for crimes against civilians and combatants alike, Redford was under no illusion that his capture was something of a coup. On hearing the news, the British had asked for him and as he was in the American sector, Redford had been assigned to interrogate the man and confirm it was indeed him. He was then to report back to the British who had a very big interest in this particular Nazi. However, he had been told that the man was denying that he actually was Finkel and consequently any involvement in any wrongdoing. Redford was not surprised at this. If indeed he was this Nazi and was to be tried and subsequently found guilty, then it would be the hangman's noose for him without a doubt. There would be no clemency for him, that was for sure.

After a couple of minutes the door behind the corporal opened and a large, brash colonel walked out. He was dressed in battle fatigues with a Colt pistol at his hip. His head was totally shaved and Redford could tell by his bold features that he was a battle-hardened soldier. He looked around the room until his eyes fixed upon Redford.

'Are you Redford of Army Intelligence?' he asked firmly.

Redford stood up and walked over to greet him. 'I am sir,' he replied, offering his hand.

As Colonel Walker shook it, he said, 'Okay, son, walk with me.'

They proceeded down a busy corridor with offices on both sides, their doors open and people hurriedly coming and going between them. Redford found that he had to step aside on more than one occasion as people barged past, as he struggled to keep up with the colonel's stride.

'The place is a fuckin' animal house,' said the colonel. 'It's all gone crazy since the Nazis surrendered. We've got people all over the fuckin' country... make that the continent... who need organising. Troops, refugees, prisoners. Not to mention the Jews in those fuckin' camps.'

'Yes,' replied Redford, half running to keep up with the big man's pace. 'I can see there is a lot to do.'

'A lot to do? Now that is one big fuckin' understatement, son. One big understatement.'

They went up a flight of stairs and continued along another corridor, not quite as busy as the ground floor and eventually they came to a room where two military policemen stood guard outside, their white helmets looking somewhat out of place amongst the other officers and soldiers in the building.

Colonel Walker stopped and turned to Redford.

'Okay, son,' he said. 'This guy is one total fuckin' asshole. He's refusing to speak to us and to be honest, I've spent enough time with Nazi shits like him to last me a fuckin' lifetime. Our guys who found him did the right thing in bringing him here, but to be honest, if you can take him out of my hair, so to speak,' he absent-mindedly ran his hand over his bald head, 'then I would be mega fuckin' grateful.'

'Right,' replied Redford. 'Thank you, Colonel. With all the confusion that's going on at the moment we can't let these people slip through the net and escape justice for what they've done. If I think it's him, then I'll arrange for his transportation to the Brits. If it's not then we can send him with the others.'

'Okay, son,' said the colonel. 'He's all yours.'

With that he turned and walked away back down the corridor without another word.

Redford turned to the door and held out his identification to the two MPs. 'Hi, Major John Redford, can you let me in, please?'

The soldier on the right opened the door and Redford stepped into the room. Inside the room another MP stood to the left of the doorway and seated at a table in the middle of the room was a German soldier, around twenty-eight years old. His wrists were handcuffed and chained to the table, which was fixed by rivets to the floor. He had thin wispy blond hair, piercing blue eyes and a nasty looking scar down the left hand side of his face. He was wearing the uniform of a soldier in the Wehrmacht, which looked slightly too large for him.

Redford knew instantly that this was no ordinary soldier. He had in his file two photographs of the man the British suspected was responsible for war

313

crimes and he was under no doubt that the man in those pictures was now sitting in front of him. The German looked over as Redford approached.

The very sight of him repulsed Redford. There was something about the eyes. Arrogance, malevolence, or just plain evil, he could not be sure, but there was something that made his skin crawl and he felt goose-bumps rise up on his arms as he looked at him.

Redford sat down on the seat opposite and placed the file on the table that separated them, shifting a glass ashtray to the side as he did so. He did not speak at first, casually observing the man who, for some reason, despite the arrogant look on his face, could not meet Redford's eyes. Redford took out a packet of Lucky Strikes and lit one from a lighter that he took from his pocket.

He caught the German looking at the lighter curiously, as though he recognised it. It was a silver lighter he had been given by one of his soldiers a few months previously, something he had picked up as war booty. The boy had claimed that he had taken it from a house abandoned by the retreating Germans but he wasn't too sure if he'd actually taken it from a dead enemy combatant. After what he had seen recently, Redford did not really care either way.

'You seem very interested in my lighter,' said Redford casually. By the reaction of the man across from him, he could tell that he spoke English. 'Have you seen one like it before?'

It was silver and had a swastika emblazoned on one side with the SS motto on the other, *Meine Ehre heißt Treue.*

'My honour is loyalty,' Redford translated. 'My honour is loyalty. Sounds a bit corny, don't you think?'

The German's eyes fixed on Redford's and he could see that he had hit a nerve. He was pleased with himself that it had taken so little time to get a reaction from the man.

'Okay,' he said after a few moments. 'Let's cut to the chase and stop all this bullshit. We know who you are and what's more, we know what you've done.'

The German, his eyes still fixed on Redford's replied in perfect English, 'And what do you think it is that I have done? I am a simple soldier, nothing more.'

'Cut the crap,' said Redford taking a drag from his cigarette and putting the lighter back into his pocket. 'It might have been easier to believe you if you'd found a disguise that actually fit.' He stood up and began to walk the room. Sitting so close to this man was beginning to make him feel sick.

'You are Otto Finkel, are you not?' he continued eventually.

The German did not answer but looked at the major as he paced the room in front of him.

'We know about you, Finkel, and what you've done.'

'And what is it you think that this Finkel person has done?' replied the German.

'Don't give me that shit,' said Redford looking at him. 'We have photographs of you... yes you. There is no denying that you are Hauptsturmführer Otto Finkel of the SS. None at all, so there's no point denying it.'

The German tilted his head slightly, a small wry smile upon his lips.

'Yes.' Redford said, noticing the reaction. He sat back down on the wooden chair to face him. 'Now that we've established that you are who we know you are, I'll get straight to the point. We have reason to understand that you were involved in a particularly unsavoury incident near Dunkirk in May of 1940.'

'Do you care to elaborate? It was a long time ago.'

'Not that long ago really, was it? Five years, more or less.'

'A lot has happened to me in five years.'

'No doubt,' replied Redford. 'Can you remember what you were doing in May of that year?'

'Clearly,' Otto replied sarcastically, his expression not changing. 'I was assisting in kicking the British army out of Europe.'

The major smiled. 'Oh right... How did that work out for you in the long run?'

Otto did not answer.

'Anyway,' continued Redford, opening up the file, 'we have a sworn statement from a British army officer who claims to have witnessed you ordering the shooting of approximately fifteen to twenty unarmed British prisoners of war in a small village square just to the east of Dunkirk. He is not too sure of the village name but the Brits believe it to be Abbeville. He also states that it was you, yourself... he even named you, who finished two of them off with your pistol. What have you to say about that?'

'I know not of what you speak.'

'Are you sure?' said the major, leaning back in his chair. He had now finished the cigarette and stubbed it out in the ash tray. 'We both know you are lying now don't we? You might as well admit it.'

'I know not of what you speak,' Otto repeated. 'Anyhow, how would this officer you talk of know my name, if indeed it had been me?'

'Because he recognised you, Finkel. He knew you.' The major leaned forward, 'It would seem that he and another soldier avoided your little round-up and were able to witness what happened before making their way to the coast. He knew you by name, Finkel.'

'It is mistaken identity.'

'Is it? You're beginning to sweat now.' Otto quickly wiped the perspiration from his forehead with the sleeve of his jacket. 'Nervous?'

Otto did not reply.

'He included in his statement how he knew it was you. He was also able to report how you got that rather ugly scar across your face.'

Otto stared at him.

'St Malo?' said Redford, driving the advantage home. 'Around 1928 if my memory serves me correctly. Let me just check the file here... yes, here it is, 1928. Ring any bells... No? Oh I think it does. I believe Big Ben himself is sounding very loudly in that ugly little Nazi head of yours right now.'

Otto tried to speak but could not find the words, opening his mouth as if about to say something and then quickly closing it again.

'You know the trouble with your lot,' said Redford calmly. 'Your trouble is that you think you are above everything, even God. Clearly you are not. How a country... a whole country for God's sake, could fall for the rhetoric of a madman and then follow him blindly is beyond me, it really is. You have marched all over this continent, killing and murdering and laying waste to everything before you and where has it left you, eh? Your little "Führer" is dead, his asshole henchmen are either dead too, or on the run, and your country is all to shit. It's totally wrecked. You're all an absolute disgrace.'

Otto stared at Redford with as much venom as he could muster but the Major laughed at him.

'When they string you up... When they put the noose around that scrawny Nazi neck of yours I want you to think of one thing. Think this. You were not just following orders or anything like that. You had a choice on what path your life was to take, we all do to a degree. You did not have to become a Nazi, you did not have to join the SS, you did not have to murder those soldiers or send Jewish children to their deaths, or do whatever it was that you did in Russia. You did not have to do any of that. You had a choice. The choices you have made have led you to the gallows and it is all your own doing.'

Before Otto could reply Redford stood up and collected the file from the desk.

'I will arrange for you to be delivered to the British. They have asked for you to be taken to them for further interrogation where there will probably be formal charges and hopefully for you, a quick trial. I have nothing more to say to you. You disgust me.'

Redford turned from him and walked to the exit. The MP at the door leaned over and gripped the handle to open it for him.

'Who do you think you are!' shouted Otto suddenly. 'Who do you think you are talking to me in such a way? I have had people shot for less. You Americans thinking you are so superior... It took all of you didn't it? All of you. Russians, Americans, British, French, all of you, to defeat us.'

As the MP pulled the door open, Redford turned and looked at the red faced German shouting at him.

'Yes,' he said calmly. 'It took all of us. But ask yourself this. Why did the rest of the world feel compelled to fight you? Who was right and who was wrong? And the point of it is, Finkel, that it is you sitting in chains right now about to answer to the rest of the world for the evil that you have done. You. Not us.'

Redford walked through the door and the MP closed it behind him before Otto could say another word.

Redford stopped for a second and put another cigarette into his mouth. Using the lighter he lit it and inhaled. He was about to put the lighter back into his pocket but instead held it up and looked at the inscription. He flipped it over and examined the swastika engraved on the other side and paused for a short moment. Then he turned to the MP nearest to him and held it out. 'Here, pal,' he said. 'A gift.'

The MP took the lighter from him and looked at Redford. 'You sure, sir?' he asked, not quite understanding why the major would do this, giving away such spoils to a complete stranger.

'Certainly,' he said. 'I've never been surer.'

Redford turned away and walked down the corridor towards the exit. He now had even more things to organise.

CHAPTER FORTY-NINE

Otto lay on his back on the bed in the cell and sighed. He had his hands over his face and was aware of the prison guard periodically looking in on him through the slot in the door, checking that he was not attempting to kill himself. The cell was quite spacious with a sink, toilet, writing desk and chair and the mattress he lay on was a lot more comfortable than the barn he had been found in with three other soldiers just a few days earlier. The window was barred but it was low enough for him to see out of, although he could not stomach looking at the American soldiers as they rushed about, beginning the administration of taking over the country he loved.

Suicide had been an option for him but it was something that he had never at any time considered. He felt that by taking his own life he would be admitting that the things he was being accused of doing had been wrong and he did not feel that way to any degree. He had not once, at any point, thought that the actions he and his comrades had carried out had been in any way incorrect, in any way unjustified. They had tried to rid the world of a disease that had spread malignantly, something which had to be stopped, a cancer that had to be cut out and removed. And to some degree they had succeeded and he, for one, felt proud of his part in it. History would determine that they were heroes and not the villains that the Allies were now portraying them to be.

He thought back to the incident near Dunkirk all those years ago. The American major had been right about one thing, five years was not such a long time, but when Otto thought about all the things he had done and seen and the places he had been to in the interim period, it felt like so much longer. The truth was that it had been such an insignificant part of his life that he had quite forgotten about it and had only recalled the events once the American had reminded him. He felt as though it was someone else who had been there and he had merely been an observer.

He had had absolutely no idea that there were two witnesses to what had happened, no idea at all. He tried to wrack his brains to think back at what had taken place in that small village during that hot early summer's day. He recalled there had been an attack on the reconnaissance squad and that his friend and others had been killed. He remembered being incensed at that. That they had been slaughtered in a cowardly ambush by a group of retreating British soldiers.

But then he thought of the actions that he had carried out over the years and knew that what the British troops had done that day was a legitimate act of war. There was nothing in it that he would not have done had their roles been reversed. However, at the time he had been extremely angry and when the British troops had been captured he had taken great pleasure in exacting his revenge. But how could the British officer who had witnessed it possibly know about St Malo and how he had come about his disfigurement? To have known he would have had to have been there when it had happened because once he was discharged from the French hospital, his parents had taken him straight back to Dortmund, and up until the war, he had never come across another British person until he had started shooting at them.

Had it been murder? He was not sure if it was. They were the spearhead of an advance and could not afford to have the problem of looking after prisoners, some of whom were wounded. It had simply not been practical. He knew that he was not the only SS officer to carry out such actions around that time and even now, all these years later, he felt no remorse and concluded that the killings were justified.

All the same, it did not matter what he thought any more. It now mattered what the Allies, and in particular the British, thought. He knew that there would be repercussions and reprisals once the fighting was over. The conquerors would be out for blood. He had heard of systematic hangings in the occupied countries for anyone who had been in any way compliant with the Nazis. Collaborators were being strung up by the lorry load and as for the SS, well, the SS were now the hunted. Being blamed for everything by both the victors and also by some of their fellow countrymen in a bid to deflect any blame from themselves.

He took his hands from his face and sat up, swinging his legs to the floor and stayed there, not moving for a short while, deep in thought.

Maybe some of what he had done had been a little "over the top". Maybe it wasn't particularly pleasant, but he remained adamant in his head that it needed to be done. And now they were going to hang him for it!

He knew that he was going to die but death did not bother him. Many times, on the Russian front, he would have gladly welcomed Death to have appeared and gathered him in his arms, but for some reason he had been spared. Now he was going to die by the hangman's noose and it irritated him that this would be the way it all ended. It was somewhat ironic that he had survived the war without a scratch, after all the combat he had seen, only to die so unceremoniously and without honour.

The only wound Otto owned was the deep scar that ran down the left hand side of his face. The scar that had been the absolute bane of his life. Many times strangers had asked how he had come about it and he would mostly lie and tell them that it had happened in combat, avoiding the truth, which he found embarrassing.

He was reminded, every single day of his life, whenever he looked in the mirror, about that day in St Malo. He remembered enjoying his holiday up to that point and had made friends with the two English brothers who seemed to also enjoy his company, despite the bad atmosphere between their two fathers. He wondered if the British officer who had witnessed the massacre near Dunkirk had been one of them but thought it most unlikely, the coincidence was just too great. Or was it fate? Had fate pushed them both together again? After all, he had bumped into another of the boys from that boat a couple of years ago. He thought back to his time in Rome and the mess that it had turned out to be in the end.

The Americans had not yet quizzed him about what had happened in Rome and he for one was not going to bring the subject up with them, that was for certain. If it was true that the witness had been one of the English boys from the boat, he could not quite recall their names, then the positive identification of him would be undeniable. But then the scar was the giveaway.

The scar that had caused so much bullying at school. The scar that had caused every girl he had ever been interested in to turn away in repulsion. He remembered back to Rome and Sophia Roncalli and the way she had looked at him. At first he had thought that it had been the scar that had caused her to be so sickened by him but now he understood that it was the uniform. But then, Sophia Roncalli was dead and none of that mattered any more.

He had not blamed anyone for the accident on the boat. Not at first anyway, but as the bullying continued and the feeling of worthlessness had taken hold of his young life, he had relived that day and had come to the conclusion that it was the quiet, strange, French boy who was to blame if anyone was. Had he not stepped into the boat, almost challenging the others to do likewise, then the incident would not have happened. If only he could have come across him during the war then he would have gladly put a bullet in that particular bastard's head.

The incident in St Malo, the scar and the subsequent bullying had indirectly led to him joining the Nazi party. They had offered him a sense of worth, a sense of purpose and belonging. He had accepted their doctrine without question, joining at first the SA and then moving onto the SS where he was quickly singled out for special training to be an officer. His father had been very proud of him, parading him about at any opportunity that he could and he had been happy to indulge him. He had not seen or heard from his father for a number of months now, since before the Normandy landings, Otto had not had a single minute of rest since then, let alone time for any leave to visit him.

He stood up and walked to the sink and threw some cold water into his face, wiping it dry with the towel that they had provided. He looked in the mirror and noticed that he was looking extremely unkempt. He had not managed to have a shave for over a week and his beard was beginning to get too long. He prided himself on his appearance normally but now he looked exactly like the rest of the German army, defeated and hopeless.

He suddenly felt anger rise within him. How dare these people treat him, a German officer, so badly, so utterly without respect. They had no right, no right at all. So they were going to hand him over to the British, he was going to be tried and he was going to be hanged. Well, he thought, we will see about that.

Otto knew that he had to get away from these people. He had no intention of allowing them to put a noose around his neck and string him up. There was no way he would allow them the satisfaction of that, no way at all. He was still quite fit, the meals he had been given were of a good quality and he felt healthy. All he needed was an opportunity to arise and then a plan of action once that freedom was regained. He sat on the bed again and heard the metal grille on the door slide back as the guard checked that he had not done anything that warranted his attention. Otto did not look in his direction but turned his head the other way, towards the window, where the light of the evening sun shone through, casting shadows within the room.

He lay back on the bed and covered his face with his hands once more and after a short while, he fell into a deep sleep.

CHAPTER FIFTY

Three Days Later.

Otto lay on the cold, tiled floor and looked across at the dead American soldier lying across the room. He tried to stop panting and steady his breathing, the exertions of the past couple of minutes causing him to suck the oxygen greedily into his lungs. He stood up and checked himself quickly in the restroom mirror before turning his attention back to the unfortunate infantryman who had been tasked, along with his colleague who waited outside, with taking him to the train station for onward transportation to the British sector.

Quickly he fumbled in the man's pockets, searching for the key that would release him from the handcuffs that he had used to strangle the man to death only seconds ago. He did not have much time. At any point the soldier's colleague would come looking to see what was taking them so long and if he did not get out of here quickly, then all hope of escape would be lost as swiftly as the opportunity to take it had arisen.

Checking the trouser pocket he found the key and released himself from the cuffs, stuffing them into his own trouser pocket before taking the man's wallet and the automatic sidearm from his holster and putting that into the pocket of his tunic.

Acting as quickly as he could, he dragged the corpse to one of the cubicles and sat it upon the toilet before closing and locking the door. He then scrambled over the top of the partition into the next cubicle and then was back in the main restroom once more, all traces of what had happened now invisible to the casual observer.

Again he looked in the mirror and sighed to himself. The sweat was pouring from his head but the adrenalin that had kicked in when he had first attacked the American was still pumping determinedly through his veins. This was make or break for him. If he was found here, with the corpse of an American soldier, then he would probably be shot on the spot. There was no way the Americans would let him get away with this. He had to get away from here and he had to do it quickly, but first he had to take care of the second soldier who was waiting patiently for them somewhere near the station platform. He needed that man to come to him, to come in search of his friend and their prisoner, who had, so he had been led to believe, come across with a sudden bout of diarrhoea. If any other person walked in before him then Otto's number was pretty much up. He needed to take care of the second soldier and he had to do it quickly. Despite it being the evening, there were still a lot of people about the station, including a handful of soldiers, coming and going about whatever business they had and getting past them was going to be a problem as he still wore the uniform of a German infantryman.

He heard footsteps coming along the short corridor outside the restroom and froze for a second before regaining his composure and rushing to the side of the door, pulling the pistol from his pocket and cocking the weapon as he did so. As the door opened, he was relieved to see that it was the second soldier, who, like his colleague was of medium height and build.

'Jim,' he said as he entered the room and then stopped, surprised to see the restroom appearing to be empty.

Instinctively his hand moved to the holster at his hip, sensing something was wrong, but before he could draw the weapon, Otto, standing behind the door, stepped out and thrust his own pistol into the man's face.

'If you want to live, you will not shout or attempt to raise any alarm,' he said calmly.

In shock, the soldier stammered, 'Where's Jim? What have you done with Jim?'

'Jim is of no concern to you,' replied Otto. 'If you want to get out of this alive then you are to do as I say. As you will be aware, I have nothing to lose and a desperate man is likely to do anything. So, please, for your own sake, and for that of your mother, do not do anything that will warrant me pulling this trigger and blowing your brains out, which, believe me, I will most certainly do if I have to.'

'For God's sake,' said the soldier, clearly petrified. 'What are you doing? You will never get away from here. You've no chance.'

'We'll see,' said Otto. 'If I get shot then so be it. That will be better than the humiliation the British have planned for me. So, you see, I don't really have much choice. Now give me the keys to the jeep.'

Fumbling in his pocket, the soldier produced a bunch of keys, which Otto snatched off him and put in the trouser pocket with the handcuffs he had taken from the man he had just killed.

'Where's Jim?' the soldier repeated. 'Where is he?'

'We are going to walk out of here and we are going to go back to the jeep. You are then going to drive me away from here,' said Otto calmly, ignoring him. 'Do not be afraid. Do not show any signs that all is not as it should be and I promise to let you go. If you don't then the first person I will shoot will be you. Now come on let's move.'

Pushing the soldier ahead of him and forcing the pistol into the small of his back, they walked along the short corridor. When they got to the door at the end, they stopped and Otto opened it slightly, all the time keeping his eyes fixed on the soldier. Glancing quickly through the gap in the door, Otto looked out and could see that there were only a few people sitting around the waiting area and the odd person walking by. The worrying thing was the group of five soldiers standing near the cigarette machine across from them talking and laughing. Each of them carried a weapon of some description.

'Okay,' Otto said quickly. 'We are going to move steadily to the exit and then make our way to the jeep outside. Anything from you and I promise you that your guts will be all over the floor. Do you understand me?'

'Yes, I understand you, you Nazi bastard,' replied the soldier viciously.

'Now now,' said Otto, smiling at him. 'Don't be like that. We were just starting to get along so nicely too.'

Otto opened the door and forced the soldier through it. With the pistol in his left hand, held across his body and shielding it as best he could, he kept the American between himself and the group of soldiers as he walked quickly towards the exit. He was aware of odd glances from one or two civilians but when they saw the scar on his face they instantly turned their heads away, their curiosity instantly leaving them.

'Hey, pal,' one of the soldiers suddenly shouted. 'Hey you… you with the kraut.'

Otto felt the sweat rolling down his forehead and the back of his neck as they continued walking, ignoring him.

'Hey you, soldier, I'm talking to you,' came the voice, agitated now at being ignored.

Otto stopped. 'Be careful,' he said quietly to his captive. 'Remember your mother.'

The soldier turned to face the group and shouted over, 'What can I do for you?' And then noticing he was addressing a lieutenant he added, '… Sir.'

'I was wondering if you had any change for this goddam machine,' replied the lieutenant but on realising that the soldier had a prisoner with him he became curious. 'Say, what's going on?'

Otto held his breath. This was the point where his hostage could give him away. This is where it could all end. He could see that he was only a few feet from the exit but he did not know what awaited him outside. If anything was going to happen then it was going to happen very soon.

The lieutenant started walking towards them, his hand going down to his holster, unclipping the cover.

'What's the matter, son?' he said. 'You look a little jumpy.'

Before the soldier could reply, Otto pushed him as hard as he could into the advancing officer, causing them both to fall in a heap on the waiting room floor. As the other four soldiers looked over in surprise, Otto fired two rounds into the group hitting one of them in the leg. As the soldier yelled out in pain, his colleagues dived desperately for cover behind the chairs.

Otto ran the short distance to the exit but before he went through the door, he turned and fired at the lieutenant, hitting him in the shoulder. He opened the door and ran out into the street and sprinted as fast as he could towards where a group of vehicles were parked, hoping he could find, in the fading light, the jeep that had brought them here. He ran past other soldiers and civilians who merely looked on uncomprehendingly as he shot past them, none of them doing anything to stop him.

Otto had been in combat many times before and this felt no different. He had acted purposefully and determinedly, completely focused on what he had to do. He had managed to let off three shots, disabling two people, all before any of them had any chance to respond and he was now in the parking lot about to get into the jeep and drive away, probably before any of them had picked themselves up off the floor. Laughable, he thought, totally laughable. How these people had won the war was beyond him.

He took the keys from his pocket, placed them in the ignition and fired up the engine. As he pulled out of the parking lot, he noticed some of the soldiers emerge from the train station and as he stepped down heavily on the accelerator, he was forced to duck his head as a couple of them fired their weapons in his direction, the bullets whizzing overhead, missing both him and the vehicle.

A few seconds later he was around a corner and gone.

Otto smiled to himself. It had all been remarkably easy in the end. He had managed to escape the detachment and get away. He sniggered to himself at the ineptitude of the Americans for underestimating him. Transporting him to the British, by rail, with an escort of only two very mediocre soldiers was either very stupid of them or very disrespectful. Either way, it had worked in his favour and for the time being he was free.

But Otto realised that he needed one more thing before he could make good his escape and that one thing was quite significant in the whole scheme of things.

The one thing that Otto needed now was a plan.

CHAPTER FIFTY-ONE

Otto drove for what felt like hours. He headed south, back towards Munich at first and then turning east toward Salzburg and the roads beyond. He had found a US Army greatcoat in the rear of the jeep and was now wearing it, enabling him to pass Allied traffic without a problem, the drivers of the other vehicles showing no interest in him as he drove by. Now and again, when an approaching convoy would come near he would become a little nervous and pull over to the side of the road, parking the jeep out of sight until they passed.

Eventually at close to two o'clock in the morning, low on fuel, he pulled off the road into a small copse and extinguished the lights. He sat for a while not moving, tiredness threatening to overcome him, but realising that to fall asleep here ran the risk of discovery if he was unable to wake. He needed to stay alert and active.

He got out of the jeep and walked to the rear of the vehicle. Squinting in the darkness, he looked into the back, rummaging around with his hands in the darkness. This was the first time he had had chance to properly look in the back of the vehicle to see what items were there, other than when he had found the greatcoat earlier, which had been unmissable behind the passenger seat. There was a jerry-can half full containing gasoline, which he used immediately to replenish the fuel tank before discarding it in the undergrowth to the side.

He found a smaller jerry-can and when he took off the cap and put it to his nose he realised it was water, so took a few mouthfuls before putting the cap back on and returning it to where he had found it. A small canvas bag was attached to the back of the passenger seat that he had not noticed up until now, and when he opened it he found a small torch inside. He took it out and flicked the switch and was pleased to see that the batteries worked and it gave off a powerful light. He quickly turned it off again so as not to be seen and then turned so that his back was to the roadway, before switching it back on to look inside the bag, using his body to shield the light.

Inside there was a miscellany of items. A pen and notebook, a small pair of binoculars, a box with the words US ARMY FIELD RATION K emblazoned upon it and, most importantly, a map.

He took out the field rations and opened the box. Inside he found a can and can opener and after a little fiddling he was able to open it and spooned the contents out with his fingers. He was unsure of what exactly he was eating but he could distinctly detect a hint of cheese. To his educated palate the food tasted disgusting but then he could not exactly be too choosy at the moment. He also found four cracker biscuits two of which he immediately consumed before taking out the map and spreading it across the bonnet of the jeep.

Using the torch he quickly assessed where he believed himself to be and upon looking at the names of villages and towns in the area he was suddenly drawn to the name of a small village just to the south of Obertrum. He figured that he was roughly ten miles to the south of the village and if he was lucky he could make it there within twenty minutes if he did not come across any Allied patrols.

The name of the village had triggered a memory. He was taken back to Russia three years previously and to his superior, SturmbannFührer Heinrich Schmidt. Whilst under attack from Russian partisans Schmidt had suffered a serious injury to his arm when a grenade had exploded only a few feet from them. The attack had been repelled but Schmidt's injuries had led to him being evacuated and later discharged from the army. Whilst lying on the stretcher, Schmidt had been worried that now he was about to lose his arm and was likely to be made to leave soldiering, he would also be of little use on the smallholding he owned near Obertrum, where his wife and young son lived and had been maintaining whilst he was in the army. However, he had smiled as he reminisced, as he was waiting to be taken away. He would once again be able to see the river flowing past the farmhouse that was such a beautiful sight, he had said, especially in the summer months.

Taking the map off the bonnet and folding it up so as to display only the area he was now in, he threw it onto the passenger seat and jumped into the jeep. Firing up the engine once more, he put the vehicle into gear and drove it back onto the road.

He now had a purpose. For the first time since his escape he now felt that he knew what he was doing and it made him feel more content and relaxed. He felt rejuvenated and alive once more. The thing that had been missing since his escape had now been found.

He finally had a plan.

*

Remembering Schmidt's description of the area it was easy for Otto to find the property, despite the darkness. The approach to the smallholding was by means of a long dirt track that ran alongside the river. The jeep was more than capable of making the journey but Otto felt that an American vehicle turning up at three o'clock in the morning might cause alarm, particularly if Schmidt no longer lived there and the house was occupied by someone else less accommodating than his old commanding officer, who, like Otto, had been a committed Nazi. He was also not entirely convinced that he was in the right place.

He decided to park the jeep discreetly off the road and get some sleep and would complete the journey by foot in the morning. It had been a long day and he was absolutely shattered, and when he placed his head on the ground to the side of the vehicle, using the greatcoat as a blanket, it took only a matter of seconds for him to fall asleep.

He awoke hours later to the sound of birds in the trees and an aircraft flying low overhead. He quickly stretched out his stiff muscles as he stood up and put on the greatcoat before eating more of the rations and taking on some water. Packing what he could into the canvas bag, and pocketing the weapon he had taken from the American soldier, he set off in the direction of the farmhouse.

After walking for ten minutes a building came into view. It was a large house positioned about twenty metres from the river that flowed slowly past it. It comprised of two floors with two dormer windows on the roof that looked out over a cobbled courtyard. A large oak door was in the centre and as Otto approached he saw a large black Alsatian dog chained to the building, secured by a steel ring that had been riveted to the wall to the side of the door. As Otto got nearer, the dog started to bark loudly and strained at the chain as it tried to get closer to him, snarling viciously, saliva dripping from its open, growling mouth.

To the left of the farmhouse stood a barn, which looked twice the size of the house and he could hear the sound of poultry coming from it, adding to the noise of the dog that snarled in front of him.

Otto stopped. There was no way he was going any nearer to the building as long as the dog was there. He had not come this far to be ripped apart now by a vicious and evil looking canine.

Before long he heard the sound of a human voice and stepped behind a tree to observe.

The front door opened and a youth of perhaps seventeen years of age, still wearing nightclothes and with his hair dishevelled, exited the house, a shotgun under his arm.

'Okay, okay. Calm down Oskar,' he shouted at the dog. 'Calm down. Now what has upset you?'

The youth looked out, up the dirt track, but Otto was still hidden behind the tree and out of his view. Otto peered around the trunk and on seeing the boy snap down the barrel of the weapon to load it, he pulled the pistol from his pocket and stepped out.

The boy looked at him, shocked at what he saw and his hand froze, still holding the cartridge above the barrel of the weapon, his mouth hanging open.

'I am sorry to do this,' said Otto calmly, pointing the pistol at him. 'Do not be afraid. I will not shoot if you do as I say.'

'Who are you?' asked the boy, evidently confused at seeing this strange looking German soldier standing before him in an American army coat. 'What do you want here?'

'Do you know where I can find Heinrich Schmidt?' asked Otto calmly.

The boy looked at him suspiciously.

'Maybe,' he said and placed the shotgun at his feet before taking hold of the dog by the collar, which continued to bark and growl menacingly. 'Depends who is asking.'

Otto looked at the boy and grinned.

'I can see you are your father's son,' he said. 'Now go into the house and tell him that an old comrade is outside and would like to speak to him. And for God's sake shut that dog up!'

As the boy was about to turn around and do as Otto had instructed, an upstairs window was flung open and a familiar, booming voice shouted down, 'Finkel!, Jesus, I thought you were dead. Or the Americans or Russians would have had you by now.'

'No, sir,' Otto shouted up, grinning at his former colleague. 'I am still very much alive. But I am in a bit of a predicament and could really do with some help.'

'I'll be down in a few minutes,' said Schmidt. 'Make yourself at home until I am dressed.' Turning his attention to his son he shouted. 'Gerhard, take that irritating animal and tie him up somewhere, then make our guest here some coffee. Where are your manners, boy?'

Otto replaced the pistol in his pocket and stepped forward as the young man unshackled the animal and dragged it, still barking, in the direction of the barn. Otto opened the door and stepped inside the farmhouse. To his right he could see a kitchen with a wooden table and chairs and moved inside. He sat down at a chair facing the door and placing the canvas bag on the floor at his feet. The room was typical of houses in the area, wooden dressers containing shelves filled with plates, pots and pans, a large oven and stove and a deep sink that was half-filled with crockery beneath a large window that faced out onto the fields to the rear of the property, where Otto could see a number of cows grazing in the morning sunshine. A minute or so later, Gerhard entered the kitchen and walked straight to the stove where he picked up a kettle to fill with water. As he did so, Heinrich Schmidt, one-time SS Sturmbannführer and Otto's former commanding officer, walked into the room.

Otto could see that the man had not changed much since he last saw him being taken away by the medics in Russia almost three years ago. He was a big man, his shoulders nearly twice as wide as Otto's and he stood well over six feet in height. His shiny bald head reflected the rays that penetrated the kitchen window and his long nose, red with sunburn, stood out amongst the prominent features of his face, which looked weather-worn from a life spent outdoors. The left sleeve of his shirt hung loose at his side, evidence of the injury he had sustained on the Eastern Front.

Otto stood up to greet him and the man took him firmly by the hand, pulling Otto close to him in a show of paternal friendship.

'My God, Finkel,' he said, smiling broadly. 'My God. I thought you were dead or captured by the Russians or the Americans. I never expected to ever see you again. Come, sit down. You must tell me everything that has happened since we were last together.'

'It is so good to see you, sir,' replied Otto, smiling broadly. 'I cannot tell you how relieved I am to have found you.'

'Gerhard,' said Schmidt turning his attention to his son who was trying to light the stove with a long match. 'Leave us in peace. Go and feed the chickens or something.'

The boy did not reply but finished lighting the stove and then left the room, closing the front door loudly as he did so.

Otto got straight to the point.

'I am in somewhat of a situation,' he started. 'I could desperately do with the assistance of an old comrade and could think of no one better than you. For some reason the Allies are accusing me of all kinds of things, some of which are true, granted, but they want to hang me for them. I have escaped custody and need to get away to somewhere safe.'

'I see,' said Schmidt thoughtfully. 'I suppose it was bound to happen in the end. It was obvious that once the war was lost there would be repercussions.

There always is. But before we go into any of that, tell me what happened after I was carted away.' His eyes went absent-mindedly to the empty shirt sleeve.

Otto ran his fingers through his hair before responding. 'I followed soon after, thank God, otherwise I would be dead by now. I spent some time in France and Italy. When the Allies invaded Normandy, I was put back into a combat unit and spent the rest of the war on the western front. I started the war going one way in France and spent the end of it going the opposite direction.'

'I take it that they want you for what happened in Rome and France then. Or Russia even, because, let's face it we were not exactly angels were we?'

'Oddly enough, no,' replied Otto. 'Maybe they haven't got round to looking into any of that yet. The Brits want me for something that happened near Dunkirk in 1940... something that I had not thought about in a long, long time. In fact I had quite forgotten about it until they reminded me.'

Schmidt stood up and went to the stove where the kettle was now boiling. He did not say anything as he made the coffee, returning a minute or so later with two cups.

'So my old friend,' he said eventually. 'What is it that you need from me? I owe you a lot, maybe even my life if I'm honest, and for that reason I am prepared to help you. I have been out of the army for well over two years now and have had time to reflect on what we did as I have watched our country being destroyed around us. It's terrible.

'The Führer is dead so they tell us, and there is little hope that the Reich will recover from this. Take it from me Otto, National Socialism in Germany is over, it is finished. The Americans and Soviets will divide the country up between them and if we think that Versailles was bad for us then I dread to think what they will decide to do with us now. They will round up anyone involved in the most minor of indiscretions and do away with them. I am still waiting for a knock at my door, which I am sure will come one day.'

Otto looked at him as he sipped at the hot coffee, allowing Schmidt to continue.

'However, all that said,' continued Schmidt, 'I cannot stand idle and let the Allies have their way without attempting to do something about it. They may have beaten us eventually, but they cannot be allowed to punish us for something that only we had the balls to do. You can stay here for a while, lie low so to speak, whilst we work out what to do with you. One thing is for sure, Finkel, you cannot stay in Germany. This country is not safe for you any more, not safe for any SS if we are being honest.'

'Thank you,' said Otto, the relief immense. 'But what about your wife? What will she say?'

'You do not have to worry about her,' replied Schmidt, matter-of-factly. 'She is dead.'

'I am sorry. I did not know.'

'How could you?' replied Schmidt unconcerned. 'People die all the time. Nothing new in that. I will get Gerhard to prepare a room for you and you can help out on the farm until we can move you on. Anyway, how did you get here?'

'I stole a jeep from the Americans,' replied Otto. 'It's parked about half a mile from here. I walked the rest of the way in.'

'Okay, I will get Gerhard to retrieve it. We can hide it in the barn for now until we decide what to do with it.'

'I don't know how to thank you,' said Otto.

'You don't have to. We took the same oath to the Führer. He may be gone now, but we still remain.' Schmidt stood up facing Otto and raised his only arm. 'Heil Hitler!'

Otto got out of his chair and stood to attention in front of him. Raising his right hand and clicking his boot heels together he shouted in reply, 'Heil Hitler.'

The two men embraced.

As they parted, Schmidt said, 'Come my old comrade. I bet you are starving and could do with some breakfast.' Otto nodded. 'Good. Then let us eat.'

CHAPTER FIFTY-TWO

The rain was pouring heavily upon the farmhouse and could be heard clearly hitting the roof above them, despite the three men being on the ground floor. The days were getting shorter and darkness was starting to fall earlier as each day passed, the summer now behind them and the cooler autumn evenings forcing them indoors earlier.

It had been four months since Otto had arrived and as Schmidt had suggested, he had spent his days helping out on the farm with the animals. It was work that Otto had never done before, a lifestyle that he would never have contemplated, but surprisingly to him, he had found that he enjoyed it. He enjoyed the peace and solitude as he spent his days in the fields or in the barn, more often than not alone and then his evenings with Schmidt and his very quiet son, Gerhard. They had reminisced constantly about life before the war, those comrades they had lost over the last few years and had occasionally touched on the many things they had done in the name of National Socialism and Adolf Hitler for which Otto was now being hunted.

Otto was not sure if the colonel was now regretting some of what they had done, or had been ordered to do, but whenever he spoke about those times it was with an air of melancholy or a sense that things may have been better done differently. Otto's own thoughts on such matters had not changed. He felt no regret or remorse, or, even for a second, thought that what they had done had been in any way wrong or unjustifiable. Okay, people had been killed. A lot of people had been killed in fact, but that was what happened in war. Those people who had died could not be looked upon as members of the human race. What had been done had been necessary and the world should be grateful that there were those around with the courage to do it.

But the world was not grateful. When they listened to the news on the radio, the BBC broadcasts in particular, they were with a tone of disgust and incomprehension. Places had been named of which Otto had been well aware. Places such as Belsen, Buchenwald, Dachau and Auschwitz. The victorious Allies putting their own spin on what had happened there. Otto knew that the people he had rounded up and shipped out to the camps were never coming back. It was something that had had to be done, something that was imperative to make the Germany he loved the pure and perfect state that it deserved to be. He never saw it as revenge for Versailles, he only ever saw it as necessary work that could not be avoided, to achieve the goals of those who knew what was best for the country. Senior Nazis had been caught and were to be put on trial. Some, like Goebbels and Himmler and even the Führer himself had taken their own lives to prevent the humiliation of being displayed in such a manner.

At times when he was alone, out working in the fields or lying in his bed at night, Otto would think of the broadcasts he had heard the previous evening and wonder at what would become of him. His life now had no direction. He was on the run and if caught then he would share the same fate as the others. It did not matter that he felt that his wartime actions were innocent, those now who had the power did not see it that way and as such there was no doubt in his mind that he would be hanged if he was caught. He could not allow that to happen. To add to what he had done he had also killed the American soldier when making his escape, so the Yanks too would be out for his blood.

Schmidt's farm had provided the perfect sanctuary. He had not once left it to deliver eggs or milk or anything else relating to the business of farming, Schmidt himself and Gerhard had done all that while he hid away from society. He was too noticeable, would arouse too much suspicion. The infernal scar on his face would cause too much curiosity and would eventually give him away, he was sure of it. So staying out of everyone's view was the best policy for the time being.

Schmidt had spoken of some contacts that he had that may be able to help with Otto's situation. He had told him of a network, albeit in its infancy, that was being set up by sympathetic people to assist in getting people away from the persecution the Allies were now conducting on anyone involved with the camps in any way. Or those involved in what they deemed incorrect battlefield tactics. It would not be long before they could get Otto to safety.

There were also rumours that some governments in South America were amenable to giving them sanctuary and although this seemed very far away, to Otto it offered the best option. The more he thought of a new life in the sunshine of Argentina, Brazil or Venezuela the more it appealed to him. He could not go back to Dortmund, or to anywhere else in Europe for that matter, as he was very recognisable and it would not be long before he was back in custody. After all, it had taken the American major only seconds to recognise him all those weeks ago.

As the rain poured outside, Gerhard placed another log on the fire and Otto and the Colonel watched it as it caught fire almost instantly, the smoke being sucked up the chimney. Otto watched his old comrade shift in the chair awkwardly as he tried to make himself comfortable. He grimaced as he moved, the missing limb evidently causing him some distress.

'Are you okay? Do you need some help?' asked Otto rising from his chair opposite.

'Ach, no,' replied Schmidt irritably. 'I will be fine.'

They sat in silence for a few minutes enjoying the peace and the warmth from the fire. Then Schmidt turned to him.

'Otto. Things may be moving along now.'

'What do you mean?' Otto asked curiously.

'I have been in touch with some of my old friends. Some of whom are able to help. There may be a route out of here for you so you must be ready to move at a moment's notice.'

'I have nothing but the clothes I sit here in,' replied Otto. 'The clothes that you have so kindly given me. I am ready to move whenever you say so.'

'There is a man...' went on Schmidt quietly before turning to his son. 'Gerhard, please leave the room. Go upstairs or something. This is not for your ears.'

Dutifully the young man stood up and left the room without a word. He knew when not to question his father.

'As I was saying,' continued Schmidt, 'there is a man in Innsbruck who can help us. I hear he will transport you... for the right price of course, I believe it to be around a thousand schillings... across the border to the Alto Adige, the South Tyrol. There are sympathisers just over the border who may be able to get you papers and maybe a visa to a place in South America. What do you think?'

Otto looked at him, unable to believe his ears. Was there a way out of this that was actually possible? Could he find a life in another country to start over again and put all this behind him? He was no fool and knew that there was no going back to his former life, the former places and to the former people. If he wanted to live then he needed to get out of the country and to start again.

'What do I think?' he said. 'I think that I would very much like to try it. But where will I get a thousand schillings from? I have nothing.'

'You have worked on the farm for the past four or five months,' replied Schmidt. 'In all that time you have never asked me for anything. I can get the money together, my friend, and a little extra to see you on your way should you need it.'

'You have put me up here and fed me,' said Otto. 'You have hidden me when you know that to do so could get yourself into a whole lot of trouble, but you have done it anyway. I ask no payment, Colonel. None at all.'

'I will give you the money and you will take it,' smiled Schmidt. 'And if I have to order you to do so then I will and you will obey like the good soldier you are. Remember, you have not been officially discharged from the army and so are under my command, even if I have retired. You will do as you are told young man.'

Otto smiled and sighed. 'I don't know how I can ever repay you,' he said. 'I really don't.'

'You can thank me by getting out of here and getting away.'

Suddenly the door burst open and Gerhard ran into the room, panting.

'My God,' shouted Schmidt. 'Whatever is the matter?'

'Outside... coming down the track... vehicles, two of them. I saw them from my bedroom window. They'll be here any minute.'

Otto could hear the faint sound of engines approaching the building and ran to the window. He looked out and could see the headlights of two vehicles getting nearer. One looked like a jeep with a truck following behind.

'Shit,' he said as they got closer. 'Americans!'

The colonel stood up. 'Don't panic,' he said. 'It is probably a routine call. Get out the back and into the barn. Hide under the tarpaulin that's covering the jeep. I will try to get rid of them.'

Otto did not need telling twice and was out of the door before Schmidt could say another word.

Colonel Schmidt went to the front door and opened it, staying just inside the vestibule as the rain continued to splash onto the cobblestones at the front of the house, bouncing out of the large puddles that had formed on the uneven ground. He watched as the American army vehicles, a covered jeep and a medium sized truck, came to a halt a few yards from the doorway. Schmidt did not move.

The drivers of the vehicles kept the engines running and the lights on. Schmidt watched the rain come down heavily in the glare of the headlights and made no attempt to move from the doorway.

Eventually, a soldier stepped from the passenger seat of the jeep. As he exited the vehicle, he put his foot into a deep puddle, splashing muddy water onto the bottom of his trousers. 'Oh crap!' he said sharply.

He was wearing the uniform of a captain, a waterproof poncho covering him. He approached Schmidt.

'Hi,' he said as he approached, stopping a few yards away. And then he said in perfect German, 'I am Captain Bill Modjeska of the US Army. Could I come in for a few moments.'

'No, you may not,' replied Schmidt curtly.

'Oh,' said Modjeska, taken aback. 'Are you sure? It is raining.'

'Yes, I am sure it is raining,' said Schmidt, his expression not changing.

'Okay,' said Modjeska drawing out the word. 'Then I will stand here then. Are you Colonel Heinrich Schmidt of the SS.'

'No,' replied Schmidt, almost smirking as he watched the American officer getting more and more drenched as he stood there in the downpour.

'Our records show that this property belongs to him.'

'It did,' replied Schmidt calmly. 'It now belongs to me. I am Heinrich Schmidt but I am no longer a colonel and have not been in the SS for some time. It's very hard to hold a rifle with only one arm,' he indicated his empty sleeve.

Captain Modjeska looked to where the arm should have been and then back to Schmidt's face. It was obvious now that he had had enough of the games Schmidt was playing with him.

'Colonel… Mister Schmidt,' went on Modjeska. 'We are currently taking a bit of a census of who is living here in the district and of anyone that may be of interest to us and it appears that your name has come up as someone we would be interested in talking to.'

'Why is that? The war is over and like I have just told you, I have not been in the army for some time. Discharged on medical grounds. I am surely no interest to you. I am of no interest to anyone.'

'You were in the SS were you not?'

'Yes. Your point being?'

'Ex-members of the SS are of particular interest to us,' replied the captain, wiping away the water from his face as the wind blew the rain into it.

'That is up to you,' said Schmidt. He became aware of a couple of other soldiers getting out of the truck. They carried M1 carbines in their hands. Schmidt began to sweat. 'What is it you want from me?' he asked.

'We would like you to come with us,' replied Modjeska, almost politely. 'We need to ask you some questions about your time in the military.'

'Why now?' asked Schmidt. 'Why tonight?'

'Why not?'

'Because it is pissing down with rain and I am busy,' replied Schmidt. 'I live here on my own with my son who has, how can I put it… certain medical needs. I cannot leave him on his own. He may do something untoward.'

338

'I fully sympathise,' said the captain, stepping back towards the half shelter of the jeep in an attempt to lessen the drenching he was receiving. 'But we really need to speak to you.'

'That's fine,' replied Schmidt. 'And I really want to help you. But I cannot leave him and let's face it, I am not going anywhere. As a compromise, I am prepared to come to your office tomorrow morning, when his nurse arrives, if that is all right with you. I have nothing to hide after all.'

The captain looked at the two soldiers who were now by his side. They had not understood a single word that had been spoken and he said something to them in English that Schmidt could not comprehend. Whatever he said made the two soldiers turn around and walk back to the truck that they had left, happy to get back inside out of the rain.

'Very well, Mister Schmidt,' said Modjeska. 'Please report to the town hall tomorrow morning after the nurse arrives and ask for me. We have set up an office there. I will hopefully not keep you too long.'

He turned around to get back into the jeep but stopped. In the darkness and the pouring rain, he had not noticed the barn door slightly ajar until now. The sound of poultry could be heard, merging with the noise of the rain. He turned his head back to Schmidt, who still stood unmoving in the doorway.

'You could do with closing that door, Mister Schmidt. You don't want your chickens escaping now do you?'

Schmidt did not reply but looked at the man stony faced.

Modjeska got back into the jeep and seconds later the vehicle was travelling back up the muddy dirt track, followed by the truck, the red tail lights gradually fading into the distance.

Schmidt returned to the living room and two minutes later was joined by Otto.

'Jesus Christ,' said Otto letting out a large sigh. 'What was all that about?'

'They are here, in the town,' said Schmidt. 'I have no idea how long you can stay any more, Otto. We have to get you out of here and quickly. Once they realise that I was your commanding officer for a time, they may search the place for you. It is too dangerous for you to stay here now.'

Otto did not reply. He knew the man was right. He had not necessarily outstayed his welcome but to stay here much longer not only put himself in danger but also the man who was helping him, and he could not allow his presence there to endanger him in any way.

'And it won't take them long to realise that I was lying to them,' said Schmidt. 'About Gerhard and a non-existent nurse, but I will cross that bridge when I get to it.'

'Thank God it was raining,' said Otto after a few moments. 'If they had decided to search the place, that could have been it for us. They did not want to get wet I suppose.'

'Tomorrow morning while I am at the town hall get rid of that jeep. I don't care what you do with it but get rid of it. Take it anywhere. I will speak to my contact and get you off to Innsbruck as soon as I can. This is it my friend. This has to be it.'

Schmidt sat back into the chair and watched as the log that he had placed in the fire only a few minutes before, crumbled to ash before his eyes. A minute later Otto could hear soft snores coming from the man.

Yes, he thought, this is it. The next part of his journey was now about to happen and only God or the devil knew where it would take him.

CHAPTER FIFTY-THREE

Sitting at the table in the kitchen of his second floor apartment, Alfred Pasche stopped what he was doing and laughed out loud. For some insane reason he found that he reminded himself of the Ebenezer Scrooge character from the English classic writer Dickens's *A Christmas Carol*, counting out his money and writing it all down in the ledger in front of him. He took great pleasure in seeing the figure rise with each trip he made.

He had never expected that joining the Red Cross would prove to be so lucrative a career choice. He had been given the job of taking mail and parcels across the border into Italy and used his own vehicle to do that. The trunk of the car was just large enough to hide a fugitive and a couple of mail bags and the rest of what he carried he placed on the back seat.

Taking money from Nazis, desperate to get away from the hunters who seeked them out with the same venom as they themselves had sought out Jews and other such "Untermensch", as they called them, seemed at the very least ironic and somewhat comical. Where the money came from was of no concern to him. Money was money, pure and simple. Whether he took it from these clowns or anyone else for that matter was of no importance to him. To think outside of that particular box was pointless. It was money that paid for everything, rent, alcohol, girls even. Money that would give him the power and respect that he had never experienced before.

He had made the trip over the Brenner Pass on numerous occasions both during hostilities and afterward and had yet to have any problems at the border, the guards waving him through without any fuss, all of them recognising his face and his familiar car as it trundled along the highway towards them. Some would stop him just to have a quick chat, to exchange pleasantries and ask after his family. It was all so very convivial and Alfred would laugh out loud as he carried on with his journey, his illicit human cargo hidden in the trunk, bound for the Alto Adige and beyond.

He usually charged around the five hundred schilling mark but on some occasions, dependant on who the passenger was or how desperate they were, he would double the price. They always seemed willing to pay it and he could see why, but he never asked any questions of their past, it was no business of his. To some degree he sympathised with them. After all, as they said, in the main they were all just carrying out the orders of their superiors. Whether they did this with enthusiasm was beside the point. The fact that some of them were the ones who had given out those orders was irrelevant to him, as in any walk of life, there was always someone higher up the chain of command who the buck could ultimately be passed to.

Pasche looked out of the window. His car was parked on the street outside the apartment block, ready for the collection of post the following day, fuelled up and ready to go. He was expecting another passenger shortly, maybe in the next couple of days or so, and this time, from what he could gather, it was someone who was very keen to cross the border and get out of Austria.

Pasche had never considered himself as German, the Anschluss of 1938 he had never taken seriously. He was Austrian and always would be. And by being Austrian he saw that any blame for what had happened during the war could be laid at the feet of the Germans and absolve his own country from any wrongdoing. The fact that Adolf Hitler was born in Branau was irrelevant and he chose to ignore it.

Beyond the car, standing at a shop front a few yards from a tram stop, stood a man in an overcoat with a hat pulled down low in an attempt to cover his features. For some reason Pasche was drawn to him. There was something about the man's eyes, peeking nervously from under the brim of the hat and looking in the direction of his window. Pasche felt a shiver run down his spine and before he knew what he was doing he found that he was closing the ledger and collecting up the money.

Who was this person? Was it the police? Maybe a client? He could not be sure. He was not expecting his next fare just yet and if it was he then the man must be desperate and would command a double fee. He stood up and took the box of money and the ledger and placed them in the bottom of the cupboard at the far end of the room. As he placed the ledger inside, he wondered if keeping a record of his transactions was a good idea. Maybe it was better to keep it simple, cash in hand and leave it at that, but he liked to see how much money he was making and to watch it grow with every trip he took.

He moved back to the window and stood to the side. He took a peek again at the shop front opposite but noticed that the man had now gone. Pasche looked up and down the street but could not see him, only the comings and goings of the people of Innsbruck as they went about their business in the cold of the early September afternoon.

Then the bell to his apartment began to ring and the unexpected suddenness of it made him jump slightly. Taking a breath he went to the door and looked through the spyhole.

Standing outside, on the landing, was the same man whom he had observed outside just a few moments ago. The man still had the collar of his coat turned up and his hat low over his face. However, being this close, he could not hide the fact that he had a large scar running down the left hand side of his face.

Pasche opened the door slightly, leaving the chain on, and looked out at the man.

'Yes, can I help you?' he asked.

'Are you Alfred Pasche?' Came the reply.

'It depends who is asking. Who are you?'

'Don't worry,' said the man with the scar. 'I am not police or anything. I believe that you have been expecting me.'

'Maybe,' replied the postman suspiciously. 'Like I said, who are you?'

'I have the money you require. A thousand schillings I have been told. The fact that I know the fare and the scar on my face should be enough to identify me. You have been told about this feature of mine?'

This was true. The contact had informed Pasche that the man he was to take across would be blond with a significant wound on his face. He did not need to know any more than that. Names only got in the way. He closed the door, took off the chain and then opened it wide.

'Come in,' he said. 'I was not expecting you for a couple of days yet.'

Otto Finkel walked in.

'I know,' he replied. 'Things got a little too dangerous at the last place and so I had to move on. I have the money you want.'

'That is fine,' replied Pasche. 'We can sort that out later. Here, let me take your hat and coat.'

Otto took them off and handed them to him and then moved to the table in the kitchen area and sat down. 'Have you any coffee? I could do with something to drink.'

'Sure,' said Pasche, following him. 'I will make some and get you a sandwich.'

Otto took out a packet of cigarettes and lit one, he offered the pack to Pasche who shook his head and Otto placed them back into his jacket pocket. Inhaling the smoke deeply, he sighed, blowing the smoke out as he did so.

'Long trip?' asked Pasche.

'There is no need for pleasantries or small talk,' replied Otto. 'I have the money and you are providing a service. It is a simple transaction between you and me and nothing more. I do not want to know about your life, your family or your reasons for doing this. All I need to know is when this can happen and what you need me to do. The less we know about each other the better it is for everyone.'

'Suit yourself,' said Pasche and turned back to make the coffee.

Maybe this strange, mysterious man was right, thought Pasche. It was definitely better that they did not know too much about each other. Anyway, he thought, he really did not need to know why this man was running away to a new life. He had obviously done something very bad and if he was capable of very bad things then it was probably better that he knew not what they were. He was clearly a dangerous man.

Handing the coffee to Otto, Pasche said, 'Very well. You can stay here overnight. First thing in the morning I will be collecting the mail from the head post office and then I am to take it across the border to Bozen in the Adige. After I pick the mail up I will return here. You will meet me in the alleyway at the rear of the apartment building where you can get in the back. We will cover you with the bags and whatever else I am taking and we will drive to Bozen.'

'That sounds very simple.'

'It is,' replied Pasche. 'That's the beauty of it. From there I would advise you to make your way to Merano. There is an inn in that town that I believe is owned by people who are very sympathetic to men like yourself. I will give you the address tomorrow. My advice is to go there after I drop you off.'

Otto looked at him expressionless as he smoked his cigarette, saying nothing.

Pasche felt a little uneasy in the man's presence.

'Now,' he said nervously, 'let us talk money.'

*

The following morning Otto found himself lying uncomfortably in the trunk of Pasche's car, having followed the man's simple instructions. They had been very careful not to be observed and as it was so early, not too many people were out, making it extremely easy for him to get into the vehicle without any curious eyes spotting him.

He had paid Pasche the thousand schillings the night before and had received a modest meal and a good night's sleep in a single bed in a small box room that overlooked the alleyway where he had got into the car a half hour ago.

Otto had been told not to move as Pasche had placed the mailbags around him, making him almost invisible from first scrutiny should any border policeman wish to take a look inside. However, by moving any of the sacks to the side, he would be easily spotted.

Although he did not know the man, Otto had to trust him. He had no option. Pasche had told him that he knew the guards personally and that they never demanded to look inside but it did not stop Otto feeling nervous nevertheless. For the second time now, since his flight from the Americans, he was placing his life in the hands of another and this time in the hands of a complete stranger. As they travelled towards the Italian border, he knew that the man driving the vehicle had as much to lose as Otto himself did should they be caught and this made him feel a little happier.

The journey from Innsbruck to the Brenner Pass and beyond to Bozen in the Alto Adige, or South Tyrol, would take a little over an hour and a half, providing there was no hold up at the border. As the car continued on the journey, Otto's mind wandered to how he had arrived at this point in his life. He was still only twenty-nine years old, a young man in real terms, but the rest of his life, his whole future, was now a total mystery to him.

Everything had been going fine until Hitler had decided to fight a war on many fronts. The initial successes in France and the Low Countries, the African campaign and the invasion of Norway, Greece and the Balkans had proved that Germany was by far the superior nation in the world. They had been unstoppable, the Blitzkrieg wiping away all before them. All nations had capitulated and bowed down before them and it allowed them the chance to rid Europe of the scourge of the Jews. Then they had invaded Russia and although they came close to winning that campaign they had been forced to retreat and it became only a matter of time before the war was lost. He had known for a long time that Germany could never win the war, especially as they had allowed Britain to be free and when the Americans had entered the fighting, defeat had become inevitable. There was no way they could sustain the fighting on so many fronts.

And now here he lay there, curled up in the trunk of a stranger's car, his life in the hands of a corrupt Red Cross worker, covered in hessian sacks and parcels, running away like a rat from a sinking ship. The irony of it all was not lost on him. The hunter becoming the hunted.

After a while he felt the car slow down and eventually it came to a stop. He was aware of other vehicles idling close by and presumed they were in a line waiting to cross the border. He started to sweat, knowing that they were at a critical point in the journey and he put his hand in his pocket, touching the American pistol that he had brought with him. If it came to it, he would shoot his way out. He was not prepared to be handed back to the enemy.

Then he could hear voices outside but could not make out what they were saying and then the sound of laughter, Pasche's laughter, and he felt at ease again, realising that the border police were about to let them through.

A couple of minutes later they were on the move again and Otto let out a sigh, his body relaxing as he understood that this was another phase of his escape that he had managed to achieve. He shut his eyes and before too long he had drifted off into a deep sleep.

*

He was awoken by Pasche as he flung the trunk open and leaned inside, shifting the bags and boxes out of the way to allow Otto to get out. He rubbed his eyes and climbed out of the car, stepping unsteadily onto the street, his body aching from the long uncomfortable journey.

When he was fully awake, he looked around. He could see clearly that he was in a large town beneath snow-capped mountains. From what he could see, it was typical of the area, many pretty white buildings, some with terracotta roofs and he could just make out a river running through the middle of the town from where they stood, on a side street away from prying eyes.

Pasche closed the trunk and turned to Otto. He handed him a piece of paper.

'This is the address of someone who can help you here in Bozen,' he said quietly, although there was no one around to overhear the conversation. 'There are many in this region who will assist you in the next stage of your journey but I know that there is also an inn in Merano where you will be able to get whatever assistance that you need.'

Pasche mistook Otto's tired expression for confusion.

'I believe it is a place where they are sympathetic to your cause,' he explained. 'In fact this whole region is. Many people here consider themselves to be German anyway. They just didn't get a chance to move from here during the "opting out" a few years back. They are more German than Italian and therefore some will give their help gladly. They will be able to help you with your onward journey. Papers, visas, that sort of thing.'

Otto had been told of the place by Schmidt the previous week and he was grateful for Pasche for providing him with the address of someone in Bozen who could help him to get there. This part of the Tyrol was German speaking and he would have no problem in finding it. He felt relieved.

Relieved that he now had a purpose to his life, something to work towards. Otto knew that his escape was far from complete, but now that he was in a place with like-minded people, people who could get him the documentation that he needed to complete the journey to South America, he almost felt a sense of contentment, as though he could see an end to it all.

He took the note from Pasche's hand and looked at him. Without saying another word, he turned from the smuggler and walked away. He did not wish to say any goodbyes to the man, after all, he was making money out of unfortunate people like himself and was nothing more than a profiteer. Otto had no time for such people.

He walked to the end of the street and joined the throng of people as they walked along in the cold morning sunshine, turning up his collar and pulling down his hat to once again hide away the ugly scar that had thwarted him since he was twelve years old. He could feel Pasche's gaze on his back as he walked away but he did not turn around, he did not look back.

He was determined to never look back again.

CHAPTER FIFTY-FOUR

'HauptsturmFührer Finkel? Otto Finkel?'

Otto put the cup back onto the saucer and turned around to see who it was that was addressing him. Approaching the table on the veranda where he had decided to take a cup of coffee, enjoying the crispness of the January air, was a man whom he had not seen for over a year, someone whom he had never expected to see again.

'Mueller, is that you?' he asked, standing up to greet his old comrade. 'My God, I never expected to see you here. Please sit down. Join me.'

Fritz Mueller was a small stocky man with thick, black curly hair. He was a little older than Otto and had served as his sergeant in France after the Allied invasion of Normandy. Mueller had been a good soldier and had caused Otto no problems, carrying out his orders without complaint or question. Otto was not sure why he would have the need to flee from Germany. He was not particularly interested if he was honest, but the four months he had spent at the inn in Merano had taught him that virtually all ex-Waffen-SS soldiers were being sought by the Allies for war crimes. He had seen plenty of people come and go but had asked none of them why they were running. Everyone had their own reasons and none were the business of the others.

He had arrived at Aunt Anna's almost four months previously and in that time he had seen many people in the same situation as himself and more were arriving all the time. He was aware that there were other places like this and had heard stories of people receiving various kinds of assistance along the way. The region seemed to be filled with them. The Alto Adige was a haven for anyone escaping the Allies, the locals helping them with papers for their onward journey or giving them jobs and false identities should they wish to settle in the area. Otto knew that staying in Europe was not an option for him personally. People he did not know had recognised him due to the scar on his face, or knew of him by reputation, which made him believe that he would eventually be caught if he stayed here. Despite all the people he had come across in the previous four months, Mueller was the first he had actually recognised back. He was pleased to see a familiar face at last and was pleased that it was someone he actually liked.

'When did you arrive?' he asked as his old friend sat down beside him.

'Only just,' replied Mueller. 'I can't believe that I am actually here. It has been some journey, believe me.'

'How did you get here? How did you get across the border?'

'I walked, believe it or not,' replied Mueller. 'Bloody cold in those mountains this time of year too I can tell you. I got to the border and finding a guide to get me across was pretty simple. There are loads willing to do it. Some for free too. It's been a trek I can tell you.'

'It has been for us all,' replied Otto taking a sip from his coffee cup. 'And thank God for this place and others like it. They have many connections and are very sympathetic to us. As are most of the people around here.'

'How long will you be staying?' asked Mueller.

'Until my paperwork comes through,' replied Otto. 'I'm waiting for a visa for Argentina and a berth on a ship to get me there. It could be a few weeks yet. The people here know how to get us what we need. There is a lot of confusion in Italy at the moment. Refugees coming and going and the authorities have no idea what's going on, which makes it much easier for us to get out of Europe. Also there are officials in the Tyrol who will provide us with papers in any name we like. Official papers, not forged. You are not looking at Otto Finkel now, erstwhile of the SS, you are looking at Heinrich Vogel, Austrian businessman.' Otto laughed. 'I'm waiting for my ticket for a business trip to Buenos Aires.'

Mueller smiled. 'I can't believe it's come to this,' he said with a sigh. 'If you think back to five or six years ago, the whole world was ours. Now look at us. Hiding away, just like the way the Jews hid from us. It would be funny if it wasn't so serious.'

'Do not compare us with those scum,' said Otto calmly. 'We are nothing like them.'

'I meant our situation,' replied Mueller, afraid that he had offended his former boss. 'Of course we are nothing like them. How could we be?'

The truth was that the irony of the situation was not lost on Otto. He had often thought the same thing over the last few months. There had been many times in the past where he had sought out Jews, ordering his men to search every nook and cranny to find them as they purged the ghettos and rounded them up to be shot in Russia and other places. He had done it without any sense of compassion, for he felt none. Otto knew that it had to be done, that the Führer had been right and the world needed to be shut of them.

But although he still felt that way, he had been disturbed by something that Schmidt had said to him before he had left the farm. Schmidt had had time to reflect on what had happened during the war and before, to ponder over the things he had witnessed in the name of National Socialism and Otto felt that those things did not sit right with his old commanding officer. Schmidt himself had not been personally involved in anything that the Allies might consider a "war crime" but he had been in charge of many soldiers who had carried them out, turning a blind eye to their barbarity. He had not necessarily shirked the responsibility and being in command made him ultimately culpable, it was just that he considered himself a soldier and preferred to fight people who wore a uniform and could fight back. Schmidt had asked Otto if he now felt any remorse for what he had done, any sorrow at all. Otto had replied, like the committed Nazi he was, that he had sworn an oath to Adolf Hitler and that would stand forever. However, Otto had not been sure if Schmidt had been totally convinced that the Nazis had done everything in accordance with what was right and wrong.

Otto, on the other hand, had no such misgivings and had gladly taken part in the killings and ordered other willing soldiers to carry out these things. The truth of the matter was that they had lost the war and lost it badly. Nazism was finished in Germany and the Jews had been freed to wreak their revenge. He found that the more he thought about it, the less he could blame them. Maybe he was having doubts himself now, but he was not prepared to accept, just yet, that he had not acted properly and correctly.

He was aware of Mueller looking at him, curious as to what he was thinking.

'It is nothing,' he said, reading the sergeant's thoughts. 'I am fine. I just need to be on the move. You know what I am like, never being able to sit still.'

'Yes, sir,' replied Mueller. 'I remember.'

'I just need to be on the go. To get moving. I just wish it wouldn't take so long to get everything sorted.'

'Yes, I understand,' replied his former comrade. 'But what a beautiful place to have to wait, eh? Despite the cold.'

Otto looked to the view beyond the veranda. Mueller was right. This was a wonderful place, the mountains dominating the landscape and the crisp, clear, winter air making him feel healthier than he had felt in a long time. He had never realised just how tired he had been until he had arrived in Merano. For the first time in years he was able to relax and to enjoy the scenery with nothing to worry about, but now he wanted to be moving again. He was not in fear of being caught here and maybe moving would put him in danger once more but he could not stay here forever. He had no idea what he would do once he arrived in South America, he would worry about that when he got there.

He had gained employment for a while, in a bar a half mile away, but he did not consider this work. The landlord had not asked any questions and the work was paid cash in hand, which he used to pay for his room at Aunt Anna's. The landlord, a man by the name of Meier, had been one of the eighty-five percent of the population of the Alto Adige that had elected in favour of the option to join Germany in the vote of 1939, after Hitler and Mussolini had agreed to solve the problem of their preferred nationality. The war had put a stop to the emigrations, so there were many people like him who saw themselves more as German than Italian. After all, they spoke German in this region anyway.

Otto had not lasted too long, only a couple of months, as the stares he received from some of the customers had started to get on his nerves and he lived in fear that someone not as sympathetic as the majority may recognise him and give him away.

'What are your plans, Mueller?' he asked his friend.

'I'm taking it one day at a time, boss,' he replied.

'Don't you think it might be better for you in the long run to give yourself in?' asked Otto. 'After all there is not much they can do you for is there? And then you can stay in Germany with your family.'

'I don't want to take that chance. I will send for them when I am settled, wherever that ends up.' Mueller looked around. 'And to be honest, this seems as good a place as any. I may just settle down here.'

'I wish I could,' replied Otto. 'I truly do.'

*

A month later, in early February 1946, on a cold winter's morning, Otto received a letter in the post. Addressed to Heinrich Vogel, he was handed it by the proprietor as he walked down the stairs to go outside for his morning stroll.

He left the building and stepped onto the snow covered street and set off in the direction of the town centre. As he walked, he opened the envelope. In it he found a ticket for a ship leaving Genoa in two weeks' time and a visa for Argentina. For a second he caught his breath.

He realised that he had stopped walking and his hands had begun to shake, his mind going blank for a short time and felt that he was watching the scene from a distance. This was it then. This was finally it. He had a way out and there was no going back. He had been content to sit and wait in Merano, never actually believing that he would find a way to get out to safety and now that it had gone from possible to probable, he found that he could not comprehend it. Did he really want it to happen? Did he really want to leave the country of his birth, the country that had given him everything? Given him pride, a sense of worth and purpose and of doing something worthwhile. Now that it had come he was not sure that he wanted it, but Otto knew that to stay meant death or the possibility of years in prison if he was caught. Staying meant humiliation for himself and for his father, wherever he was.

He placed the paperwork back into the envelope and put it into the pocket of his coat and continued on his stroll. He looked around at the mountains that surrounded the town and breathed the cold air in deeply, enjoying the purity of it as it filled his lungs. He attempted to smile to himself, to force himself to be happy that his flight was close to an end, that there was a light at the end of the tunnel that was now within reach. All he had to do was to keep on walking towards it.

What he would do once in South America he did not know. What had become evident was that there was a growing expatriate German community that he would seek out and join. He would hopefully get a job and who knows, get married and raise a family. He had it all to look forward to. The future could be bright if he let it be, all he had to do was to embrace it.

*

That afternoon Otto found Mueller in the bar where he used to work. Mueller was spending more and more of his time drinking beer to see away the days while he waited for his paperwork to arrive. He had been offered work on numerous occasions but had not, as yet, taken up any of the offers, preferring to spend his days getting drunk and feeling sorry for himself instead. Otto found it hard to criticise him. After all, his life had been turned upside down.

'Ah, Otto,' he said drunkenly on seeing his former comrade enter the building, kicking the snow from his feet as he walked into the bar. 'Come and drink with me, my old comrade.'

Although it was a bright sunny day outside, inside the room was dark. Small windows and dark oak furniture gave the place an illusion of night time although it was only mid-afternoon.

Mueller stood at the bar alone. He was the only customer, it being so early in the day and the barman raised his hand in casual greeting to which Otto nodded in acknowledgement.

He approached Mueller, taking off his coat as he did so and laying it over the back of a chair.

'Do not call me by that name,' said Otto slightly annoyed. 'My name is now Heinrich, as you know. I might as well get used to using it.'

'Ach,' said Mueller raising his hand in annoyance. 'What does it matter? It is your name is it not?'

The barman sensing the awkwardness that the conversation was creating between the two and not wanting to get involved, walked away to a room at the back as though he had urgent business there, leaving them both alone.

'I have told you before,' said Otto. 'You must refer to me by my new name. I am now Heinrich, not Otto… anyway, I have come to give you some news. I am leaving in two weeks' time. My visa has arrived. I just wanted you to know.'

'So you are getting out of here then are you?' slurred Mueller contemptuously. 'So you are running away then. Off to pastures new and all that?'

'I am,' replied Otto. 'And I really think that you need to take control of yourself. People are starting to talk and you need to be careful. Your indiscretions are being noticed now and they don't like it.'

Mueller turned to Otto and looked into his eyes before turning away to take a swig from his beer glass, then placing it back down heavily on the bar and facing him again.

'You know what, Ott… Heinrich?' he laughed. 'I don't particularly care what people think.'

'Well you should,' said Otto calmly. 'You really should. I cannot help you for much longer for I will be gone. You need to take care of yourself.'

Mueller took another mouthful of beer and then started to shout. 'Barman! Barman! Two more beers here please. Two more. One for myself and one for my old comrade here who is running away to Argentina.'

The barman returned and pulled two more beers. As he placed them on the counter, Mueller looked at Otto.

'You couldn't, could you?' he slurred and Otto sighed and put his hand in his trouser pocket and put some change on the counter. The barman counted out what was owed and put the money in the till. He then turned around and walked away once more.

As Mueller put the new drink to his lips, Otto stood watching him, leaving his own untouched on the counter.

'You know what the trouble is, Otto,' he said wiping froth from his top lip with the back of his hand. 'The trouble is we are running because we are guilty.'

'What do you mean?' asked Otto picking up his own drink and taking a tentative sip. 'What are you talking about?'

'You know very well what I'm talking about,' replied Mueller.

'You are drunk.'

'I am… that is true… but not drunk enough to wipe out the memory of all the shit we have done in the name of Germany… and the fucking Führer.'

'Be careful what you say,' warned Otto.

'The time for being careful is way gone. What do you think of what you did, Otto? Do you think that it was right what we all did? Do you, really? I have had time to think… If it was so right then why have our illustrious leaders all either run away like cowards or killed themselves… If what we did was so right then why did they not stay and argue their case to the Americans and the British and the Russians, eh? Tell me that because I would like to know.'

Otto did not reply.

'If what we did was so right,' continued Mueller, his voice rising a pitch. 'If what we did was so right, then why are we here now, you and me? Here, with false names running away to Argentina or Venezuela or wherever the fuck it is we are all running away to. If we truly believed in what we were doing then why are we running?'

'To live to fight another day,' replied Otto, but he did not believe his own words, them sounding hollow and phoney, even to his own ears.

Mueller laughed loudly. 'Who are you trying to kid? We are finished, my friend… All of us. We are going to spend the rest of our days looking over our shoulders and, in my opinion… rightly so. Have you seen what happened in those camps? Have you? Dachau, Belsen, Sachsenhausen, Auschwitz? We murdered them, Otto, murdered them… All of them… Children too. Little babies forced from their mothers' arms and taken away and shot… or gassed. We should all burn in hell for this… All of us… Join Hitler and that other gang of bastards who made us do it… They warped our minds, Otto. They turned us all into murdering automatons and we did it gladly, even with smiles on our faces. What the fuck is wrong with us?'

Mueller stumbled and sank to the floor, spilling his beer as he did so. Hearing the commotion the barman came out from the back and looked at Otto.

'I think it best you take your friend away from here,' he said sternly. 'Take him away and neither of you return. You are not welcome here anymore.'

Otto bent down and helped Mueller to his feet. 'Come on, let's get you out of here.'

Mueller had given up and allowed Otto to place him in a chair while he collected their coats, under the stern, watchful eye of the barman.

A minute later they were outside, Mueller leaning heavily on his friend as they struggled down the street towards the inn.

'Let's get you back home,' said Otto. 'You have had too much to drink. You need to sleep it off.'

Mueller began to weep. People passing looked at them curiously as they walked by, which made Otto feel more and more uneasy.

'I miss them,' slurred Mueller after a while. 'I miss my wife and children, Otto. I do not know what has become of them. I wrote to them and they have not replied. They could be dead for all I know or in difficulty and I can do nothing to help them. I have abandoned them.'

Otto did not know what to say. He felt sad at the way this once strong man had sunk so low in despair and he genuinely worried for him. Mueller had started to say some things, after drinking, that was making a whole lot of people uneasy and Otto genuinely feared for his friend's safety. He knew that once he was gone and Mueller was left alone, there were many people who might do something to shut the man up for good.

Mueller leaned all of his considerable weight onto Otto who struggled and slipped in his attempt to keep him upright. Finding it too difficult to continue, Otto found a bench, just inside the entrance to a small park and sat him down. Mueller sat back sharply, his head falling straight back with his face turned up to the sky.

'It is so beautiful, don't you think?' he said staring upwards. 'The blueness of the sky and the whiteness of the clouds.'

Otto sat beside him, panting from the exertion, and looked up.

'Yes,' he replied after a while. 'I suppose it is, yes.'

Mueller turned to look at his friend, the only friend he had left in the world.

'Can I ask you a question, a personal question?'

Otto looked at him.

'If you must,' he replied indulgently.

'Have you ever been happy, Otto? Truly happy, I mean. You see... I can't remember the last time that I was.'

Otto looked back to the sky and sighed.

'I suppose I must have been at some point,' he replied. 'But to be honest, it was such a long time ago.'

'Don't you think it is sad? How young are we? Late twenties? Early thirties? And our lives are pretty much over without ever having been truly happy. I think I may have been when the children were born but I was never there to enjoy them and now I may never see them again. Ever.'

'You don't know that do you?' replied Otto. 'You don't know what lies ahead for us.'

'Maybe not... But this guilt I am feeling, Otto, I cannot shake it. I cannot shake out of my head the images of the people I have killed. I know that when the day comes I will not be able to face my maker. I am damned, Otto. We all are and we all deserve to be.'

Otto looked at his friend and sighed. What if this man, who sat distraught at the side of him, was right? What if what he was saying, although coming from his drunken mouth, what if all of it was true? Had he behaved in an evil way? Had what they done been against all that was holy and just? He thought back to the time he had spent in Rome and what the Italian priest had said to him. He had told him the same things that Mueller was now saying. Could they both have been right and Otto had been wrong all along? Had what he done been so wrong that he was now damned for all eternity?

'Why did you never marry, or have children?' asked Mueller, breaking his train of thought suddenly.

Otto thought about the question before replying. 'I don't suppose I ever had the time or the inclination for women. I was always so busy.'

Mueller looked at him curiously. 'Have you ever been with a woman, Otto? Have you ever...'

'Enough,' said Otto interrupting him. 'I think you have said enough now and it's time you got back to the inn and slept off the beer. You are beginning to irritate me.'

'Okay,' said Mueller, sensing the change in mood, realising that he may have pushed his friend too far. 'You are probably right. Probably best I got some sleep.'

Otto assisted him to his feet and as they slowly made their way back the quarter of a mile to their lodgings, neither of them said another word.

*

Two days later, in the early evening just after dark, a carabinieri patrol was called to sounds of an altercation at the rear of a bar in central Merano by a concerned resident who lived nearby. It took them ten minutes to arrive from receiving the call, which was pretty quick for them. The two policemen entered the alleyway and there they found the body of Fritz Mueller lying face down in the snow. He had multiple stab wounds to his chest, his tongue had been cut out and an SS dagger was embedded, virtually to the hilt, in the back of his head.

CHAPTER FIFTY-FIVE

Otto stood on the deck and looked to his right as the ship slowly sailed through the Strait of Gibraltar. He could clearly see the rock that stood out prominently in the morning sunshine, rising above the British Overseas Territory that lay on the southernmost tip of Spain. He could also see many warships of the Royal Navy docked there, the greyness of their hulls reflecting off the clear waters of the Mediterranean Sea.

The fact that this was probably the last view of Europe he would ever have was not lost on him. He had come to accept, over the last few weeks, that if he made this journey then he was unlikely to ever return to the continent of his birth, the continent where he had lived and was a part of. He had considered changing his mind and going back to Dortmund to find his father, but he knew that if he did so it meant capture and death and at the age of twenty-nine years old, he was not quite ready for death just yet.

He had a very sketchy plan as to what he would do once arriving in Buenos Aires. He had been given the names of a few ex-SS who had travelled ahead and he would seek them out and hopefully they could provide him with some sort of plan. He contemplated getting work on a farm, there were plenty of them over there after all, as he had enjoyed the short time he had spent at Schmidt's place before he had been smuggled to the Adige.

He knew a little Spanish but not knowing the language fluently just yet did not concern him. He was fluent in many others and knew that he would soon pick it up, his aptitude for foreign tongues inherited from his father.

And then he thought of his father. What had become of him? He had not heard from the man for such a long time, since before the Allied invasion of Normandy nearly two years previously and did not know if he was alive or dead. Otto's mother did not concern him and he only gave her a fleeting thought. She was a weak woman, subservient to his father in every way and he had never respected her because of it. The last time he had seen her she had hardly said a word to him and if he thought back hard enough, he now wondered if she had been ashamed of him and the uniform he had worn. She was French after all and had seen how quickly her home country had capitulated during the first stages of the war and Otto's own personal part in that French defeat could not have pleased her.

He looked above as a number of seagulls swooped low onto the deck in search of scraps of food that may have been discarded by the passengers and then turned around and found a long bench, fixed against the ship's infrastructure, on which to sit.

Otto had left Aunt Anna's four days ago, getting a train from Merano and then changing at Bozen for the onward journey to Genoa. The travelling had been long and tedious and on arrival at the Italian port he had taken a room for one night at a small hotel not too far from where the ship he was to sail upon was docked. He had boarded the *Santa Cruz* the following morning without any fuss. After all, the passport and visa were not fakes but official documents that the network in the South Tyrol had provided for him. However, when he walked up the gangplank onto the ship, he had never felt so nervous in all of his life, expecting at any time for someone to grab his shoulder and arrest him. The border guards had looked at his scar curiously but had not said anything, even if they had suspected he was not whom he was claiming to be. He imagined that the Italians, as a whole, were happy enough to see anyone with any kind of suspicious past leave their country and take their issues and troubles with them.

The berth he had been allocated was simple and pleasant enough and he had been quite happy with it, storing the meagre possessions he had accrued over the last few months into an overhead locker above the bed. So he had settled down for the long journey, which would take him across the Atlantic Ocean and to his new life in South America.

Sitting on the bench, watching the Spanish coastline disappear from view, Otto drifted off to sleep, his head falling forward onto his chest. A couple of hours later he awoke and sensed someone looking at him. Turning to his right, he saw a man standing opposite him, dressed in an ill-fitting grey suit, looking at him curiously. He was in his mid-thirties with greying black hair, which was parted to the side, the fringe hanging limply just above his dark eyes.

Noticing Otto had woken up, the man approached him. Standing in front of him and without saying anything, he held out a pack of cigarettes that he took from his jacket pocket, a single cigarette protruding from the rest.

Otto took it and put it to his lips. The stranger bent down, holding a silver lighter in his hand and flicked it. At first it did not fire but on the second attempt a flame appeared. Otto cupped it to prevent the wind from blowing it out and sucked in the smoke as the cigarette caught. He indicated for the man to sit down beside him.

They smoked in silence for a few moments before the man said, 'It is very sad, don't you think?'

'What is?' replied Otto quietly.

'That we have to flee like this.'

'I have no idea what you are talking about,' replied Otto suddenly alert. He had no idea who this man was. He could be anyone and Otto found that he was suddenly very nervous.

'Come now,' said the man, half laughing. 'I know who you are… or who you were, just as you know that I am the same as you.'

'Like I said, I really have no idea what you mean,' replied Otto. 'I am Heinrich Vogel, a businessman from Austria.'

This time the man laughed loudly. 'Yes? And I am the crown prince of Sweden! I know exactly who you are. I was under your command in Rome a few years ago. You are amongst friends, you have no need to worry,' he said, almost casually.

'Like I just told you,' said Otto. 'I am a businessman from Austria. I have never been to Rome in my life.'

'Suit yourself,' said the man calmly and went on smoking his cigarette.

Otto looked at him again and tried to place him but he could not find any memory of the man's face, no matter how hard he wracked his brain. But then Otto had only been in the Italian capital briefly in 1943 and had been overseeing a large amount of troops, not many of which he took much notice, so it was possible that this man was telling the truth. However, it could also be a trap, he could not be sure.

Sensing Otto's unease, the man in the grey suit said, 'I was at the cordon. I smashed my rifle into the face of some mad Italian who pulled a knife on you.'

Otto shivered involuntarily at the memory.

'Ah, I see you remember me now,' said the man in the grey suit, smiling. 'He was furious if I remember rightly,' he continued. 'He absolutely hated you. I could see it in his eyes. They were like a demon's as though he wanted you to suffer badly. I have never seen hate quite so personified.'

Otto turned to him, his face not changing expression.

'There's one thing that I don't understand though,' continued Otto's former subordinate. 'One thing that I have often wondered about regarding that day.'

'Yes,' said Otto, 'And what would that be?'

'Why did you let him go? I thought you were going to shoot him with that funny looking pistol you used to carry.'

Otto put the cigarette into his mouth and took a long drag before replying.

'Why did I let him go? I often wondered about that myself afterwards,' he replied. He paused for a few moments. 'I let him go because he was my friend.'

*

Otto and the man in the grey suit, who gave his name as Erich Steigel, (he could not be sure if this was his real name or an alias) spent the rest of the journey mostly in each other's company. Between them they made plans as to what they would do once they arrived in Argentina and Otto was grateful that he now had a companion with whom he could face the future. They were both in the same situation and decided that two heads may be better than one once they arrived in the new continent.

Otto had not, since he was a child, given anyone so much of his time willingly and he soon found that he grew to like Steigel, enjoying the man's company and bright outlook on life, despite their current position in the world. Otto was able to forget their uncertain future for a while and enjoy the moments spent with him in the ship's bar and walking on the deck when the weather permitted it.

They spoke of many things, mainly of what the future could hold for them and rarely looked back at the time they had spent in the SS, only briefly mentioning a character they may have known or a mutual situation they may have shared. Otto realised that if he was to have a future that was productive and bright, he could not dwell on the past or what he had done there. After all, it was now another time, a different world.

Steigel had no family. He had been born and raised in Stuttgart and joined the SS in 1936, after the Berlin Olympics. Otto had pretended not to be particularly interested but came to learn that Steigel too had served for a time on the Russian front, something that bound together all the survivors of that campaign for life. There was a bond of brotherhood between all who had endured that particular hell. A lifelong bond that could never be broken.

Otto now dreaded the ship arriving in Argentina. The end of the journey would mean an end to the brief happiness that he was now feeling and he, for one, did not want it to stop.

'What are your thoughts?' asked Steigel on the evening before the *Santa Cruz* was due to dock. They sat together on the foredeck, passengers bustling around them as they prepared their luggage to be taken ashore the following morning.

'My thoughts?' replied Otto. 'I don't know Erich. I feel a little cold if I am honest with you. I feel that I have shaken off a former life and I do not want that life to ever return. It is best left in the past and forgotten about. My life will begin from here, the moment I step off the ship, everything that happened before it is now of no consequence to me.

'I have had time on this journey, and since I escaped the Americans, to think and reflect about things and I am not too sure about what conclusion I have come to. I don't know if what we did back then was correct. At the time I did, but now? I just don't know, if I am totally honest.

'A friend asked me recently, a friend who is now dead unfortunately, he asked me if I had ever been truly happy and I could not give him a straight answer. When I think now, I can answer the question honestly and the answer is yes. I was once truly happy but that was such a long, long time ago. Before I had this,' he indicated the scar. 'I was a child and I was on holiday with my parents. I used to go and visit my grandparents on my mother's side in St Malo, you see, and one year I met some children who were the same age as me. British children. There was an Italian and a French boy too. We were a mini league of nations, I can tell you.

'For a few of those days I could not have been happier if I had tried. That was the time when I found true happiness, my friend, and if I am totally honest with myself I have never been happy a single day since.'

'That is so very sad,' replied Stiegel, not taking his eyes from Otto's face. 'So sad.'

Otto stood up.

'Come,' he said. 'Enough of this melancholy and feeling sorry for ourselves. We have a bright future ahead of us and it starts tomorrow morning when we get off this ship.'

'I couldn't have put it better myself,' he smiled.

Otto let Stiegel walk away and he moved to the gunwale and looked out to sea, letting the salty sea air blow into his face. He ignored the hustle and bustle behind him and closed his eyes and mind to the world for a few moments, drinking in the peace that he was suddenly feeling. He took in a number of deep breaths through his nose, breathing the air down deep into his lungs, which instantly made him feel alive and invigorated.

He opened his eyes and looked once more out to sea before turning around. He walked away with a new confidence in the direction of his berth, to pack the things that he would take with him to his new life in Argentina.

Otto Finkel was dead. Heinrich Vogel was born.

PART SIX

BRITANNY 1964

CHAPTER FIFTY-SIX

The man in the dark suit and grey overcoat raised the pistol higher and pointed it menacingly at the man calling himself Heinrich Vogel.

'Stay where you are, Finkel. That is close enough,' he said forcefully. 'Just sit back on the bed like the good little Nazi you are.'

'What do you intend to do with me?' replied the German. 'If you are to finish this then please just get on with it.'

'All in good time,' said the Englishman calmly. 'All in good time. I want you to answer some questions for me. You need to give me an understanding as to what turned the boy I knew, albeit briefly, from the quiet, gentle person he was, to the murderous Nazi he became. I really would like to know.'

The German sat back further on the bed and leaned back, using his arms to prop himself on the mattress. 'I am not that person anymore. I have not been that person for such a long time, Jack. As far as I am concerned, that person died in Germany in 1945. I am Heinrich Vogel now and I think I like being Heinrich Vogel a lot more than I liked being Otto Finkel.'

'That's as maybe,' replied the Englishman. 'But you can't just stop being one person and start being another as it suits you. You have never answered for the crimes you committed, which, may I say are quite numerous. People died, Otto... do not look at me like that, for it is your name... people died and they died badly. Many at your hand and many because of you.'

'Maybe,' said Otto, brushing back his blond fringe, the scar almost glowing in the light from the lamp. 'But like I said, that man is now dead.'

'That man sits on the bed in front of me,' replied the Englishman calmly. 'That man is still very much alive and needs to answer for his sins.'

'You speak of choices,' said Otto, ignoring the veiled threat. 'You speak of choices like you think I had any. If it had not been me then it would have been someone else. I was by no means the only one.'

'And that justifies what you did, does it?' The Englishman frowned. 'To say that if it wasn't you then it would have been someone else, like you? You may be right but the fact remains it was you. You, Otto Finkel, not this made up person you have been calling yourself for the past twenty odd years. Heinrich Vogel does not exist. You are Finkel and you will always be Finkel, no matter what your paperwork says.'

'And another thing about choices and the decisions we make,' went on Otto, ignoring him, 'What about the choice you made all those years ago, not two miles from here. Maybe you should have all left me to drown. You would have saved a lot of people a whole lot of heartache. Including me.'

'Undoubtedly,' replied the Englishman. 'I have regretted that day for the last quarter of a century, believe you me. We should have let you die, but you see, we were not like you. We were children, all of us, including you. Innocent children trying to have a little bit of fun and nothing more. We could not let a child die when we could prevent it. Maybe that's what makes us different.'

'This scar,' said Otto, indicating the deformity on his face. 'This thing that day left me with has been a curse all of my life. It would have been better for you all if you had left me to drown instead of that retarded janitor, or whatever he was. I have had to live with this thing all my life.'

'So that's what made you so bitter, that's the excuse you have for becoming a Nazi and the atrocities you have committed?' The Englishman could not believe his ears.

'Adolf Hitler gave me a purpose to my life,' replied Otto, the memories he had tried to forget now flooding back. 'He gave me the respect and the sense of worth that had been lacking through my youth. Because of this,' he indicated the scar once more. 'So becoming a Nazi and joining the SS and the rest of it, it all goes back to that day in the cove. Had you not been arguing with your brother, had not that French boy got into the boat and had not we all followed him, then none of this would have happened. I would not be sitting here with you now and you would not be pointing that gun at me.'

'Bullshit,' replied the Englishman. 'Do not blame everyone else for your own crimes. You made the choice to become a Nazi, you made the choice to join the SS, you made the choice to kill British soldiers in cold blood, round up Jews and send them to their deaths and all the other shit you've done in your life. Take responsibility for your actions, you arrogant bastard.'

'But do we have choices?' said Otto. 'Really, do we? Are not our lives pre-planned for us? Do not circumstances dictate how our lives are mapped out?'

'I don't believe that for a second. And let's be honest, neither do you.'

Otto made to move forward but the Englishman lifted the gun once more and he sat back down.

'So why are you here?' the Englishman asked. 'Why have you come back here, and to this hotel of all hotels.'

Otto let out a huge sigh.

'I don't know,' he said after a while. 'I really don't know. A good friend of mine died recently. Cancer of the pancreas. I had to watch him deteriorate and die a slow and painful death. It was terrible. Whatever he had done, he did not deserve that. When he was in the last stages, we spoke at great length. About our pasts and other things and although I had wanted to forget, I thought a lot about that holiday. I told him that it was the only time in my life, up to arriving in Argentina, that I truly felt happy. I suppose I had to come back and take a look at the place one more time, call it nostalgia if you wish.'

'How very sad and romantic,' said the Englishman sarcastically. 'Bit of a mistake in the end don't you think?'

'Not really,' sighed Otto. 'Not really.'

He closed his eyes for a while, not saying anything and when he opened them, the Englishman was still sitting there, looking at him.

'Tell me, Jack,' said Otto. 'Do you know what happened to the others? The other boys from the boat.'

The Englishman looked at him and sighed. 'I tried to find out what had become of everyone a couple of years ago. All I know is that my brother died during the war. The Italian, Marco, is still alive and is now a parish priest in a little town just outside of Turin, where he was raised. The French boy, Jean-Luc is probably dead. He was a member of the French resistance for a while and then ended up in Drancy. He was deported to Auschwitz in the summer of 1943 under an assumed name. He probably perished there.'

A brief feeling of déjà vu hit Otto, a vague recollection of a transport he had overseen, but it was a fleeting memory that was instantly forgotten.

'Do you know that Marco and I met in Rome during the war?' asked Otto. The Englishman did not reply. 'We got to know each other a little when I was there. Do you know that he pulled a knife on me? A Catholic priest attempted to murder me. Can you believe that?'

'It's a good job he was just that... a Catholic priest,' replied the Englishman. 'Anyone else would have stuck it in you.'

'I have tried to live a good life since the war, you know,' continued Otto. 'Erich and I built up a very nice business and have given a lot of the money we made to the underprivileged. Did you know that?'

'No I didn't. But it does not detract from what you have done. For which you have yet to be punished.'

'Maybe not,' replied Otto. 'Maybe not. Maybe I have come back to face that punishment, to face up to the things that I have done.'

'When I arrived here, I had the express desire to kill you,' said the Englishman after a short while. 'I fully intended to put a bullet into your brain, primarily in revenge for those soldiers you murdered in France in 1940. But for some strange reason putting a bullet into your head is not enough for me. It is too final a thing. I am at a loss at what to do with you.

'You seem more to be pitied than to be punished, Otto. More to be ignored and disregarded for the nonentity you have been all your life. Your life is insignificant to the rest of society... to the rest of world for that matter, but do not blame that world because it is a world that you and people like you created, so live with it. That same world has moved on and you have wallowed in self-pity while it has been turning. Whether that self-pity is for the guilt you may feel for things you have done in your past or for what you are now, or losing your friend, who, frankly, I really don't give a shit about. Living your life alone, unloved and forgotten is probably the best thing for you and for all of us. I will now make my final decision regarding you... You see I now have another choice before me where you are concerned, to kill you or to leave you to live your life with your own internal sufferings and demons.'

Suddenly the Englishman stood up and walked to the door, passing Otto who lay back on the bed with his hands over his face.

The Englishman put the gun into the pocket of his grey overcoat and with one glance back at the former Nazi lying sobbing on the hotel bed, he opened the door and walked through it.

CHAPTER FIFTY-SEVEN

Henri Le Bot should have retired a long time ago. That's what his wife kept telling him. He had been in the gendarmerie for close to thirty-eight years and at the age of fifty-seven he had decided to stay until his sixtieth birthday. He loved the job, he always had, and he still felt very fit and healthy. There was no need for him to retire and he knew that as soon as he did, his wife would regret the decision as much as he would.

He had served the community of St Malo for all that time, since well before the war and during the dark times that followed. The post war years had been good to him. They had provided him with a good living, a happy lifestyle and three grandchildren whom he doted upon. He had never gone for the promotions that he had been capable of, preferring to stay at the rank of sergeant so he did not have to be moved on. All in all, Henri Le Bot was a happy man.

The station had received the call at ten thirty that morning when the maid from the Hotel Britannique had found the body of one of their residents in the bath when she had gone in to change the linen. He had decided to tag along with the young gendarme who had been assigned to investigate what had happened, as he was still under probation and this would be his first death.

They had driven the short journey to the hotel, which stood just outside the town centre facing the English Channel and had been met by the hotel manager, a short wiry, man with thinning hair and small round glasses, as soon as they got out of the car.

The man looked fraught with panic. This was a situation that he had clearly not come across before.

'Thank goodness you are here,' he said as they approached him. He was wringing his hands together. 'I have cordoned off the room and given Matilda, that's the poor girl who found him, a glass of water. She is in the dining room now in tears. I have not been in the room myself, I believe it is a little gruesome.'

'Okay,' said Le Bot. The man was already irritating him despite only just having met him. 'We'd better get inside then and speak to her.'

The manager, who introduced himself as Michel Dupont, led them into the reception area and to the dining area beyond. Le Bot had been in this hotel a number of times in the past, the last being some years ago, to speak to a resident that was causing trouble with management over a disputed bill. As he sat down at the table to face the young maid, who was shaking as she held her glass of water, his mind wandered back to early in his career when he had had to interview a young boy regarding a missing janitor who was feared drowned. If he remembered correctly, they had found a body on the beach the following day, but it was a faint memory now.

The young gendarme, Arnold, sat down at the side of him, taking his notebook from his pocket.

'I'll ask the questions, Arnie, you take the notes,' he instructed him.

Turning to the girl, whose face was streaked with tears, he said to her, 'Okay, my love… Matilda isn't it?' She nodded, then took a sip of water. 'Do you want to tell me exactly what happened this morning.'

'It was horrible,' she stammered. 'I have never seen anything like it. Have you seen it? All that blood.'

'No,' replied Le Bot, 'Not yet. We want to speak to you first so you can get yourself home. I believe Monsieur Dupont has given you the rest of the day off.'

'Yes,' said Dupont from behind him. 'Yes, yes, of course.'

Le Bot smiled and winked at the girl across from him. 'Go on, dear. Tell me what happened.'

'Well, it was a normal morning,' she said, wiping a tear away with the back of her hand. 'Nothing special. My job is to clean all the rooms on the second floor, change the linen, towels, that kind of thing.' Le Bot nodded encouragingly. 'Well, I got to the third room, the one the strange German man was using. I knocked on the door and there was no answer so I presumed that he was either still asleep or had gone out or something. I knocked again and when there was no reply I let myself in with my key.'

She stopped talking as the memory of what happened a few short minutes ago came back to her.

'Okay,' said Le Bot. 'And then what happened? Take your time now.'

'Well, I went in and the curtains were still closed. The bed didn't look like it had been slept in because I tuck the sheets in tight and they were still like that, although it did look as though it had been sat or lay on at some point. I went to the curtains and opened them to let the sunshine in. Then I turned round and could see the bathroom door was open… You see this is a nice hotel and all the rooms have bathrooms… then…'

She began to cry again and Le Bot left her for a while as she gathered her thoughts together.

Then she continued. 'So I went into the bathroom and found him there. He was in the bath and there was blood everywhere. He had no clothes on and all the water was red. I just started screaming with the shock of it and ran from the room… I think there was some writing on the mirror in the bathroom too.'

'What did it say?' asked Le Bot, intrigued.

'I didn't stop to read it but I don't think it was French.'

'Okay,' said Le Bot rising from his chair. 'Thank you Matilda. Arnie, did you get all that?' he said as he strode towards the door.

'Yes, Sergeant Le Bot,' replied Arnie standing up and following his superior out of the room.

'Monsieur Dupont, please take me to the room in question.'

Following hurriedly behind, in order to keep up with Le Bot's long stride, Dupont said, 'Yes, yes, of course.'

A minute later, as they approached the room, Le Bot turned to Dupont. 'What do we know about him?'

'Nothing at all,' replied the hotel manager. 'He has been here for a couple of days, that's all. He has an Argentinian passport but he spoke with a German accent. Very good French if I remember rightly.'

'Argentinian? That's a little odd.'

'Very much so. I hadn't seen one before so I looked at it closely. His name was German… Heinrich Vogel. He said he was originally from Austria but had emigrated there some time ago.'

Le Bot looked at Dupont and raised his eyebrows.

'Very strange,' he said. 'Has anyone else had access to this room? Anyone who may have been able to get in beside him?'

'No,' replied Dupont. 'Security here is very strong. We take good care of our customers. They have a key, we have a master at reception and keep the other master keys in the safe overnight before we give them to the cleaners in the morning. So the answer is that it is most unlikely that anyone could get access to the room other than the resident himself.'

'Okay, thank you.'

Leaving Dupont in the corridor, Le Bot opened the door and walked into the room, followed closely by Arnie. He had a quick look around the room and saw that it was as Matilda had described it. Basic but clean, the curtains open letting the light in from the window that faced the sea. A double bed was in the centre with a wardrobe opposite. There was also a chair pushed back against the wall near to the window.

He moved to the bathroom, the door still ajar and opened it wider.

In the bath, which was filled virtually to the top with water, lay the corpse of a man who looked to be in his late forties. His lank, blond hair had fallen over his eyes as his head had fallen forward, but Le Bot could distinctly see a large, ugly scar running down the left hand side of his face. The left arm stuck out over the bathroom floor causing the tiles to be soaked red in the blood that had fallen from the large, deep cut that ran the length of his forearm.

It looked to Le Bot that this was a clear case of suicide, the blade that had caused the cuts was probably somewhere in the bath with him, but he would not know that until the body was taken out.

'Shit,' he heard Arnie say behind him, 'What a mess.'

'It certainly is,' said Le Bot quietly, 'There's no denying that.'

He looked to the mirror and saw writing on the glass, a marker pen loose in the sink. It said simply *Mein name ist Otto Finkel. Ich sollte ertrunken.*

'What do you think it means?' asked Arnie. 'I don't know any German.'

'Let me translate for you,' said Le Bot quietly, his mind drifting back over thirty years to something in his distant memory. 'It says, "My name is Otto Finkel. I should have drowned".'

'What do you think that's supposed to mean?' asked Arnie. 'Why would someone do such a thing?'

'Who knows?' replied Le Bot, still looking at the mirror. 'Who knows what goes on in a person's mind? Maybe he was looking for something that this world could not give him. Some sort of absolution maybe. I guess we'll never know will we? Come on, let's go and make some calls.'

CHAPTER FIFTY-EIGHT

Off the Dunkirk coast, May 31st, 1940

Jeff Watson looked at the devastation all around him. The Messerschmitt's bullets had smashed the wheelhouse to bits, shattering the windows and wrecking the instruments in front of him. The shelving behind had been ripped from the walls scattering splinters of wood and charts all around the floor. He had been pushed aside by young Toby who was now clambering to his feet, a cut across his forehead where the flying glass had struck and cut him. Young Harry, Toby's brother sat crying in the corner.

'Are you okay, Skip?' Toby asked. 'Jesus that was bad!'

'I'm fine,' said Watson, looking at the cut on the young man's head. Seeing that it was only superficial he said, 'Take your brother to the rear and find some shelter in case we are attacked again. I'll see if I can guide her out to the destroyer.'

As Toby set to move to the rear of the boat with his brother, still slightly dazed from the air attack, Watson looked at the deck in front of him and saw that a number of the soldiers he was taking had been hit. Blood was now mixing with the spray on the boards of the deck as men rushed to assist those who had been wounded. It was obvious to Watson that some of them were dead and he felt a lump rise in his throat and tears well in his eyes. Steeling himself he grabbed hold of the wheel and felt it respond under his grasp, relieved that he still had control of the vessel.

Ahead of them, perhaps three quarters of a mile away, was the large destroyer that he was headed for, cargo nets draped over the side to allow access for the soldiers being taken home. He knew that this time he would be going with them. The *Margaret Rose* had done her bit and now needed to get back to England, a fourth trip to the Mole now impossible. Plus he could not put young Toby and Harry in any more danger.

Across the deck he could see soldiers working frantically to save their comrades who were wounded badly and his eye caught one young lieutenant who had quickly holstered the pistol that he had fired ineffectively at the attacking German plane only moments ago. He rushed to assist a fallen comrade and Watson was immediately impressed with the young man's composure and calmness in the most dangerous of situations.

As he set his sights on the destroyer and pointed the *Margaret Rose* to that heading, he became aware of more anxious shouting above the noise of the battle around them. Some on the deck were shouting and readying their weapons once more as the others continued to provide what medical aid they could to their fallen comrades.

Watson looked to the right and could see that the Messerschmitt had circled around and was now coming back for a second attack. They were sitting ducks. There was absolutely nothing he could do to avoid it and the only defence they had were the small arms belonging to the exhausted troops he was ferrying.

Instinctively he ducked down behind the wheel housing as he heard and felt the bullets rip into his fishing boat once more. It was like nothing he had ever experienced in his life before. Again splinters and debris flew all around him and more glass fell from the already shattered windows onto him as he crouched down, making himself as small as possible.

Seconds later it was over and it took him another few seconds to realise that he was still alive. Slowly he stood up and looked out onto the deck. The devastation was complete. The foredeck was riddled with bullet holes and more troops lay dead or dying. Those that had attempted to assist the wounded from the first attack were now wounded or dead themselves. It was a total nightmare and to make matters worse, the *Margaret Rose* was listing badly to the left and he could see smoke billowing from the hatch that led to the engine room.

Above the sound of the screams of the wounded he could hear the German aircraft and realised that one more pass and they would all soon be at the bottom of the English Channel and there was nothing he could do about it. He searched the sky for the murderous aircraft and was relieved to see that it was flying away, back to shore, and he nearly cheered. Instead he looked to the skies and thanked God.

Again he took hold of the wheel and was relieved to see that he still had control of the rudder. The power was failing fast but they were not very far from the ship and with a bit of luck they could make it. If he could just get alongside, they may be able to cross over before the *Margaret Rose* sank, which he now knew to be inevitable.

He was tapped on the shoulder and saw that Toby and Harry were both fine, having been at the rear of the vessel during the second attack, the wheelhouse giving them the cover they had needed and again he thanked God for sparing them.

'Jesus, Skip, we're sinking,' said Toby.

'I know, my boy,' said Watson calmly. 'That's what happens when your boat gets filled with holes. We may just make it to the ship but get your life jackets on right now, just in case.'

As Watson fought with the wheel to maintain the course, a face appeared before him through the broken window. It was that of a major with a large moustache.

'I say, Captain,' he greeted him. 'Major Harding, Royal Fusiliers. Do you think you can hold her until we get to that destroyer over there?'

'Yes,' replied Watson. 'But we won't have much time before she goes down. So you had better get your boys ready for a quick disembarkation.'

'Okay,' replied Harding and turned around to assist with the wounded once more.

'There are some life jackets in those boxes over there,' called Watson after him. 'But not enough for everyone, I'm sorry.'

The Major raised his hand in acknowledgement without turning around and walked unsteadily down the sloping deck.

Watson gritted his teeth.

'Here, Toby,' he said to the bigger of the two brothers, 'Give me a hand with this wheel. It's trying its damnedest to fight me.'

Together the two men held the wheel steady as the boat sailed very slowly, losing height in the water as it did so, seawater below decks pouring through the holes and flames taking hold in the engine room beneath them.

'If you believe in God,' he said to his two crew members. 'I think now is a good time to start praying.'

*

Major Harding left the wheelhouse and walked along the deck, careful not to lose his footing as he did so. The German plane had done for the boat, of that he was certain, so his priority now was to save as many of his soldiers as he could.

The second pass had taken out more of them and he had to take control of himself and remain stoical even though all he wanted to do was scream in frustration. These men had come so far, been through so much, only to have it all ended here, in the Channel so close to safety.

Sea water mixed with blood was settling in puddles against the portside gunwale as more spray splashed over the side. The captain of the vessel was doing an excellent job in keeping the boat on course and he could see the ship they were heading for getting closer with every lurch forward.

He approached Lieutenant Wilson who was desperately attempting to apply a field dressing to a soldier lying on his back with a bullet hole in his chest. Harding could tell straight away that he was wasting his time. The man had only minutes to live, if indeed he was still alive. His eyes were closed and blood was pouring around the sides of the dressing.

'Dan,' said Harding, placing his hand on his shoulder. 'There's nothing you can do for him. You need to let him go.'

'But he's my friend,' replied Wilson. 'I have to help him.'

'I know, son. You need to get your men organised, this is not going to be easy getting across. Take care of the wounded as best you can but we are going to have to leave the dead I'm afraid.'

Lieutenant Wilson turned his head and looked at Harding, tears pouring down his face.

'Come on,' said Harding. 'Let's get these boys home.'

Wilson knew that Harding was talking sense. There was nothing he could do for his friend. It was those with a chance of survival that he had to help now.

Wrenching himself away from his fallen comrade he turned to Harding.

'Okay, sir,' he said. 'What do you need me to do?'

*

Wilson stood with Harding on the deck of the destroyer and looked back at the *Margaret Rose*, which by now was virtually on its side in the water. Flames and smoke could be seen billowing from the engine room hatch and as the sea water entered it, the black smoke turned to steam in the air.

The skipper of the fishing craft stood a few feet away from them, his head turned away, unable to watch the boat he loved die. His two young crew mates, however, watched with a morbid fascination as it listed and almost turned fully over.

The only thing that pleased Harding was the fact that all the men who had survived the air attacks, both able-bodied and wounded, had successfully made it onto the Royal Navy vessel and that was in the main part due to the three civilians who had crewed the fishing boat. He knew that everyone who had survived owed their lives to those three unassuming fishermen.

He looked at Wilson with a fatherly concern. The man seemed to have aged in the short space of an hour, for that was how long it had been since they had left the East Mole. Harding realised he was getting too old for all this shit. He had had his war over twenty years ago and he really did not need another one. He feared that this one would be much worse, if that was at all possible. The last one had been played out on the battlefields of Flanders and northern France over the course of four years, but it had taken the Germans only a few short weeks to force the British off the continent. He feared for the future and what was to come.

As they watched the *Margaret Rose* finally give up the ghost and succumb to her injuries, both Wilson and Harding did not speak for there was nothing more to say, no words were appropriate. The corpses of many of their man had been left on the deck as the survivors had scrambled up the cargo nets to the relative safety of the destroyer, those with injuries being assisted as best by their comrades.

And as the small fishing craft that had brought them to this floating sanctuary disappeared beneath the waves, taking the bodies of the fallen, including that of Lieutenant Jack Graham with it, they both found that they were weeping.

CHAPTER FIFTY-NINE

Heathrow Airport, London, 1964

The man in the black suit took off his grey overcoat and placed it over his arm as he walked to the Hertz rental desk. He had arrived from Paris a half hour ago and after going through passport control he had collected the small suitcase he had taken with him and made his way through customs.

He was only stopping in London for a few days, to tidy up the rest of the administration and to speak to the letting agent about renting out his apartment whilst he was away. He had sold his car the previous week, letting it go for a fraction of what it was worth, so now had to use a rental for the few days he had left before his flight to Washington and the three year posting that he had secured.

It was not something that he had volunteered for but he was not too bothered about going. It was supposed to be a step up, a promotion of sorts, and since his break up with Jenny a year ago, he saw it as maybe a good thing to get away. She had moved on and that was what he needed to do. He would miss the children, of course he would, but he could fly them out in the school holidays and take some time out with them then, to explore the east coast of America.

He needed a focus now that he had put the affair with Otto Finkel to bed. He had been surprised at how he had felt so calm upon meeting the man again after so many years and even more surprised that he had found that he felt only pity towards him, and not the hatred that he had known until that point.

He had come close to getting him, back in 1945, just after the war, but the Americans had somehow let him slip through their fingers when they were transporting him to the British sector. The American major... Redman or Redford, he could not quite remember the name, had confirmed beyond doubt that it was Finkel and he remembered the frustration he had felt when learning of his escape.

The trail for Otto Finkel had grown cold from that point and it was only a few days ago when he had been given word that a man fitting his description had flown into France from Buenos Aires on an Argentinian passport. The authorities had a particular interest in anyone coming to Europe from South America with German sounding names and it was not long before a picture of his passport had landed on his own desk. He knew instantly that it was his man. After all these years the chance to finally get him had come totally out of the blue and he had immediately asked for a few days off so he could follow up the lead. He did not take it through the official channels. This was personal.

The man in the black suit had spent the flight to France thinking back over his life and how he had ended up in the position he was now in. He thought back to that sunny day in the cove near St Malo and what had taken place there. His thoughts also took him back to when he had joined the army and of being recruited for the new Special Operations Executive due to his fluency in French. The offices on Baker Street where they had planned out missions, the code names of "Grey Man" and "Francois" that he had used during those times. He thought again of having come across Jean-Luc Descartes very briefly, and how he had not revealed his identity to him for fear of compromise should the man be caught. It was just as well because he eventually had been, that whole cell being taken down by the Nazis in 1943, Jean-Luc included.

He had no idea why Finkel should return to Europe. His father had committed suicide shortly after the war and he had no other family, his mother seeming to have disappeared off the face of the earth. There seemed no reason for it. The ugly scar on his face, that had been there since he was twelve years old, was a total giveaway to his real identity.

He had taken a chance and driven to St Malo, back to the Hotel Britannique, where they had spent that holiday back in 1928 and on checking the register with a very friendly receptionist, he found that a Heinrich Vogel was staying there, the same name as the person on the Argentinian passport that the French authorities had handed on to his bosses at British Intelligence. He even managed to persuade her to give him the room number.

Finkel had surprised him. He had always thought that if the day should ever come when he would be able to confront him, he would find an unrepentant Nazi. Instead he had found someone quite different to what he had expected. Whether it was genuine remorse or that the man had simply given up on life after the death of his close friend, he did not know, but whatever it was it left him pitying him and not hating him. He could not muster up that emotion, no matter how much he wanted to.

The man was responsible for the murders of British prisoners of war and the transportation and killing of untold numbers of Jews but he had found that he could not despise him the way he thought he should. He found that the person he saw before him, in that hotel room, was merely a reflection of the young boy he had met on holiday so long ago and not the evil Nazi that was wanted the world over for crimes against humanity. He had discovered that no matter what this man had done in his adult life, it would feel like he was putting a bullet into that mild-mannered blond boy who had tagged along quietly with him and his brother all those years ago. He had realised that he could not do it. He was not capable of murder and, if he was honest, he was quite pleased about that.

The young girl sitting behind the reception desk looked up at him and smiled, revealing a set of perfect white teeth. 'Can I help you sir?'

'Yes,' he replied placing his coat over the suitcase at the floor and taking out his wallet. 'I need a car for a few days. Anything will do.'

'No problem sir,' she replied. 'I'll see what I have available.'

'Thank you,' he said and placed his passport on the counter.

Again his mind wandered to things that had passed. He felt no guilt at having let Finkel go. There were many others after the man anyway. All those he had mentioned, Mossad, the CIA, the French, the Italians and the Russians. There was no real escape for him now that he was in Europe. Maybe that was what he wanted, he thought. Maybe he was sick of running and wanted it all to be over. Maybe he welcomed the punishment that his actions had deserved. It was just that the man in the dark suit was not the man to give it out.

He concluded that he really did not care anymore. For him it was over now. He had cornered the man and had confronted him and that was enough for him. His thoughts now had to move to the future and the three years he was about to spend working at the British Embassy in Washington DC.

'Can you just sign here for me?' said the girl, pushing a contract across to him. He used the pen chained to the counter to sign it and handed it back. 'Thank you,' she said and when he had paid her she said, 'Here are the keys, and a map to where the car is parked. I have put a cross on the map for you to show you the parking bay.'

'Thank you so much,' he said.

'Have a nice day, Mr Graham,' she said as he put the keys in his pocket and put on his overcoat.

Picking up his suitcase he smiled at her.

'You too, miss,' he said. 'But please, call me Frank.'

The man in the black suit and grey overcoat turned away and headed towards the exit.

Author's note

Jack's Story

The massacre described in Jack's Story, although purely fictional, is loosely based on two events that took place in that area of France on the retreat to Dunkirk by the British Expeditionary Force in May and early June of 1940.

The first occurred on May 27th of that year at Le Paradis in the Pas-de-Calais region. Ninety-seven prisoners of war of the 2nd Battalion, Norfolk Regiment were machine gunned to death by 14th Company, 3rd SS Division (Totenkopf) under the command of SS Hauptsturmführer Fritz Knochlein. Knochlein was convicted of war crimes in 1949 and hanged.

The second incident occurred a day later at Wormhoudt and was carried out by 'soldiers' of the 1st SS Division Leibstandarte SS Adolf Hitler. British prisoners of war of the Royal Warwickshire Regiment, the Cheshire Regiment and the Royal Artillery, with some French POWs, totalling just under a hundred were rounded up and put in a barn. They were attacked with grenades and machine guns. However, some prisoners managed to escape. No one was ever brought to justice for this.

Jean-Luc's Story

This book does not wish to criticise the actions of French people during the war, but it remains a historical fact that the number of Jews taken to Drancy and then deported from France to Auschwitz and other such places could not have been so high without the compliance of the Vichy government and the gendarmerie. These people did the Nazi's work for them before the Germans occupied the south of the country (or the Free Zone) in November of 1942 and this part of French history remains an embarrassment to them to this day.

There were, however, many French people who resisted the occupier extremely bravely and any criticism should not be of the nation but of those individuals who were involved.

Marshal Petain, the head of the puppet Vichy government (and First World War hero), was tried for treason after the war and sentenced to death. The sentence was commuted by Charles de Gaulle to life imprisonment and he died in 1951 at the age of ninety-five.

Klaus Barbie and the Gestapo occupied the Hotel Terminus, a hotel near to the railway station in Lyon in November of 1942. Barbie became known as "The Butcher of Lyon" due to his violent interrogations of prisoners. He is known to have actively taken part in some of the tortures that took place there. After the war he escaped to Bolivia (with the assistance of US Intelligence allegedly) but was deported to France in 1983. He stood trial and was sentenced to life imprisonment. He died in prison at the age of seventy-seven, unrepentant. He was in his late twenties when he carried out his crimes.

Marco's Story

On the morning of October 16th, 1943 SS Hauptsturmführer Theodor Dannecker (the former commandant of Drancy Deportation camp in Paris) ordered the Jewish ghetto of Rome, near the Portico D'Ottavia, to be emptied of all Jews. Three hundred and sixty-five German soldiers arrived that morning and took away over a thousand people for shipment to concentration and death camps. Of those people deported only sixteen survived the war.

Over the years there have been many criticisms of the way the Vatican handled the Nazi situation and of Pope Pius in particular. Whether maintaining a relative silence was the only course open to the Church at the time is a matter of debate. I leave it to the reader to form their own opinion on that particular issue.

Otto's Story

The route taken by the character Otto Finkel to escape Germany to South America was widely used by ex-SS members and other Nazis fleeing justice at the end of the war. There were many such "ratlines", as they came to be known, but by far the easiest method of escaping Europe came via this Northern Italian route.

In 1938 a referendum was carried out in The South Tyrol, or Alto Adige, in Northern Italy, as to which nationality the residents there wished to be, Italian or German; this being a matter of debate between Mussolini and Hitler. As this is a widely German speaking region, the majority of the populace voted in favour of Germany and many emigrated to Germany and Austria (which had been annexed in the Anschluss of 1938) shortly after. However, the outbreak of war prevented any further emigrations. This affinity to Germany by so many in the Adige was maybe the reason why Nazis did not find it too difficult to get the help they needed when fleeing justice. There was also much confusion in Europe at that time due to so many displaced people moving across borders etc., which, if anything, made it much easier for them to simply 'disappear'.

A lot of those who helped them were public officials, so many of the documents they used, passports, visas, etc., were not fakes and obtaining new identities was relatively easy.

Aunt Anna's inn, mentioned in the novel was a real place and acted as a haven for fleeing Nazis.

The character Alfred Pasche also existed. He worked as a driver for the German Red Cross as a postal courier, taking mail (and people) between Innsbruck and Bozen. He was arrested by the carabinieri in September 1945.

Acknowledgements

There are many people that I wish to thank for their help and support during the writing process.

Firstly, I would like to thank my wife, Dawn, for her patience and love. I would also like to thank my sister, Barbara, my daughter, Jessica, and my friend, Deborah Parden-Bell, for taking a look at the draft and offering words of wisdom. Your help is very much appreciated and has prevented me from embarrassing myself. Many thanks also to all at Pegasus Elliot Mackenzie and Vanguard Press.

I have read many books during the research for this novel and those that have particularly helped are the publications of the Forgotten Voices series. Where better to get an insight into what took place other than from those people who were actually there? The two that assisted me greatly are: *Forgotten Voices of Dunkirk* by Joshua Levine and *Forgotten Voices of The Secret War* by Roderick Bailey. However, all the books in this series are highly recommended.

Nazis On The Run – How Hitler's Henchmen Fled Justice by Gerald Steinacher particularly helped with Otto's Story and I would recommend this to anyone with an interest in the subject.

However, the one book that assisted me greatly and opened my eyes to the horrors of Drancy Deportation Camp is a little known book that is currently out of print. I had to scour the internet for an English language copy and found it in America, published by M-Graphics Publishing. This book is *From Drancy To Auschwitz* by Georges Wellers.

Georges was an inmate of the camp and his description of the layout, the administration and what took place there have proved invaluable to me. Unfortunately Georges is no longer with us, but I hope to have done justice with what I have written regarding Drancy and what took place there in those dark years. His book deserves to be read.

Others that may be of interest are *The Nazis: A Warning From History* and *Auschwitz : The Nazis & The Final Solution* both by Lawrence Rees.

A final thank you to my two daughters, Jessica and Sophie, for lighting up my life. I love you both.

Now for the next one!